Praise for novels by Tracy Groot

"[*The Brother's Keeper* is a] lyrical and affecting first novel."

   BOOKLIST, starred review

"Groot vividly portrays both the heroism and the horrors of World War II. With the release of Christopher Nolan's film *Dunkirk*, there is bound to be interest."

   LIBRARY JOURNAL on *The Maggie Bright*

"Groot's well-researched, inspirational historical tale . . . will be compelling and memorable for a diverse audience."

   BOOKLIST on *The Sentinels of Andersonville*

"Groot has done good historical homework. . . . The pacing is page-turning. . . . This Civil War–era story grapples with fundamental moral questions about decency and conscience—questions that can be asked about all wars."

   PUBLISHERS WEEKLY, starred review of *The Sentinels of Andersonville*

"Richly detailed, engrossing historical fiction."

   KIRKUS REVIEWS on *The Sentinels of Andersonville*

"If the truth hurts, [*The Sentinels of Andersonville*] is like a knife to the heart. . . . This story of a Good Samaritan shines brightly as the characters place themselves in

   ROMANTIC TIMES, Top Pick review

"Groot . . . does good historical work with details and subtle psychological work with her characters. WWII-era novels are popular; this is a superior, page-turning entry in that niche."

PUBLISHERS WEEKLY on *Flame of Resistance*

"Scrupulously researched and lovingly written, *Flame of Resistance* plunges the reader into an exhilarating story of courage, grace, and one endearing woman's leap of faith."

THE BANNER

"[A] well-paced, beautifully written historical novel. . . . Entertaining and compelling."

PUBLISHERS WEEKLY, starred review of *Madman*

"Groot cleverly combines historical research, Scripture, and thrilling imagination to create an ingenious story built around the Gerasene demoniac described in Mark's and Luke's Gospels. It's one of the best fictional adaptations of a biblical event I've had the pleasure to read."

ASPIRING RETAIL MAGAZINE

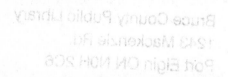

The Stones of My Accusers

Tracy Groot

The Stones of my Accusers

Tyndale House Publishers, Inc.
Carol Stream, Illinois

Visit Tyndale online at www.tyndale.com.

Visit Tracy Groot online at www.tracygroot.com.

TYNDALE and Tyndale's quill logo are registered trademarks of Tyndale House Publishers, Inc.

The Stones of My Accusers

Previously published in 2004 by Moody Publishers under ISBN 0-8024-3106-2. First printing by Tyndale House Publishers, Inc., in 2018.

Designed by Mark Anthony Lane II

Published in association with Creative Trust Literary Group, 210 Jamestown Park Drive, Suite 200, Brentwood, TN 37027. www.creativetrust.com.

Some Scripture quotations are taken from *The Holy Bible*, English Standard Version® (ESV®), copyright © 2001 by Crossway, a publishing ministry of Good News Publishers. Used by permission. All rights reserved.

Some Scripture quotations are taken from the New American Standard Bible,® copyright © 1960, 1962, 1963, 1968, 1971, 1972, 1973, 1975, 1977, 1995 by The Lockman Foundation. Used by permission.

The Stones of My Accusers is a work of fiction. Where real people, events, establishments, organizations, or locales appear, they are used fictitiously. All other elements of the novel are drawn from the author's imagination.

For information about special discounts for bulk purchases, please contact Tyndale House Publishers at csresponse@tyndale.com or call 1-800-323-9400.

Library of Congress Cataloging-in-Publication Data
Names: Groot, Tracy, date- author.
Title: The stones of my accusers / Tracy Groot.
Description: Carol Stream, Illinois : Tyndale House Publishers, Inc., 2018. | Previously published in 2004.
Identifiers: LCCN 2017057769 | ISBN 9781496422187 (sc)
Subjects: LCSH: Jesus Christ—Crucifixion—Fiction. | Bible. Gospels—History of Biblical events—Fiction. | GSAFD: Historical fiction.
Classification: LCC PS3557.R5655 S76 2018 | DDC 813/.54—dc23 LC record available at https://lccn.loc.gov/2017057769

Printed in the United States of America

24	23	22	21	20	19	18
7	6	5	4	3	2	1

For the one who threw no stones.

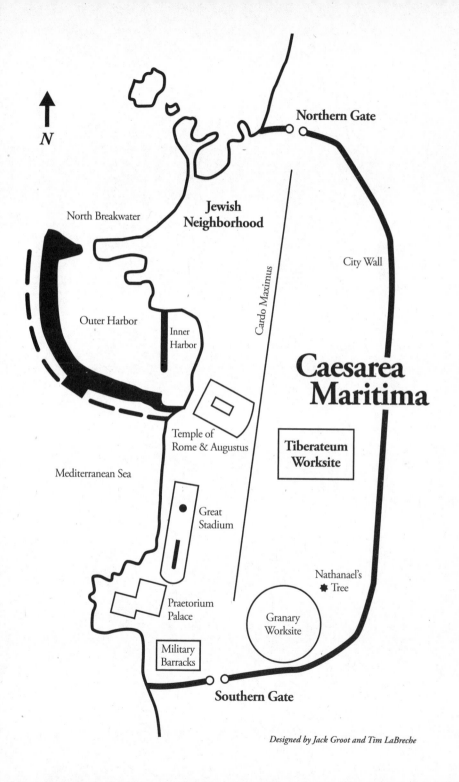

N

Northern Gate

North Breakwater

Jewish
Neighborhood

City Wall

Outer Harbor

Inner
Harbor

Cardo Maximus

Caesarea
Maritima

Temple of
Rome & Augustus

Tiberateum
Worksite

Mediterranean Sea

Great
Stadium

Nathanael's
Tree

Praetorium
Palace

Granary
Worksite

Military
Barracks

Southern Gate

Designed by Jack Groot and Tim LaBreche

Prologue

JORAH WATCHED as Annika marked the height of the child with the flat of her hand and scored the limestone wall with her thumbnail. The child stood back and watched the addition of his newest notch.

The occasion was a solemn one, Jorah could tell, a mysterious bargain struck between the old woman and the little street scamp. After making the mark, Annika pursed her lips and, with a mistrustful look at the boy, bent to examine the distance between the last notch and the fresh one. The mistrust turned to surprise, and her fists went to her hips. She regarded the child with suspicious interest.

"Well, Jotham. What have you to account for nearly two finger-spans of growth? Are you wearing sandals?"

"No, Annika," the child said, lifting a foot for examination. "I have been eating the loaves."

One eyebrow came up. "Every day?"

"Every day." He nodded, dark eyes large in his thin face.

She glared at him a moment more, then the eyebrow came down. "Good boy."

His face broke into a sunny smile, and he turned to skip to the tall cupboard in the kitchen. He waited until Annika got there, and she reached to take down a wooden box. Jorah could not see what she gave Jotham, but the boy received it with a smile, then scurried through the kitchen and out the door.

Annika watched him go, smiling fondly. "Little rogue."

Seated at the table, Jorah looked out the window to watch him dash away. "Little ungrateful wretch. I didn't hear a thank-you."

Annika replaced the box. "One thing at a time." She turned to the shelves and took down the cups to set them on the table. She waved a few fruit flies from the pitcher of watered wine and set it next to the cups, then she set out a loaf of spiced honeycake and fetched a few plates.

Gazing out the window, chin on her fist, Jorah murmured, "It's hard to think of him as a boy, but he was, you know. A little boy like that."

Annika hesitated only a second as she sliced the bread. "Which him would you be speaking of?"

"You know."

"I do. Try and say his name now and again. Else it would be as if he never was."

Pain surged. As if Nathanael never was? But he was. And never would be again.

Jorah made her lips small to keep them from quivering. Annika was busy with the serving, she would not notice when Jorah pretended to adjust her head covering to wipe away tears.

Three weeks since they had buried Nathanael at Bethany. Three weeks of endless tears, and they did not appear to be slowing. There was too much to grieve over. The loss of the man she would marry. The loss of her old life. The loss of . . . but she could not think about Jesus. She lost him long ago, the day he left their home.

Annika was speaking. ". . . family from Sepphoris still interested in your place?" She shook her head and gave a heavy sigh as she slid a slice of honeycake from the knife to a plate. "I never could have imagined such a thing: no tribe of Joseph left in Nazareth. My steps may stop at the well, but my heart will ever wander past it. Up that old hill to that old home."

"They are interested. But Jude and James do not want to sell until they talk to Simon about it, and he's off on some crazy lark to Decapolis. They want to talk with Joses and Mother too, but that's not the reason they're going to Jerusalem." No, it was the same old story. People leaving her for God. Jorah never seemed to figure in.

"So," Annika said as she slid onto the bench across from Jorah. "Caesarea Maritima for you."

"Someone has to tell her."

They fell silent. Jorah's glance kept straying to the uncut portion of Annika's honeycake. What was it about that loaf . . .

Annika was right. Soon all of the children of Joseph would be gone from the home forever. In just a few hours, Jorah and James and Judas were leaving, she for Caesarea Maritima, they for Jerusalem. The home would be an empty shell. As she was without Nathanael.

Why would a loaf of bread . . .

She remembered. This time she could not conceal the tears.

"Child," Annika said softly, reaching to grasp Jorah's hand.

"He brought them bread," Jorah gasped, and bit her lip. Sorrow wrapped around her like an old black garment.

Nathanael had brought them bread, one of Annika's loaves. He went back to ask the strangers to join their party on the road to Jerusalem, so they would feel safer traveling in a larger company. For bread, they gave him blood, his own. He died days later of the wounds.

Jorah sagged and rested her forehead on the table. Grief upon grief. Nathanael and Jesus, dead within days of each other, both murdered. One was said to have risen again. Well, Jorah never saw him. The other lay beneath a pile of stones in a common grave outside Bethany. No rumors of resurrection there.

Her face became humid with her breath on the table. "I would kill Joab if I could," she breathed into the old oak. "I would kill him, Annika, God help me I would."

"I would lend a hand."

Jorah looked up, scowling. She drew her sleeve across her face. "You would lend a hand," she sneered.

Annika smiled sadly, cheeks pushing skin into a multitude of soft wrinkles. "You and me both, Jorah. We'll be the terrors from Nazareth. Instruments of God's vengeance. What do you say?" She balled her fist and held up her arm to show she still had some muscle.

Jorah couldn't even smile.

Did everyone change as much as Annika had in the past month? News of Jesus, and news of Nathanael . . . Annika had gained ten years with all the news from Jerusalem. That made her old indeed.

"You would not kill a fly if it bit you twice." She hated the sound of her own voice. All the crying made her speak through her nose.

Annika snatched her fist from the air. "You would not either," she retorted. "Judas tells me that boy was not responsible for Nathanael's death. He said that Joab tried to save him—that he killed the one who attacked Nathanael. Stop making him responsible for your pain. That's cowardice, Jorah. You are not a coward."

"Joab could have prevented it!" Jorah spat.

"Jorah, Jorah," Annika said, voice low. "Sorrow is enough to bear."

"He was going to marry me, Annika."

The old woman nodded heavily. "I know, child. I know he loved you."

Did Nathanael talk about her? Jorah scrubbed her eyes, then poked at the honeycake on her plate. "You knew he loved me?"

"He was addled over you."

"I didn't—know if he loved me as—" She swallowed the words and scowled at her plate. She didn't want to cry; she was tired of sounding ugly.

Honeycake. The way her mind worked these days, sluggish as an overfed ox. Annika told her a soul hobbled in grief moved slowly for a time, like a wounded animal. She felt doubly dosed with pokeweed.

She touched the cake on her plate. Touched the wine cup and watched a fruit fly imbibe on the rim. These days she would do crazy things, like see a flower sprig in the midst of a crying spell. She'd take and hold it close to her face and see satin sparkles, pattern, and color. She'd take an orange peel and squeeze oily spray on her hand, and marvel at the fragrance. She'd examine a pinch of sand. So many colors. How could someone say, "It is the color of sand," when sand was a rainbow up close? Marveling at orange peel and sand did more than speaking with a rabbi.

She picked up a slice of honeycake. "I used to make them exactly as you told me, and mine would always turn out dry," Jorah murmured. "You probably told me wrong on purpose, else lose your reputation for the best."

But Annika was in her own thoughts. "Even Judas leaves me," she grumbled unhappily, "and he is my least favorite. What is Nazareth without a single member of the Joseph clan?" She hesitated. "Jorah. I know what James believes of Jesus. How does Jude feel about . . . the rumors?"

Moist and delicious. Or it would be, if its flavor hadn't fled at the mention of her oldest brother. Jesus! *Oh, God . . .* But no—no. Jorah had piled that way with boulders. She set the bread down and brought her palm close to inspect a few crumbs. "Why don't you ask Jude?"

"Fair enough. One thing at a time." Whatever she meant by it, Annika left it. "How long will you stay in Caesarea?"

"As long as it takes me to find her."

"You are sure your father's cousin still lives there?"

"Yes. Simon and Joses visited Thomas on the trip to sell the benches. He lives across the commonyard from a famous mosaicist. I should like to visit his workroom. I have a talent for mosaics, you know." She brushed the crumbs from her palm to her plate.

"Child?"

Jorah looked up.

Annika looked at her long. "You do a good thing. A hard thing. To tell a mother her son is dead . . . I am proud of you, Jorah ben Joseph."

Jorah hoped her smile did not look fake. Annika would not be proud if she knew the real reason she was going to see the woman.

"Oh. I nearly forgot." Annika got up and went to her bedroom in the back of the house. When she returned she was folding a long cloth, a narrow linen tablecloth. "I made this for Rivkah. Please take it to her for me."

Rivkah? But of course. Nathanael's mother. It was hard to think of her with a name. She who gave him birth . . . she who gave him scars.

"Annika." Jorah hesitated. "Did you know of Nathanael's scars?"

Surprise, then wariness came into Annika's face. "What scars?" she said sharply.

"When Abi and I wrapped Nathanael's body for burial, we found—" She squeezed her eyes shut. Orange peel fragrance. Flower petals. "There were—scars on his thigh. Old ones. From childhood." She clenched her teeth. Grains of sand. A mosaic. "Nathanael told James his mother did it. To let the evil out."

When Jorah looked at Annika, she found she had aged again. She was looking out the window, chin in her hand, tears brimming.

"Six different shades of ugly, all of us," she murmured, and a tear dropped away. "He wanted to tell me. He tried to tell me, but couldn't bring himself to do it. It would have shamed her more than him." She sniffed. "Poor thing."

Through her own tears, Jorah suddenly smiled. "He would have never let anyone call him a poor thing."

"I wasn't talking about Nathanael." Annika wearily pressed her fingers against her eyes.

The smile dropped. "Why is *she* a poor thing?"

"She hated herself, not Nathanael." Annika wiped her nose with a fold of her tunic. "Oh, Jorah, what we are capable of. God have mercy on us."

Jorah could only stare, then look away. Annika could say what she wanted, but she had seen the scars with her own eyes. God would not have mercy on that. Never that.

He's dead now, Jorah would tell Nathanael's mother. She knew exactly what tone she would use. She had rehearsed it several times, whispering to a fingerprint of sand. *I know what you did. I've seen the scars. And now your son is dead. You never deserved him, and now he's dead.*

It was the only thing to give true comfort. The only thing to help her breathe. At the times when the grief would consume her, when she would suffocate and go mad, she would think on these words and allow them to calm her.

She owed it to Nathanael if only to raise a voice against an old, horrific deed. If only to not allow it to go unnoticed. It was God's justice, after all. God knew what Rivkah had done, and he would expose it through Jorah. It was Jorah's mitzvah, her responsibility to Nathanael's memory.

Calmness came, like wine warming her blood, and she actually smiled at Annika.

Annika smiled back, if uncertainly.

Yes, Jorah would go and tell a woman that her son was dead. *Let those words score that heart as she had scored Nathanael's leg. Let her take those words to her grave, as Nathanael took the scars to his.*

Nathanael was dead. Joab lived. This is what he knew for now.

The road from Jerusalem would break west, and he would bring Nathanael's last words to his prostitute mother in Caesarea. Bring them, yes, but how to give them? They were tricky, treacherous words. Not Nathanael's words at all.

Tricky, too, telling a mother her son was murdered.

Joab sat on his haunches, tunic tight over his knees, trailing his knuckles back and forth in the dirt. He stopped when it made him think of what the doctor said, that Jesus had his fingers in the sand too. He folded his arms instead, and lifted his eyes to the silver box a distance away.

The box on the boulder, with the wrapping cloth splayed beneath, picked up a scrap of the descending sun and put a painful gleam in his eye. He stared at it until white blindness came. He couldn't see it now, but he knew every detail. The lid was etched with a strange design, pagan symbolism for all he knew. It was inlaid with cut stones of lapis lazuli. Threads of white laced through the indigo stones. Glitters, half the size of sand grains, shone golden in the blue.

Nathanael was dead. Joab lived.

He had fancied the box had powers, maybe, because it once held frankincense for the Teacher. He had brought it to Nathanael, hoping it would save him. It did not. The Teacher was dead too; so much for a magical box. There were crazy rumors he came alive again, and that was much to think on, but Joab couldn't think past the words he was charged to carry. Why couldn't they be "Mother, I love you," "See you on the other side," that kind of thing?

How could he be doing this? He was the son of a dye works owner. Lived in Hebron all his life. He knew color. He knew what iron salts and alum could do, he knew which plants produced the best color for the cheapest price, he knew he should never have listened to Avi and his Zealot friends. Everything had been fine until Avi came along. Avi was dead too. Joab lived.

What if Nathanael had been his friend instead of Avi? They wouldn't have cared about the land and the Romans. They would have paid mind to things at hand—playing tricks on Joab's older brother, hauling in a good harvest, working hard and laughing hard and getting drunk on occasion and goading each other to talk to a pretty girl and—

The blood and the knife. There was a great deal of blood.

Joab looked away from the box. He had found out things about Nathanael after he was wounded. Found out he had quite a sense of humor, and he was fiercely loyal—that, Joab knew already. He'd discovered that the day Nathanael kicked him out of the carpenter's shop. And even as Joab had fled the home, he put a backward glance on the house and thought maybe he was in the wrong company . . . that he should have been in the shop, laughing as James did, watching the Zealots run away.

He didn't know much about Nathanael, he who was loved of Jorah, only that he should not have died. Mostly he knew Nathanael had quality. He learned of the quality in the way Jorah tended Nathanael after he was wounded. The way James, the oldest brother, never left the cart. Learned it by the way Jude, the quiet one, hovered with hawk eyes on the wounds and the way Simon, a fellow he suspected of a normally grim nature, rivaled Avi himself with furious, anxious brooding. What little he learned in words, he learned from Simon, information resentfully given by a man who hated him as much as anyone in that party traveling to Jerusalem for Passover.

Where is he from?

Caesarea.

Which one?

By the sea.

Who are his parents?

He has only a mother, a prostitute.

What is her name?

What do you care? Get out of my sight!

Joab flicked an ant off his toe. Curious that he should think so much about Nathanael. He remembered feeling jealous, watching Nathanael in that cart, even the way he was, slick with sweat and his breath coming hard, face pale against those colorful cushions. Jealous because the way they acted, you would have thought the worst thing in the world was for that apprentice to die. And him trying to act as if his wounds were nothing but an inconvenience.

Nathanael had quality, a mystical kind, the kind the Teacher had. The kind that had Joab heading to a place he had never been, to give a stolen box to someone he had never met, to tell her words he feared would stay in his throat for the consternation of them. The quality made him do it, and the knife and the blood.

Why—he scrubbed up his hair—why did it take that long? Why had he been so blinded to Avi's madness? Avi's madness, his own madness . . . why did it take blood to bring the truth? Why were the words *these* words?

You're the one, Nathanael had said. You go and tell her, no stones.

Who? What are you talking about?

No stones . . .

I don't understand!

Tell her what Jesus said.

The doctor had taken him aside and told him what Nathanael meant. Told him of Jesus and the adulteress and the ones who would throw the stones. But it was no explanation at all. It drove up new thoughts he wished would stay put. He went to flick another ant, but his fingers left the ant to hesitate over the sand.

What did Jesus write? Was he buying time because his words would change everything? Maybe he was working up the courage to say them. Did he and the woman look at each other, there on the ground, he on one side and she on the other? Did she look at him just as amazed as the others; did she wonder what he was doing? Writing in the sand in the middle of a conversation. What kind of craziness was that? The doctor told the whole story; it was the most troubling thing Joab had ever heard.

Joab wrote *no stones* in Aramaic, then erased it to write the same in Greek. He would soon be in Caesarea. His father said they spoke mostly Greek where the Romans had set up their government in Palestinia. Avi had refused to speak in Greek. Called it the tongue of the oppressor. Soon, from Joab's own tongue would fall words in defiance of the Torah he had been raised to revere.

He rose and dusted off his hands. He rewrapped the box and stuffed it in his shoulder sack, slipped the strap over his shoulder, and took up again for Caesarea.

The sack thudded softly on his hip. He hoped it looked like nothing more than an extra set of clothing; a silver box inlaid with lapis lazuli was a prize indeed.

Joab gazed at the green appearing in the brown hills. It was late spring in Judea; color came up everywhere in this tawny land. About this time he usually helped his father and brother bring in the first blossom harvest from the cultivated field, where the bees worked with them. He could hear the hum, smell the sun-warmed flowers. He lifted his face to the sun, closed his eyes, remembering.

Where would he go after Caesarea? It didn't matter. Catch the next vessel out of the harbor. Go to Rome, go to Gaul. He could never go home. Never again see the field or the bees, because Nathanael was dead and Joab lived. This is what he knew for now.

❧

They had kicked the stones out of place. They had to go far out of their way to do that, up here on the slope facing the sea. The tree was not an obstruction to their beast building project, not even in the way of foot traffic. Not yet. The stones were a warning.

Rivkah knew they watched her replace the stones into the ring around the cedar tree. She thought about spitting, "Fah!" and hissing like a cat, but they might not recognize a good Jewish insult. They would only think her mad, and she was, a little bit, but at least they would not see her fear. When every stone was back in its place, she stood back to look at the tree. It was an eighteen-year-old cedar, nineteen next month. It fared well.

Half the time Rivkah feared she'd come and find the branches stripped. Her worst fear she could not name, because if she allowed the thought it might happen. If God heard the prayers of a prostitute, it wouldn't.

She looked past the cedar, let her gaze travel every rueful inch to the top of the slope. She did it to torture herself. Ever since the threat came upon Nathanael's tree, she wished she had planted it at the top. But who could have foreseen Caesarea would grow so much? Eighteen years ago the southeast part of the city was neglected and barren. She had chosen the site for that reason.

She was only fifteen then, and alone. If anyone had seen her plant the tree for her baby boy, they would have scorned her to dust for the hope she had for her son. If she had planted it where her old friends had planted theirs, the tree would have been cut down long ago. By Mother. Or maybe Zakkai.

She ran her hand over the comforting roughness of Nathanael's tree, then turned and sat against it where she could watch the sea, and more importantly, where she could watch the ugly beast pigs at the work site.

Two months now Nathanael had been gone. She had much to tell him when he returned. His grandmother died two days after he left. His friend Hepsominah married a rich Egyptian and moved to Alexandria.

Kyria might fret about Nathanael's long absence, but Rivkah wasn't worried. He could take care of himself. Wasn't he her boy? If she was a little mad, so was he, and madness had a curious quality of preservation. If Kyria said she knew Nathanael could take care of himself, it was other people who worried her, well, Rivkah refused to allow Kyria to scare her. Sometimes she screamed in Kyria's face to force the bad words back and prevent them from creating havoc—something Mother had taught her, and you had to scream yourself hoarse to make it work. She'd stiff-arm Kyria's evil words and think only on the letter Nathanael had left.

Do not worry about me, Mother. I am going north for a
time. I will explain all when I get back. I should return by
the next full moon. Ho, the stories I will tell. Just you wait.

If Nathanael did not return by the next full moon, or the next, wasn't he still her boy? She'd taught him to take care of himself. Kyria taught him things too. From her he learned to hit a gecko at fifty paces.

Rivkah squeaked a yawn and pressed her fist against her mouth.

She was used to sleeping at this time of day. At least she had some coin to live on for a while, and enough possessions to sell or trade if things got bad. Or she could live on Kyria; Kyria had lived on her enough times when business was slow, when the Roman garrison was out on field maneuvers. She would sleep here if she had to. Kyria could bring food if she could not leave.

Day after day, brick by brick, the walls of the granary grew. It seeped toward the tree like an incoming tide. Day after day Rivkah went to the Praetorium to try and stop the tide. Day after day she petitioned for Nathanael's tree. Pilate's chief secretary, Orion Galerinius, came to expect her visits.

He had a different expression on his face this morning. When he looked up from the table and saw her next in line, his face cleared. *You again,* he had said, folding his arms and sitting back. *Me again,* she had replied, folding her arms to copy him. His eyes had a tiny twinkle, and she wanted to say something to make him smile, as she had done before.

He'd have been disappointed had I not shown up, she thought, and the idea made her laugh out loud.

The sound brought attention from a worker at the wall. He leaned toward another worker and said something to make him sneer as well. She made her own sneer six times as ugly—she could hood her amber eyes, fill them with rage, and make them look hellish as a demon-cat. She wished she could scream curses, but couldn't risk it. Instead she cupped her hands and whispered a curse, then blew the ugly words to the workers and deepened the demon-cat look.

Muttering and sullen, they went back to their work.

The tide seeped daily, brick by brick. So the fear grew, brick by brick. She looked out to the Mediterranean, saw a ship bound for the harbor. Rivkah ground her heels into the earth to push her spine harder on the tree. If God heard the prayers of a prostitute, and Kyria thought maybe he did, then somehow Rivkah would stop the swelling tide. Or she would chain her neck to the trunk and drown with the tree.

Orion tried another note on the pearwood pipe. That was closer. He added it to the last note, and it sounded promising. He wet his lips and started the tune from the beginning, ending with the new note; it didn't work.

He'd have it right one day, but he wondered if memory played tricks on his ear. It was a tune that had made him lift his head when he passed a stall in the marketplace. He had slowed his steps to hear more, but the crowd carried him on. He passed the same stall on other days, listening, but never heard anyone play there again.

At the rare times he took out his pipe, he closed his workroom door. A closed door to the people of the palace meant serious discussion lay within, and Orion could enjoy a little peace. Duty always made him open the door after no more than a few minutes, but today he was bearing down on half an hour. He played in defiance of the two matters that lay in wait.

Protecting Jews had been a game up until now. Petty defiances that amounted to no more than a stuck-out tongue behind Pilate's back. Protecting Jews was an easy way to look like a benevolent man, a quick and cheap way, because protecting Jews had never cost him. He lowered the pipe and looked out the window to his bit of the Mediterranean. Hazy out today.

If he brought the matters to Pilate, disaster would come of it. But there was no *if* about it: the two matters had escalated to the degree that if he did not put them before the governor, Pilate would learn that Orion had delayed them. And that would make Pilate wonder what else Orion did around here. It might expose the gleaners' program he had granted to the soldier Cornelius for hungry Gentiles—and Jews. It would threaten the little son of the Jewish laundress. It would lay bare his arrangement with a cruelly poor old Jew who paid his taxes in dried-up dates.

So he allowed Jews to eat Pilate's scraps, so what? The scraps filled the bellies of the Gentiles too. It used to be things were not alarming. Now, anything with a tiny taint of Jew was touchy as a mad scorpion. Things had changed over the last five, six years, he wasn't sure when or how.

One woman wanted to keep her tree, and one man did not want to work on his holy day. Orion had looked; it was only a tree. Orion had inquired; the man was a hard worker. Simple requests borne from custom. If they were Roman requests from Roman customs, there would have been no delay. But they were Jewish requests, and that is why Orion played his pipe.

It was either the pipe or heavy drinking. A tent filled with poppy smoke sounded nice. Wasn't he second in command? Couldn't he ask around for the local poppy tent? He pictured fat pillows and people lolling and laughing. He'd like to loll and laugh. He'd never been in a poppy tent before. He'd never defied Pontius Pilate before. Not like this.

His eyes went to the top of the recessed shelves. He couldn't see it from where he sat, but upon the top shelf was a small wooden box. In the box was an iron collar, made to fit the neck of an eight-year-old boy. The collar had belonged to his father.

When courage was as scarce as barley after gleaners, Orion thought of the box. He had taken it out only once in the six years of his Palestinia sojourn, when he had to tell a palace slave his wife was dead. He went to reach for the box—

No! He would *not* bring the matters to Pilate. He did not need a collar to tell him what to do. He'd fire the stonemason and tell them to cut down her tree. What did he care? Gods and goddesses and all their mincing offspring, these people *vexed* him! Two weeks trying to come up with solutions. He'd wasted enough time. Didn't he have a palace to run? What did he care? He didn't care, he was too tired to care.

If he took the matters to Pilate, and only a majestic idiot would, he would have to make them sound fresh from the petitioners—as though the majestic idiot had not taken two weeks to puzzle over them. If the idiot took the matters to Pilate, and only a pox-brained lackwit would, he had to sound casual as he stated the matters . . . as though he didn't care about the outcome one way or another.

It was only a tree. It was only a day, just one day away from work in a week. They were not unreasonable requests. They were simply wishes. Pilate could grant them as easily as saying hello.

They were Jewish wishes.

Orion rewrapped the pearwood pipe in felt and placed it on the recessed shelf, then pulled his stool to his table. He took a tablet, freshly filled with beeswax. He took a stylus from the vase and picked off old wax. He blew on the stylus and glanced at his bit of the sea. After a hesitation, in which he wondered what poppy smoke was like, he went to work scratching into the wax two new items for the attention of Pontius Pilate.

1

Pontius Pilate, Governor of Judea, the Eastern Imperial
Province of Rome, to the honorable Decimus Vitellus
Caratacus, Primipilaris, greetings.

I am heartened by your consideration to an appointment
within my administration. This position of Chief Secretary is
held by Orion Galerinius Honoratus. Orion is unaware of the
precariousness of his employ; he knows only that an old friend
is coming to Judea for a visit. I will appreciate your discretion
upon arrival.

You may have heard of the recent event in Jerusalem,
the matter of one Jesus of Nazareth, leader of a Jewish sect
in my province. It was a distasteful matter, typical to the
trials involved in ruling a people as obstinate, rebellious, and

seditious as the Jews. I look forward to discussing this event with someone of true Roman sensibility.

Most important to me is your witness to the veracity of my reports of a people as difficult to manage as the Jews. The jeopardy of my secretary's position testifies to this: he is a Jewish sympathizer, a vexatious man bewitched by whatever spell these people hold over the weak-minded and frail.

How fares Sejanus? I hear disturbing reports that he falls from favor with Tiberius. A pity . . . he was my sponsor, you know. Bring what news you can.

I anticipate your arrival, and will begin to look for you. May your journey be accompanied by fair winds and good fortune. Long live Tiberius.

Pontius Pilate, by my own hand.

Herod may have been Jewish—Jewish enough—but at least he had taste. He had chosen the best place in Caesarea for his palace, right on a dramatic promontory, right in the spray of the Mediterranean. The first story withstood any threats from the sea, and the second story afforded a magnificent view. It was arguable that the mighty harbor to the north was built only to grace the view of the palace.

Pilate leaned on the window and caught the salty tang of the sea in a billowed mist on his face. The glorious harbor; the sumptuous Praetorium Palace; the Temple of Rome and Augustus; the theater and the statuary and the gardens; the Great Stadium with clashing tournaments, its sands dark and foamy with blood . . . because of these things, these alone, Pilate could feel at home in a gods-blasted outpost like Judea.

Because of these alone Pilate could ask his old friend Decimus to come from Rome. On the way, he had surely put in at the decrepit harbor at Phalasarna in Crete, then at Paphos on Cyprus. Either harbor would provide perfect contrast to what Decimus would soon find upon arrival at Caesarea.

If Decimus were at the bow, sea spray on his face, gazing at shining green-blue crests in the perfect weather of early summer, perhaps he would see a white speck upon the horizon. He would squint and ask of a deckhand, and be told, yes, that is Caesarea; the white speck is the Temple of Rome and Augustus. And Decimus would wonder out loud, You can see it so far out? And the deckhand would assure him, Just wait until you come into the harbor.

He would have heard about Herod's harbor, the better between it and the mighty Piraeus in Athens. This sweep of coastland, from Antioch in northern Syria down to the Egyptian border, provided no natural harbor, not for major trade. Herod the "Great" built a harbor so glorious, so sweeping in size it took a Roman to fully appreciate it. Indeed, Caesarea—he had named it for Augustus— became Herod's little Rome. It was Herod who built the pagan temple for Augustus. Herod who built the Roman amphitheater. Herod the Jew.

Decimus will remember that when he sees the colossal statues at the harbor mouth, and the colonnaded temple on the hill, the majestic centerpiece of the quay. When his ship comes under tow by a smaller vessel, and when he passes, openmouthed, beneath the sculpted stone arch connecting the towers at the harbor entrance, perhaps his skin will rise from a chill not induced by sea spray. He will think, astonished: *This, from the hand of a Jew!* And in the marveling, his childhood friend will be elevated in his estimation— Pilate is governor here. Pontius Pilate!

Pilate smoothed his hand on the damp stone windowsill. Maybe it was built on the promontory because it was closer to Rome. He pushed off from the window, away from the view, away from the pull of Rome. Orion Galerinius was waiting. Orion was a poor substitute for the view.

When he knew he had the governor's attention, the slightly built man opened and consulted his tablet. "Theron," Orion stated. "He is waiting in the audience hall with a few other candidates. Remember Theron? He repaired the mosaic around the drainage hole in the pool last winter."

Would Decimus trade his freedom for the tablet and stylus? Decimus was free. Free, after twenty years of military service, ready to take a pension and a wife and head for family land. Would he run back to Rome when he realized what sort of smug, cantankerous people he would have to deal with? Or would he see it as a challenge, just the sort he loved?

He would soon see what the Jews had put Pilate through. A mere letter could not convey the vexatiousness of these people. He'd rather face Jupiter in a bad mood than a cohort of these circumcised subjects of Rome. . . .

Orion Galerinius was waiting for an answer.

"Theron does fine work," said Pilate. "Hire him. Have him bring samples of borders, as well as any new patterns from Pompeii."

"You plan for more than a border for the walkway?" Though Orion kept his eyes on his tablet, over which his hand busily worked, his brow came up ever so slightly.

"If it pleases me," Pilate snapped.

"As you wish, Excellency. Theron and his people will be honored to be in the employ of Rome."

"Has the Primipilaris arrived?" Primipilaris, ex–first spear. Decimus had earned that title.

Orion finished pressing a note on the waxed tablet. "Not unless he has come in the last hour. I have a man waiting for him."

"His rooms are ready?"

"Have been for days."

"Good." Pilate would miss Orion's efficiency. He had a way of anticipating the governor that was both pleasing and irritating. "This Theron did fine work. Talkative, if I remember. Went on and on about the barbarian mosaicist who had done the original pool tile."

Orion's mouth twisted wryly. "Opinionated, sir. The good ones always are. His work rivals that of Dioskurides."

Pilate felt himself brighten. Dioskurides of Samos, one of the most brilliant mosaicists ever. So Caesarea had a Dioskurides. Another thing to tell Decimus. "Yes. Theron is an excellent choice. Put him to work right away. As soon as the hole is punched through."

"As you wish, Excellency."

"Next?" Pilate said, and Orion fell into pace beside him.

"Another letter from a place on the Galilee. Magdala. Owners of a dye works protesting an import tax on the Phoenician purple."

"Reply standard. Inform me when the letter count reaches five." Pilate trotted down the stone steps and rounded the corner. Orion kept pace, jotting as he went.

Pilate suddenly stopped. "There is a Phoenician-purple dye works at Joppa. Since when is the purple imported?"

Orion's lips pursed. "It isn't."

Who had slapped an import tax on the dye? Was Rome getting a cut? He continued down the steps. "Inform me when the count is five. Contact the magistrate who originated the tax and tell him we get 10 percent. Next?"

Orion pressed the notes in the wax, then hesitated as he consulted the other side of his tablet. "Conscription of a Jewish stonemason for the Tiberateum."

Pilate stopped, and Orion continued a step before he stopped as well.

"Well, what is it?" Pilate demanded. "He's purple over the fact that it's in honor of Tiberius? Tell him his own Herod built the Temple of Rome and Augustus."

"He has agreed to work on the Tiberateum—"

"Generous of him."

"—but will not work on his holy day." Orion's brown eyes met Pilate's briefly, then dropped.

Pilate stared down at the diminutive man, even smaller for standing a step lower. Will not work on his holy day. Will not. Pilate scratched his nose with his fingertip. "Well," he said softly. "Curse me if I cross the creed of the Jew. Of course, reply Jewish standard: give him his way."

Orion began to jot, but fury came. No. Pilate couldn't let this one go, not so soon after Jerusalem. The Jews needed a reminder of who was in charge. Every seventh day is their Sabbath?

"No, Orion. This: let him be scourged with seven times seven every day he does not work his Sabbath. If the others think to get out of work because of his example they will think again." He cut a quick glance at his secretary—yes, Orion was slow to record it on his tablet. *Don't think I did not see.* "This evening their Sabbath begins. The day after tomorrow I want you to be at the work site just before the men leave for the day. Assemble them and give the decree. The man will have one week to ponder his indiscretion." Scourge him seven times seven. It was lyrical. He drew a breath and said brightly, "Next?"

They came to the bottom of the stairwell and out into the colonnaded corridor. The columns bordered the swimming pool on all sides. It was a vast area that would be called the atrium back home.

A small room near the stairwell, of what purpose before imperial occupation Pilate was unsure, now served as the palace shrine. In it he could see Janus Bifrons, the palace priest, arranging a grain offering in the corner. Fussy as a prissy grandmother, that was Janus. He positioned the bronze dish, stood back to look, repositioned it. He glanced up as they passed and gave a ridiculous smile, as if pleased to be caught at his duty. Pilate ignored him and looked past the shrine to the triclinium.

A glance told him the dining room was ready, as was Orion's way. The table was set with refreshment, the serving ware polished to impress. Each day for the past week the table had been laid at the ready. Pilate hoped Decimus would prove as efficient. He had known Decimus since childhood; yes, he was a fine soldier, and ever the Roman competitor. But had he the talent for detail? Patience for it? Pilate had his doubts. Orion would have to train him well.

Pilate's fists closed. By the favor of the gods—and Janus Bifrons had taken his vow to the temple—he would secure Decimus. Decimus's father, Vitellus, was instrumental in Pilate's own posting; Vitellus had been friends with Sejanus, and Sejanus had been the confidante of Tiberius. Though scuttlebutt said Sejanus had fallen from favor with the emperor, time was Sejanus had his ear . . . and the gods had favored Pilate through suggestions whispered there.

Vitellus had always been good to Pilate. Ever since he was a boy, throwing makeshift javelins with Decimus, he had been treated by Vitellus as another son. It pained him to know that good Vitellus heard the rumors, too.

Why couldn't the Jews act like a subjugated people? *Why* couldn't Tiberius see their insolence? All the emperor heard were reports. Jewish reports. Whining and griping about the way Pilate ran things. Caesar was deceived into thinking *Pilate* was the instigator! Caesar should come to Judea himself. Give him one month here, just one month. He'd kick them out of their own country as he had kicked them out of Rome.

His smirk disappeared. If only Tiberius knew of Pilate's devotion, of his loyalty. If only he knew the inspiration he himself was to a patriotic governor on the outskirts—no—on the *expansion* of the Empire.

He quelled the growl in the back of his throat. Curse the Jews for turning his devotion into humiliating scandal. Curse them for making his name a mockery! He knew what they thought in Rome. *Pilate is weak. He cannot control as simple a folk as the Jews. What makes him think he will ever rise above a provincial governor?*

Decimus was the key. Pilate's good name could be restored with the witness of Decimus. They would believe him; his father was Vitellus.

"... a delicate matter. Her name is Rivkah. She is a Jewish prostitute. It appears she has—"

"Do not speak in my presence the name of one so insignificant as a Jewish prostitute!" Tiny missiles of spit landed on the tablet. "If that contains one more Jewish matter, you shall lunch on it."

"As you wish, Excellency." Orion discreetly slid his sleeve over the spit.

Pilate tugged down the sides of his toga. "Next?"

Orion doubtfully studied his tablet. "It appears our business is concluded. I will see to Theron."

"Good. Ready my escort. It is a beautiful day; I will walk to the harbor myself to see if Decimus has arrived."

"As you—"

"Tell me, Orion, what matter involving a Jewish prostitute is so cataclysmic it must be brought to the attention of the governor of Judea?" Pilate watched Orion color. "What matter could not be solved by a common magistrate? By a harbor sweeper!" Pilate now stood his tallest, gazing down on Orion. "What matter involving a Jewish *whore* could not be solved by the Chief Secretary to the Governor of the Judean Imperial Province of Rome?"

Orion had closed his tablet. He kept his eyes appropriately averted and appropriately did not answer. He had been told, after all, that he would eat his tablet if he said one more Jewish word. Orion was smart, if not wise.

Pilate let the moment linger, then said, "State the matter."

Orion opened his tablet. "It involves the granary going up in the southeast quadrant. There is a certain tree planted within the perimeters of the project. Apparently it is a custom of the Jews to plant a tree for a child when it is born. Work has not progressed to the slope, but the woman has—" for an instant, Orion's cadence faltered—"taken up residence in front of the tree. Because she is a prostitute, she has caused a bit of—" again that very interesting hesitation—"a scene. According to the foreman, some of the men have a hard time keeping attention on their work. The woman attends the Praetorium daily to plead for her tree, and the foreman on the project wants to know what is to be done." Orion closed his tablet.

Pilate stared. It was a perfect example of a Jewish matter poisoning the natural reason of a man normally talented in his work. Anyone who could not deal with a situation like that deserved to be kicked all the way back to Rome. Any misgivings at losing Orion evaporated once and for all.

He put his palms together and tapped his lips with his forefingers. "The foreman wants to know what is to be done with the tree . . . gods, what a perplexing situation. Would that I had Cicero at my aid. Perhaps I should write to Seneca. Shall we appeal to Tiberius?" Orion's face was growing dusky red. Pilate couldn't wait to tell this to Decimus. "Or . . ."

Pilate caught sight of a slave girl kneeling at a poolside planter, picking through the lavender plant, plucking out dead leaves. "You there!" The girl froze, fear making her eyes huge. "Yes, you. Come here."

She stood quickly, knocking over her watering can. She stared in horror at the can, jerked as if to right it, caught between instant obedience and her clumsiness. She left the can and scurried to Pilate. She stood trembling with hands clasped and eyes on the floor.

"A tree blocks the progress of a granary. What should be done about it?"

Her head jerked up. She gaped at Pilate, quickly averted her gaze, eyes shifting wildly. She even appealed to Orion with an astonished glance, but Orion's eyes were rigid on his tablet. "I—I—"

"What should be done about the tree?"

She swallowed. "I suppose . . . it should be . . . cut down?" She waited, wincing, for Pilate's response.

Pilate smiled warmly. "You may return to your duties."

She ducked her head and murmured with obvious relief, "Thank you, Excellency." She scurried back to the planter faster than she had come.

Orion should be plucking dead leaves from planters. Were he not so well organized, were he not so capable . . . yet his capability slipped bit by bit. An issue like this would have been too trivial to reach Pilate's ears a year or so ago. He could snap that scrawny neck in two, a Roman should not—yet suddenly—unexpectedly—Pilate felt compassion for him. Of all people Pilate should know what befuddled Orion's sensibilities: the man dealt daily with Jews. Daily.

"Orion Galerinius Honoratus." Pilate spoke his name with weary tenderness. With the compassion a father would have for a son. *It isn't your fault,* Pilate wanted to tell him. *It is the way of things, Orion. You were simply not strong enough. A lesser man would not have lasted as long as you did. Do I not know it? A perplexing thing, this corrosion from Jews, a disease, Orion. You had the misfortune to contract it.*

Pilate laid his hand on Orion's shoulder. "Here is what you do: Have the foreman cut down the tree. Have him send the Jewish whore away. If you have any other Jewish matters, bring them to me, we will work through them together." He wanted to tell Orion of the pity he felt for him, but could not risk *too* much compassion. Compassion weakened, it made the receiver feel sorry for himself. Whatever backbone Orion had left Pilate would need until Decimus arrived.

Orion slowly opened his tablet, took up his stylus. His hand paused over the amber-colored wax, then he pressed in a few notes—written in Greek, at least, Pilate noted, not Aramaic or Hebrew, thank the gods—and slipped the stylus back into its loop.

"I will call up your escort, Excellency," Orion murmured. "Enjoy your stroll." He inclined his head and took a few deferential steps backward. Clutching his tablet to his breast, he turned and strode away.

Pilate watched Orion walk past the long pool and disappear around the corner. He would miss Orion, the way he used to be. He would grieve for this son of Rome, as surely as if he had been murdered by a band of Zealots.

Would there was a cure for the madness. Only one Jew ever offered a glimmer of interest in Pilate's entire tour of duty in Judea, and now he was dead. He was only another stubborn, intolerant Jew. But . . . *Everyone who is of the truth hears my voice . . . ?* It still made Pilate laugh. So gloriously outrageous. Beautifully arrogant, even for a Jew. That was one Jew Pilate would have invited to dinner. His smile faltered.

He was leaning against one of the columns lining the pool. Next to the column was a planter filled with lavender flowers. Green and lavender flowed gracefully from the planter, the green-leaved tendrils perfectly trimmed to barely brush the marble floor. The same planter with the same array stood beside each column lining three sides of the pool. There were forty-five columns, eighteen each on the long sides. Pilate counted them the first day he came to Caesarea.

The swimming pool was open to the sky, and the waxing sun warmed the fresh water. The pool was nearly half the length of the private wing of the palace, its grand centerpiece. Pilate liked to come here. Not to swim, which was nearly un-Roman. The mesmerizing symmetry of the pool attracted him. Symmetry soothed.

Even in the main triclinium, the one with the view that waited for Decimus, symmetry prevailed; the mosaic was a transfixing marvel of pure pattern: tiny black-and-white tiles formed squares within ever-smaller squares. Though others found the floor hard on the eyes, it was there Pilate could breathe deeply. There, with the soothing rigidity of pattern, he felt most Roman.

He unlaced his sandals and set them neatly at the poolside, then sat and put his feet in the water. He stared at the gently rippling surface of the pool, until his eyes focused on the bottom. The mosaic in the center of the pool bottom was created by the same master who had done the triclinium mosaic. Overlapping concentric circles this time. Pure pattern. Pure order. Decimus will be impressed.

Orion heard his own footsteps echo back from the walls. He kept himself rigid, he walked with precision. If he looked over his shoulder he'd see Pilate seated at the pool's edge again, sandals at his side, feet in the water. Reveling in his many clevernesses. He came to the end of the corridor, turned the corner, and closed his eyes. He could wail like a woman over the memory of Pilate's hand on his shoulder.

Sympathy! Pilate was showing him *sympathy*! Didn't he feel like a little boy who just had his head tousled? Shrieking gods and goddesses and all their mincing offspring. But the thought of shrieking gods reminded him of the look Janus Bifrons had given him when they passed the shrine . . . that simpering smile. It only started his flesh on a crawl, and now Pilate's sympathy. What a day this was going to be.

He pried the tablet from his chest to look at the nonsense he had pressed into wax. Scourge the Jewish architect with seven times seven? Every time he did not work on the Sabbath? Brilliant, Excellency. Ho, brilliant. And cut down the tree? Cut down *her* tree? Gods, he had to think. How could he cover for him this time? Why not leave the Jews to their peculiarities? They did no harm. Even the Caesars saw that, Augustus a long time ago, Julius well before. Tiberius was another matter.

Pilate's renovation to the northeast stairwell was about the only impressive decision he had made lately. The new entry from the private wing of the palace to the public auditorium would save Orion countless steps. He came to the place where workers would soon punch a hole through the Praetorium wall. Already a man was measuring and taking down notes on his own waxed tablet. He gave Orion a glance.

Pilate was foolish to order an entire mosaic for the walkway. A border would have been sufficient. Tasteful and unpretentious. The expense would be astounding, for Theron of Caesarea did not come cheaply. It was one more thing local magistrates could fling in Pilate's face regarding his excesses with public money. But Orion couldn't stop a smile; he would see Theron every day. With his own duty to oversee the project, life in the palace had a sudden warmth to it.

But the worker was looking strangely at him. Orion stopped smiling and escaped around the corner and out the entryway. Already the day was hot, and it was nowhere near noon. Ornamental trees lined the flagstone walkway and would soon give shade from the early sun. The Great Stadium just beyond the Praetorium blocked the sun for now. From there came the faint sound of metallic clashing. Cornelius would have been running the auxiliary troop through drills since dawn.

He stopped a moment to kick a few pebbles off a flagstone. His stylus slid out of the tablet, and he bent to retrieve it, glancing at the inscription etched into the ivory on the flattened end. It had been a gift from his father before he left Rome over five years ago. He tucked it back inside his tablet.

He entered the doorway to the business half of the great Praetorium; here, rooms and corridors had bewildered him for the first six months of his new position. He would constantly turn a corner into a dead end, or come into a hallway when he expected a wall. It was as frustrating as a garden maze in Annapolis. Once Pilate's renovation was complete, Orion could avoid the extra steps in this honeycomb and go straight to the auditorium. It would be the best decision of Pilate's tour, and not even Orion could see how it could offend the Jews—unless Pilate decided to make the mosaic a tribute to Caesar or a god. Or make it Jews dining on pork. Ha! Pilate would even invite the Jewish Council to come see its unveiling—and expect praise for it! Orion laughed out loud.

He wound his way deftly through the halls and came out into the huge auditorium. He looked for Theron, and found him already studying the floor at the northwest corner.

Orion went to dismiss the other candidates. There were only four, but each seemed resigned to the fact that Theron would get the job; indeed, scowls had formed on their faces when Theron was the last to arrive this morning. Orion thanked each of them and watched them go, then strolled across the auditorium to Theron.

Not many people were shorter than Orion. His height had prevented him from joining the Roman army, had fated him to a life of scholarship or politics, and only an unexpected summons from Tiberius himself had delivered him. Only Tiberius could have changed the course of his stars. Tiberius or Theron's god.

Theron of Caesarea was nearly as thick as he was short, and hairy as a bear. Tufts of hair came out the top of his tunic. He did not wear the hair on his face, which was not particularly Jewish of him, and the only time he did not wear a scowl was when his wife, Marina, upbraided him for this or that. He looked like a tiny giant at those times, abashed and found out. Marina was the only one to confound the fearsome Theron.

Theron also had the biggest lower lip Orion had ever seen. It looked like a fat earthworm. Sometimes it was hard not to look at it. It stuck out far now, as Theron studied the pavement.

"He wants it to match the border, or he wants a different one?" Theron asked when Orion joined him.

"Most people would find your presumption irritating."

Theron glared at the existing border. "I hope he wants a different one. I could complement it nice. Who knows where Herod got his tesserae; a match will be impossible without sourcing it. You got some wear, you got some variations from the lighting. See? Look at the lighting in here, it's terrible. What did you say?"

"I said you have the job."

"Oh. You coming tonight? Marina is making fried fish balls."

Orion pretended casual surprise. "It's your Sabbath already? The week has flown." But the thought reminded him of Pilate's latest decrees. He was supposed to give Pilate's order for the stonemason day after tomorrow, but the punishment didn't go into effect until next week. That was when Pilate would inquire if the man had changed his mind. He would buy himself thinking time with that one week. Thinking time? Only a fool wouldn't give the order.

Only a fool would. Orion pinched the space between his eyes. What could he do this time? Whatever it was, Pilate would find out.

He would want to know how the Jew had held up under the whip. He would want details. And what of the tree? No, he couldn't think that far, the scourging overwhelmed it. Forty-nine? Every time he did not work the Sabbath? The full import settled in. No one could survive a straight forty-nine; the tree was nothing compared to this. A woman could lose her tree, but a man would lose his life. A woman would lose her husband; children, their father. Flaming gods and goddesses and all their mincing offspring, where was that poppy tent?

"You like the fish balls. What's the problem?"

Orion glanced about before he replied. "A tricky one this time."

"What's Pilate up to now?"

"Keep your voice down, Theron," Orion hissed through a smile. "We're not at your table, we're in the Praetorium Palace. You will have to remember that every single time you enter that doorway."

Theron shrugged and put his glare back on the pavement. He scratched his black curly head. "Well? What's it gonna be? Match it or complement it?"

"You don't look like an artisan. You look like an ornery stonecutter."

Theron glanced at Orion, bemused. He shook a thick finger at him. "You know, that's why I like you. You got a sense of humor with a nice nasty streak."

Orion laughed. It didn't take long, around Theron. "Fish balls, eh?"

"And fish gravy. Marina wants to impress our new apprentice."

"You hired someone? He must not be from around here."

"He's out on the steps. Trying to decide if he's a good Jew or a bad Jew. I says to him, 'You coming in? Good Jews don't.' He says, 'What does that make you?' I says, 'Rich.'" Theron chuckled.

"He must have decided he's a good Jew."

But at that Theron's amusement disappeared. He pursed his thick lips and shook his head. "No, he don't think he is. Marina says he's got a bunch of heart trouble. You can't tell by looking at him. I leave such things to Marina."

Orion gazed across the auditorium at the Praetorium entrance. *Marina is probably why the lad even got hired.* "You've got a good wife, Theron," he said quietly.

Theron looked at the entrance too, and sighed so deeply it became a groan. "He don't know a template from a tile."

"Where is he from?"

"Hebron. He's been in Caesarea awhile looking for someone. Couldn't find him, needed to eat. Marina found him in the marketplace and brought him home for dinner."

Marina had an uncanny knack for spotting the lost.

Theron bent to examine the color of the border. He wet his thumb and rubbed it on a tile. "So. What does the Illuminated One say? Match it or complement it?"

"Complement it. And he wants a mosaic for the entire walkway. Bring your patterns tomorrow. See if you have anything new from Pompeii. He specifically mentioned Pompeii."

Theron rose and rubbed his chubby hands together. "Good, good. I'll be on the job for a year."

Orion shook his head. "You, a whole year. A whole year of daily insolence."

"Palace food, every day." Theron patted his protruding gut.

Orion cocked his head. "Or is it a year of comic relief?"

"Wait, wait—I got it. Tell them the artist will not work without a pistachio pastry every day. Two of them. Tell them it inspires me."

"I'll have to offer extra sacrifices for patience . . . Janus will have to bribe the *di penates.*"

"Which god is that?"

"The spirit of the pantry. Protector of the household stores. It will have to go on extra duty with you around."

"Well, you got a god for wine? Tell your priest to throw in extras for that one too. And only the good stuff. Tell them the artist works better with the good stuff."

Orion laughed. "Go tell your new apprentice the artist got the job. I have to call up Pilate's escort before the governor drowns himself."

"See you tonight."

"Tonight." Orion left him and entered the honeycomb of rooms.

His duties did not often allow time for personal things, like writing letters home. Orion had long since taken a habit of sending them on the wind until he had time to put ink to parchment.

"To my beloved Father," he dictated under his breath, "from your son, Orion Galerinius, greetings. I pleased a god today, Father, I don't know which. But Theron will work in the palace for a year."

Theron in the palace for a year. Not even Tiberius could have pulled off that one.

⁂

Theron watched Orion leave. He did not believe the man had forgotten it was Sabbath. Orion never forgot. He hadn't missed a Sabbath meal for nearly a year.

Marina had found him, too, same marketplace. Theron thought maybe Marina was like the story of the angel in Jerusalem, with the pool. Maybe the marketplace got stirred up, and Marina was there to make a lame one well. At least get him on the road to well. Last year she brought home Orion. Before Orion, Bereniece and her mother. Before Bereniece, Lucius and what's-his-name. Before Lucius, Rivkah and her boy, Nathanael. He frowned at the border tiles. This new one, though. He was a case even for Marina. Orion, she had drawn out. After a month of his awkward visits every Sabbath evening, he began to smile. Another month, and he was laughing with everyone else. Another month, and he was making the jokes himself.

But this young Joab. He had a black cloud snugged over him that even Theron could see. And Theron usually did not see. That was for Marina. Maybe it was twenty-five years with her that did it. He would have never noticed before. He wasn't sure he liked it that he noticed now.

He slowly strolled to the entrance, taking his time to gaze all around. He liked to work on-site. Some transferred their designs by portion to the pavement; not Theron. He worked classically, like Samos, and wasn't about to stop now. Once he had the preliminary sketches complete, once the construction workers put in the archway, and once he sourced out enough tesserae, he would work in this posh place every day. Unless of course, this turned out to be the right place for his ribbon pavement. A long time he had been waiting for a place for the ribbon pavement. He'd have to wait and see what those construction workers did with that walkway.

He couldn't wait to tell Marina: he was now on the payroll of the Roman government, every shekel guaranteed. Regular pay, and at the price he was worth. His stroll became a swagger. They would do some celebrating tonight. He paused halfway across the auditorium to regard the bema seat, set on the dais in the center of the great room. All the swagger suddenly went out of him.

Pilate's latest act, the crucifixion of that prophet from Nazareth, still had Jewish Caesarea buzzing. It was cruel even for Pilate. Theron shook his head. The lad was a good man. Did good things. Wasn't Jesus the main topic of every Sabbath meal for the past few years? Probably didn't have enough money to barter for his life, and Pilate could be bought. Surely he worked hard to line his pockets as much as possible before his term in Judea was up, like any other Roman official.

Theron left the bema and came out, squinting, into the morning sun. Joab sat on the steps with his chin on his fist, gazing at the curved wall of the Great Stadium. Next to him was the bundle that never left him. He rose when he saw Theron.

"You got the job?"

"I got it. We'll celebrate more than the Sabbath tonight. Pilate will keep me in pastries for a year."

"Good," Joab said, and looked again at the Great Stadium. The tinny sound of steel meeting steel came from there; it was where the auxiliary troops learned the Roman method of warfare. The stadium was impressive, but Theron had lived in Caesarea most of his life. He barely noticed the things Joab gawked at.

He was a Judean country boy, complete with accent. And he didn't speak much Greek. Most of Caesarea was going Greek, had been for a while, since the days of Herod. It was good for Theron to practice his Aramaic with Joab. His mother would be proud.

"Come, boy, we have much to do before tomorrow. Pilate wants to see patterns of Pompeii. Patterns of Pompeii, we will give him."

"But . . . tomorrow is Sabbath," Joab said doubtfully as he scooped up the bundle and followed Theron down the steps.

"Aye, and the Lord of the Universe is aware of the fact that it doesn't mean much to Pilate, save for some peace and quiet from his Jewish subjects. Besides, you constantly forget that I am a bad Jew." He reached over to flick him on the head. "You have been with us for a week, this you should know."

"Yes," Joab said, squinting at the stadium. "I have been with you a week, and you are not a bad Jew."

"Neither are you."

To this, the boy did not respond. He kept his gaze on the Great Stadium as long as he could, walking backward to do it, until the road put it behind them.

"Pompeii," Theron muttered. "Whatever I come up with has to be from Pompeii. If he asks you, it's from Pompeii."

"Do you have anything from Pompeii?" Joab ventured.

Theron tapped his head. "Right here, boy. I was trained in Pompeii, seven years. So anything I come up with is from Pompeii. And anything I come up with is new: there you have it. New patterns from Pompeii."

They walked in silence for a while. At least Theron would get the exercise Marina spouted about; the palace was nearly a mile from their neighborhood. He was already sweating from exertion. He glanced at the morose boy next to him and grimaced. The lad had barely spoken all week. Made for awkward times in the workroom.

But he seemed willing enough. Theron could see the blisters on his hands from chiseling stone boards, and the boy didn't whine about them. And often he forgot he was a bad Jew and kissed the mezuzah in the doorway. It seemed to take deliberate thought for Joab *not* to kiss it. Theron would learn his story soon enough.

"Fish balls tonight," he said gruffly.

Joab did not answer, lost in a brood that rendered him deaf. Theron fancied he could reach out and touch the shroud that walked with the boy.

Presently, the quiet one spoke. And it was Theron's turn to be speechless.

"Do you know where I can find a Jewish prostitute?"

Theron slid him a glower the lad did not see. He was too busy staring at the back of the Temple of Rome and Augustus. Theron shook his head. Some people's children. If Joab was his own boy he wouldn't sit for a week, asking a question like that.

He sighed. Well, Joab wasn't his boy, and it was none of his business. "Does she have to be Jewish?"

Joab broke from his stare at the temple. Interestingly, his cheeks went red as a sunset. "No—that's not what I—"

"There's a place, an inn—the kind no honest mother's son has business being at—in the west part of the Old City. It might have what you are—" and on behalf of the boy's mother, he scowled his blackest at the lad—"interested in."

The boy's face went redder, and Theron scratched the back of his head. Well, did he want directions or not? Who could figure out young people these days?

Joab stammered, "I don't want—I'm not—" but he didn't finish the thought. He simply sighed deeply.

Maybe it was a good time to change the subject. "Did you find your friend yet?"

The boy gave a strange half chuckle, then said, "No, not yet."

"Are you sure he is supposed to be in Caesarea?"

Joab gazed at a lawn party of affluent Romans in the back of a stately villa. He murmured, "It's not a he."

Ah. This was an important piece of information. Not a he the boy was looking for, a *she*. No matter that it took a week to find it out. He would bring this to Marina, and she would be pleased. He clasped his hands around his belly, delighted with himself. Eh, someday he would be as good at this as his wife. And he knew enough not to proceed further with Joab. Like a perfect mosaic, he would walk around it, study it, give it time. Then place the tile exactly where it should go.

Heart matters required finesse, he was learning. After twenty-five years, Marina was finally getting her hands dirty and learning how to create a mosaic; so, too, Theron was learning Marina's craft.

"Fish balls tonight, my boy," he boomed cheerfully. "And nobody makes them like Marina."

2

Tucked into the shadows, Pilate watched Orion shut the door to his personal quarters. Under his arm was an amphora of wine. Every seven or eight days, Orion left the palace near sunset with an amphora of wine. He disappeared into the city for the entire evening, returning late. He was never late for duty the next morning. If his eyes were tight at the edges from less sleep—or much wine—Pilate could not confront him for dereliction of duty. Nor could Pilate accuse him of pilfering wine from his reserve; Orion was fastidiously honest. He would not steal from Pilate.

A woman? A *man*? A prostitute? Was the wine a special libation to a god? Did he give a weekly vow at the Temple of Rome? Pilate could never ask him where he went. To question Orion on personal matters would be distasteful.

Orion's quarters were near the stairwell. He could hear the slap of the secretary's sandals as he descended the marble steps. He counted the steps, sixteen, seventeen, eighteen, nineteen. The footsteps faded and the palace was silent. Pilate emerged from the shadows and looked long where Orion had gone.

⅋

Theron and Marina lived in a decent enough neighborhood, if a Jewish one. The northern part of Caesarea had the densest Jewish population. Here were a few synagogues and quiet Sabbath days. If Orion ever had a day off because of a festival, and if the festival happened to be on a Sabbath, it was there Orion would go. He would walk the close alleys off the main street. He would listen, and watch, and enjoy the peace. Orion was born and raised in Rome. It was never peaceful in Rome. To take a day off from the hustle, every seven days without fail, was an eerie and pleasant idea. Someone should present it in the Senate.

Caesarea Maritima was still called Straton's Tower by most, and by the Jews its Hebrew name, Migdal Sar. Herod renamed it Caesarea in honor of Augustus, and Maritima set it apart from inland Caesarea Philippi. But it had been Straton's Tower for centuries, and a name took a few generations to change.

"Migdal Sar," Orion murmured. The Hebrew words were interesting on his tongue.

Caesarea snugged the Mediterranean coast like a great god lying on his side, languidly trailing fingers in the sea. The main street was called the Cardo Maximus and ran from the Roman barracks, south of the palace near the city wall, up to the gate near the old north harbor. The route from the palace to Theron's took Orion past the prestigious southern villas, past the temple and Herod's Harbor. There was always something to see, and anything was welcome after a day in the Praetorium. Almost anything—he was passing the site for the new Tiberateum, Pilate's soon-to-be monument to his beloved Tiberius. The site Pilate had chosen evidenced his ambition, just north of the mighty temple Herod built. It would likely overshadow it.

Herod was much like Pilate, Orion mused. They would have been infamous friends, the Jew trying to please the pagans, the pagan trying to please the Jews. Herod's temple, built in honor of Augustus Caesar, evidenced the point perfectly. It was built along the Corinthian influence but kept in check with its obvious lack of ostentation—it was Herod trying to please Augustus while maintaining some inscrutable Jewish sensibility. Laughable, considering it was a pagan temple. Perhaps it would have been more beautiful if it had been wholly Jewish or wholly pagan.

Usually Orion enjoyed the walk. Today the newest Jewish dilemmas wouldn't let him.

Theron had to help him. How could he disobey Pilate this time? How could he save that poor wretch from Pilate's madness? And what about the tree? *Her* tree? Orion could not see a way out, but Theron would know what to do.

He passed the quay of the inner harbor with no more than a glance at the waters washed in sunset. Smoke from the lighthouse on the northern breakwater momentarily took his attention, that and the smells he caught on the sudden breeze: burning charcoal and roasting fish, ocean salt and rotten seaweed. Clematius had better be on the quay with his eyes out for the arrival of Decimus Caratacus; he had more of an eye for the women who walked the quay than he had for the ships themselves.

Orion's gaze left the lighthouse smoke and settled again on the cobbled pavement. Life was much easier before he met Theron and Marina. Morality in its first form had always been duty to the State of Rome. It's how he was raised, how any decent citizen of Rome was raised. He'd never much considered anything else. Caring about the treatment of Jews was still so foreign and new that it itched.

He came to the cross street with the bank of storefronts and remembered the directions Theron gave a year ago . . . take the Cardo Maximus to a street called Mer. Go past the storefronts and enter the gate of the first commonyard you see. The last house on the left. The one with the mosaic in front.

Orion smiled as he unlatched the gate. Theron didn't tell him the "mosaic in front" was actually a mosaic set right into the wall of the house. An upright mosaic! A pavement standing up. Theron told him later that this was an innovation learned in Pompeii. He said one day it would be fashion. Orion didn't think so. You couldn't walk on it, what kind of mosaic was that?

The courtyard was alive with people hurrying to finish tasks before the sun set. Women surrounded a common-use oven in the middle of the commonyard. Children played or scurried to do errands for their mothers. Men came in from fields, or market, or smithies, or halls of study. One murmured to him, "Good Sabbath," as he passed, and he replied in turn; it was getting dim, the man did not see he addressed a Gentile, the toga-wearing Roman kind.

He came to the last home on the left, the fourth one down, the one with the mosaic in front. The mosaic was a lovely pattern of white sea crests. Look at it another way, and it was blue crests. Orion had seen much of Theron's work in Caesarea; some of it even contained images of birds and animals—things forbidden to make image of, according to the rules of their sect. This mosaic, embedded on Theron's wall, evidenced his respect of his people. His other work, gracing the pavements of rich southern villas, evidenced the independence of his art.

Orion smiled; Theron's brand of Judaism allowed him to break bread with a Gentile, something for which most Jews around here would choke on their own tongues. To the right of the mosaic was the window. Orion gazed inside before he knocked.

Marina's table was set for Sabbath. Upon a white linen tablecloth were candlesticks and little dishes filled with nuts and dried fruit and salt and herbs. And oh, the aroma coming through the window. Orion closed his eyes and inhaled. Savory fish gravy that only Marina could make. He could hear the fish balls sizzling in the olive oil on the charcoal brazier in the kitchen alcove. Marina was talking to the gravy; he couldn't catch what was said. He could already feel the warmth of the kitchen.

Once Marina had asked him to bring a friend to enjoy the meal. By her dancing look he knew what she meant. But life in the palace afforded no time for romance. Briefly, the face of the woman filled his mind. No, there wouldn't be romance with that one. Her romance came at a price, and Orion was saving for a tract of land in Ostia. Still, those amber eyes. Her other features did not dazzle, but the eyes made her beautiful. He'd seen more lovely cheekbones, more perfect noses. True, her lips, shiny and sticky with cosmetics, were beautiful. But it was the eyes that demanded one's attention. They made up for ordinary features, and surely she knew it. The ground kohl lining her eyes, giving stark contrast to their golden hue, proved it.

She had been to the palace every day for two weeks. Sometimes Orion had a difficult time listening to what she said, so—he felt himself flush—distracted he was with her eyes. What was he to do with her tree? By the gods, it was a predicament.

"You going to stand there and just smell your dinner, or you going to come in?" Marina stood in the doorway, smiling that crooked smile, fists on her hips.

Her dark eyes were in a long and lovely face; she was probably considered very pretty in her younger days. Well, these were her beautiful days. She was taller than Theron, infinitely more elegant, and Orion often wondered what the ugly, ornery mosaicist had done to capture her heart. Her eyes carried the gleam of humor and kindness, and a smile was never long from her lips.

Her apron was spotted with grease stains, and her chin was tipped in meal. Marina looked at him more closely. "What—I thought you liked fish balls."

He handed her the amphora. "Good Sabbath, Marina."

"Say it in Hebrew and I'll be impressed. What's the matter?"

"I can barely manage Aramaic, and you want Hebrew?" He followed her into the house and pulled off his outer tunic. As he hung it on the peg near the door, he looked around. "Where's Theron?"

"Back in the shop. Cleaning up with our new helper."

Orion went to the brazier in the kitchen alcove and put his nose over the pan. He rolled his hand, beckoning the fragrance, and sighed. "Why are you not a palace cook? I am tired of the latest dishes from Rome."

"They could not afford me. Besides, they want pig. Can you imagine? Me, cooking pig? I wouldn't know how to do it." She took down plates from the shelves. "Can you see me asking for recipes?" Her tone grew animated. "'Esther, Esther . . . how do I make pig balls?'"

Orion turned to look out the window at the home across the commonyard. "Where is Thomas? It's dark over there."

"He is not coming tonight. His cousin just came in from Nazareth. They are taking the Sabbath meal with his sister-in-law on the west side. Here, put that on the table."

Orion took the willow mat and placed it in the center of the table. He took the stack of plates from her and began to distribute them.

He smiled as he remembered the first few visits here. How foolish he had felt then. "I will miss Thomas tonight." He missed Sarah too. Thomas's wife had died in early winter. "Will his cousin be staying long? I'm glad he'll have some company."

Marina took two dishcloths and lifted the hot pan from the brazier. She brought it to the table and set it on the willow mat. "I'm not sure. Lovely little thing, she came to visit while Theron was at the palace. She was so taken with the outside mosaic." Marina looked out the window to Thomas's place. "Poor lamb. Her brother was the one who—" She caught herself and slid a look at Orion. "He was the one Pilate crucified in Jerusalem."

Orion looked to Thomas's home. "Really."

Marina followed his gaze and shook her head. "Poor girl. She must have adored her brother. She's a walking wound and doesn't even know it. Perhaps it isn't real yet."

"Perhaps it is too real."

Marina sighed. "Perhaps." She looked a moment longer, then turned to the cupboard.

Orion kept a thoughtful gaze on the darkened home. He never knew the old man was related to Jesus of Nazareth. Thomas had never mentioned it.

How many times had Pilate called for that particular record from the archives? How many times did Orion have to pull the scrolls only to reshelve them? What was Pilate trying to decide? A copy of the report had been sent to Rome, as was procedure for any execution. What was wrong with it that the governor needed to reexamine it every other week? There were two other reports that Pilate repeatedly called for: the report on the standards and the report on the aqueduct. Two of the most notorious incidents in his term. The Jesus incident had joined them.

It was common knowledge Pilate had erred grossly with his

conduct regarding the standards and the aqueduct; he had deeply offended the Jews, and if he continued it would one day cost him his position. Or start an uprising. Of this, Orion was certain. But the matter of Jesus . . . Orion had read the report himself, and it only perplexed him. Pilate had pleased the Jews this time. This time he did what they wanted, without his usual resistance, something very un-Pilate-like. This report did not seem to match the others.

Orion had not been in Jerusalem that day. It fell to him to look after matters in Caesarea when Pilate was away. Prometheus, his undersecretary, had accompanied Pilate. Orion knew this Jesus had raised the roof in just about every Jewish household in Palestinia, but he had not paid much attention. He had a Praetorium to run.

"Did you know Thomas was related to Jesus?" he asked.

"No," Marina replied. "It was news to me."

Many Sabbath-meal discussions had included this Jesus. Theron, and especially Marina, had been interested in the young man. They had talked about going to listen to one of his discussions. Marina had called his death a cruel shame—at times like those he felt most acutely in Pilate's employ.

"You are grumpy again. What are you thinking of?"

Orion realized he was still holding a plate. He set it on the table. "You know, if Pilate knew I came here every week . . ."

Marina raised her eyes to the ceiling. "May the Eternal prevent such a thing . . ."

". . . I would be on the next ship to Rome. On my merry way to exile." Orion flicked his forehead. "I'll tell him tomorrow. What have I been thinking?"

"You will do no such thing," Marina chided, and gave his arm a firm, twisting pinch. "Where would our people be without you? You have done much to prevent needless—oh, now what is that look? Will you please tell me what ails you?"

"Pilate."

"Pilate ails everyone," Theron boomed as he came in from the back room. "So what is new about that?"

"Good Sabbath, Theron," Orion greeted him. He nodded to the lad following behind Theron. Heart trouble, Theron said he had. That could mean anything from women to . . . well, women. The young man nodded back, ducking his glance away.

"Say it in Hebrew—"

"And I'll be impressed," Orion finished with him. "Do you speak Hebrew?"

Theron shrugged. "I'm Jewish. Close enough." He gestured to the boy. "Joab? I give you Orion the Magnificent. He works for a fellow you may have heard of: Pontius Pilate."

The lad's eyes widened, and Orion watched the color drop from his face. The boy glanced quickly at Theron and Marina, as if he couldn't believe Orion stood in their home. "What does he do for him?" Interesting that he would not ask Orion himself.

"Well, now, that's a good question. I have a hard time getting that right myself," Theron said. "What do you do for Pilate, Orion?"

Orion smiled. If he were back home the answer would be simpler. In the province, his office was more complex. He was Pilate's nomenclator, supplying the names of all the important merchants and magistrates who came to the palace. He was quaestor, Pilate's financial secretary, paymaster to his staff. He was aedile, heading up administration of local authorities. And he made sure the palace didn't run out of candles or lentils or coal or Pilate's favorite wine. In the province, where they could not quite get things to run as they did back home, it culminated to one title.

"I'm his chief secretary."

"That's right, chief secretary." Theron reached to flick Joab on the head. "Pilate's number one—you better behave around him."

The sullen look on Joab's face meant he was either uneasy or determined to be unimpressed.

"It's all right," Theron assured him. "He's on our side."

"And which side would that be?" Orion wondered.

"The right side."

Orion chuckled. "The Jewish side, then? This from a self-proclaimed bad Jew?"

But Theron grimaced, and gained a muttering tone. "No. This from a human being. Why in God's name people like Pilate have to be in power . . ."

"Theron . . . ," Marina warned gently. "Come, my men. Let's eat. Tonight is a night for celebration." She gestured them to the table. Joab glanced at Orion and seemed to pick out the seat farthest from him.

They stood around the table while Theron the bad Jew invoked a blessing on the meal. A surreptitious glance showed Joab with his eyes closed, rocking gently on his heels in that Jewish custom, mouthing the words. The blessing said, Marina touched a twisted bit of cloth to a coal in the brazier and lit the candles.

Orion's plate was soon full of the bounty of Marina's table. Fish balls covered in a savory herb-speckled gravy. Marina's delicious bread. Spiced olives and cinnamon-scented dates. Roasted barley, perfectly seasoned. A tangy cucumber salad. Orion made sure to keep himself extra hungry on this day; woe to the man who did not eat enough of Marina's food.

She poked Joab's arm. "How about those fish balls?"

Joab nodded, chewed, and swallowed. "Very good."

"They make them like this in Hebron?"

The lad shook his head. "Not like this. My mother would—" But he broke off and looked at his plate.

Marina smoothly took up. "She would probably want the recipe." She took the dish and pushed more fish balls onto his plate.

"My mother put onions in hers," Joab said quietly.

"You gotta quit talking so much," Theron said with his mouth full. He looked at Orion. "I never heard him talk so much."

"I should get Thomas's cousin over here," Marina said as she broke off a piece of bread from the loaf. "So pretty she would leave you speechless. Oh, and Theron—she wishes to learn the trade."

"Ah. A sensible girl."

"Thomas had to drag her away from the wall." She looked at Orion. "You can meet her at the next Sabbath meal."

Orion's mouth twisted. "It was hard enough for you to get Thomas to eat with the fearsome Gentile. How will his cousin feel?" He put his gaze on Joab. "How do you feel, lad? Breaking bread with a Gentile? A *Roman* Gentile?"

If his cheeks colored just a trace, the boy replied evenly, "Is it a political or religious question?"

Orion's eyebrows shot up. He exchanged a look with Theron. There was more to this boy than met the eye. "Very good. How about an answer to both."

Joab wiped his mouth with his napkin. "Religiously? The decision to eat with you is not mine. It is that of my host. My employer."

Theron banged the table approvingly. "Well put, boy! What do you think, Orion?"

But Orion put his elbows on the table and looked at the boy over folded hands. "And politically?"

Up until now the lad had not looked him in the eye, not for any real length of time. Now, he tore a piece of bread from his loaf and put it in his mouth, chewing deliberately—never taking his eyes from Orion's. Orion returned the gaze, and found it hard to keep from smiling. By the gods, this lad had backbone.

Marina took a sip from her cup, cleared her throat delicately, and said, "It is hard to answer Pontius Pilate's closest employee, isn't it, Joab?"

"Make no mistake, Marina," Orion said wryly. "He answered it." Someone had raised the boy to be a good Jewish nationalist. What decent nationalist worth his weight in hidden weapons wanted to sit with someone who represented the conquest and occupation of his land?

Theron reached to thump Joab's shoulder. "No worries here, Joab. Remember what I said? Orion is on our side. You can speak freely around this table."

Orion leaned back and appraised the mosaicist. "Yes, Theron, let's talk about that. Tell me what is the right side again."

"The Jewish side."

"But you're fond of telling people you are a bad Jew. You're proud of it." He gestured at Joab. "Don't you worry about corrupting the innocents?"

"That he can take care of himself," Theron said, easing a strange grimace at Joab. Interestingly, Joab flushed at the comment.

"How many bad Jews are there like you, Theron?" Orion asked.

Theron dipped a big chunk of bread in a dish of mashed olives and oil. "Not so many," he said regretfully, and took a mighty bite of the bread. Around the mouthful, he said, "Many are good. Too many."

Conversation dwindled and eating revived, and with the settled silence came the thoughts that ceaselessly troubled Orion. He didn't want to talk about it, not yet. He was enjoying the meal. The company. He was enjoying this part of his life that Pilate and the palace and Rome could not touch. He gripped his cup. But conversation usually came down to Pilate, the palace, or Rome. It came in particular to those delicate intricacies that lay below the surface of his occupation. Delicate things he kept from Pilate.

His first breach of Pilate's protocol came before he knew Theron and Marina. Pilate had a palace edict in effect that Orion had followed without thought . . . until he met little Benjamin and his mother.

Pilate did not want the small children of palace slaves to remain with their mothers during the day. At the age of five, the children were placed in the care of a supervisor who taught them various jobs, like cleaning out the dung pits and sorting the charcoal. One day an upper-level servant, a Roman citizen who tended the triclinia, had dragged a laundress to Orion's workroom. The laundress was a Jew and a palace slave, placing her two steps below the free Roman servant. The servant was a nasty woman named Rhodinia who announced to Orion that the Jewish slave had a son who stayed at her side during the day—even though the child was five.

The Jew was terrified, her eyes desperate and her face white with fear. She tried to keep her son firmly behind her, but he peeked out, interested in the doings. Rhodinia, in the midst of her tirade, seized the child's arm and jerked him out to display him to Orion.

"I have a five-year-old son," Rhodinia had screeched, "and he is not allowed to stay with me—a Roman citizen! This woman is a Jew, and her child stays at her side!"

Orion had looked down on the child, who looked up, black eyes full of uncertainty. The uncertainty caught Orion. Another child his age would have been fearful. He merely stared from adult to adult, unsure yet interested in what was happening. His face had an open and rather vacant look, an expression not normal on a five-year-old. His lower lip hung, adding to the wide-eyed bewilderment. He blinked up at Orion.

"What is your name, boy?" Orion had asked.

The mother bent to repeat the words to the child in Aramaic. The child thought it over carefully and said to Orion, "Benjamin."

Then slowly he said something to his mother and waited for her to say it to Orion. The woman hushed her boy, but Orion asked, "What did he say?"

And the woman, blushing crimson, replied in halting Greek, "He wishes to touch your face, sir. His father and his uncles have beards, and he has never touched the smooth face of a man."

Orion went to his knee and put his chin out. The child first inspected Orion's cheeks, then reached and put his palms on either side of Orion's face. He rubbed his cheeks and patted them, serious as a merchant in a barter. Then, satisfied, the child smiled at Orion and looked up at his mother. Orion rose, and looked at Rhodinia.

"This child is not five. He is four."

Rhodinia shrieked, "He is almost six! He is older than my Theophocles! And he is a *Jew!*" Then she realized with whom she argued. She dropped her eyes and cut a furious stare at the mother.

"He is four. He just turned four. He has another year with his mother," Orion informed her. Rhodinia, with a white ring about her lips, had nodded and excused herself. Benjamin's mother followed after, shepherding her child, and gave Orion a backward look he never forgot. It wasn't gratitude, exactly, unless it was a stunned sort; it was a look he had never been able to define. Was it hope? Fear? Confusion? It was a look to visit him now and then, at the oddest of times.

Orion rubbed back the beginnings of a headache. "Where are you from, Joab?" he asked, deliberately shutting away the look of the Jewish laundress.

"Hebron."

"Hebron. Isn't that near Jerusalem?"

"South of it. East of Beth Ophra." Joab flickered a look at him. What was that look? Then Orion remembered. Of course, Beth Ophra. Early this year Pilate had sent a cohort there to snuff a minor rebellion involving, as ever, the Zealots. Political tensions ran particularly high in the south, owing to the celebrated Jerusalem—and any sort of inflammation could usually be laid at the feet of the Zealots.

It made him think of the man who was to arrive any day from Rome, Pilate's friend Decimus Vitellus Caratacus. Pilate had made a comment the other day, how Decimus would find the shenanigans of the Zealots amusing. He wondered if Decimus would find Pilate's decree for the Jewish stonemason amusing.

"More gravy, Orion? Orion?"

Orion looked up. "Yes. Please."

"You are making me crazy," Marina said as she spooned the gravy onto his plate. "What are you trying so hard to not talk about?"

"What did Pilate put his paw into this time?" Theron asked.

Orion sat back. "Two problems tonight. Both have my stomach boiling."

Theron tore off another hunk from the loaf. "Talk, my friend! Rabbi Theron is here. Soon your mind will be eased and your conscience at rest."

"You may have to call in the rabbis on this," Orion muttered. "You may have to take it to the Council."

Theron stopped in mid-chew and regarded Orion. "You are serious." He looked at Marina. "He is serious." He sighed and tossed his bread on his plate, shoved it away. "Why do I get the feeling I am about to lose my appetite?"

Orion chuckled despite himself. Theron had already eaten enough for two. But the matters made the smile disappear. He put his elbows on the table and gripped his fist. "Here is the first: a Jewish stonemason for the new Tiberateum has refused to work on the Sabbath. Pilate's judgment is this: grant him the Sabbath off, but punish him for it. He is to be scourged seven times seven . . . for every time he doesn't work on the Sabbath."

Shock froze the table. Joab paused with his cup halfway to his lips. Theron stared. Marina's face went from disbelief to belief to anger. Her lips pressed into a thin line, and she and Theron exchanged a long, grim look.

"Forty-nine?" Theron finally demanded of Orion.

Bleakly, Orion asked, "What am I to do? Tell me what to do. Pilate will want details on this. I have one week to come up with a solution."

"*Forty-nine?*" Theron growled. He rubbed his forehead. "And he wants details? Such as, will he survive forty-nine?" His hand dropped to the table. "What if this man changes occupations?"

"No chance, he was conscripted for service." He glanced at Marina and dropped his eyes. "He has a family. Eleven children." He hated to admit his helplessness. He liked being Marina's sometime champion for her people, but it was always in small ways. This was huge. It did not involve a few whispers or slipping someone a coin. It wasn't a game anymore. "If I don't give this order, Pilate will find out."

"Why do the evil always preside?" Theron demanded angrily, his thick black brows plunged into a scowl. "Why are not good people in power? Herod the Great was never great, he was an idiot. He had a chance to do something for us, but cared only for himself. And God help us from the procurators. Well—Valerius Gratus was better than Pilate. . . ." He held up a tiny space between his thumb and forefinger. "By about this much."

"Gratus would never have paraded Roman standards in Jerusalem. Gratus would not have dipped into the Temple treasury for a Roman aqueduct. Gratus would not have crucified Jesus of Nazareth. We are not talking about Gratus, Theron." Orion picked up his cup of wine and took a deliberately slow sip.

Marina had her chin in her hand, thinking furiously, to judge by her frown. She shook her head. "This one is not so easy, Orion. Sometimes Pilate can be led about like a placid donkey. This time . . ." She blew out a breath, then looked at Joab. "What do you think, Joab?"

After a quick glance at Orion, the lad licked his lips and said, "I think it is time for the Zealots to depose him."

Orion sat back, rolling his eyes. By the gods, he had enough to deal with. He didn't need the ignorant rhetoric of a young Zealot.

Theron lifted his eyebrows and appraised Joab. "So. My apprentice shows himself."

Joab took his napkin and wiped his mouth. "Raziel of Kerioth has an idea that if all the factions can be brought together—"

It was too much, and Orion's hands went into the air. "Raziel of Kerioth!" The name could set ablaze a heap of wet laundry. "Theron, can you tell your apprentice that for me to sit in earshot of that name is treason?"

Theron ignored him and said musingly to Joab, "I would not have taken you for a Zealot."

Joab raised a defiant chin. "I am not a Zealot." The defiance came down. "Not anymore."

Theron threw a look at Marina. "Not anymore . . ."

But Joab looked at Orion. "You said there were two situations."

The lad had intelligence in his eyes—for a young fool. Only a fool would talk of Raziel in front of Pilate's number one. Yet he had the temerity to look Pilate's number one straight in the eye without glancing away—and his question made Orion look away.

The other situation. "Yes. In some ways as tricky as the first." Theron grunted at that. It didn't make Orion feel better, but at least this matter was not as heavy as the other. It was nearly a relief compared to it.

"A woman has been coming to the palace for a couple weeks."

He already felt his face begin to warm. By the gods, he hoped Theron and Marina wouldn't pick up on his admiration of her. He would be teased without mercy. "A Jewish woman. Eighteen years ago she planted a tree in the southeast quadrant when it was empty scrubland. It's near a slope facing the Mediterranean . . . right where the new granary is going up. Apparently it is a custom of yours to plant a tree when a baby is born?"

Theron shrugged as he looked at Marina. "Yes. For some."

"It is in Hebron," Joab offered. "A cedar for a boy, an acacia for a girl."

"We have different customs," Marina explained. "Sometimes according to region."

"The branches of the tree will be used to construct the chuppah," Joab said.

"The what?" Orion asked.

"The wedding canopy," Joab said. "For when the child is married."

"It is a nice custom," Marina said softly, nodding.

Orion inwardly winced; she and Theron did not have children. That was one subject of which the plucky Marina did not speak.

Theron put it together. "A Jewish tree planted where Rome is building a granary. So go on with what is about to become a heartbreaking story."

"Pilate says cut it down. That's what the workers tried to do from the beginning. The woman says the tree belongs to her Nathanael and will be cut down only if they take the ax to her as well."

He happened to be looking at Joab when he spoke, and Joab's eyes had gone wide. Perhaps it was a very important custom in Hebron. Theron and Marina did not seem so offended.

He scratched the back of his head. "Anyway, I feel sorry for her. That she has managed to save the tree this long is amazing. The foreman doesn't know what to do with her." *He* didn't know what to do with her. "Stubborn thing. I should pit her against Pilate. Put them in a room and see who comes out worse for wear." He chuckled. "*She* would make a great procurator."

Theron cleared his throat. "This woman. What is she like?"

"Well, she—" But he caught Theron's face. He had a funny little smile. And Orion certainly didn't like that tone. "What do you mean, what is she like?" he snapped. That was the last thing he should have done.

Theron's face suddenly shone in delight. If a face could caper, Theron's did. He shook his finger at Orion and beamed at Marina. "Ah, Marina, set another place next Sabbath!"

Orion held up his hand. "No, no, no. You don't understand."

"I understand plenty!"

"She's a *prostitute.*"

Theron's glee came down. "Oh." But then he raised his arms in an expansive shrug. "So what? We shall reform her of her wicked ways. I have not seen a woman unsettle you yet. Not even Nashir's daughter, and she could turn the head of a eunuch." He banged the table and laughed loudly at his own joke. "She could make a eunuch curse the day he was born, let alone curse the day he—" He caught Marina's look.

"Oh?" Marina said archly, folding her arms.

Theron's expression changed so fast it was Orion's turn to laugh. "Marina . . . turtledove . . ."

"How would you like to curse the day you were born?" she asked him sweetly.

"Marina," he pleaded, hands on his chest. "I am an artist! It is hard for me not to notice beauty."

"I'll give you something to notice."

Theron did not deserve to be rescued, but Orion took the

conversation back with, "Listen . . . the Jews on the job are clearly in a dilemma. I went to the site myself and spoke with one of the Jewish workers. They want to support her because she is Jewish. But she is also a prostitute. For the Jews to take her side would mean condoning her occupation. 'How can we support her? What kind of example is that to the pagan workers?' That kind of thing."

"What is her name?" The question came from Joab. Strange, the question. Stranger yet his tone.

"Rivkah."

The name was an explosion.

Theron and Marina gasped as one. Shocking enough, their reaction. But Joab . . . his face went the color of ashes. He stood up so fast his chair fell over.

Marina and Theron pulled from their distress to stare with Orion at Joab. He was flat against the wall, pale as the plaster.

"I—I don't feel so well," the boy stammered. "Onions do not sit well in my stomach. Please . . . excuse me." He stopped short when he saw his overturned chair. He righted it, then hurried back to the passage and ducked through the curtain.

Marina stared after him. "But . . . I didn't serve onions."

"How would he know Rivkah?" Theron demanded to know.

"How do *you* know Rivkah?" Orion snapped.

But Theron did not answer. He thoughtfully tapped a thick finger against his lips, looking to where Joab had left. "He said he was looking for a Jewish prostitute. And I am now thinking he did not mean in *that* way."

Orion looked at the curtain flap too. The little reprobate was looking for Rivkah? What then? Was this prostitute's—talent—known far and wide?

Theron had shrunk into a deep brood. He pinched his lower lip and rolled it between his thumb and forefinger. Considering how huge the lip was, it was not a pleasant effect. "I wonder if he is a friend of Nathanael's," he murmured to himself.

Orion took his eyes from the rolling lip and said to Marina, "How do you know her?"

"We invited her to a Sabbath meal, a long time ago," Marina murmured. Her mind seemed only half on her words. "Nathanael was only a little boy then. They came every Sabbath after that, for nearly a year. Until she feared for our reputation. As if we ever cared about such a thing." She threw a scornful look out the window. "Not many people around here could countenance her visits. They treated her shamefully."

Such a defiant thing she was. A little younger than Orion himself, maybe in her early thirties. He remembered the first day she came. Throughout her impassioned speech, Orion had to constantly train his mind to her words. She did not wear a decent head covering like every other Jewish woman. She wore that filmy green-blue veil, secured by a circlet of bangles that tinkled every time she made a vehement point. Which was often. She was not tremulous with the intimidation that usually accompanied anyone who brought an appeal past local magistrates to the doorstep of Pilate.

Daily she haggled her request under his nose as if good bargaining could make both walk away pleased. It wasn't that simple. No, she couldn't clean the palace floors for a year. No, she couldn't work in the kitchen. And no, thank you very much, but it would be inappropriate for Pilate's chief secretary to—and she had laughed at his blush—accept other . . . *services*. (On that score, he kept his gaze fixed on his tablet while hastily assuring her the proposal itself was not unappealing. It was simply, well, the wrong time and wrong palace.) Thankfully she only offered that bargaining chip once. Orion had a measure of fortitude, and did not care to discover its limitations.

The last few days she had tried a different tack, throwing reason on her request. *To save this tree is for the good of Rome,* she had declared.

For the good of Rome? Orion had countered with an incredulous grin. *This is interesting. Tell me how it benefits Rome.*

She had drawn herself up, haughty as a patrician lady, and replied, *Many of my*—and here she faltered, just for a blink—*my clients are Roman. Important Romans,* she had direly assured. *Romans in Caesarea only on business. It would not do to have those very important Romans know about the way things are run around here. You place great importance on diplomatic relations, and this is nothing short of a matter of diplomacy. It could very well become an incident.*

Orion had just stopped himself from laughing out loud. He was doing well, he thought, acting as though it were no different looking into her eyes than looking into Pilate's. *An incident?* he had repeated, wide-eyed, folding his arms.

And the woman came close to laughing herself.

Every day she had acted as though Orion himself could grant her request, and he should do so immediately—with remuneration. She had all the imperiousness of a woman who had justice coming to her on a solid silver platter.

"What are you smiling about?" Theron demanded. Then he said, wistfully, "Perhaps you see she is more than just beautiful."

"More than what she is . . . ," Marina said softly, to nobody in particular.

"She is so fearless," Orion murmured. "She sits in front of that tree like the Furies couldn't chase her away."

"She's a wonderful woman," Marina said. "She just doesn't know it yet. She doesn't believe it."

Orion blinked. Reality came wriggling back, and with it, pure irritation at his own helplessness. "A wonderful woman?" He snorted. "Marina. You know what she is."

Marina nodded, her gaze far away. "I do. But she does not know, not yet. Would to God she will find out someday."

"I am not in the mood for your riddles," Orion snapped.

"There is no riddle. She is loved by God. Made in his image. She does not believe this. Not yet."

He rose, folded his napkin, and set it on the table. "I must leave. Thank you for the meal." It was as stiff as it felt, but there was nothing for it. "Take the matters to your Council. Perhaps in the matter of the stonemason, they can do something. Maybe your god will see fit to make a concession for him so he can work on his Sabbath. Else he will die."

"Do you have to give that order, Orion?" Marina asked sadly.

"Does your god have to be so stingy with human life?" Orion returned. "What does a day matter, Marina? Theron, it's no wonder you are a bad Jew. I would be too."

Theron rose from the table and stood his tallest. Chin high, he said, "It is true I do not look upon things in the same way as most Jews. But whether a priest or an *am ha-aretz*, I am a Jew. And I will fight for the beliefs of my people."

"You'll fight for the belief of a day? That doesn't make sense!" Orion nearly shouted, exasperated. "Gods and goddesses, it's only a *day*! Tell your priests to have pity on this poor man and make a concession. They can do that, can't they? I could help them frame it. They can have the fellow put in extra time at the synagogue if it makes them feel better. He could—"

Marina cut in with, "The man will not work on the Sabbath because of his conscience, Orion, and conscience is what it is all about." Wearily, she pushed up from the table and came to stand next to Theron. "The question is, what kind of pity can *you* have on this man?"

Orion stared from Marina to Theron. "You make it sound like

it's up to me. You make it sound like it's my fault! By the gods—'Orion, see what you can do about this. Orion, we have a situation.' No. You are on your own with this." His face burned, he was trembling. He had never spoken this way before, not to Marina and Theron. He started for the door and reached for his robe, but turned. "It was enough for me to put the matters before him. Don't you see that? Do you know what I risked in that simple act? I could lose my position for it."

"A man could lose his life," Theron said. "Perhaps that would be the beginning of something quite catastrophic. You think they had fits about the standards in Jerusalem? There would be an uprising, Orion. This is one I would join."

Orion could only stare. He put out his arms and let them drop. "What am I to do, Theron? I can help you people in many small ways under the table, but not like this."

"You people," Theron muttered. "Now we are 'you people.'"

"What do you want? Lots of small ways, or the single one that will end it all, and my career in the bargain? Do you know what that would do to my father? Pilate could charge me with treason—treason, Theron!—and I'd lose more than my job. I'd lose my freedom or my life. I can't do that to my father. I'm all he has." *Iron collar in a small wooden box. Fashioned for the neck of an eight-year-old.*

"You can't do it to your father, or you can't do it to yourself?" Theron asked very quietly.

The words slammed like a blow. Sick at heart, Orion nodded at Theron. "The cause is everything, isn't it? That's your Jewish slogan. Your cause is more important than the life of one insignificant secretary. I see it now, Theron. I see now, Marina. I see what all these Sabbath meals have been about. By the gods, I have been blind."

Theron's darkened face said he was wrong. The tears in Marina's eyes said he was wrong, and he knew he was, knew it because he knew them. But he said what he said, just as Theron had, and there was no taking it back. He said it because it felt good to say it.

He had waited all week to come and suddenly could not leave fast enough. He ducked out the doorway, for the first time without a good-bye.

Candlelight spilled from windows onto the commonyard walkway. Ten steps away and the evening chill told him he had forgotten his robe. He folded his arms tightly; he'd freeze before going back to fetch it. He glanced bitterly into some of the windows as he passed. Orion would never be allowed to cross the threshold of most of these homes. Some purified themselves for even touching a Gentile. Who wanted their god if their god was as quarantined as they? If these people thought to beguile the Gentiles from their wicked ways, they had better start acting like—he grimaced. Like Theron and Marina.

How could a people be so *stubborn*? For things that did not matter? They brought it on themselves, they got what they deserved because they would not play Rome's rules.

They would suffer again. One will lose her tree. Another will have his back laid open with forty-nine lashes. He will die from blood loss or infection. What would come of it this time? There would be a fourth file. He knew it. He had the same bad feeling he had when Pilate cheerfully dipped his pagan hands into the Jews' sacred Temple treasury to put in the aqueduct. In his inexorable, obtuse, enthusiastic way, Pilate was making for himself another incident, the repercussions of which would reach Rome. He was the only man Orion knew who would spear his foot and call it good.

There would be a bloodbath, for the Jews would not put up with it. They would come to the aid of their man and people would die, same as when they protested the standards. People would die.

He hated the day he left Rome. Hated the day he met two people who changed his mind about Jews. Hated that the people he loved on earth had grown to a grand total of three.

"To my beloved father," he dictated out loud, "from your son, Orion Galerinius. Greetings. How is Aunt Vesta? Better, I hope. Well, it's just another day here in Judea. Another gods-cursed day."

3

Jorah handed Cousin Thomas the bundle of his prayer shawl and tefillin, and stood on her toes to kiss his cheek. The old man took the bundle absently, a delighted smile on his face. He wasn't used to having someone fuss over him.

"You will introduce me to the mosaicist today?" Jorah asked him.

"To Theron. Of course. He will be delighted to meet you. He has a new apprentice."

"Yes. You told me. Several times." Cousin Thomas was getting old indeed. He was supposed to be off to synagogue but took his time about it. He plucked at the bundle, smiling at her.

"Synagogue, Cousin," Jorah gently reminded him.

"Ah, yes. It is Sabbath morning. Good Sabbath morning, Jorah." He beamed at her, plucking the bundle.

"Good Sabbath morning."

"Today you will meet Theron. He is a good man. His wife

was Sarah's friend. She's very kind. They have a new apprentice."
A frown briefly pulled his face. "Theron does not go to synagogue."
The childlike cheerfulness returned. "Marina is a good cook."

"So you have told me, Cousin. I am glad they take care of you."
She guided him to the door and opened it for him. "Enjoy your
morning."

He shook his finger at her. "Good neighbors are hard to find."

"Yes, Cousin. Synagogue, Cousin."

He stood in the doorway plucking and smiling, then finally
kissed the mezuzah on the doorjamb and left. Jorah sighed as she
watched him go. At least he fell in step with another man emerg-
ing from a doorway farther down the row of houses. She hoped he
remembered the way home.

Her gaze left him and went to the mosaic across the commonyard. A standing-up mosaic! There it was—embedded on the wall
of his home, proclaiming to the world what he was all about. So
daring and fresh and delightful. Nothing like it in Nazareth, nothing that even felt like it.

It was transfixing. Perfect crests of the sea, now blue, now white,
in some places touched with sunlight. Sunlight! At least that was the
effect. It was astonishing. Where did he get that blue? Where did he
get the yellow? She wanted to go and run her palms over it again.
A work like that beckoned. She could not believe everyone in the
courtyard did not come daily to admire it. To respect such talent.

Perhaps they were used to it. Not a single person gave the mosaic
even a glance yesterday, and she had watched to see. If anything, it
seemed Theron's place was ignored. Were they so used to living near
such brilliance? And why did he live here? Why didn't he have his
own villa instead of a home with a commonyard?

She had watched anxiously for the mosaicist to leave for synagogue with the new apprentice Thomas spoke of, but nobody

cracked the door this morning. A curtain was drawn over the window. Well, Cousin said he didn't go to synagogue.

Shame on you, Jorah, she told herself as she pushed off from the door and turned into the house. Spying on people. You're just not used to living in a city, living so close to so many people. She had always pitied Annika for living in town. Perhaps it wasn't such a bad thing.

She hummed as she gathered the plates and set them in the washtub. She covered the dirty dishes with a towel; they would be washed this evening, when Sabbath was over. She placed the washtub on top of the cupboard so she would not smell the dishes when the day grew hotter.

She wandered about the little home, gazing at the way Sarah had set things up, the way she had kept house for Thomas for over fifty years. It was evident she had had a lingering illness; the corners of the home were thick with dust that had been there a very long time. The place also had an odor to it. It was the smell of old people and old cooking. The kitchen needed a good scrubbing, that was certain. Jorah had clucked like an old housewife at the dirt under the kitchen table. She couldn't wait to get at it tomorrow. It was fun to clean someone else's home.

Jorah was happy to think of making this place shine again. She liked gentle old Thomas. She remembered when he and Sarah came for visits to Nazareth. More, she remembered coming here. There wasn't much in Nazareth; here was everything. Herod's Harbor. The Praetorium Palace, a huge marvel of a place. The Great Stadium, and most of all, the sea. Once she had this place thoroughly scrubbed, she would visit the sea. Find a solitary place to gaze on it for hours.

She paused at a little table. A small lamp stamped with a seven-branched menorah sat on an embroidered—and very dusty—cloth. She bent close to examine the perfect, tiny stitches in the cloth. She brushed her finger over them.

Perhaps she could forget what brought her here, for a time. Perhaps she could forget why she left Nazareth. Nobody here knew who she was. The moment she came into Caesarea, she had felt the cloak of who she was lift away, leaving her in a relief of anonymity.

Thomas did not seem to bear the onus of one related to Jesus of Nazareth. As far as she could tell he was treated the same as anyone else. Perhaps coastal people were different. Perhaps he had never told anyone. There was a great deal of hope in that. Marina had not mentioned Jesus' name.

Here, she could be a different person. She could breathe again.

She lifted the lamp and shook out the cloth. Yes, she came to Caesarea for a reason, but it could wait. It could wait for a very long time as far as she was concerned, because for the first time in a very long time she was free. For once it was Jorah's turn to leave Nazareth. Maybe Jorah's turn to never go back. The thought made her eyes widen, and she straightened from the table.

Well, and why not? Why go back to scandal and notoriety? Why go back to where they whispered behind her back and sometimes right in front of her? She hated Nazareth. Yes, she was to go back and live with Annika once she told Rivkah the news . . . once she breathed to her of certain scars. She was to stay with Annika until word came from her family in Jerusalem. But what if she couldn't find Rivkah?

Nathanael was dead, and nothing would change that whether she found Rivkah or not. She who gave Nathanael those scars wouldn't care anyway. Why waste time searching for her? She centered the lamp on the embroidered doily and continued her tour of the home.

The sitting area was small, just a couch and two tripod chairs with old leather seats. Two rooms opened off the sitting area, the room that belonged to Cousin Thomas and the storeroom in the back where he had set up a cot for her. Jorah went to the doorway and pulled aside the goatskin curtain. She smiled sadly at the bed;

there were still two pillows at the head. Cousin Sarah's beautiful clothing chest, stained in a lovely light brown, so light it was nearly yellow, was at the side of the bed. On a recessed shelf above it was an assortment of things collected over a lifetime.

Jorah wouldn't be surprised if her father had made that chest. There was a time when nearly everything he stained had that color, no matter the wood. She looked at the recessed shelf. Hairpins, a comb. Some jewelry. She reverently picked up a simple bracelet set with a single stone. She put the bracelet on her wrist and held it out. Poor Cousin Thomas. What would that be like, living with someone for over fifty years and then that person is gone? No wonder he seemed bewildered half the time.

"Oh, Cousin," she murmured softly. She was putting the bracelet back when her eyes fell on a small wooden trinket box. She froze, bracelet in midair. She knew those crosscuts in that wood. The bracelet dropped with a small clatter. She stared at the box for a very long time.

They were his crosscuts. Jesus made the same box for James, only bigger. Same smooth lines carved to look like a braid. Same corner squares filled with tiny crosscuts.

She backed away from the shelf. What ever made her believe she could leave Nazareth? Reminders were everywhere. In the face of Thomas, who looked like Father. In unexpected wooden boxes. She was his sister. She could never leave that behind. Who she was and what had happened . . . it pursued her like a distant thief on a road.

The moment Jorah had turned into the home, the door of the mosaicist opened. A young man came out, pulling the door shut behind him.

Joab's face felt like a cold, tiled board, one of Theron's sample patterns. Today he would tell a mother her son was dead. Today he would tell the last words of Nathanael, which were not his words at all. His arm tightened around the bundle. He hunched his shoulders and made for the gate.

Even in the commonyard he noticed the way people treated him. He learned quickly that people around here either loved Theron and Marina or hated them. How could anyone hate Marina? He found his teeth clenching at what happened last night. From behind the curtain flap, he had heard the man's raised voice. And when he had left, he heard Marina crying. That haughty Orion had made Marina cry. The memory brought fury. Wasn't he ready to fly out the door and flatten his Roman face for whatever he had said to make her weep? He had disliked Orion the moment he saw him. What were Theron and Marina thinking, entertaining Pontius Pilate's closest employee? Their trust in people went too far. One day they would pay for it.

They were stupid even to trust him. How did Marina know he wasn't a common brigand the day she found him in the marketplace and asked him home for dinner? The same evening, Theron hired him without so much as a reference. His father would never have done such a thing. It wasn't good business. Theron and Marina were good people, kind people, but not very smart.

If there was one thing that bothered Joab about Marina, it was the way her kindness toward other people came before obligations around the house. Though he loved her kindness, that same kindness had a distraction about it. She would be three houses down, showing a young wife how to make a lentil and onion salad while her own lay half-assembled on the cutting board. She'd help the crabby old woman across the commonyard with her laundry while—Joab sniffed his tunic. His spare tunic had been in the laundry pile since the day he arrived.

Theron was a different case. He was not in danger of over-abundant kindness, but that workroom—how could he get anything done in such a place? Joab spent three hours the first day just cleaning up. It seemed Theron was always ready to erupt when he started on a new area to clean. He wondered what held him back—not much kept Theron from explaining exactly how he felt about anything.

He was up and gone by the time Joab woke this morning. When he asked Marina if Theron had gone to synagogue, she merely chuckled. When he asked where he did go, she said (evasively, Joab thought), "Oh, he had to see a few people." A few people? That early in the morning? Theron did not rise until late. Whom would he see?

A granary going up in the southeast of Caesarea couldn't be hard to find. He didn't tell Marina where he was going—he could be as evasive as she—only that he would be back in time for midday meal. Joab frowned; Theron should be coming up with the design for the palace walkway, the pattern from "Pompeii." Weren't they supposed to bring the patterns to the palace today, despite the fact that it was Sabbath? Where was Theron off to? It didn't seem very responsible. As far as Joab knew, he hadn't even looked at the sample boards.

Joab left the commonyard and fell in behind a group of men on their way to synagogue. They walked along the main street, past the main marketplace where Marina had found Joab. On the other side of it, streets led to alleys, which led to the bad part of Caesarea. He had found the bad part his first day in Caesarea. He was referred to an inn by a man who had stood with his friends on a street corner—probably the same inn Theron told him about. It was not the sort of inn where his parents would inquire for lodging. He had gone in and asked a serving girl—if that's what she was—if she knew where he could find a prostitute named Rivkah. She had looked him up and down and said, *You can't afford Rivkah, but you can afford me, country boy.* His face flaming, he tried to explain he just needed to talk to her. Soon a burly man he took to be the innkeeper came and escorted him to the door.

He had hung about that corner for a few days, figuring if they had at least heard of Rivkah, she must be about somewhere. But the people coming and going in this part of town did not like to be questioned. And if he asked a woman her name, he got a variety of answers. Nobody asked a woman her name around here. The question they asked was, "How much?" His cheeks warmed just thinking of it. If his parents could see him now.

Seagulls cried in the harbor. The smell of the sea came in on a breeze, and with it the smell of smoked fish from the smokehouses on the quay. Such different smells from those in Hebron. Everything was different. Caesarea was a port town, a worldly, wonder-filled place. So much to see. It reminded him of Jerusalem because of all the foreigners. It was a place where business was transacted between Romans in their white togas and locals in their decent tunics. Ships of every size came and left the harbor, laden with spices, cloth, grain, wood, balsam, and travelers. Warehouses lined the quay, bustling with people coming and going. Women came to see their men off or welcome them home. Certain women came to pick up business from sailors; Joab had looked for Rivkah here too.

He was coming up on the Great Stadium. He gazed past it to the Praetorium Palace on the promontory. The sight of it brought a curl to his lip. The man had made Marina cry. One day Joab would like to make him answer for it.

The expanding part of south Caesarea—the New City, they called it—was planned out instead of built around. Here the streets were laid out in parallel lines. Here were new villas, expensive ones

from the look, and much more expensive shops. This is where
Caesarea was the most Roman. Yesterday, on the way back from
the palace, Theron had pointed out to Joab a place where he had
put in a mosaic.

"A retired Roman general lives there, Antony Scarpus. I did a
copy of a Sossus for him. Over there is the home of a woman named
Camilla. I did a Sossus for her too. It is in her triclinium and looks
as though foods have fallen off the table. Get it? The floor looks like
it needs to be swept after a feast—nutshells, fish bones, olive pits,
lobster claws—all done in tile. Quite amusing."

Joab smiled. Who would take him for a master mosaicist? He
looked more like a cheated merchant. One minute he shook the
heavens with his complaints of the mortar Joab had mixed—apparently, mosaicists were very touchy about their mortar—and the next
minute, he cooed like a new mother over the color of some stones
Joab had found on the beach.

"I did a labyrinth over there. Theseus killing the Minotaur.
Marina helped me on that one. She did a wonderful job. Well—
pretty good. Ho, what a lot of money in those tiles. Gold leaf under
glass. An exquisite pain to work with such tiles, but Joab, you should
see it. You don't want to be a mosaicist, do you."

"I—"

"No, it's all right. I don't understand it, naturally, but it's all
right. You have to find what you want to do. What kind of trade
were you brought up in?"

"Dye. My father owns a small dye works in Hebron."

"Ah. So you know color. I knew that much."

The Great Stadium was probably the best part of Caesarea. He'd
like to see a chariot race someday; Theron said Pilate was an avid
supporter of the races. From the stadium he soon heard the same
thin sounds as yesterday.

Maybe he should join the auxiliaries. Wouldn't that raise Avi from his grave. Jews and Judean Gentiles who actually joined forces with Rome. But did Joab care? Truth was—and if he had ever mentioned this to Avi he'd have been asking for a slit throat—Joab felt the Jews were beaten. The last true Jew on the throne was Aristobulus, and that was a long time ago. Why not try and make the best of it in this Roman world? Except for the taxes it wasn't so bad. Why spill any more Jewish blood over an enemy too strong? That was what had haunted Joab, in deep secret thoughts, that people would die needlessly because it would take every single Jew in Israel to rise against them, and there was no way that was going to happen. Raziel of Kerioth thought it could, he honestly did, and for a time Joab allowed the man to beguile his hopes to action. But it turned out as his father had warned him: the Jews could not be united. Until that happened, Rome would remain in control. A courageous fool is what Father had called Raziel, with a sadness that spoke of his own bitter longings.

The Teacher from Nazareth had renewed some nationalism, but he made it clear he was not interested in the restoration of Israel's former glory. The only clear thing was that everything he said would *not* be clear. And now he was dead—or was supposed to be. Joab tried to push off thoughts of Jesus. It wasn't easy, considering the words he was charged with.

Before the doctor told him the story, he thought maybe he had seen enough and thought enough of Jesus to shore up what belief he had and cast it toward him. But the story of the adulteress and the stones and no accusers did more to set Joab at a distance from Jesus than anything else. It was an act of mercy, and that was appealing. But it was also a clear defiance of the Torah. And that was unsettling. Torah was Law, Torah was God's Voice to his people. What Jesus did was much more than an astonishing act of mercy.

Well, and Father was right, wasn't he. Today he wouldn't be thinking of issues fit only for rabbis if it wasn't for his own passion to leave home. Passion for anything got him into trouble. He'd still be mixing dyes with Father, were it not for listening to Avi or Raziel. *The cause is everything.* Hollow words now. Avi was dead, Raziel likely would follow. Why had he wanted to leave home so desperately? It wasn't such a bad life.

One thing had happened that perhaps changed Joab for the good: he learned he had an opinion. All his life he had allowed others to shape and guide what he thought. He noticed, lately, that he stood his ground on what he really believed and that felt good. They were his own opinions; they might not be right in the whole scope of things, but they were his own. He was thinking for himself. That counted for something, maybe even with God.

Joab squinted at the curved stadium wall as he passed. Would the auxiliary troop be so terrible? Three meals a day. Lodging. Something to do. He hated working with stone. All week Theron had him chipping out tiny squares. Chiseling strips of stone, chiseling nicks, then breaking off tiles at the nicks. Sorting the tiles to be sanded later. He tucked the bundle under his arm to look at his palms. He'd soon have more cuts on his hands than hairs on his head.

How did he die? Joab imagined Rivkah saying as he stared at his hands.

He died because I did not act in time. He died because I was a coward. Your Nathanael would be alive today, were it not for Joab ben Judah of Hebron.

❧

His tablet under his arm, Orion stood at the edge of the granary work site looking for the foreman. Some of the workers glanced his way and nudged one another. Look, Pilate's number one. What is he doing here? Investigating the matter of the Jewish whore? Maybe he can see how overworked we are in the bargain.

Orion snorted. They did not appear to be in danger of overwork. Some lounged at the half-finished wall, languidly chatting. Three men threw dice near the cement-mixing barrel. One sat examining the sole of his sandal. Two men at the wall noticed Orion and made a show of labor; one slapped a trowelful of mortar on a stone block, another set a block in place. The one with the trowel scraped away the excess, exaggerating his movements, acting as fussy for the outcome as if setting the block for his own home. Orion rolled his eyes away; when he looked again the man had resumed conversation, leaning on the block he just set, displacing it bit by bit. Orion watched the block press out a curve of mortar.

All the while he was aware of the tree on the slope. He had looked for her the moment he came on site. There she was, knees drawn up, arms about them, gazing out at the sea.

He was here to give the order. What was he thinking to try and talk it over with Theron and Marina? Did he think to buy her time? She had pressed the appeal for two weeks. The foreman had no more patience for her presence. There was no more time left. Orion had his orders straight from Pilate. The tree would come down. Today.

He risked another glance at her. The look on her face, he had not seen this one before. Her features were smooth, features not resolved for battle. He could call the expression tranquil but for the tightness of her eyes. What was that tightness? Worry? She wasn't worried she would lose her fight, was she? Not she. She had lost it, of course. But she didn't know that.

What did she see on those waves? Did she think of the one whose tree she guarded? He must be some boy. Orion wondered if the son had as much grit as his mother.

Then she was looking toward him, and his stomach dipped. She was smoothing a long strand of black hair from her face, and her hand stilled when she saw him. He knew the expression would change, would assume that wry haughtiness he knew. But for a moment she gazed at him with the sea expression. For a moment they regarded one another, both faces smooth.

Then wryness came, the superior set to her lips. He in turn allowed his face to go its usual way with her. He felt his face say he was a schoolmaster with a recalcitrant student who amused him. He gave her a nod and turned back to observing the site.

His schoolmaster face dissolved as he became aware of the weight of the tablet. This morning he had scraped the old beeswax from the tablet's wooden recess and pressed in fresh. He carefully scratched in the words of Pilate's new decree, copying it from the one he had made on papyrus for the archives. He did not try to word it gently, he gave it as bald as it was. They were Pilate's words, not his own. *Regarding the foreman's appeal: Cut down Jewish tree. Send Jewish whore away.*

Irritation grew as he tried to spot the foreman. He didn't have time for this, he had to get back to the palace. He could see the matters pile up on his writing table from here. The quicker he was done with this the better.

"I heard you were looking for me," a voice said behind him. Orion turned to find the foreman, and caught sight of someone else.

Past the foreman, mostly concealed by a tall pile of stone blocks, was the lad from last evening's meal. Joab. He was holding a bundle and gazing intently at . . . Orion turned to see. And his teeth ground of their own accord.

Rivkah. The lad was gazing at Rivkah. She did not notice him. She had gone back to the sea, her face more expressionless than before. A look nearly bleak, and it jabbed like a thorn. She rested her chin on her knees. A waft of breeze lifted her filmy veil. It billowed, then settled like a tamed wind. Slowly he turned back.

"You want me to take him away, sir?" the foreman was saying.

Orion blinked.

The foreman gestured with his head to Joab. "The lad . . . you're looking murder at him. What's he done? I could have a couple of men—"

"That won't be—" He broke off to clear his throat. "That won't be necessary. He's leaving."

Joab had turned away. Had stumbled away, actually, and broken into a run.

"He must've seen your face, sir," the foreman snickered. He looked to where Rivkah sat. "Probably came to look at the whore. I hope you plan to do something about her, and soon. I'm tired of the disturbance among the men. The lesser of my men leer at her all day. She even had one of them in the shed over there. I keep telling her to take her filthy trade elsewhere, and she curses me to make a barbarian proud." He folded his arms and sneered at her. A look not far from a leer itself. "I can't wait to hear her howl when I cut down that tree."

"Pilate says the tree stays."

The man took his slobbering face from Rivkah and looked uncertainly at Orion. "Pilate says . . . what, is she Pilate's whore? But she's Jewish."

It took the space of a heartbeat, maybe the time it took for his own gaze to cut to Rivkah. Pilate's whore. Pilate's whore, and therein safety lay. The chance to save her tree came through a coarse foreman.

Orion, you majestic idiot . . .

Orion slid his gaze to the foreman. He glanced about as if for privacy, then leaned to the foreman. Through stiff lips, without looking at him, he said deliberately, "Of *course* she's not Pilate's whore. You said it yourself. She's *Jewish*."

In a moment, the man had a sly grin on his face. Now in Orion's confidence, he grew bold. Just as conspiratorially, he replied, "Who would have guessed, a Jewish whore. Eh, Pilate has taste then. Jewish or not."

"So you understand the . . . delicacy of this situation."

The foreman nodded. "I understand plenty."

You can still back out. Right now . . .

"It cannot become common knowledge that she is . . ."

". . . in Pilate's services." The man pressed his fingers to smirking lips. "Too bad I can't cut down that tree, but we know women, don't we. She don't get her way, Pilate don't get his."

Orion made himself grin. "You are a discerning man—what is your name again?"

"Raman."

"Raman. I would like you to let it be known—in the discreet manner you seem capable of—that the woman and her tree are not to be touched. Do not let the men know why." He gave him a significant, amused look. "Only you and I have to know that."

Orion, you fool.

"Yes, sir." Then, after a lingering grin at Rivkah, whose wary attention was now on the both of them, Raman said, "You have the new plans from the architect?"

Orion moistened his lips, then opened his tablet a little to let his stylus fall out. He bent slowly to retrieve it, and bent, allowed his face to make a vicious fist. The architect! No, by the *gods* and all their *mincing offspring* it wouldn't be as easy as that. The granary would have to be modified to accommodate the tree. The whole place would have to be resurveyed. He would have to spend time he did not have to find and bribe an architect to engineer the changes and keep the reason quiet. Gods, gods he had to think.

Could an eighteen-year-old cedar be transplanted? Or would that violate yet another suffocating custom? With Orion's luck, such a thing would end up worse than cutting the thing down. He straightened, and on the upswing shot a dark look at Rivkah.

He tucked the stylus into the tablet. "The architect has not yet been informed," he said briskly. "You know how slowly these matters move. I will get the plans to you in a day or so. The wall is certainly not in danger of reaching the tree any time soon."

If Raman caught his jab at the slovenly pace he didn't let on.

Orion surveyed the site. He would have to study the original drawings in the archives. He would have to change the wall to stop short of the tree by at least, what, twenty feet? But ho! Perhaps an additional custom said the birth tree could not be within twenty feet of a Gentile establishment! And what would Orion do then? He'd like to roll up the whole thing and shove it up the nose of the nearest Jewish official. He'd like to laugh himself to weeping, if he had time for it.

To my honorable father, from your Orion, greetings.

What curse was laid upon our lineage to visit every male by the time he turned thirty-seven? Which Fury is fast on my trail? Life, Father, is suddenly surreal, and if I survive the week it is because some god stayed my hand from plunging a knife into my heart.

Orion's bleak gaze somehow ended up on Rivkah. The worst thing in the whole rancid mess was that he had just made her Pilate's whore. A rift of wind from the sea stirred the tree branches. Customs. How he hated customs.

❧

She watched until he disappeared, thinking maybe he would turn around. Look up one more time before he left. He never did.

Why had he come? What was he talking to the foreman about? She would find out when she visited the palace tomorrow morning. Today was Sabbath, and as a rule no Jews were heard at the palace on Sabbath—it was assumed they would not show up for business. A new rumor said that all Jewish matters would be heard by Pilate only once a month. Once a month! She would have to ask Orion Galerinius about that.

What did he talk to the foreman about? If it had nothing to do with Nathanael's tree—and if God heard the prayers of a prostitute then it didn't—he would simply tell her it was none of her business.

She picked up a stick to stir the sand. What made him so sad? When the foreman went back to work, Orion Galerinius Honoratus had looked up at her with none of his usual airiness. It was a look to catch her breath, she'd not seen that look before. Then he turned and walked away.

She pitched the stick aside. Her arms resting easy on drawn-up knees, she thought on Orion. . . . He needed something. He needed out of that stuffy palace. He needed to take a walk on the quay at midnight, get a faceful of stars. Someone should throw sand at him, throw him in the sea, wake him up, startle him.

That's what he needed. He needed to be startled. He was so in control, so efficient. She smiled wryly. Well, she had startled him once. And what she offered him he was too decent to receive. At that moment, not for the first time but for the first time in a long while, she had felt shame. She also felt a crazy contradiction in the offering; if he had accepted, she would have liked him less.

She sighed hard. She hoped Orion Galerinius would have Pilate's answer soon. Why was it taking so long? Not that this daily vigil was so terribly awful. She'd never had two weeks to do nothing but sit and stare at the sea . . . or amuse herself with fantastical thinking . . .

She was a cloth merchant from Spain! A cosmetic dealer from Egypt! She was a rich woman traveling in Corinth, and in her exotically draped sedan chair borne by handsome slaves, she chanced to pass the temple of Artemis (or whatever god it was called by). There she would call a halt to her slaves. She would descend and enter the temple and ask to speak to the person in charge. While she waited she would not make eye contact with the temple prostitutes. When the person in charge came, and after some astonishing negotiating, she would clap her hands, and her slaves would bring forth chest after chest filled with gold coins. She would purchase the freedom of those cult prostitutes she did not make eye contact with.

They would imagine they were being purchased for their function. How astonished they would be, led away and taken to the harbor and each given a purse filled with gold. They would be told, "Go! Anywhere you want, you are free! Go back to your home, if you can, make for yourselves a new life. Go, you are free!" Free.

Sometimes in the fancies all would leave, they would board the next ship and look long behind them at the woman on the harbor who watched them go. Lately she made the fancy have one of them stay. One wanted to stay with Rivkah and serve her as handmaiden for the rest of her life.

It was a client who had told her about the cult prostitutes in Corinth. He tried to persuade her to come with him, told her grand stories of Greece and that she would be the most sought-after temple prostitute because of the striking color of her golden eyes.

Nathanael had been nine or ten. The client suggested that he would be sought after as well. When Rivkah asked what he meant by that, and when the client explained, she rose in a screaming rage and beat him all the way out of the brothel. Later she was told the truth about the temple prostitutes. They were slaves, sold to the temple by merchants like the client. They had no choice in what they did, and while Rivkah did things decent women wouldn't, they were forced to do things that made Rivkah tremble in fury and fear.

Rivkah had cried in despair that Nathanael had been thought of in such a way, cried in rage at herself for her naïve stupidity, cried because the man had nearly beguiled her to go. That night she was thrown out of the brothel for her treatment of the man, told never to return. That was fine with her, she could make it just fine because she had her own home and what did she need them for?

She and Kyria had a better setup than others. They had their own clientele—mostly soldiers from the Roman garrison—and had only to pay a percentage if someone sent business their way. Sometimes business was at the inn, but never again at one of the brothels. Some prostitutes begged to come live with them, but Rivkah and Kyria turned them away; they didn't want to run a brothel. Ha—that seemed indecent.

Once she asked a sailor on the quay which way was Corinth. He turned and looked, then pointed across the sea. Northwest.

Was there a Rivkah at the temple in Corinth? Did she have a son? Was he forced to do unthinkable things, and did it tear her apart? Did she want to kill herself, did she want to kill whoever stole her and sold her? Even if it was her own mother?

Nathanael, Nathanael. I hope you never come back. I hope you've made a life for yourself. I hope you forgive me for the life you had to live with me, and I hope you will forgive me—

—for the other.

That shook her from the sea and fancies.

Because he loved her, because she knew him, Nathanael would be back. He said he would. If Kyria cast doubt on that with her nasty silences when Rivkah spoke of his return, well, that was Kyria with all her miserable pessimism. She could look at an array of springtime flowers and find something depressing to say. She didn't see much point in Rivkah's determination to save Nathanael's tree. Rome was all-powerful, and Pilate hated Jews. What chance did a tree have when it was in the pathway of Rome?

Rivkah would do anything she could to make sure he stood beneath his wedding canopy. Then, somehow, her son would be ensured of a decent life. If she had stood beneath her own chuppah, maybe . . . but at least he had the blood of a priest in him.

That accounted for something. If God heard the prayers of a prostitute.

※

Joab hardly remembered the walk from the granary to the common-yard. Here he was, ready to unlatch the gate. He stared stupidly at the leather thong hooked on the peg.

A coward twice. She was not what he expected, whatever that was. If she had looked mean and ugly it might have been easier. She sat like a sentry at that tree. He closed his eyes. At the tree of her dead son.

He could not. Even with the bundle, and he had fancied the box could help, he could not tell her. Not with what he had overheard at the curtain flap last night, when Orion spoke of her determination to save the tree. How she faced down Roman authority daily at the Praetorium. Joab wouldn't dare do that.

He put his hand on the latch, and desperate thoughts came. He could leave right now! He could take the first ship out of the harbor, he could trade service for passage. He would leave the poor woman at the tree, let her live in the illusion that her son lived. What was wrong with that? Wasn't it mercy?

Tell her for me. No stones.

She'd find out someday, but not from him. She'd live a lot of years without grief until then. Wasn't it mercy, after all?

The silver box in the burlap felt like a sack of stone. Did he think to appease her grief with a stupid box? What would she care who owned it? The Teacher was dead, and it never did help Nathanael. What foolishness, that the box had powers and could help him do the impossible. It was only a box.

He unlatched the gate. It was still Sabbath, still early in the day. According to law he could only travel a Sabbath day's journey . . . but he was lawless now. He would have to get used to that. He had let Nathanael die, as surely as if he had plunged the knife himself; what did it matter if he traveled on Sabbath? He wasn't his father's son anymore.

Joab slowly started for the mosaicist's home. He would say good-bye to Marina and Theron. Maybe collect his wage, whatever was due him, pack his extra tunic, and hope that Marina would send him off with some food. He thought she probably would, she was good that way—

Joab stopped, stared, and his life came to an end in the commonyard.

Marina stood in front of the home, in front of the upright mosaic, with a girl. Talking, smiling with . . . Jorah. Jorah ben Joseph, sister of the Teacher, Jorah who had loved Nathanael. The bundle slipped from his hands.

How God hated him for his cowardice. Images flashed. Avi's malevolence, the streak of the knife. Joab held Nathanael. Oh, God—oh God, he held him while Avi . . . Why hadn't he done something sooner?

How God must hate him, to bring her here.

He gazed helplessly on Jorah while she did not see him. He

should run, now, before she looked up! She was excited . . . so different from when he last saw her at Nathanael's side. She was bedraggled, then, lovely in her love for Nathanael, dark circles under eyes set in an ashen, desperate face. Now she was groomed, with color in her cheeks and sun on her face. Now she was smiling eagerly at Marina. He had not seen her smile before. How lovely she was.

Run, Joab, run away. You still have a chance.

It was what he deserved, her here. And he suddenly knew he would not run anymore.

God had done his worst. In a moment, Jorah would look up and see him, and the sweetness on that face would turn to hatred. The face of Joab ben Judah of Hebron would scour the sweetness away. He would be to her what she was surely trying to escape. He was the living reminder of the murder of her beloved.

Joab died, then, he snapped in half and sank away and who stood there now did so by the vengeance of God. God would force him through this, make him witness her pain. It was only a matter—

—of time.

She looked up. She saw him.

He only thought he had died.

She was smiling from something Marina said, but now the smile froze. Her eyes grew large, and the sun on her face vanished. She took a step toward Joab, staggered back two, put out her arms for balance and turned as if to go to Thomas's home. She did not make it three steps. She collapsed as if her life strings were severed.

Marina cried out and moved to her, but Joab's shout was a roar. "Leave her!"

He was at her side in the beat of a heart. He gathered her up and lifted her. Marina rushed to their door, and Joab carried Jorah into the home.

He would be there when she woke.

4

EVENING HAD PASSED, and it wasn't a bad dream. He was Joab.

Lavender dawn slowly illumined the boy in the corner. He was sleeping, and sleeping, not the person she had seen in the commonyard. He was huge in the commonyard. She tilted her head to match his. He wasn't as old as her memory of him. She remembered a man, a faceless man, barely there. She remembered someone who hovered anxiously in the background. She remembered wishing he weren't there, that he was a discordant intrusion.

He sat on a pallet slouched against the wall, one leg drawn up. Arms folded, head sagging on his shoulder. He was Joab.

Joab, the friend of Avi, who had killed Nathanael. Joab, who had killed Avi.

He was maybe eighteen. Through the hair fallen across his face, she could see his face was smooth, Roman style, but his hair was not Roman short. Not even Jewish short. It came nearly to his shoulders, wavy and straggly.

What would she do when he awoke? Everything had changed.

The pretending was done, over before it began. Maybe Cousin Thomas couldn't remember who his relatives were, or maybe he never owned up to them; with Joab here, she was Jorah ben Joseph, sister of the crucified blasphemer. For the first time, she wondered what Joab was doing here. It was as if the thought shook him awake.

He pulled in breath like a snort, unfolded his arms, drew his hair behind his ear. He froze at the sight of her.

Her head spun briefly at his eyes on her, but something had changed. All she knew was that he had been reduced. Everything he had been to her came down to what she now saw . . . just an ordinary boy. To her great surprise she did not hate him. She tested it, like a toe in the water . . . no, it wasn't hatred she felt for him. It wasn't anything at all. What wonder was this?

"What are you doing here?" she said softly.

A chuckle burst from him. "That's not what I expected."

"What did you expect?" she said, and this time he didn't chuckle.

It occurred to her how little she had noticed him. The first time she saw him he had come to the shop with Avi to vex the family with yet another curiosity visit, perhaps to abscond with tokens of wood or stone, like pagan amulets. When was that? Months ago, years ago. They wanted to convince James to convince Jesus to join up with Raziel and his Zealots, to throw in his miracles with their military strategy to overthrow Rome and regain what the Hasmoneans had lost.

The second time she saw him was on the road to Jerusalem after Nathanael had been wounded. She remembered looking on him with hatred when she sat on a boulder and watched him scrounge for firewood. She didn't recall when he had left their traveling party, before or after arriving in Jerusalem.

"You're not what I remember," Jorah murmured without thinking.

"Neither are you."

She blinked. "What do you mean by that?"

"Nathanael made you beautiful."

Did he—*dare* he speak Nathanael's name? Did he *dare* speak it so casually?

"You're still pretty. And you can stop looking like that; I speak as plainly as I like. Nothing matters anymore. You've changed everything."

She was speechless and blinking. Finally, "*I* have?"

He put a finger to his lips and glanced at the curtain partition. "If I know Marina, she's trying to listen."

She had to calm herself. She had to think clearly. "How—" she swallowed, and tried again. "Why are you here? How do you know Theron and Marina?"

"I work for Theron."

"You *work* for him," she repeated dully.

"I needed to eat." His next words were less clipped. "I came to tell her. Just as you did."

They were quiet words, but stark as a slap. So. Rivkah already knew. And not in the way Jorah intended to tell her. She had been cheated out of her carefully prepared speech, thanks to Joab.

"How did she take the news?"

But his gaze dropped, and he did not answer.

Jorah sat up straight. "You didn't tell her."

He didn't answer. Didn't look at her.

"How long have you been here, and you haven't told her?"

His gaze shot back. "What about you? When were you going to tell her?"

"I—I've only been here a few days."

"You will not find it any easier than I."

"Oh really?" she snapped. "It will be perfectly easy to tell her he's *dead*. I know things you do not."

His lip rose in scorn. "Likewise, maiden." Glowering at her, he stood and went to the partition. He peeked out, then turned to Jorah. "The way I see it, we have a choice to make."

Uncertainly, she looked him up and down. "What choice?"

He studied her. "It seems you don't want to tell her any more than I do. Who says we have to tell her at all?"

❧

"Can you hear anything?" Theron said in the loudest of whispers. Marina furiously waved him down. From her post at the loom she leaned as far as she could toward the curtain. She had even grabbed a wool comb and a fat ball of wool in case either of them came out.

"They're awake. They're arguing," she finally whispered to Theron, who sat at the kitchen table. He was supposed to be mending a broken chisel.

"What are they saying?"

"I can't make out the words," she said, frustrated. "Only that they argue."

Theron nodded. "That is good. It is as you thought: they are former lovers."

Marina frowned, and noticed the ball in her hand. She idly picked at bracken in the wool. She had never seen a former lover stagger and collapse the way Jorah did. She had never seen a former lover look fresh from the grave, like Joab. There was no joy at their reunion.

Of course they were former lovers, but it must have been a devastating breakup. What preceded it? Were they mismatched? Was Joab a servant, and Jorah—well, Jorah was the sister of the prophet. It meant she . . .

The fat ball of wool tumbled to the floor.

Marina gasped, pressing one hand to her chest, clawing the air with the other. *"Theron!"* She hurried to the table and dropped next to Theron. "Of course! Oh, the poor things!" She clapped her hands to her cheeks and gazed at the curtain. How tragic! How exquisitely tragic!

"What?" Theron followed her gaze.

"You will not believe it." Marina slowly shook her head at the majestic conundrum. "Jorah and Joab have been desperately in love. Oh, so in love! But Theron, my heart, who is Jorah but the *sister* of that *young man* who was crucified! The *sister of Jesus of Nazareth!*" She gave his arm a thump. "Didn't the Council from Jerusalem declare that anyone who held to the teachings of this man was banned from synagogue?"

Theron's eyes went wide. No intellectual slouch was her man. She nodded sadly at him, and delivered the rest with the slow weight it deserved.

"Yes, my love. The family of the young prophet had been shunned. And Joab's family, knowing of his love for Jorah—" she poked his arm with every word—"forbade . . . any . . . further . . . contact with her."

Her man was dazed, then, as she expected, angry. His face darkened, and he rubbed his hand over his fist. "Do we not know of such things . . ."

"You see why they have come to our doorstep?" Marina shook her finger. "This is no coincidence."

"Who could understand but us?"

"Joab could not endure his family's treatment of Jorah."

"They treated her like garbage."

"But he could not disgrace Jorah by taking her without his father's blessing."

"I knew he was a good Jew," Theron said darkly. "He doesn't fool me."

Marina gazed at the curtain. "So he broke his own heart by running from Nazareth. He meant to sail for Rome, but oh, he stopped right when he put his foot on that boat. Couldn't do it. He realized that though he could never see her again, his feet were still upon the same land as hers. He knew he could never leave." She clicked her tongue. "Joab, Joab."

"You know, I didn't buy it that he was from Hebron. I knew that was a fake accent."

"You should have *seen* him in the commonyard! Oh, Theron, so manly. Oh, that shout of his. *'Leave her!'* Swept her up like a child. That heartbroken look. It made me want to weep, and I didn't know why."

Theron sat back and appraised his wife. An affectionate smile slipped through. "You knew it all along, my turtledove. 'Joab has heart trouble,' you told me from the first." But his admiration drooped to puzzlement. "But I thought he came looking for Rivkah. I thought maybe he brought word from Nathanael."

She patted his hand kindly. "Well, it is clear why *God* had him come. How could Joab know that Jorah's cousin is our neighbor? And now Jorah is here." She wagged her finger. "No, no coincidence, absolutely not. By their very meeting it seems our work is half done." A light leapt to her eyes. "Or perhaps it has just begun." She grasped her chin and fell into thought.

"What do we do?"

"Do?" She tapped her lips and frowned as she thought. Then

she nodded briskly. "We do nothing. We *say* nothing. We go carefully—in fact, we go delicately. As delicately as . . . pressing gold leaf under glass."

"Ahh . . ."

"We keep our wits and say little. Our hands must come away; it is time for God to do his work. *Maybe* an artful word here or there, but much healing needs to take place. Jorah lost her brother and her Joab—for good, she thought. The poor thing! But by God's mercy she has her love again, and that is where our work lies. She may have hardened herself to any happiness. Who can say?" She rapped her knuckles on the oak table. "Follow my lead, Theron, at all times. Do *not* let on that we know. Theron, that is *very* important. Innocence is the road we take for now."

"As you say, my dear," Theron said happily. He gazed at her dreamily. "You thieved my heart and devote your life to fixing others'. Do you do it with pieces of my own?" Then his eyes went wide, and he banged his palm on the table. "Turtledove! I have the most astonishing proposal!" Face bright with excitement, he put a thick finger to his lips, then nodded. "Yes, it is perfect! As you say, no coincidence."

"What?"

"The mosaic walkway at the palace!" Craftiness deepened his smile. "I will need an extra hand with the walkway. Joab, I have. What do you think about—"

"Hiring Jorah? Oh, Theron!" She reached to seize his face for a kiss, but his eyes skipped to the back of the room. The curtain flap had swished aside.

※

Joab held the curtain aside for Jorah, and she stepped meekly past him into the room. He himself felt a wave of awkwardness. Alone in a room with a girl, a pretty girl at that. All night! His father would've laid out his hide like a—but he stopped short at the faces of Theron and Marina.

They sat at the kitchen table with the most perplexing looks on their faces. They gazed at Joab and Jorah with . . . pure delight. They beamed. They radiated joy. He could have groaned out loud. What they thought couldn't be plainer than a thump on the head.

"Feeling better, Jorah?" Marina practically sang. Marina was never this sweet. She looked from Jorah to Joab and . . . *sighed*! Theron gazed with pride at them, as if he'd just given his blessing for marriage. Joab slipped a look at Jorah. What could she be thinking?

"Yes, thank you," she said to Marina. "It must have been a sun spell."

"Of course it was," Marina crooned, and on her way to the kitchen she gave Jorah's chin a quick caress. "Hungry? I have some bread and mashed olives . . . sit, both of you. You're probably starving."

"Cousin Thomas . . . ," Jorah said.

"He's fine. I told him you were fine, you'd had a spell and were resting. I told him you would spend the night here."

"Thank you," Jorah murmured, and sent a furtive glance to Joab. No, she didn't catch on. She didn't know them well enough.

She had no idea Theron and Marina had just paired her with *him*. Insane laughter threatened to burst from his throat. He swallowed it down and escorted her to the table, where Theron waited with that dancing, knowing look. Joab bit back the groan and went to take a seat across from Jorah. It was then he noticed what sat in the middle of the dining table. A silver box. Inlaid with lapis lazuli.

Unwrapped. Open to the sight of its former owner.

He could feel her eyes. He could feel her wonder, and her accusation. And he loathed her, then, because he could never explain why he took it. She would never understand, because he didn't either. Flaming with self-consciousness, he reached for the cloth the box sat on and pulled it to him. He wrapped the box and tucked it under his arm.

"I'm not hungry," he muttered, and left the room.

❧

It was late morning, and the apprentice had not returned. Well, and when he did, he'd come home to another new apprentice.

There was no place on earth like his workroom. More sacred than a synagogue. More comfortable than his bed. Here Theron lived and moved and had his being. Yes, Joab slept on the pallet in the corner. It made Theron put up a screen there for privacy. Theron's privacy. He did not want to see a pallet in his workroom, it didn't belong. To see a screen was better, it reminded him of a blank pavement waiting for a coat of mortar.

"This is . . . this is . . ." Jorah was speechless.

It delighted Theron to his sandal tips. Jorahs were few and far between in this business.

She had unwrapped the four tiles he was bringing to the palace this afternoon and arranged them on the floor. Correctly, and he watched to see if she would. She stood back to gaze on them, hands clasped, the fever light in her eyes. The idiots who took themselves to his door did not have the fever light. They had the money light. They knew what a perfect mosaic went for. They knew the fame of the few. They knew nothing.

"You like the design?"

"Oh, Theron," Jorah breathed.

These were no ordinary tiles. They were his ribbon tiles. It was a pattern he had conceived of when he was a child and perfected along the way. He was waiting for the perfect place for installation, and a walkway could not have been more perfect. The design was as if a flock of children had run on ahead, each trailing a different colored ribbon behind. It was smooth, it streamed, it sinuously overlapped. It beguiled one along and would make the walker wonder where the ribbon trail led. Of course, he would have to add at least eighteen tiles for the length Orion proposed, but what was that? Only a chance for the walker to wonder some more. He only wished the walkway would turn a corner. What drama in that. He'd like to go to heaven like that, treading a mosaic of ribbon.

He came next to Jorah to point out the golden ribbon in the design. "Because we are on the payroll of the Roman government, this will run throughout. A single thread of it through the entire walkway. You see the way it moves? Thin strips of lead will outline each ribbon. The tricky part is where the ribbons overlap. The intersecting strips will—"

"What sets the little tiles?" She folded her arms and strolled around the mosaic.

"Tesserae. The little tiles are called tesserae."

"Tesserae." She tried out the word. "What sets them?"

Lovesick, Theron sighed. "Between them, grout. Beneath them, mortar. Three layers of foundation."

"Which are . . . ?"

"Vitrubius says, and I usually agree, the first layer is pebble. Gives a good solid base. The second is mortar mixed with brick. Third is a thin layer of finely ground brick with fine mortar—run from anyone who tells you differently. Into this layer, the tesserae are set. Joab is probably off looking for red right now. Said he found a cache of red rocks." He peered sharply for any reaction at the name of Joab.

But Jorah crouched next to the tiles and placed her palm flat on the surface. Didn't move her hand, simply rested it there. Theron forgot Joab and watched in wonder. It was himself he was seeing, so many years ago.

"I can't thank you enough for letting me work here." She glanced at him. "I have heard of you all my life, of course. I even visited here with my father when I was small, before you had the mosaic out front. I never imagined I would work here one day."

It had been a long time since he'd had a Jorah in his shop. There was that young Junius who came from Cyprus to study with him. Arrogant knucklehead. He had talent and he knew it, though that didn't bother Theron. It was his presumption. Thought he could bypass technique and go straight for design. Cared more about popular pattern. Theron could not mash it into the idiot's head, and God knows he tried, that *technique* was all part of it. Technique was the . . . roaring of the volcano, the fury and the flow. What was boring about foundation? What was boring about the consistency of mortar or the substance of a tessera? Part and parcel! Like it or get out of the business! Go lay bricks for all your talent is worth. You want to learn, then learn, and learn it all. Tear your nails digging for the perfect pebble. Bloody your knuckles. Starve to save every pruta you can to set sail and study with the best. The best, and if you settle for less you deserve it. Cheat and charm and commit glorious atrocity to *learn* the craft and *own* your talent, and if ever a thought comes to make money at this . . . if it ever enters your mind, then go lay your bricks and stop wasting my time.

Sure, the money was nice. Theron liked money. But it usually came as a pleasant surprise, a vague thing at the end of it all. Many of the woodenheads saw only money, that and popular pattern to get the money. Only pattern, never technique, ninety-nine out of ninety-nine of them. But the way Jorah was looking at it now . . . she saw the mosaic entire. She saw surface and foundation at the very same time. By the bit of wildness in her eyes he knew how her brain was working—it was in a galloping fever with thoughts and ideas of her own. She gazed at the pattern, creativity crashing with creativity, and from the flying sparks would come brand-new marvels. She couldn't wait to snatch a slate and a piece of chalk and sketch her own designs. A young Dioskurides is what he saw. A young Theron. He sniffed, and roused himself.

"A denarius a week, to begin," he growled. "We did not speak of terms."

She pulled her gaze from the mosaic to him.

What was that troubled look? Did she wonder where her Joab was? What on earth did she see in him? *He* would never be a mosaicist. He nearly spoke this out loud, but Marina said go carefully. Not a word, Theron. He pressed his lips firmly.

Jorah's face, momentarily troubled, now cleared and she nodded. "A denarius. That is more than reasonable. It is . . . very generous."

"You can expect it weekly."

Jorah rose. She looked at him uncertainly. "I don't understand."

Theron went to get the mortar buckets. First lesson, mortar. He never forgot how disappointed Junius was when he pulled out the buckets instead of the pattern plates.

"I will be paid weekly, meaning so will you." Theron grinned at her. "Benefits of studying at the school of Sossus in Alexandria. It means they pay me however I want. I usually work it half now, half later, but I prefer a steady income. That doesn't happen often in this business."

The maiden was still confused. He set the buckets on the table, glancing at her as he reached for the box with the stirring sticks. "What don't you understand?"

"*You* are going to pay . . . *me*?"

Theron of Caesarea stopped rummaging for stirring sticks and lifted his head. He chuckled. Chuckled some more, then put his head back to laugh. He'd dance a jig if his gut didn't hold him to the earth. When he quit laughing he wiped his eyes. Jorah was smiling a bewildered smile. He pointed a stirring stick at a bucket. "Lesson number one. Mortar."

She quickly moved to grab the bucket. "Mortar."

"A mosaic is only as good as its foundation, I don't care what the pattern is. Pattern will—" He broke off suddenly and eyed her sideways. "You know what? Sometimes I dream in mosaic."

Jorah gasped. "So do I!" They grinned at one another until Theron felt ridiculous. He took the mortar bucket from her.

"Don't worry about pattern right now. Forget pattern. For the next few days you're gonna slop mortar until you know each flavor blindfolded. You think I'm joking? An artist works with all his senses." Her eyes were so wide, so eager, she'd be spooning into the first batch if he didn't stop her. "I am joking. Do not eat my mortar."

"I won't eat it." Then, grinning, she said, "Can I taste it?"

He laughed himself helpless until a mystified Marina peeked in at the curtain flap.

⁊⹁

"There's someone here for you. He's not a customer." Kyria let the beads fall into place.

Not a customer? Who would it be? Orion Galerinius? Rivkah snorted and dipped the brush into the charcoal mixture. She adjusted the bronze mirror and pulled back the corner of her eye. She lined her lower lid, dipped again and lined the upper. She paused as she considered who might be at the door; maybe another sent from Zakkai. He had an odd way of atoning for his sin—he tried to convert her from her own.

Not that he had ever once shown up himself. And she wasn't

supposed to know these Zealots were from him. A year or so ago she had asked one straight out, "Did Zakkai send you?" The lad about choked on his tongue.

Ah, it wasn't their fault. Some of them were genuinely concerned. They had some sort of . . . mitzvah to try and change reprobates from wicked ways. She had fun with one and said, with much wide-eyed innocence, "But my little honeycake, I *like* what I do." Then she gave him a pinch. He went crimson as a couch cushion and all but ran away. She had felt a *weensy* bit bad about that. He cared, or seemed to. And he was different from the rest. He was Zadok ben Zakkai . . . Nathanael's own half brother. The irony was they had been friends since childhood. Neither knew common blood flowed in their veins.

She sat back and gazed at the mirror. That was going to change. She had decided it one afternoon at Nathanael's tree. Nathanael had to know, it was his right. It didn't matter about Zadok, he was Zakkai's concern. But why did it take her this long to decide to tell Nathanael? Why this need to protect Zakkai? Why did *his* sin have to be covered? It had taken a long time to realize she had been the one seduced. The realization brought at least a bitter comfort.

She would tell him. Nathanael was smart, he may have figured it out by now. Or maybe he had been near his grandmother during one of her drunken slops. In a wine-soaked minute she may have let slip that the priest Zakkai was Nathanael's father.

"Rivkah! Get the door!"

"I'm coming!" she snapped.

She pushed through the hanging beads and went to the door, glaring at Kyria on the way. Kyria slouched on the couch, picking at a pastry.

"You're going to plump up like a ball of dough," Rivkah sneered.

"Shut up. Cat eyes."

Rivkah pulled open the door and groaned. Sure enough, he had to be from Zakkai. Real customers did not come at this time of day, late in the morning. She leaned against the doorway. She already knew the Ezekiel passage, better than he did.

"You are Rivkah?"

"Yes. Are you going to quote me Ezekiel?"

"I—I've been looking for you for a long time." The boy could not look her in the eye. None of them could. "Someone at the inn told me where to find you."

"You found me. Why don't you do a little dance for me while you quote it, that would be new." Maybe he was a customer, though small chance. She didn't remember seeing this one at the tavern. If they were potential customers sometimes they hung about in twos and threes, observing her and goading each other to violate the tradition of their fathers. At least the Jewish ones did. Not many Gentiles had moral dilemmas over it. Except Orion.

He had long scraggly hair, all one length, and didn't wear a grimlet around it. She sniffed. Nathanael wouldn't be found dead without his grimlet. This boy did not have much sense of style.

"Look, lad, I have a relatively new policy. I don't do anyone my son's age or younger." The boy went red as a berry. Rivkah sighed. "Quote me Ezekiel and leave."

Instead, he pushed a bundle at her. She took it in surprise.

"What's this?" she demanded. He was already backing away.

"That's for you. It was . . . meant for you."

She swiftly set it on the ground and kicked it to him. "No thanks. I don't take anything from someone I don't know. Another new policy."

The lad first stared, dumbfounded, then scrambled for the bundle. He held it to his chest, clearly unsure what to do next. She could not shut the door on him yet, this whole thing was just too crazy.

She tilted her head. "Will you just quote Ezekiel and get out of here?"

"What does it say?"

"'Repent and turn away from all your transgressions, so that iniquity may not become a stumbling block to you. Cast away from you all your transgressions which you have committed and make yourselves a new heart and a new spirit!' You want me to say it in Hebrew?"

His face changed. This lad was too young to look so bleak.

"Those words are not possible," she thought she heard him say. Louder he said, "That's not why I'm here." He looked down at his bundle. "I'm here to give you this."

"I don't want it."

"You don't know what it is. A treasure, such as you've never imagined."

"It could be poisoned. That happened to some women in Jerusalem, you know. They were given poisoned perfume for payment. Seven died. You haven't heard about that? You could be a crazy out to rid the world of prostitution." A smile twitched. She was enjoying this, because interesting things like this didn't happen. The lad didn't have crazy in his eyes, nor Ezekiel. Nobody came to give a gift and expect nothing in return.

He unwrapped the bundle and held it out to her. Her smile faded.

It was a silver box, a beautiful thing. It was inset with stones so deeply blue they could only be lapis. "That must be a bribe. Is Zakkai up for temple service?"

"I don't know anything about that."

"Invite him in," Kyria called from behind her. "That will get rid of him."

"Shut up," Rivkah said over her shoulder. She tucked her hair behind her ear as she turned back to him. The lad had a strange look on his face. It was . . . full. Saturated with something he felt deeply. Perplexing as the look was, it made her uncomfortable, and that made her edgy.

Rivkah darted a glance into the street. The box gleamed in a bit of sunlight. The young fool didn't know this was the wrong part of town to flaunt a thing like that.

"Nathanael—"

Her eyes snapped to his. "What about Nathanael? You know Nathanael?"

He was pale. He did not answer, did not look at her.

The door went wider. Kyria was at her side. "What do you know about Nathanael?" she demanded.

"This is from him," the lad replied.

Kyria went and snatched the box, glaring at the boy as she handed it to Rivkah, whose hands trembled as she took it.

"Where is he?" Kyria asked.

The question startled him. He pulled his gaze from the box. "It's—a gift. From Nathanael." He began to back away. "I'm sorry."

"What are you sorry about?" Kyria demanded. "Where is he?"

But he turned and ran.

"Wait!" she shouted. She started after him, but Rivkah grabbed her arm.

"Kyria. It's from Nathanael." The cloth wrapping dropped to the ground, and she turned the box in every direction. She worked off the lid and looked inside, then replaced it. "It's from my boy. A gift from my baby."

Kyria frowned after the lad. "What is he sorry about?" Then she moved to block the view of the box from any potential thieves. "Let's get it inside before someone wants your baby's gift." She bent to snatch the dropped cloth, then they went inside and Kyria shut the door. "You ever see him before?"

Rivkah shook her head, staring in wonder at the box. What a beautiful thing. What a lovely thing.

Kyria frowned. "Nobody gives you a box like that. Nobody just comes to your door and says here, have this. All that lapis? It must be worth a hundred denarii." She went to the couch and dropped to her stomach. "He says it's from Nathanael, but says nothing about him. He runs away. What is that? Seven kinds of odd, Rivkah." She cocked her head and one eyebrow came up. "I will say he was nice looking. You think you're too old for him, but I'm not. Maybe he'll be back. And you have charcoal all over your face."

Rivkah sniffed and nodded, rubbing at her cheek. She didn't know she was crying. She had never seen anything more beautiful. Nathanael had taste, always did. He had an eye for beauty.

"You know what this means, Kyria? He speaks to me with this. It's a message."

But Kyria was silent.

Rivkah could barely breathe sometimes for the ache of missing him. But how happy she was that he had the guts to shake off what he was, go out there, and make himself a life. How proud she was. Perhaps, in the two months he had been away, he had gone to work for a wealthy merchant and saved for this box. It was a message.

She didn't deserve him, never would. Prostitution? Not even sin compared to what she had done to Nathanael. Not even Kyria knew. Only Rivkah's mother knew. And she was dead.

She absently pressed her palm on the top of her leg. Sometimes customers asked about the scars.

This box meant maybe Nathanael forgave her, because he had an unnaturally good heart. This box could make her delirious for a month. It meant maybe God really did hear the prayers of a prostitute.

"He couldn't remember his aunt Kyria," Kyria sniffed, and rolled to her back. She picked up her plate and set it on her stomach. "Fix your face, you're scaring me."

Holding the box to her cheek, Rivkah drifted to her room.

❧

Kyria watched the beads sway until they stilled.

No word in two months, and that wasn't like Nathanael. He'd said he'd be back by the next full moon. She'd known the boy since he was a baby, and it was not like him.

What could that box mean? Didn't Rivkah see the look on the lad's face? That bleakness. That misery. It put fear in her, fear for Nathanael and fear for Rivkah. But try and make Rivkah see something was wrong. Rivkah flounced about with that fake cheerfulness that all was perfectly fine; Kyria felt foreboding snake in. All was not fine. Try and make Rivkah see.

5

Rivkah sat with the others on the steps of the Praetorium Palace. At least, she sat on the same steps. They sat on the other side.

She looked over her shoulder at the great guarded doors and sighed. What was taking him so long today? It was close to noon and getting hot.

The undersecretary was taking petitioners now, and it never seemed to be her turn. Prostitutes did not have rights, after all, not even the right of place in line. A woman who had come five persons after Rivkah gave her a triumphant look when the guard called for her to approach the table of Undersecretary Prometheus Longinus. Whenever Orion was at the table, from that first day, Rivkah kept her place in line.

She scowled at the number of people ahead of her. It would be a long day if Orion did not soon appear. She had eaten a barley loaf purchased on the way to the palace, had drunk a cup of sweet water, and the sun was making her drowsy. The warmth of the wide stone step beneath, the warmth of the sun above . . . she would love to melt down onto the step and sleep the day away. Sabbath ended at sundown last night, and Sabbath was the day she usually slept extra—Jewish clients did not appear then—but guarding the tree had taken extra sleep. She gave her cheeks little rows of pinches to stay awake.

Whose child do you think it is, Mother?

Surely not! I will tear out that evil tongue if you continue to speak such lies!

Why, Mother? Why did you ever send me there? Zakkai already had two serving maids. He did not need another! Why, Mother?

He asked for you—what am I to tell a priest?

Do you know what he did? Do you care?

There would be no wedding canopy for Rivkah.

"Prometheus calls for you."

Her eyes flew open, and she looked about. Everyone else was gone. The sun was high noon. The shorter of the two Praetorian guards stood on the step above her. It would be the shorter one—the taller one would have roused her with his boot.

This guard—Marcus, Orion Galerinius had called him—had been on duty the first day she came to plead for Nathanael's tree. Why was he standing there? Then she rose quickly. She realized he was blocking the view of Prometheus so she could order herself.

She rearranged her veil and righted the circlet securing it. She smoothed her tunic, wiped the corners of her mouth and set her face. She looked up at Marcus, but his gaze flickered down. She glanced down; a portion of her tunic billowed disproportionately from her belt. She tucked it in and flashed a smile at Marcus. He winked and turned on his heel. He went back to the door and assumed his position.

Undersecretary Prometheus had known perfectly he had skipped her all along. He sat back on his stool, an amused sneer on his ugly Roman face. She knew how to handle idiots like this.

She approached the table in a slow, emphasized sway, one she had never conceived to use on Orion. She let her eyes travel slowly over the man, long enough to let his eyes travel over her. It didn't take long at all with this one; she saw the desire light in his eyes.

"I need to see the chief secretary. He knows my business."

"I'll bet he knows your business."

She turned to half sit on the table. She yawned and stretched and gave a little shiver, making her jewelry tinkle. She brushed aside a filmy fold of her veil, then seized the edge as if examining a flaw. Then she looked over her shoulder and pretended surprise that he was still there. "Well? May I see him, please? I regret that I do not have all day to spend with you, good sir."

"Sure you don't. But you have all *night*." His look lingered over her. "What do you want Orion for when you could have someone who is a real soldier? I'm shocked he sends for you. Everyone knows he's saving for a place in Ostia. He wouldn't pitch a copper to his starving mother." He pretended to peek into the purse strapped to his waist. "Me, on the other hand. I can waste a few coins."

She smiled then. She lowered her chin until she was looking at him from hooded lids. She leaned forward, close enough to know he breathed her perfume, and crooked her finger to beckon him to a secret. He flicked a grin at the tall guard, then moved his head closer to hear.

"Orion is free, you ugly lout," she breathed in his ear, and watched her breath make his arms prickle. "I'd bed Pilate before you. Now fetch Orion, or I'll tell the guards I saw you at the inn asking for a man . . . not a woman." She withdrew, smile in place.

The leer dropped off his face so fast she had to bite the inside of her cheek to stop a laugh. He stood quickly, too quickly he realized, and covered for it by snatching a leaf of papyrus from the table to examine. "I have to get this to Orion," he said loudly. He looked at the guard and said, "Make sure she doesn't steal anything." He disappeared past the massive doors into the Praetorium.

Once he was gone she did laugh, and drummed her palms on the table in delight. She caught the look from the guard Marcus. He was grinning, had a twinkle in his eye like Orion. It warmed her to her toes.

She hopped off the table with a light heart and settled into a stroll on the top of the steps. Here she was, pacing the steps of the Praetorium, looking forward to seeing a *man*. Wouldn't Kyria laugh! She had not felt this way since she was fifteen, and it was so ridiculous she could laugh. She was thirty-four, a prostitute, and Jewish. He was a high-ranking official, the highest beside Pontius Pilate himself, and Roman.

Strangely, she wanted to tell him all about the box from Nathanael. It was so beautiful! She'd never owned such a thing! She'd thought about it all the way here. Surely it meant one single thing—Nathanael forgave her.

But Orion would soon arrive, and thoughts of what Nathanael had to forgive did not belong. She made Orion's face replace the silver box. She had been doing that lately, inserting his face in the oddest of places. Wouldn't he be surprised to know he appeared in Corinthian fancies, now a slave bearing her sedan chair, now sharing the sedan.

Orion Galerinius did not have the stature of a gladiator, or even a Roman soldier. She had certainly known men more handsome. But she loved early gray in black hair. And though he didn't smile much, once she realized how entrancing his was, she tried to get him to smile at least once at every interview.

Then she happened to catch the look of the tall guard, and it quenched the smile on her own face. Did Orion ever see her as this guard did? She knew how to handle lust, accept it or shove it away. But this in the guard's face was an old thing she had never learned how to handle. It was the look of an elder or a rabbi. Or her mother.

Contempt was a mystery. It tripped her up at the oddest times, because she knew what she was and it didn't bother her. What someone thought of her was the least of her worries. But every now and then, there it was, an issue. Every now and then she did care. There had to be a secret to dealing with contempt. She would discover it one day.

She pulled her outer vest closer, lifted her chin, looked away. She was a fool. Entertaining Corinthian thoughts of Orion Galerinius. She would ever be what she was, and decent men would give her no more than a kind smile and a twinkle in the eye. Decent men could stand next to her and be a country apart. She started down the steps. She didn't want to be here anymore.

"Rivkah."

Curse it that her heart stopped at his voice. And her steps as well. Fine fancy, Rivkah, that you thought you could leave without seeing him.

She set her face in the way that amused him and whirled about. "You think you can hide from—" But her words dropped.

He was not amused. He had the same look that had caught her breath yesterday. Grim and bleak.

"What's wrong?" she snapped. "What is that face?" She hated to see him like that. It unsettled her worse than—and she gasped, clutching her belly. "Oh God, no."

"The tree is safe!" he said quickly, coming down a step. He moved as if to touch her shoulder, but didn't. "It is safe. You do not have to guard it anymore." He quickly gave her a smile—as if he knew she liked his smiles—and then a little bow of his head. "Your worries are over. You can go in peace."

Her heart was beating again. "If my worries are over, why is your smile so fake?"

He drew himself up. Coldness replaced the smile. "It may surprise you to learn I have other matters to attend to. Jewish matters make up only six percent of my total occupation."

"What did you say to the foreman yesterday?"

"Why do you ask?"

"No reason, just . . . nobody bothered me yesterday."

He was silent. His face eased a bit. "Had they been . . . bothering you, then?"

Three times the foreman had dragged her to the tool shed after the other workers left for the day. He said it wasn't rape because she was a whore.

"I can take care of myself. But . . . if you said anything to him . . . thanks."

Those brown eyes locked on hers, making her stomach twitch, but then they skimmed past her. His face went grim, and he backed up a step. "I have other matters to attend to." He backed up another step. "Your tree is safe. Do not go to the site anymore."

"Marina expects you at the next Sabbath meal, you miserable pile of fish guts," boomed a loud and familiar voice. She turned slowly.

Only Theron would call Pilate's chief secretary such a thing. She had not seen him in a long, long time. Not since Nathanael was a boy. He didn't seem to notice her.

He stopped several steps below Rivkah, set down a flat and wide cloth-covered bundle, and pressed his face into his shoulder to blot sweat. "You must think mightily of yourself if you believe the hope of Judaism rests upon you," he cheerfully told Orion. "We were persecuted long before Orion the Mighty came to work for Pontius Pilate. Hello, Rivkah."

"Weren't you supposed to be here yesterday?" Orion said coldly.

"Hello, Theron," Rivkah said as her stare went to Orion. If his face was grim before, it was black now.

"This man ever tell you he's the hope of Judaism?" Theron asked.

"Close that trumpet of yours and get those patterns inside," Orion snapped.

"Did he save your tree yet?" Theron asked.

"Theron!" Orion barked. Rivkah watched his face turn crimson.

"Yes, Theron. The tree is saved. He told you about Nathanael's tree?"

"He did," Theron told her. With an amused squint at Orion, he said, "So you found a solution, did you? We knew you would. Maybe you are the hope of Judaism. Maybe you're the Messiah. Ha. A Gentile Messiah, now that's an innovation. And what about the Jewish stonemason? What miracle did you work with that one?"

Rivkah fancied if she poked Orion with a needle, he would shoot to the stars.

"No miracle there, Theron," Orion said between his teeth. "Next week his back will look like a skinned ox. Next week he'll die. All because of custom." He turned and trotted up the stairs, vanishing into the Praetorium through the space between the doors.

Theron's shoulders came down. "I talk too much," he said quietly. He hoisted his bundle and started up the stairs, then paused. "How did he save your tree, Rivkah?"

She lifted her chin. "I suppose Pilate decided the tree was worth saving."

"Pilate told him to cut it down."

He continued up the steps and slipped into the Praetorium, to leave her gazing after.

❧

Orion heard Theron's sniff behind him. He could pick that sniff out of a crowd. It always made Orion want to tell Theron to blow his nose and be done with it. He couldn't tell him anything now, he was too furious. But he felt the fury abate at each step. Anxiety swallowed fury whole.

The ugly scene at Theron's meant nothing now. Yesterday at the granary site Orion had joined the roster of corrupted officials with his impromptu plan to save Rivkah's tree. That was nothing: today he did not appear at the Tiberateum work site to announce Pilate's decree for the stonemason. He was suddenly very aware of . . . everything. Every footfall in the corridor. Every person he passed.

Twice Orion had to pause in the tangle of rooms past the great hall and wait for Theron to catch up. The Jew had not been to his office before. He heard Theron mutter, "What is this? I feel like I'm in the labyrinth mosaic." Then a breathless, "No wonder you're skinny."

Orion's office was past the small audience hall that served as Pilate's council room. He glanced in as he passed; Pilate sat at the table with Cornelius and a few of Cornelius's men. Some of the men were laughing, and Pilate had a self-satisfied look. Cornelius was not laughing.

Orion took the corner and after several paces realized Theron was not on his heels. He rolled his eyes and leaned against the wall to wait for him to catch up.

"Orion Galerinius. Honoratus."

Just the tone could set his flesh to creeping. Orion hadn't heard the clack and clatter of the jewelry, else he would have ducked for the nearest doorway. He closed his eyes. *Hurry up, Theron!* He put a careful smile on his face—a smile so businesslike it could freeze the sun—and turned to Janus Bifrons. "Hello, Janus."

The priest folded his arms and leaned against the wall, as delighted as a child discovering a cache of—Orion swallowed—sweets.

He must have been on his way to the Temple of Rome and Augustus; he was in his full priestly vestments. He wore a sleeveless vest of rich indigo, banded with golden embroidery, as long as the rust-colored tunic it covered. The tunic was long-sleeved. Orion did not know how the local priests in this land regarded long-sleeved tunics, but back in Rome they were considered effeminate. Well, Orion didn't know everything about priestly duties or Roman priests. Perhaps a long-sleeved tunic was one of the requirements.

Perhaps not.

Janus toyed with one of his wooden necklaces. He didn't wear a single piece of metal jewelry, it was all wooden. Why, Orion did not know. But he usually heard Janus coming from all the clacking and could dash the other way or dive into the nearest room.

The priest gave Orion a head-to-sandal glance that put him in an instant sweat. "Has the Primipilaris arrived yet?"

Orion glanced longingly in the direction Theron should be coming. "Noooo, not yet. Any day now." If he were lucky, any second now.

"A pity. All of this waiting is exceedingly hard on His Excellency. It troubles me to see him so."

"How is that?"

Janus shrugged and set his ornaments to clacking. "Oh, the *genius* of a man should not be so confined. Pilate is harnessed tighter than a vestal. Poor man. A person shouldn't have to live like that . . . don't you agree?" He entwined his fingers into the necklace and lowered a look at Orion.

Shrieking gods and goddesses, where was Theron? Orion cleared his throat and wished for his tablet to consult. It wasn't that Janus Bifrons was such an unpleasant person. He had more insight than anybody else into the goings-on around here—and he seemed to take special pains for Orion to notice it.

Or was it all Orion's fancy? They had come over on the same ship, with Pilate and the rest of the entourage bound for the Praetorium Palace of Caesarea Maritima. Orion had enthusiastically shared with the middle-aged priest the hopes and dreams he had for his new position as chief secretary, spilling his soul in the giddiness of the adventure, the excitement of the voyage. He had spent the ensuing years feeling as though he needed to disabuse Janus of any . . . notions.

Truly, the man had a sense of humor and could be counted upon for an accurate assessment of the political plays that went on in the palace. Several times Orion had sought him out for information on local religious proceedings, and had even asked his advice on the occasional servant-and-slave dilemma.

The older man lifted his arm and shook his wrist. It was an unconscious motion, making the bracelets fall down his arm to his elbow. One of the bracelets, so pale it was nearly silver, caught Orion's notice.

Janus followed his gaze. "What, this? This was a gift from Augustus, given to my mother." He smiled fondly. "I daren't take it off, it has brought me much luck."

"If I have to come through this honeycomb every single day—hello." Theron nodded at Janus. "I will insist on *four* pistachio pastries just for the exertion."

Orion could have collapsed in relief. "Come, Theron . . . I don't have all day." He gave Janus a long-suffering glance, jerked his head at Theron, and rolled his eyes.

Janus in turn gave Theron a haughty up-and-down look.

"You could have helped me carry these," Theron complained as he shifted the load on his shoulder.

"Brute," Orion heard Janus mutter before he lifted his chin and strode away, ornaments clacking.

"Who was that?" Theron asked when the clattering died away.

"Janus Bifrons, the palace priest."

"Friend of yours?" Theron set his boards down to wipe his forehead. He looked at the sweat on his palm and wiped it on his tunic.

Orion glared at Theron. "What's that supposed to mean?"

Theron glanced at him, surprised. Orion's glare made him glare. "What's the matter with you?"

"Understand immediately I am not in the mood for *anything* today."

That made Theron scowl. "You should've put more honey on your bread this morning." He picked up his boards with an air of sullen injury and followed Orion to his workroom.

He had a notion, conceived earlier that day when he realized Theron would show up with the mosaic samples, that it was very important for Theron to see the place where he worked. Maybe if he saw the order of his room he would understand a little of what Orion was about. Orion had seen Theron's own workroom—what a mess. Boards with half-finished patterns propped everywhere, broken and scattered tesserae crunching underfoot. Bowls with hardened mortar, stirring sticks stuck fast. Old orange peels and fruit pits on the floor. Theron never noticed the disarray, or didn't care.

Here he would see that Orion's work involved much more than Jewish dilemmas. The scourging of a Jewish stonemason was one item on a long list that included *Send small cask to Quirinius, Prepare guest list for the Festival of Luna, Pilate's mother's birthday, Check on arrival of Decimus, Order more wax, Fire Solonus, See Claudius on renovation, Report from Prometheus,* and twenty other things all for one day's work. It did not include the daily parade of problems and requests that never made it to the tablet.

He hoped to be interrupted several times while he reviewed the Pompeii patterns. Orion was more than a colorful tile to be pushed about on Theron's pattern board. More than useful for Marina's schemes, no matter how good they were. He had a job, something those two never seemed to consider. Let Theron try and do Orion's job, let Marina. They'd founder in the first five minutes.

Orion loved his workplace. He wasn't here often enough; he was usually chasing about the palace on Pilate's heels or with a servant on his own. Here was the kind of order Orion imagined the palace had, beneath the flurry of activity. If the order of the Praetorium could be compared to a single thing, Orion hoped it would look like his workplace—in particular, his writing table: free of clutter, organized, at-the-ready.

The long narrow table against the wall—he had placed it under the window for the partial view of the sea—held clean rolls of fresh papyrus, still smelly from the maker. Neatly arranged next to the rolls were stoppered ink pots, a vase filled with pens and styli, a new kind of tablet from Rome, sent by his father. It had eight folded sheets of papyrus stitched together at the folds, topped and bottomed with wooden boards. It was awkward and impractical, but it was from his father. Placed neatly next to it was a pile of ready-use tablets, freshly filled with beeswax. In front of all this was his palace calendar, bordered with notations arranged in order of importance. The entire writing table was neat, ordered, and spoke of a man who had little time for what did not concern the efficient operation of a palace staffed with fifty-four—and that, half his job. The other half was daily attendance to a governor who was just as static as he was surprising.

Theron stood in the doorway. "So this is where Orion the Mighty works." He lowered the boards from his shoulder to the floor, then carefully leaned them against the wall. He put his hands on his hips, then reached for the small lumpy vase on the candle table next to the doorway. "What's this?"

Trust Theron to pick out the one thing not in keeping with the order of his workplace. "A gift from one of the cook's children."

"And this?"

Trust him to find the one other thing. It was a tiny bronze figurine of a charioteer in a quadriga, a four-horse chariot. The charioteer was painted red.

"A present from my father, when I was a child. I was a fan of the Reds."

"Ah." Theron replaced it and looked about the room with undisguised interest. "I've always thought you can learn a lot about a person by his workplace. It's quite clear to me now. No wonder at all."

Orion squinted at him. "What's no wonder?"

"I didn't know you played the pipe." Trust Theron to find the *other* thing. He had spied it on the recessed shelf on the left side of the room. He picked it up and gave it a blow—the vexing shriek it had when the holes were uncovered. Little Benjamin's screeches made Orion sure he never wanted children.

Theron held it up to the light from the window. "This is pretty. What wood is it?"

"Pearwood. Where were you yesterday? I dislike you taking advantage of our—friendship—to excuse your absence. I expected you."

"I had something to do. Something important. How long have you played this?"

"Awhile. Show me the patterns, Theron. I don't have all day." Not a single interruption yet. Where was everyone? Midmeal was long over. He should have had four intrusions by now.

Theron set the pipe on the shelf above the writing table. Orion snatched it and replaced it where it belonged, bringing Theron's attention to the other objects on the recessed shelves . . . to the small wooden box on the top shelf. Theron reached for it.

"Don't!" Orion barked, and Theron froze. "It is sacred to me."

The mosaicist withdrew his hand and respectfully murmured, "Apologies, Orion."

He was in no hurry to get to the boards. He patted his stomach absently as his eyes flittered over everything in the room. His attention came to a little shelf above the table, then rested on—Orion scowled. He had meant to put that away. Theron was not seeing his workplace the right way at all.

"Why, Orion . . . this is a charming thing."

It was a tiny replica of a wine amphora, cast in bronze, ringed with brilliantly colored enamel. It had a removable stopper, which Theron naturally tugged off to squint inside the tiny hole. He sniffed it, then replaced the stopper.

"That was my mother's," Orion said, his tone softened. "It was Father's last gift to her before she died. She collected little things like that."

"I regret my words from the night before." Theron examined the amphora a moment more, and replaced it carefully.

Was that an apology? It came as casually as a cough. "I probably regret my own words, but I don't remember what they were." A few things had happened since then.

Orion picked up the boards and brought them near the light of the window. He unwound them and set them on the floor, pushing them into a line. He stood back to look.

Theron groused and stomped over to the boards to realign them. "*There,*" he declared, and stood back with Orion.

Orion could feel his face soften. Each board was its own pattern, whorls and convolutions of color as though someone had dropped a handful of ribbons on the floor, pretty enough. Placed correctly, the four separate boards made a long, sinuous pattern. More boards would continue the pattern. It was quite astonishing. Not only the design, but the brilliant colors. It would make for an entrancing walkway.

"You're a genius, Theron," Orion murmured.

And if there was one thing Orion loved about Theron, it was his inability to fake modesty. With his hands clasped about his belly and his eyes lovingly on his tiles, the fat little man swiveled back and forth on planted feet, beaming like a child at the praise.

"You think so?"

"From Pompeii . . . ," Orion said.

"Of course," Theron assured. "Except this mosaic is not classically worked."

"Meaning . . ."

"Not done on site, saving the actual installation. Most of the work is done in my workroom. Meaning—" and his tone went mournful—"fewer pistachio pastries."

Meaning he would not see Theron every day.

"At least I have an apprentice, and Thomas's cousin wants to learn the trade. Pilate will have his walkway in less than half a year. And *they* will be the ones to carry the boards from my workroom." Theron gave his tiles an indulgent smile. His chin came down, producing a few more chins as he admired his work. "You like my tiles?"

It wasn't so charming anymore. "I said I did."

"You think Pilate will like them?"

"Theron, let me ask you something." Orion leaned back to look both ways out his door. Suddenly he didn't want anyone to interrupt. He scratched the back of his neck. He was no good at this. Whispering, he said, "I have to bribe an architect. How does one . . . ?" He gestured helplessly. "How *much* does one offer?" Would he have enough in the Ostia fund?

The adoration left Theron's face. He squinted at Orion, then pushed his hand upside his head and blew out a breath. "You have to *bribe* an architect. What architect?"

"That's what I'm asking *you*."

"What for?"

"I need—" He jumped at the face at the door.

"Orion Galerinius Honoratus?" a woman inquired formally and fearfully. "Sir? I beg forgiveness for the interruption."

"What do you want?" Orion snapped.

"Undersecretary Prometheus Longinus sends this report, sir."

Or so he ascertained from her mangled Greek. She held out the tablet, keeping her eyes properly downcast. At least Portia had trained her correctly.

He took the report and tossed it onto his writing table. "Tell the undersecretary to deliver it himself next time."

The woman broke protocol to gaze, fear-struck, into Orion's eyes.

Quickly, Orion flicked his forehead. "Ah—what am I thinking? I have a meeting with him this evening. Never mind, I will tell him myself. You are dismissed."

She bowed her head and scurried away.

Theron had a curl to his lip.

"What? Is she Jewish?" Orion demanded. "How did I offend this time?"

"You didn't. It's that Prometheus I do not like."

Neither did Orion, but he wasn't about to agree with Theron. Prometheus never liked to be reminded who was his superior officer. He never failed to remind Orion, however subtly—like sending a slave to deliver a report, for instance—that Orion had never served in the army. Perhaps if he began to grunt unintelligible phrases, Prometheus would have more respect for him.

"What an ornery face. You don't like him either."

Orion scowled—then froze. Did he hear footfalls?

"So you want to bribe an architect. About what?"

"Shh!" Orion listened carefully for a wide-eyed moment, then eased. To the point of mouthing the words, he whispered to Theron, "I have to change some sealed plans. The sooner the better. Pilate cannot know why the granary is moving west twenty feet."

Theron's face softened. "You are a good man, Orion Galerinius Honoratus. What does Honoratus mean?"

Orion's breath seized and he held up his hand. *Did* he hear footfalls in the corridor? At length he took a breath and whispered, "Latin for 'esteemed.'" Is this how all corrupted officials lived? An ear to the passageways and a hand to a hidden dagger?

"Why do you ask me about bribing?" Theron said in a very loud whisper. "Isn't that the first thing junior officials learn?"

"Amusing. Are you going to help me or not?"

"Sure. I am in daily league with tricky characters such as bribable architects." But he held up his hand and said, "Do not worry. Uncle Theron will look into it. I consider this a Jewish cause." He thought on it. "Tomorrow I will bring back more boards, as if you were not satisfied with these, and I will have your answer. Who and how much."

For the first time all day, Orion took a relieved breath. Who else could he talk to about this? Prometheus? His head would decorate a platter before dusk. Or worse, he'd be shipped to the mines in Spain and chained to a gang of angry slaves. They'd be Spaniards or Gauls or Germans or Britons. They'd be bigger than him. They would hate him because he was Roman, and one would have an unholy appetite for short and reasonably handsome men. Gods. He wouldn't last a day.

Orion had no one else to talk to except Janus Bifrons and a

father consulted by air letters. He thought he could trust Janus, but how far? What sort of sentiment did Janus have toward the Jews? Really, there was no one he trusted more in Caesarea than Theron the Jewish mosaicist.

"There is, of course, a fee."

"What do you mean, a *fee*?"

"Don't give Pilate's decree for the Jewish mason."

"Theron—"

"Who can survive forty-nine?"

"Theron—"

"Lie. Next week tell Pilate he suffered mightily. Tell him his flesh was in shreds, blood like a river. Tell him you could see bone." He lifted his finger in inspiration. "Tell him his wife and eleven children watched. Maybe you could work up a tear."

Orion pinched hard the space between his eyes. "Lie. To Pontius Pilate." *To my honorable father from your lying son . . .* A thought came, and he took his hand away to peer at Theron. "How did you know I didn't give the order yet?"

"You did not scratch through it on your tablet. You scratched everything else."

Orion's gaze jerked to the tablet on his writing table. He had not seen Theron look at it.

"And don't worry about lying to Pilate . . . you are already bribing an architect, what's another lie?"

Orion resumed the pinch. He could hear the clank of the chains. Smell the sweat. "Go away, Theron."

"I can't, not until you see these."

Orion looked to see Theron wriggle a sheaf of papyrus from his inner tunic. He handed the pages to Orion.

Orion took them, trying to ignore the unpleasant fact that the sheets were warm and damp with Theron's sweat. "What are these?"

They were old sheets, that was evident. Rolled and pressed and cut in the old fashion. They looked like dirty woven linen. They rustled despite the dampness.

"Copies of documents."

"What documents?"

Theron came and glanced at the one Orion was looking at. "That one is a copy of a letter from a man named Lepidus Servilius, from Ancrya. Can you read Aramaic? It says, 'Wherever the Jews have been following their ancient custom of collecting money for religious purposes and sending it to Jerusalem, they may do so without let or hindrance.' It means the Jews can send the half-shekel to Jerusalem without interference. Their rights were disputed by the local authority but challenged—and upheld—by the proconsul."

Orion put that leaf behind the rest, and Theron pointed at the next. "This one is pre-Augustus, but nonetheless it is a copy of a document regarding the same rights for Jews. The Jews were supported in their endeavors by Roman authorities. You heard me, I said *supported*. Read it, Orion. These are imperial edicts."

Slowly Orion said, "Where did you get these?"

Theron pointed at the next document. "That one names Ephesus and Libya. That one names Sardis. The other names Miletus. They all deal with the rights of Jews to send the half-shekel donation to the Temple in Jerusalem. The rights were challenged in every one of those cities, and defended by each local proconsul."

"Where did you get these?"

"Don't ask foolish questions. You want to know where I was yesterday? That's where I was. Had to miss synagogue because of you."

"You always miss synagogue. What do you expect me to do with these?"

"Present them to Pilate."

Orion shuffled through the papers. Here was a letter from one

Proconsul Jullus Antonius—a letter written at the request of the Jews. It reaffirmed the provisions made by a previous ruling to allow the Jews to collect and distribute the half-shekel to Jerusalem.

"Theron, these are dated. Some are decades old. This goes back to Julius Caesar! A lot has happened since then—how much weight do you suppose these will have with Pilate? His own Tiberius drove the Jews out of Rome ten years ago. I was there, Theron. I saw some of them leave."

"Ah, but they didn't leave completely, because of Tiberius's mediocre hate. Many already returned because he doesn't care enough to oust them again. It's that Sejanus who stirred him up, and we hear Sejanus—because God is not mocked—now has precarious footing with old Tiberius."

Orion flicked the papers impatiently. "What does the collection of money have to do with not working on a holy day?"

"Implications! Allowance to adhere to ancient customs."

"That's very thin, Theron. I'm not a lawyer. I can't make these look like more than what they are. Pilate is not an idiot."

"They are imperial edicts," Theron implored.

"They are not imperial edicts on keeping your Sabbath. Get me some edicts like those. These are worthless."

Theron stuck out that fat lower lip. "This is all we have. They dug these up when Valerius Gratus questioned the half-shekel practice. They presented these very papers to Gratus, and he dismissed the charges. Take them to Pilate, Orion. He impresses easily. Once he sees his own predecessor treated the Jews more fairly, perhaps he will change his mind with the stonemason. Maybe it will help other Jews around here who are harassed about the Sabbath."

Orion tossed the sheaf of papyrus on his writing table. He put his foot on his stool and leaned on his knee, kneading his forehead. Good Theron. How could he tell him, after his effort to procure these documents, that for him to wave these under Pilate's nose would be the same as asking for exile? It would prove to Pilate what Orion knew he suspected, that Orion was pro-Jewish—and that to be pro-Jewish in these parts was to dally with treason.

It was not a hundred years since Pompey sacked Jerusalem, too short a time for Jewish dreams of independence to die. With Jews, Orion suspected it would take a lot longer than a hundred years. The others who made up the "Gentile" portion of Palestinia—to the Jews, they were all Gentiles, not Syrians or Greeks or Parthians—did not seem to have the same drive for the old autonomy.

"Think on it." Theron nodded at the papers. "See what you can do with those. It wasn't easy to get them, and you got a whole week to work with them. Orion . . . sure, you can run a place like this. Maybe that very same talent includes the chin to finesse old Pontius Pilate."

Orion did not respond.

"Now. I will see what I can do about an architect for your granary plans. I'll be back tomorrow with 'new' boards." He grinned suddenly, happy as a child. "This is exciting, don't you think? I've got a chance to do something for my people, and that is fine. They'll be calling me Theron the Maccabee. What's the matter? You look uptight."

Exciting? When was the vomiting kind of fear exciting?

Theron began to rewrap the tiles. Loudly he exclaimed, "What do you mean, not good enough?" He gave Orion a delighted grin, one Orion could not return. Bribe an architect. Disobey a direct order. What else would he do before sundown?

"It was good enough for Sossus, you barbarian! It is good enough for the majestic Pontius Pilate!"

To my honorable father from your corrupted son . . .

Theron had the boards on his shoulder and was backing out

of the doorway. "You wouldn't know beauty if you drowned in it! You wouldn't see brilliance and dignity and emotion and grace if it slammed you on the head! I'll be back tomorrow, you offspring of a Cretan, with a pattern to make the emperor weep. He would weep over *this* one! You have the discernment of a—"

"Good enough, Theron," Orion whispered.

"Right." He looked both ways, winked at Orion, and departed.

Orion watched until he disappeared, then turned into his workroom. He went to the window. It wasn't a bad view. When he leaned left he could see the entire length of the Great Stadium. He could see where the charioteers careened around the corner. The harbor was straight ahead, and when he leaned right he could see a good portion of the Mediterranean. He felt for his stool and dropped heavily onto it.

After a moment he pulled the stool to the table and pushed Theron's documents aside. He began to pick through the notes by his calendar. He was working on the guest list for the Festival of Luna, and had the month of Augustus laid out—a specially cut piece of papyrus large enough to accommodate various addenda. Augustus. It used to be Sextilis. Become a Caesar and they rename a month for you. Would September become Tiberius? Who would replace November?

Eyes on the calendar, he reached for a stylus in the vase and drew a hard line through the unscratched item on the tablet. He blew the curls of beeswax from the stylus and dropped it into the vase. Then he took Theron's documents and slid them under the calendar. He made sure it was flat and smooth, as though nothing was underneath. He weighted the edges with objects from his table, a stoppered inkwell and a tablet, a small sack of withered dates. Then he reached for the smallest tablet at the corner of his table and looked at what he had written.

Write Father.

Pick up fish sauce at Falnera's.

Get sandal fixed.

Beneath the last item, he added *Confirm balance in Ostia fund.*
He pulled open the table drawer and took out a small correspondence roll. He unrolled it flat, selected his favorite pen, dipped it, and touched the excess ink to a scrap of felt:

*To my beloved father, Appius Galerinius Libertus, from your
son, Orion Galerinius Honoratus, greetings.*

*We are putting in a mosaic walkway, Father, and the
design is splendid. I think you would like it. Before I forget,
thank you for the new tablet. It arrived precisely on my
birthday. Well, precisely a day later. Truly a fascinating Roman
innovation. I look forward to its use.*

The pen stopped. He lifted his gaze to his view.

Today I will disobey a direct order, Father. Today Pilate keeps a Jewish whore.

I've been thinking about her. It's ridiculous. It doesn't make sense. Sometimes I want to ask her about it. I want to say, What are you doing? What are you thinking? Because you can see it in her eyes, she was not born for what she is—so much for Stoicism. What she is, Father, is a whore.

A vile word, I hate it. *Prostitute* does not lessen it, but *whore* is vile. I use it for reality. Like I'm taking up a handful of the beach to rub my face. I need reality, Father. She is a whore. I even made her Pilate's whore.

The pen started.

*What are your plans for the Festival of Luna? What, your
gilt invitation from Tiberius has not arrived? I'll see what I
can do. I'm practically wearing purple here. Not bad, for the
son of a freedman. Well, it is hot here, and that on the coast.
Hot! Hotter than summers in Rome, and I never imagined to
say such a thing. How is Aunt Vesta feeling? Better, I hope. . . .*

He finished the letter and carefully blotted the ink. He took
a wooden dowel and worked the edge of the parchment into the
long slit in the dowel and began to roll up the letter. He paused
and stared at his hands. They were trembling. He held them out to
stare at them.

He could not tell his father, not even in an air letter, how afraid
he was. He had talent to run a Praetorium Palace. He had talent
to present to the public a Pontius Pilate free from wrinkles in his
purple-bordered toga, a Pilate knowledgeable of local customs and
up-to-date on the latest names and faces and situations. Orion knew
what he could do. What he could not do was tread the grapes of
deceitfulness for long. His fear would expose him, he would blun-
der. Today began a course to he knew not where.

He rose and went to the recessed shelves. He took down the box.
He held it long, then brought it to his table. He sat on the stool and
looked at the sea, put his hand flat on the box. One thing was certain. Two things. Today a woman's tree was safe. Today he did not
give a cruel decree. The splayed fingers on the box curled to a fist.

6

JOAB DROPPED THE BUCKET of shells on a workroom table. Jorah was crouched at one of the tiles, examining the edge. She rose and came to the bucket, inspected a shell, and clicked her tongue. "How many days have we been working together, and you still cannot tell the difference between crimson and scarlet?"

He should have expected that. He gets a pinch in his back gathering all these shells and that is what she says, not thank you, Joab, not a single word of appreciation. "That is not crimson *or* scarlet. That is *pink*. There are no crimson or scarlet shells to be found anywhere on the beach. And we've been together four days now. Four very long days." He glanced to make sure Marina was not at the curtain flap.

Jorah tossed aside the shell—not into the bucket, but on the floor as if she were Theron himself—and took a mortar stick. She stirred up the shells, then stopped when a shell seized her attention. She examined it closely, holding it to the light at the doorway.

Joab picked up a broom and started to sweep debris from under the worktables. His father would have had a fit if even a portion of the dye room looked like this. He glanced at Jorah. Four long days. She hadn't said a word about the silver box. "What are you doing with those shells, anyway?"

"I'm trying to come up with a new color," she murmured.

"A *new* color . . ."

"To maybe border the tiles. I want to try grinding up shells like this—exactly this color, see? *This* is crimson, this rippled edge—and I'm going to mix it with mortar. I'd like to paint it on the border, like a paste. I want to see what Theron thinks of it."

"It would crumble away. It wouldn't be consistent with the surface of the tiles."

Glaring at him, Jorah went back to the bucket and took up the stick. "How do you know? Have you tried it?" She stirred up the shells until she saw another she liked. She took the shell, then yelped and dropped it.

Joab came close. He bent to warily examine the shell. "What? Is there a spider?"

"No. Seaweed."

Slowly, Joab looked at Jorah. *"Seaweed?"* He regarded the shell. It had a teeny tiny gob of stringy seaweed on it. The size of a thumbnail. "You're afraid of seaweed?"

She drew herself up. "I'm not *afraid* of it, I don't *like* it."

Joab scooped it from the floor with a half shell. "It's a plant. People dry it and eat it. What are you scared of?"

"I'm not scared," she protested, but backed away when Joab came closer to her with the seaweed-filled shell. "It's disgusting."

Joab took the shell and dumped the bit of seaweed onto his palm. He held it out to Jorah. "It's time to face your fear, Jorah."

"Joab . . . ," she warned.

He came closer, palm out front. "That's what my father says. You have to face your fear."

She gave a nervous giggle and backed up a step. "Okay, that's funny. Now throw it away." But he edged toward her. "Joab . . . !"

"You can do it, Jorah. Just touch it."

"Go *away*! You're acting like one of my brothers."

"I think you should taste it. Come on, you can do it. It's only a little plant."

"Stop it!" she pleaded, then shrieked a nervous giggle as he took a step closer. She ducked around him and grabbed a mortar stick. "I will beat you with this!"

"Here, look. Nothing to be afraid of." He held up the gob to his mouth. She clapped her hand over her own. He popped it into his mouth, pretended to be surprised at the glorious taste, and chewed it as if luxuriating in the flavor. "Delicious." He looked at the bucket with interest. "Is there any more?"

"Disgusting! Hideous! I can't believe you did that." She dropped the mortar stick into the bucket, snatching her hand back as if the seaweed would slither out and grab her. She went to the tile and squatted next to it. Presently, not looking at Joab, she said, "How did it really taste?"

"Awful."

After a moment the curtain flap, which had been parted an inch or two, eased back into place.

❧

He tried another note on the pearwood pipe. He'd never get it right. It was a tune that came and went, stirring his soul only to disappear. He didn't sleep a minute last night, and once he realized sleep wouldn't come, tried tricking his brain into remembering the tune. He made himself go back through the marketplace, made himself see the same sights and smell the same smells, hoping the tune would show up. It never did. He shoved the pipe aside, knocking things off the table, and rubbed his forehead.

A sound in the corridor—he froze, heart seizing. He listened, breathless. It didn't come again.

The implements of his treachery were laid out before him. A land-grant scroll from the archives with the most perfect seal he could find. Soft clay to mold the seal. Wax to make a seal from the mold. More wax for the forgery, dyed deep purple, Pilate's signature color. A small knife to scrape the forgery clean.

Here was the scroll Theron brought to him this morning. It came blank except for the signature in the bottom left corner. Orion spent the entire morning copying the granary plans to the scroll. The only thing left was to forge the seal.

Alexander Jannaeus was the name at the bottom of the scroll; apparently the architect was named in honor of the great Jewish leader. Orion had seen his name on various documents in the past few years.

This Jannaeus risked much. He had knowingly and willfully put his signature to something that could one day implicate him if Pilate ever found out. Did he know it was for a prostitute? Orion rubbed his eyes, and tried to tuck his heavy eyelids under his brows. They fell down. It would be a long day before he could drop to his couch. He had to *do* this. He had to get it over with before the daily parade of problems began. He'd wasted an hour fooling with the pipe. Was he trying to find a nice accompanying tune for treachery?

He tried to think on the injustice of Pilate's decree. It was just a tree. It would have been a benevolent thing to do, sparing that tree. What kind of leader would Pilate be if he actually listened and cared about the petitions brought before him? He didn't even have to care so terribly much, just listen. But he never really did. In any situation he only focused on whatever course should be taken that would most benefit Rome. Or his own career. Orion waited for the anger to come, as it had before when he would allow himself to think on Pilate's decisions.

He closed his eyes and tried the look of the Jewish laundress. Nothing. He even tried to imagine, as Theron suggested, a man whipped forty-nine times. He saw a splayed-open back, crisscrossed with lashes, dangling ribbons of flesh. He made the back bleed, heavily. He put in that image a wailing wife, added a few children. Nothing. Rivkah appeared next to the wife and waved at him. A corner of his mouth came up, and he twinkled his fingers back at her.

It was futile. He could not conjure a wisp of indignation. Not even compassion. Which god had cursed him with this fate, to suddenly have need of that which he did not possess?

So he picked up the land grant and blew the seal clean of dust with no bravery to do so. He took the soft clay and began to warm it in his hands to an easy malleability, with no anger. He didn't even have a twitch of satisfaction that Pilate's unjust decree would be thwarted today. He had only a surging headache. He raised tired eyes to his bit of the sea. What did he have to make him do it?

Fear, he supposed. The only thing he had was fear he wouldn't do it at all.

Pilate told him to cut it down. Rivkah shut it out and put the two lengths of cloth next to each other. The one on the left had faded to a bluish lavender; the one on the right was a few shades deeper.

"Kyria, look—I soaked this in alum before I put it with the hyacinths." She held it up to show her.

Kyria looked over from the pile of beads she was sorting and shrugged. "So?"

"These were dyed last year, and all year I washed each cloth according to a normal month's wear. Six days a week all year long I put them both in the sun for about two hours—except when I forgot. Now look at this one—the one with the alum kept the most color."

Kyria eyed it more closely. "Not much of a difference, for the trouble or the cost. Or the stink—I think I remember the stink."

Rivkah considered the difference between the two again. "Nooo . . . but it's something. It's cheaper than Tyrian purple. Do you know how much murex costs? If I could sell something close to the same color that wouldn't fade in the sun . . . I'd be rich." *Then I could live in a southern villa. Nathanael would never again be ashamed to have his friends visit, because I would be a cloth merchant and not a whore.*

"You don't think someone else has thought of that? You don't think someone else has tried it? Nothing new under the sun."

Rivkah smoothed a wrinkle in one of the lengths of fabric. Kyria was right. She was a whore, not a cloth merchant.

"You know what? I don't care what you say. Maybe there's nothing new, but what if I make a little modification to what's not new? And what if someone really hasn't tried it? Or they did, but they live in Briton and not in Judea? It would be new around here. Kyria, you could look at the face of God himself and find something to criticize."

Pilate told him to cut it down. Rivkah rubbed her middle finger on the headache at her temple.

"You don't face reality." Kyria shrugged again. "Why set yourself up when you know it will disappoint you?"

Rivkah ignored her.

It wasn't surprising, now that she knew. Why had she expected sympathy from Pontius Pilate? Her tree was a Jewish tree, and she was a whore. So why was it now safe? When did Pilate tell Orion to cut it down? What did he do to circumvent an order from Pontius Pilate, and why would he do it for her?

A hard fast rap came at the door, interrupting Kyria's drone and Rivkah's thoughts. Kyria chirped, "That's for you. Clients don't knock like that."

Rivkah realized she was fingering the two different cloths. She had heard that iron salts worked to keep the dye in the cloth. What if she combined iron salts with alum? What would that do? She left the cloth and strolled to the door.

"Yes?" she asked of the young man. He was already sweating as though he'd been sitting in the sun box at the jail yard. His fists were fast at his sides, and they convulsively opened and closed as he shifted from one foot to the other.

"You are Rivkah?" he asked in a shrill voice.

"I am," she replied, and for the first time she felt pity for these poor messengers of Zakkai. They didn't *want* to do what he made them do; they did it because he made them. Because they thought they had a moral obligation to do so.

The young man launched loudly into the scripture, never pausing, never once looking into her eyes. He didn't even know she mouthed the words along with him.

"Repent and turn away from all your transgressions, so that iniquity may not become a stumbling block to you. Cast away from you all your transgressions which you have committed and make yourselves a new heart and a new spirit."

The young man fled. Mitzvah fulfilled. Or whatever it was.

Rivkah slowly closed the door. She walked through the sitting room, past the table with her dyed clothes, to her beaded-curtain alcove. Kyria was saying something to her. She brushed the beads aside.

She had a lovely bed, draped with gorgeous and tasteful fabrics. She had beautiful tasseled pillows she had made herself and a shelf lined with vases of perfumes and ointments. Antony Scarpus had given her an amphora of balsam. She had a small alabaster vase, so beautiful with overlapping tones of creamy translucence that she often picked it up to wonder at it and roll its smooth cool curves against her cheek. It shone with milky lavender sparkles in the sun.

She had beautiful clothing and beautiful jewelry. And now she had the most precious treasure of all. She went to the silver box on the end of the shelf and she took it in her arms. She crawled onto her bed and wrapped herself about the box.

If the tree was safe . . . and if Nathanael forgave her . . . why did pain claw her, why did it slash inside like a ravening demon? Prostitution? It wasn't even sin. Not compared to what she had done to her baby.

She clutched the box and rocked with it on the bed. Then she began to weep. Scars and scars. Innocent child flesh. Precious child skin.

She held up shaking hands before her eyes. These, her mother-hands, had taken a razor to her own child. *To let the evil out!* Rivkah had said, as her own mother did long ago. *It will protect you!*

Kyria was at the doorway holding the beads aside, face stone cold. She watched Rivkah, and Rivkah was embarrassed, but pain made her weep and there was nothing she could do about it. She was smearing her lovely fabrics with her cosmetics.

"I hate them!" Kyria shouted. "I *hate* that Zakkai most of all! And you are *stupid* to let them do this to you!" She whirled away, the long strands of beads swinging and clicking behind her.

The weeping settled into soft crooning. She could not tell Kyria for the monstrous shame that it wasn't Zakkai at all; it was never Zakkai. It was so easy to blame him. She and Kyria could be just as self-righteous as he.

She had only done to Nathanael what her mother had done to her. . . .

She had only done what she had been taught. . . .

Mother's family converted to Judaism when Mother was a child, but of the old traditions, of the old ways, bloodletting stayed. The old belief said to bleed the evil from the child, if you really loved him. She had only done to Nathanael what her mother had done to her.

She knew it wouldn't prop her before God.

She couldn't blame Zakkai anymore, she couldn't blame her mother. She had done what she had done, and for the very first time she heard the words of the prophet. If repent meant that she would never again take a razor to her son's leg . . . if that's what repent meant, she had already done that.

The other young man who had brought the box, he was right about Ezekiel—how could one make a new heart and a new spirit? Nothing was more impossible. The tree didn't matter, it never had. Nathanael's leg had scars on it.

God did not point at the whoring because he knew it was not sin compared to what she had done to Nathanael. Others saw the prostitution—God looked past it to a crying boy who cowered from his mama. That's where God looked. That's what God saw. And if it made Rivkah wonder about God, that he loved a little boy and hated what she had done to him . . .

She lessened her stiff hold on the box to look down upon it. If this box said Nathanael forgave . . . well and good . . . but what of the demon inside? He would never leave. She didn't deserve for him to leave, because she had hurt her baby. Weeping came hard again, and she heard the slam of the front door.

7

ORION AND HIS SACRED WALKWAY. The little flutterby used it as an excuse to dump more responsibility on Prometheus.

For nearly a week the fat mosaicist had scuttled to the palace every day with the two young Jews trailing after him. For nearly a week Prometheus had to endure the offhanded way Orion tossed him one errand after another because he was busy with the walkway. "Get Pilate's signature on this." "Ask the cook for the menu for the Luna feast." "Get a slave to clean the walls in the west corridor, they look disgusting." He made it sound like Prometheus himself was responsible for the condition of the walls. Bad enough, scurrying after him like a slave. Having to yessir someone who had never served a day in the Roman army galled him to his marrow.

He clapped his hand over his helmet as the cart jostled down the alley. Its wheels found every single uneven cobblestone in Caesarea. It wasn't dignified to bounce so, not for the undersecretary to Pontius Pilate.

"Stop here!" he ordered the driver. He would walk the rest of the way to the tavern. He slid off the back of the cart and left without paying the man—he'd just borne the undersecretary on his cart, payment enough.

He didn't know the name of the tavern next to Falnera's import shop on the quay, or if it had one. It was an exclusive drinking house, Roman soldiers only. Legionnaires could gather and talk of the latest incident they'd smothered, talk about the pathetic auxiliary units. Or when they were further in their cups, speak of the days of real action back in Germania or Gaul. Some of the older ones spoke of the conflicts on the German line, some spoke of their days stationed at the mines in Spain or Britannia. Talk was usually anything but Palestinia. Palestinia was fine until you got here.

And once a soldier was home? It was all about quelling riots in Samaria. Crucifying Zealots in Jerusalem. Tension at the Parthian borders. Rome was fine until you got there.

The serving maid saw him when he entered and was already fetching his wine. He spied a small empty table and made his way through a forest of smelly soldiers to get to it. He removed his helmet and placed it on the table, disinviting any company.

The girl arrived with his drink. She had a new hair color today, German blonde. Probably a wig from Falnera's, gotten from a German captive.

"Greetings, Prometheus Longinus," she said with a flirty smile. She put the cup in front of him and hugged her tray. "Haven't seen you in a while."

"Been busy." Thanks to Orion. He took a coin from his belt

purse and gave it to her. "There. Get yourself another wig. Blonde is ridiculous on you."

The smile went stiff, and she whirled away.

He had only settled into his second sip when someone said, "Prometheus Longinus?" He savored the swallow and set down his cup, then looked over his shoulder to see who had spoken.

The man was not a soldier, but in the company of a few. It was the only way he could get into the tavern. Even that wasn't supposed to happen, but the proprietor wasn't going to argue with a six-foot Roman soldier.

The greasy man grinned a gap-toothed smile at Prometheus. He seemed familiar. He was not Roman, that was easy to see—easy to smell. He could pick out a national by smell alone. Was he an auxiliary soldier? Prometheus nodded and turned back to his drink.

"So what's it like, working for Pontius Pilate?" the man said.

Two things wrong with that. By his comradely tone the man made himself equal with Prometheus. Orion was the only one between him and Pilate, and the three of them stood higher than anyone else in Caesarea—whatever local magistrates might fancy. Those idiots minded waterworks and gutter cleaning and festival organization. They could not walk the palace as Prometheus could. They could not sip wine with Pilate when he was in a gregarious mood.

The other thing was that Prometheus simply didn't want to talk, especially with a guffawing foreigner. Gods up-in-arms, his helmet square on the table should have told the man that—maybe he didn't know the Roman custom. He spoke only to make himself look important to his friends. Why was he so familiar? From wherever he knew the man, he would not acknowledge him now, groveling fool. He took a long sip and set the mug on his table, rolling it between his palms.

"Quite a woman he has," the man said loudly.

Prometheus turned. "Are you still speaking to me?"

The granary. That's where he'd seen this cur. He was the foreman at the new granary in the south quadrant, past the city wall where the new Cardo Maximus picked up again. Orion had Prometheus deliver a sealed scroll to the site a few days ago, on one of the errands he could have well done himself if he didn't have the excuse of the almighty mosaic walkway. This foreman had been screaming at a worker, and Prometheus didn't have time for it. He'd left the scroll with another.

"Eh, Pilate prefers his handsome palace slaves," one of the soldiers jeered. "And I ain't talkin' women." A round of laughter erupted.

"Where's his wife?" another said. "I thought he had a wife."

"She lit for Rome after Pilate crucified the Zealot from Nazareth."

"I heard she killed herself," a burly centurion from another table put in.

The man from the granary held up his hand. "No, gentlemen. I speak of his *woman*. Finer than Oriental silk. And I oughta know." He belched then, and laughed. It wasn't just the foreign stink Prometheus could smell. He'd been draining the amphoras long before Prometheus came.

"Eyes like pieces of honey-colored amber. Hair like a black waterfall."

Prometheus's cup stopped halfway to his lips.

"Body to make a man curse the gods. She may be Jewish, but Pilate's not blind."

Prometheus looked over his shoulder again and caught the eye of the foreman, who snorted and guffawed with the others. Oddly, his eyes grew round and he dropped his gaze. Suddenly he looked like a man who had said too much.

"You work at the granary," Prometheus said.

"Yes, sir." He wet his lips, then grabbed his mug to wet his throat.

Prometheus moved his chair so he wouldn't have to turn. He kept a dead stare on the man until he squirmed. Then he lifted his cup. "Hail Pilate."

"Pilate!" the foreman quickly replied, and drained his cup. He wiped his mouth on his sleeve and set the cup down. Then he rose and said to his companions, "That's it for me, lads. My woman is a jealous one. She'll think I'm shopping the quay." He slapped a coin on the table and left.

Prometheus drained his cup and picked up his helmet.

He caught up with the man near a piling on the dock. The foreman probably thought himself safe. When he realized it was Prometheus calling to him, he stopped dead and got that interesting look on his face again. The guilty one.

Prometheus strolled over to him, strapping on his helmet. He said pleasantly, "Raman, isn't it? I knew I would remember."

Raman bobbed his head, clearly wishing to be anywhere else. "Yes, sir. Raman."

"I saw you at the granary the other day. I came to drop off the sealed scroll from the chief secretary."

"Yes. I got the scroll. Thank you, sir."

"Pilate's woman, you said." Prometheus looked at the shimmering surface of the inner harbor. A luminous glow from the lighthouse wavered on the water. He wouldn't have to say much. This man had something to hide, and he knew Prometheus knew it. "Amber eyes, you said." Only one woman fit that description.

The man went as sickly yellow as the glow on the water. His eyes darted wildly and he rubbed his mouth. "I've had a bit too much to drink, sir. It's not an excuse, I know. I will try and keep my mouth shut. By the honor of the gods, I will try. No! I—mean I *will* keep my mouth shut!"

Silence was a useful tool. It worked wonders with this lout. Without permission to leave, the man fidgeted where he stood until he finally blurted, "I'm sorry, sir, I truly am! Please don't tell Orion Galerinius Honoratus. I know it was supposed to be secret, her being a Jew and all."

"Orion told you . . ."

"Only because of the tree. He had to because of the tree."

The tree? What tree? She came to the palace every day, two or three weeks running. She had said Orion knew her business.

He hadn't seen her all this week, and he'd been looking. His eyes narrowed. The haughty whore was *Pilate's* whore? She came to see Orion, not Pilate. It didn't make sense; Pilate would fall on his sword before he'd bed a Jew. Before he had danced about like an entertainer, trying to please them. Now he acted as if he wanted to erase the way he had tried to accommodate them. What then, would a Jew whore and Pilate and a tree have in common . . . and what would betake the chief secretary to be involved?

On impulse, Prometheus said, "The scroll, Raman." He kept a cool gaze on the water. Maybe he wouldn't have to say anything else.

The man was scratching the back of his head, looking longingly in the direction he wanted to go, when he stiffened at the mention of the scroll. His eyes now searched, unsure what Prometheus wanted. "The plans are fine. Just what we needed."

Then it must have shone through his wine-bleared brain. In that moment he realized he knew something Prometheus didn't, and it bloated him more than the wine. The fear on his face dissolved, replaced by cunning.

"We all know women, don't we?" The lout grinned, indulgent now with his information. "They get their way, we get ours. Pilate keeps her happy, she keeps him happy. It's what Orion Galerinius told me. That's why the granary is moving, because of her tree.

Course we have to take down a portion of the east wall, and my lads weren't too happy about that. Fine workmanship in that wall. Pilate must sure love that woman."

The granary was *moving*? For the sake of a tree? Prometheus watched the water a bit longer, then looked at the man. "You may leave."

The cunning faltered. He suddenly didn't seem so eager to go, not with his newly won position with the third in command of Judea. He bobbed his head and reluctantly turned away.

"I may wish to speak with you in the future."

Grateful as a dog thrown scraps, the man's teeth shone in the dimness. "As you wish, sir." He left the wharf cheerful as a newly paid soldier.

The lighthouse kept the harbor illuminated in the night, and Prometheus observed a ship being loaded with sacks of grain. A miniature crenellated tower, an amusing boast for the ship's cabin, rose in the stern of the ship. A man stood by its doorway, watching the on-loading of the grain. He had to be the captain; he had the stance of one in command.

Prometheus wouldn't have suspected intrigue from Orion Galerinius. It was pure nonsense to consider that Pilate kept a Jewish whore. His tenuous tolerance of Jews had snapped with the incident involving the Nazarene. He was different when he came back from Jerusalem. Not markedly, but enough so that those close to him saw the change.

Pilate reminded Prometheus of his father. When Prometheus was a boy, his father would fly into a screaming rage at something stupid Prometheus had done; the screams would alternate with deceptively serene moments where his father calmed himself and tried to show reason for his rage. It was precisely during those quiet moments that Prometheus trembled most.

That was exactly how Pilate treated the Jews. They should have been wary at the times of his calm, suspicious of his seasons of tolerance. Those were the times they should have feared him most. Ah, but they were learning, now, weren't they. Not so vocal these days, the proud Jews. They now treated Pilate with the respect afforded a scuttling scorpion.

Prometheus stared at the ship's crenellated cabin. Pilate had his pick of palace slaves, like every other senior official in the Praetorium; an insignificant thing like lust would not beguile Pilate from his hatred of the Jews, for it had become a cause. Interestingly, Pilate now had the same sort of contempt for the Jews that the Jews had for the Gentiles. Pilate, by his passion, was more like the Jews than he knew. But to say so would invite torture and death.

"What are you up to, Orion Galerinius?" Prometheus murmured. He pushed off from the rail and began the stroll back to the Praetorium. Prometheus Longinus did not get to where he was by ignoring opportunities, and chief secretary was not his end vision. One day he would be procurator. Today put him one step closer. He knew it by instinct.

8

SABBATH TOMORROW. One week since the scene with Orion. Theron said it was a repaired relationship, which meant maybe Orion would come. Marina could not countenance a Sabbath meal without company. And she would plain miss Orion if he didn't show. Orion made Theron laugh with that crazy sense of humor. And now that Rivkah's tree was safe . . . why not make things a little interesting?

"I'm thinking about inviting Rivkah for Sabbath tomorrow," Marina said as she pulled and stretched the ball of wool. She worked the big tuft into the iron-toothed comb, pulled out the tuft, shook the bracken from the comb, and dropped the cleaned tuft into the basket at her feet. She brushed the bracken on the table into a pile and swept it into her palm. "What do you think?"

Theron only grunted as he swabbed his bread in the herbed olive oil.

She went to the window with her handful of bracken bits. Her eyes on Thomas's place, she stuck her hand out the window and brushed her palm clean. "What do you think?"

"Sure."

Orion and Rivkah. It delighted Marina to think about Orion's face the other night. Her Orion was actually distracted, and by none other than one who'd sat at the very same table many years earlier. What a delightful coincidence—if that it was.

"I remember when I met Rivkah."

Nathanael was six. He had been capering around Rivkah while she was trying to bargain for cloth in the marketplace. Marina had watched the child from the corner of her eye as she waited in line to haggle for cucumbers. While his mother spoke with the shopkeeper, Nathanael tried to make the woman's daughter laugh by taking edges of fabric and poking it up his nose and crossing his eyes. The little girl shrieked with delight, which only encouraged Nathanael. Rivkah alternated between haggling and hollering.

Marina had looked at the woman who owned the stall, wondering if she noticed what the little boy was doing . . . then she saw that the owner wasn't concerned with Nathanael at all. It was Rivkah who had her full and disdainful attention.

Marina looked at Rivkah then, and it became clear—the young woman was obviously a prostitute. Nobody wore that much jewelry. Nobody wore so much eye cosmetic. Marina drew herself up and looked away. How could a young woman treat her body so? How could she *employ* herself so? It was disgusting. And she, with a little boy. How was that poor child being raised?

"Twenty-five dinars," the owner said.

The young prostitute had stared. "Twenty-five?" She looked at the fabric. "I want *linen*, not silk."

Marina glanced at the cloth in the girl's hands—and glanced

again. She herself had purchased the same cloth in a different color just a few weeks ago from Collina. She certainly had not paid twenty-five dinars for it.

"Go somewhere else then," the owner said.

"I need the cloth." The young woman's tone lowered. "The others won't trade with me."

At that, Marina looked to see what the owner would say.

A hard smile came to the woman's face. "I have to raise my price for all the customers you are scaring off at this moment. I will take twenty dinars for it, and that is all the sympathy you're going to get."

Twenty dinars! She could get twenty amphoras of oil for that. For twenty dinars Marina could have a fine cloak custom-made for Theron, and bless her man, that was a quantity of cloth. *Four* dinars paid the rent every month.

"She's not buying your entire stall," Marina snapped at the owner.

"You stay out of this!" the woman barked back.

Yes, to interfere with bargaining—that was a disgrace. But the way the young woman hesitated meant she was actually considering paying such a price. That was the real disgrace.

"Come," Marina said briskly, as she abandoned her place for the cucumbers and seized the young woman's arm. "Let us go to Collina's. This woman is not getting twenty dinars for that cloth."

The young woman in turn snatched the arm of her son, and as the trio marched from the stall, the owner called after, "Go ahead and try Collina! She won't trade with her!"

And Marina had shouted over her shoulder, "No—but she will trade with me!"

She realized she was still looking out the window at Thomas's place. She turned from the view and went to sit next to Theron.

She put her chin in her hand. "So you think Orion isn't angry with us anymore?"

Theron said through his mouthful, "No. He's too scared to be angry."

"Poor Orion."

Theron chewed thoughtfully and took a drink of watered wine. "Actually, I think it will be good for him to come. The day after Sabbath is when the fellow is due for his scourging." His tone darkened. "At least, it's when Orion will not give Pilate's—" his mouth pinched as he tried and failed to find a suitable expletive—"order. Maybe it will help take his mind off it. Orion is as nervous as a new bride."

Marina sent him a twinkling glance. "I wasn't nervous."

Theron's darkness disappeared and he grinned at her. He tiptoed stubby fingers across the table to her, in that way that always made her laugh, made his fingers tiptoe on her hand and up her arm. He snatched his hand away when the curtain flap swept aside.

"Nonsense," Jorah was saying briskly to Joab, who was drying his hands on the front of his tunic. "It's *scarlet*, not *crimson*."

"What's the difference, I'd like to know," Joab answered. When Marina met his glance, he jerked his head at Jorah and rolled his eyes. "Crimson and scarlet. She acts like a variance the breadth of a hair will make Pilate choke on sight."

"Who cares about Pilate?" Jorah insisted as she took two plates from the cupboard and handed one to Joab. "The fact that there *is* a variance is all that matters."

"You see why I love this child?" Theron said. "You should be my daughter."

"What are you children arguing about?" Marina demanded, folding her arms.

"Do you know how hard it is to match color?" Joab demanded

of Jorah as they each sat at the table. Then there was an awkward moment, that hesitation where Joab wondered if he should say a prayer before he ate.

Theron was right, the boy was raised a good Jew. His hesitation made Marina feel a flash of sympathy for his mother. She wished he would just say the prayer for the sake of his conscience. It seemed to go against his instinct not to, and that made Joab momentarily sullen. There was a quiet and uncomfortable moment while Jorah bowed her head and whispered while Joab lowered his eyes and fiddled with his cup.

"Of course I do," Jorah resumed, breaking the moment. She took the wine pitcher and first poured a cup for Joab, then herself.

Interestingly, that wasn't the order a few days ago. Marina wondered if Theron noticed.

"And that is why your job is so important," Jorah assured Joab with all the diplomacy of a woman married twenty years. "It *is* difficult. Color is everything."

Slightly appeased, Joab relaxed and took a loaf of bread from the basket. He tore it in half and handed a piece to Jorah.

Marina glanced again at Theron.

"That's what my father says."

Jorah took the loaf. "Thank you. Which is why it is so important to differentiate crimson from scarlet."

"Jorah—" he groaned.

"I don't know where you got that last batch of stone, but it won't work." Then she hastily added, "Of course, Theron can use them for a future project. They are very good quality. They simply won't do for this one."

Joab sighed and fell to his meal without further comment.

"It is coming well then?" Marina presently asked no one in particular.

Theron answered. "It's coming too well. You both need to slow down; I would like this project to last at least six months. At the rate you are going, it will be half-finished by the end of Augustus."

"Oh, I wouldn't worry about that, Theron," Joab said lightly. "Not with Jorah's color preferences."

"Theron, I don't know why you hired this barbarian. Olives?" Jorah offered the dish to Joab.

"Please," he said, and took the dish.

Theron finally looked at Marina, and she hid her smile. Barbarian? Things were progressing well indeed. The first few days this unlikely working arrangement did not have happy insults like these. In the last day or two there had been a subtle change. Jorah and Joab were no longer stiffly polite to one another. They seemed to forget themselves in the business of paying attention to the Praetorium project.

Often, without drawing notice, Marina would peek into the workroom to find the two of them paying serious attention to what Theron was saying. To watch them without their knowing, in that innocent concentration of theirs . . . and to see the occasional look one gave the other when the other did not see . . . the looks themselves were *very* interesting. They were glances of appraisal. Of . . . well, Marina wasn't sure. But at least they no longer tolerated one another. And sometimes when Theron was out of the shop, she would hear Jorah laugh. It always made Marina pause and lift her head. It made her want to scurry back and find out what Joab had said to make her laugh. Yes, things were progressing well.

It's just that things were confusing too.

Once when Jorah had left the shop to fix a meal for Thomas, Marina went back to put a stack of clean rags on a workroom shelf. There she saw Joab sitting on a stool with such a look on his face . . . oh, it wrenched Marina. It was the same look she had seen in the commonyard when Jorah had collapsed. She could nearly feel it in that room, a sense of—she frowned.

What was it . . . misery? No, not misery. It was closer to despair. He hid it well when Jorah was around. He hid it well when he took meals with Theron and Marina. It was in unguarded moments like those when Marina saw it, and felt it, clearly.

Did her man sense the despair that hovered around Joab? He never mentioned it. Marina could sense it like rain on the wind. Young people did not possess enough guile to hide their feelings well. Young people did not have the years to lay like bandages upon their wounds. What had wounded Joab so deeply? Jorah, his eternal love, was at his side again. Shouldn't he be happy?

Marina reached for the pitcher and topped off Joab's cup. She returned his smile and went to fill Jorah's cup, but it was full. Yes, and then there was Jorah.

What fragrant air she brought! So young and cheerful and delighted to be working with a mosaicist for whom she obviously had a great deal of respect—and it was long past time people gave Theron the respect he deserved. She was talkative and opinionated and truly enjoyable to be around.

Marina loved it when she gave Joab the business for this or that. Her superiority made it quite clear she was used to having brothers to manage. Joab really did not seem to mind her ordering him about. "Joab, please fetch another pound stone for me. Joab, this mortar needs more sand. Joab, could you reach that? Joab . . ."

It was precisely Jorah's cheerfulness that had Marina worried. At times it was a deliberate cheerfulness, one that shut out the possibility of any questions that could be raised about her famous brother.

Marina had longed to travel and hear the young man speak. She'd heard of the truly astonishing things he did, if indeed it was fact and not rumor, but it was the words that accompanied the deeds that took her attention. Collina, the Greek woman she often traded with, had gone to see Jesus a few years ago. Such stories Collina had told her! Very interesting things he had to say about the Sabbath. Things that made such sense. "Man came not to be for the Sabbath, but the Sabbath came to be for man." When some had bellyached about an alleged healing that had occurred on a Sabbath, Collina said Jesus replied, "Is it lawful on the Sabbath to do good or to do harm, to save life or to kill?"

Such implications! That to *not* offer healing when healing was needed was as good as killing? At least, that's how Marina thought about it. Oy, what a thing to think. Collina told her other things too. Things even Marina, born and raised a largely unconcerned Jew, had a hard time reconciling. She was religious enough to feel alarm at things like, "I am the way, the truth, and the life." Could any man say such a thing? How could God allow this man such gifts of healing when he had the temerity to say such things? Perplexing, it was. It boiled up a kettleful of questions. Here was Jorah, sister of the very man who had long captured her imagination—and Marina could not ask of her a single thing.

"I hired him precisely because of his knack for color," Theron was saying. When Joab gave him a look, Theron added, "Well, his background in dye turned out to be fortuitous."

I am the way, the truth, and the life, and there his sister sits, right at my table.

Did he say things like that growing up? He must have been ten years older than Jorah, maybe fifteen. Perhaps they didn't have much growing-up time together.

"How old are you, Jorah?" Marina suddenly asked. And instantly regretted the asking.

Jorah was pushing the crumbs on her plate into a little pile.

Her fingers hesitated, then resumed. "Seventeen. Eighteen in two months."

Eighteen in two months—and not married. That's how the question was perceived. Marina winced.

"Eighteen?" Theron exclaimed.

Marina squeezed her eyes shut and held her breath—*no, please, Theron . . .*

But Theron cheerfully barged ahead. "Well, you're certainly not ugly," he boomed. "What are you doing eighteen and not married?"

Theron! she wanted to shriek. Have you forgotten our intrigue? Have you forgotten who else is at this table? Her hand went to cover her eyes. Lord love her man, he could embarrass her to ashes sometimes. Just as her cheeks were flushing, Joab gave Theron a response.

"It's because her parents wanted us to live in Galilee. And my parents wanted us to live in Judea and take over the dye works."

Marina peeked at Joab between her fingers. He was calmly sipping wine. And if Jorah's face was as flushed as Marina's felt, her silence supported Joab's words. Cautiously, Marina drew her hand from her face. This was the first acknowledgment of their previous relationship. *Theron! Please do not mess this up!*

"Oh, really?" Marina said brightly. "You knew each other before you came here?" She turned a wide-eyed look on Theron. "Why, this is news, *isn't it*, Theron?"

And Theron, who had realized his mistake, gave her a quick look with an apology in it and said, "Why, yes. This is news. Who would have known?"

Well done, Theron! Marina could relax. In a tone carefully balanced with surprise and joy, she said, "Joab and Jorah, what a delight. You are . . . betrothed?"

Joab smiled a curiously stiff smile first at Marina, then at Jorah, who had her back turned, clearing away the midmeal things. "Yes.

Betrothed. There is still the question of where we will settle. It will all work out, eventually. My parents are . . . confident it will."

"Congratulations to you both," Theron said. He added, "You know, I'm not really surprised. It seemed as if you knew each other."

Nice touch, my heart!

"We did," Joab said, his gaze drifting.

"Tell you what," Theron said suddenly. "How about if you two take the afternoon off? Jorah, you've not seen the city since you've been here, have you?"

Jorah, who still had her back to them, scraping off the dishes in the alcove, did not respond.

"No, you've only seen the inside of my workroom, and while that is commendable, you need some fresh air. Go look at the sea! Go to the harbor! Joab, you take her and show her how Caesarea has grown up since she was last here."

"I should find a match for that crimson," Joab began.

"I need to see about Cousin Thomas," Jorah quickly said over her shoulder.

"I will see about Cousin Thomas," Marina assured her as she got up and went to Jorah. She took the plate from her. "Theron is right, it is time for . . . time. You've both been working hard, you need a break. You need some catching up. Now go."

Jorah did not meet her eyes, and didn't wait for Joab. She wiped her hands on a dish towel, adjusted her head covering, and went to the door. She quickly kissed the mezuzah and left.

"Well, go on, boy," Theron urged.

Joab slowly rose, went to kiss the mezuzah but did not, and left.

They waited about a minute.

Marina collapsed at the table. Theron fell back in his chair and stared at the ceiling. Presently, still staring at the ceiling, he said, "What do you think?"

"I think that went well. I think."

"You don't think they knew we knew?"

"No." Pause. "I don't think so."

"I'm glad it's all out in the open now," Theron sighed. "I couldn't have stood it much longer."

Marina didn't think he could either, but this she did not say. She drew herself up and smoothed the front of her tunic. "Well. That's *one* thing around here on the road to healing. Other things await us." She looked at Theron. "So. I will go and ask Rivkah to come to Sabbath meal tomorrow. And you go ask Orion."

"I can ask him tomorrow." Theron shrugged. "When I deliver a few more tiles."

"No! You must ask him today. We must be sure he makes no other plans for tomorrow evening."

"I can't imagine what those would be . . ."

"Nevertheless, I will not rest unless I know Orion is coming." She ignored Theron's sigh and tapped her fingers on the table. "What shall I make tomorrow . . . fish balls again? They're Orion's favorite. What did Rivkah like? I'll have to get more meal. I think I'm out of sage too. And Rivkah will sit here, and Orion will sit there." A little smile began. "Oh, Theron."

"All the way to the palace just to ask him to the meal? It's kind of embarrassing. Why did I send those two off?"

"Pistachio pastry!" Marina banged the table. "That's Rivkah's favorite." She rose from the table and hurried for her market bag. "I have no pistachios, just a few stale ones, and the dessert tastes much better the next day. I'll have to make it today." She went to the money box, took out a few coins, and put them in the market bag. "And I have to make it in the common oven, which means I better get it in there before Velina takes over the whole thing . . . so much to do!"

She paused to put the items on her fingers to remember. Thumb for sage, forefinger for meal, middle for pistachios. She added parsley and cucumbers to the other fingers, gave the sighing Theron a kiss, and hurried out the door.

9

CAESAREA WAS A YOUNG TROUBLEMAKER trying to resemble an older, cleverer, more elegant troublemaker. But the young wasn't as guilty as the old. Caesarea was safer than Rome, and seemed indignant over it. When it tried to match Rome for violence and corruption, it came up shamefully short.

True, there were some places in Caesarea so rank they made Pilate feel he had never left Rome. Some places had the familiar taint of poverty, crime, and hunger. Places that ran with rats and dripped with stink and incubated new diseases. Like some places not far from the Circus Maximus.

In other places, Caesarea tried to copy Rome the way Rome copied Greece. It only made Rome superior to Caesarea, the way Greek art and science and philosophy and finery would always be superior no matter how Rome tried.

"When is he scheduled to arrive, Excellency?" Prometheus Longinus asked.

"Any day." Pilate took a deep pull of a sudden breeze on the wharf. Herod's Harbor, he loved. He loved the audacious sculpture adorning the entrance to the port, the delicate arc joining two towers at either side. "It's possible they had to wait for a shipment before leaving Cyprus." All for the better. Let Decimus absorb all he could of the inferior condition of the Paphos harbor.

Pilate leaned on the wharf rail. The haze today prevented distant sightings. Perhaps Decimus was behind that haze, looking through it to the harbor, enjoying more of a breeze than Pilate, that was sure. The air hung thick and sticky, with rare bursts from the sea. It was hot enough to make him want his cool marble couch in the triclinium. But it would be a perfect day for Decimus to arrive. He would see Pilate leaning languidly on the rail, with the backdrop of the massive white Temple of Rome and Augustus.

The undersecretary stood formally near him, eyes alert for any threat of danger to his procurator. A distance apart stood four rigid Praetorian guards who had accompanied them from the palace. They were Roman soldiers to the bone, ignoring everything and missing nothing. Pilate was safe as a baby in his mother's arms.

"Do you suppose they put in at Alexandria instead?"

"Possibly." It was a stupid question. One thing about Orion: he did not speak unless he had something to say. Orion's undersecretary, on the other hand, was ever eager to bend Pilate's ear with any trifle he thought could possibly provoke Pilate's interest.

"I understand you served with Decimus Vitellus Caratacus."

"Primipilaris," Pilate added sharply. "He earned that."

Longinus blanched. "Of course, Excellency."

Primipilaris, retired First Spear. Tribune could replace that, or Camp Prefect, but lucky for Pilate, Decimus ever wanted to keep a clear road before him. He loved his options. Lucky for Pilate, becoming a chief secretary was one of them. Pilate rubbed a corner of his eye. Perhaps he could change that title to something else. Something closer to procurator. Underprocurator, perhaps.

"You served in the Augustan Second, Excellency?"

Pilate's eyelids fluttered. Fawning fool. "Yes."

"Were you ever stationed in Germania Superior?"

Pilate glanced at him. "Briefly. Before my appointment here."

"Did you know a Publius Cassianius, sir?"

He put full attention on Longinus, looked him up and down. "Yes. Of course I knew Publius. He was . . . over the third or fourth cohort, I believe."

Prometheus Longinus chuckled nervously. "I've always wanted to ask you that, Excellency. He is my cousin."

"Really." Perhaps this wait on the wharf would be more interesting than Pilate had anticipated. "Is he still serving?"

Longinus smiled. "He was princeps under Decimus Vitellus Caratacus—Primipilaris."

Pilate leaned back in pleased astonishment. "*Really.* Your cousin was his princeps."

Longinus leaned to show Pilate the brooch at his neck, clasping his cloak. "See? He gave this to me before I shipped to Caesarea Maritima. He's like a brother to me."

Pilate looked. Cast in bronze, it was a relief of the Pegasus, the emblem of the Augustan Second. He found himself smiling. It had been a long time since he'd seen one of those brooches. He looked at Prometheus Longinus. Ruefully, he said, "Your cousin once blacked my eye."

Longinus gasped. "No."

"Yes, and I had it coming to me. I had cast my attention on a girl who turned out to be his fiancée." He chuckled, then asked suddenly, "Did he ever marry her? I think her name was . . . Antonia?" He didn't think—he knew.

"No. His wife is named Coventina. He met her on his last tour, while stationed in Gaul."

"Ah. Then I'll black his eye, next time we meet." They shared a genuine laugh. Still smiling, Pilate resumed his slouch at the rail. "What about you then, Prometheus? You've served under Orion Galerinius for—"

"It will be two years, sir, on the Kalends of December."

Pilate nodded. He watched a half-eaten bloated fish float by. The inner harbor needed a good cleaning. The breakwaters prevented a free flow, and when the sea was still the water went stagnant quickly. He'd have to make sure Orion got with the public—

"Sir, would you like me to check with Hermenes about doing a harbor sweep? Looks like it needs another."

"Yes. Do that. Orion has been quite busy with the new walkway. What do you think of the mosaic so far?"

Prometheus Longinus was looking at the water when he smiled, and a softness came to his eye. He shook his head, saying, "Sir, that Theron is a genius. From the few tiles he's installed already, I think his work could easily show up the palace back home."

Pleased, Pilate said, "You think so?"

Longinus gave Pilate a look that wondered if he was crazy. It delighted Pilate. Rigid Orion would never allow himself this casualness.

"Of course, Excellency. All I can think is how impressed Decimus Vitellus Caratacus will be."

"Primipilaris," Pilate reminded him.

Longinus winced. "Primipilaris. Sorry, sir."

"Longinus? Do you miss Rome?" He had never asked Orion such

a thing. Never thought to ask him. Longinus was a Legionnaire, and with any soldier he felt a certain amount of ease.

Longinus stood tall, hands clasped behind his back, gazing out to sea. He was a handsome man, he had to know that. He had a fine firm face, firm jaw. More handsome than Orion, and certainly Roman-soldier tall. He was looking toward Rome. He knew where the direction lay. He considered the question, then looked sideways at Pilate.

"With every breath, Excellency."

Pilate returned his gaze, then nodded. It was a risky response. Soldiers of Rome were not supposed to miss Rome; that was too much like complaining about their station. Together they looked out to sea, over the Mediterranean to Crete, past Crete and over the sea to where Rome lay.

❧

"See that man over there?" Joab said. "That's Pontius Pilate."

Jorah, whose attention had been on anything but their own company, stopped walking. "Where?"

"There, at the rail with the guards. The other man is the one from the palace, Prometheus Longinus."

Jorah followed his finger and regarded the man in the distance at the harbor rail. He was dressed in a brilliantly white Roman garment, a toga she thought it was called. It had a bar of purple at the bottom. She couldn't see his face very well, but he seemed to be in earnest conversation with the other man. So that was Pontius Pilate. She gazed a moment longer, then looked away.

She was surprised to know the harbor wasn't far at all from Theron's home, just a five-minute walk. She'd been in Caesarea a week and was five minutes from the sea. Why hadn't she come before now?

"That was a dumb thing to do," Joab said quietly.

Surprised, Jorah said, "What was?"

"Pointing out Pontius Pilate to you. I don't think sometimes." He put his hands on his hips and looked up at the soaring roof of the Temple of Rome and Augustus. "I'm sorry."

Very nearly Jorah asked him what he was sorry about, in the stupid cheerful way she would have earlier in the week. But she was so tired, so bone-weary tired of pretending that things did not happen. That she did not shut away Joab's words meant maybe she was . . . maybe she knew it was time to look on things that did . . . indeed . . . happen.

She adjusted her head covering and said briskly to Joab, "My father is dead. You will have to remember that."

Joab was in the middle of shaking a pebble out of his sandal. He paused.

"You said my parents wanted us to live in Galilee. My father is dead. And just to let you know, my mother is in Jerusalem. Or Bethany. I think."

Joab straightened. "Well, my betrothed, perhaps we should learn a bit about each other if we are to continue with this ruse."

Jorah smiled a little. "That's a good idea. I didn't know your father owned a dye works."

"*That* would have been a slip."

Jorah gazed at the temple. She looked around at the vast buildings on the quay and at the still water inside the arms of the harbor. The water beyond had occasional white crests. "I don't want the city anymore. I want the sea."

Joab glanced at the quiet harbor water. "There it is. There are places to sit over there."

"Not this sea. It's too captured. Let's go somewhere else."

They followed the edge of the quay until it gave way to a less polished place. A place where smelly seaweed huddled in fly-swarmed patches on the rocks. Just when Jorah expected Joab to say something, he did.

He pointed at the nasty patches of seaweed and said cheerfully, "Look, Jorah."

"Yes . . . maybe you're still hungry."

"No thanks."

The buildings were older here, and here they sprawled brokenly. There was none of the precision of place the buildings near the harbor had. This unpolished area soon met the city wall, and they turned into a neighborhood to follow the city wall to the gate.

The northern aqueduct, another product of Herod's reign, brought fresh water down from the foothills of Carmel and ran parallel with the sea. It came into Caesarea at the city gate, and here Joab and Jorah followed it out of the city. Then they left it and picked their way over knolls covered with long sea grasses until they came to the shore of the Mediterranean.

Joab sat down on a chunk of rock. Jorah took off her sandals and dropped them near Joab. She walked out straight to the water's edge with her back to him, so that when she stopped with her toes in the water he would not see her close her eyes and smile at the scent of the salty sea air. She lifted her face to the sun. Here she could not hear the yells of the sailors on the quay, nor the scuttle and hustle of people coming and going. After a time, standing where she did, eyes closed, she began to listen; she heard the gentle shush of the water upon the shore, washing and foaming and trickling. She heard the occasional cry of a gull, the song that went with the sea. She soon tasted salt on her lips. She made fists with her toes, and heard the squeak of the coarse wet sand.

After a time she opened her eyes. She folded her arms and gazed upon water now light blue, now dark blue. Lines of white crested here and there, and near the horizon the sky was hazy lavender. A gust of wind brought prickles to her arms and made her head covering whip around her. She pulled off the covering and shook out her hair; it felt like going barefoot, exhilarating as sand on the soles of feet closed up too long in sweaty sandals. She tossed her head covering behind her and worked her fingers into her hair, giving her scalp a luxuriant scratch. She put her head forward and shook out her hair again, delighting in the sea breezes. Then she swung her head up, whipping her hair behind her, and looked for a dry place close to the water.

Joab did not join her for a long time, time enough for her to get fully reacquainted with the sea. Nearly an hour had passed before he finally appeared a few paces from her side, wind rippling his tunic. He sat down near her and pulled up his knees, gazing at the water.

"What is it about the sea . . ." he murmured.

Jorah pulled a strand of hair from her mouth. "It's bigger than we are. That's why we need it so badly." She looked at him sideways.

"What's that smile for?" he asked, a very small smile of his own beginning.

"I don't know. I haven't felt like this in a long time."

"Like what?"

She looked out at the sea. "Like that."

"I don't know if I've ever felt like that." Then he shrugged. "Well, we have this big field, this patch of flowers we cultivate for the dye. You should see it in full spring."

"Is it beautiful?"

"It's beautiful."

Jorah wiggled her toes in the sand. "Tell me your story, Joab ben . . . ?"

"Judah."

"I have a brother Jude."

"I know. How many brothers do you have? I know of James, Jude, and Simon. And the other we were going to meet in Bethany. . . ."

"Joses."

"This is good," Joab said, brightly mocking. "Getting to know the number in each other's families, we who have been betrothed for a year."

"*Betrothed,*" Jorah repeated. "I'm going to have to remember that."

"Yes. We're going to have to *act* betrothed."

Jorah considered it. "I think we've been doing a pretty good job. We've been arguing. You've been teasing. That's good, don't you think?"

"Yeeesss . . . I've been thinking about something more natural. We need to make sure they think our betrothal is real." He frowned, musing hard. "I should kiss you in front of them. Make it look like they walked in on it—we could act embarrassed. That would be more nat—"

"I'd give you such a slap."

"No, you'd have to act like you enjoy it."

"Joab ben—!"

But now what was he doing—laughing! He was only teasing her again! She gave him an indignant glare, then turned away to hide her smile. With her head turned, and she couldn't be sure because of the sea breeze in her ears, she thought he murmured, "A slap might be worth it." And suddenly the absurd thought came that a kiss from him wouldn't be the most gruesome thing to ever happen . . . and the thought shocked her into quickly searching for another subject. Brothers—didn't he ask how many brothers she had?

She tamed her hair down from the wind. "I have—" But here she faltered. She burrowed her toes farther into the sand. "I have four brothers."

Joab did not reply for a time. Presently he asked, "Do you have any sisters?"

"Only one. Devorah. She is married and lives with her husband, Matthias, in Bethany. She just had a baby, the sweetest little thing. Micah."

"Devorah. Matthias. Micah," Joab repeated carefully. "James, Joses, Simon, Judas."

"What of you? How many brothers and sisters?"

"An older brother, Alexander. An older sister, Hepsibah."

"I have a niece Hepsibah. That will be easy to remember."

"And a younger sister. Marya." His face softened. "She's the one I miss the most. She's six years old." Half his mouth curved in a smile. "Such a scamp. She never walked, she danced. Could never go from one place to another in a straight line. She'd hop and leap. Her favorite thing was pretending the ground was 'hot lava.' She'd go from rock to rock, chair to chair. She'd walk on the tops of our feet, sometimes, so she wouldn't burn hers."

Jorah smiled, and another thought came that he was rather nice looking. He didn't make her lose her breath the way Nathanael had, but—Her toes burrowed. "She probably misses you. When do you plan to go back to Hebron?"

But he looked out to the sea, and the curtain descended. That same dark curtain she'd seen on his face when he thought she didn't see. "I'm never going back," he muttered. Then he stammered, "I mean . . . not right now, of course."

"Of course," Jorah said lightly. What would *he* have to hide? "And do you really have a . . . betrothed?"

"Sure I do," he replied, returning to his calm self.

Calm . . . *that* was the difference between him and Nathanael. Joab had a calm about him. He carried himself in a way that said he knew everything would turn out right. Except when that curtain came. But—what had he just said? He had a betrothed. Jorah blinked. "Oh."

"You." They grinned at each other, and his grin became rueful. "A fake betrothal is probably the closest I'll come to getting married. I liked a girl once. She didn't like me."

"Oh. Well, I like you." Jorah ben Joseph! She cast about to cover for it. "And . . . Theron likes you. Marina likes you. A lot." She winced within.

"Theron likes *you*."

Jorah looked at him and could earnestly say, "No, I really mean it. Theron likes you. You're good for Theron."

Surprised, he said, "'Good for Theron.' What does that mean?"

"You tend to things he doesn't think about. That surprises him and that makes him respect you."

Joab got a quizzical look on his face, so she continued. "You take care of things. You sweep up. You clean the mortar buckets. You put the tools back. You don't complain. You don't talk too much. And you treat Marina with respect. Believe me, we've had enough apprentices for me to see the difference between you and them. Theron has too. Once when you were gone I heard him say, 'I've never seen this place look so good, not since we first built it. Joab's a good apprentice.'"

Joab picked up a shell and tossed it into the water. "Was Nathanael a good apprentice?"

Her heart squeezed, briefly. She would have ignored his words—but it was time. "Yes, but he talked too much. They were always telling him to be quiet and get to work." A smile came. "He told us stories all the time. He was so funny." She glanced at him, and her smile left.

That curtain again. Didn't she just try to make it go away? But he put that hard stare on the waters again. She wanted to ask him what made him so angry. Was it because he felt guilty—as she did, if she was truly honest—about not telling Rivkah?

"Jorah . . . what do you believe of the reports of your brother?"

A ripple of panic. This was a great deal of looking on things that happened. She dug her toes until they met with shells. "I—well . . . James believes the reports; he has a report of his own. I think Jude believes. I don't know what Simon thinks, or Joses."

"What do you believe?" He was persistent, but gentle.

She noted this on the periphery of the agitation. For that is what she felt, terrifying agitation. It was not comfortable at all, looking on things that happened.

She went to dig her toes again, but made herself stop. "Who would not want to believe that one's—crucified brother has come back again? But how could I believe such a thing?" She looked sideways at him. "How could you? How could anyone? I will not let myself believe. I won't let myself imagine it. You know why? Because they all leave, and they never come back. Everything changes, and so far there hasn't been a thing I could do about it. He appeared to his disciples, and he appeared to strangers. He appeared to James, or so James said, but you know what? I haven't seen him. Until I do, I have nothing to believe."

What a strange thing, to sit with one who had been there. A strange thing that this person of whom she knew little, whom she was getting to know, shared with her the two most devastating things of her life. He was there the day his friend attacked Nathanael, and he was there the day they killed Jesus. There when Nathanael died.

When Nathanael died.

Sometimes she ran her hand over her thigh, imagining her flesh ridged with scars. What had never entered the mind of any loving mother had entered Rivkah's mind not once but several times.

"Joab. What did Nathanael say before he died? Did he say anything at all?"

Joab stood suddenly. His face was dark, and growing darker. Jorah rose warily. She'd never seen the placid Joab like this.

"I wouldn't be in Caesarea if it weren't for Nathanael's last words," Joab said in a strange tone.

"What are you talking about?"

"'No stones,' he said. 'No accusers.' How could he say such a thing?" He glowered at the sea. "How could he do that?" His furious gaze went higher, to the sky. "An act of mercy is what it was, and that is what I don't understand."

Now he was just plain scaring her.

Joab began to walk the shoreline. "I can think for myself now, and that's a relatively new thing, but I don't know what to think about this. Was it just to torture us? Because if he meant it, if he really meant it, it changes everything. That's how big those words were." He scrubbed up his hair. "Why do I have to be thinking about this? I'm not a Pharisee, I'm not an Essene. I'm nothing. I'm only recently with an opinion."

To Jorah's amazement he stopped and looked full in her face, searching her eyes with desperation. "Jorah—it was the most wonderful thing I have ever heard, and it was the most terrible thing I have ever heard."

"Nathanael's last words?" she whispered.

He sniffed, and drew his sleeve across his nose. Then calm returned. Not calm, really, more like resignation. "They were never Nathanael's words. He was only saying what Jesus said."

Her lip curled. "Of course he was. It always comes back to Jesus."

While they were on the subject . . .

Because he had been there, she would ask him. She would ask what she dared not ask her brothers, though they had been there too. She would ask of that day they had arrived in Bethany, on Passover. It was nearly noon, and the sky was notably blue. Blindingly bright, not a single cloud—not a single cloud, and that fact was terribly important.

"Joab . . . that day we arrived in Bethany. Remember that? Remember the moment we arrived in Bethany? It was noon. Did . . . the sky really go dark?"

Silence. Then, "Yes, it did."

"I mean *black*."

"Yes."

"And it was that way for a few hours."

"Yes, it was."

Eyes on the sea, Jorah nodded. "I thought so."

Seagulls wheeled and cried overhead. In the distance a ship came, heading for Herod's Harbor. They watched the ship lift and fall in its passage to the shore, and said no more.

❧

Prometheus took a sip of wine, then hid his smile behind his mug. Pilate was weak. Prometheus could read him like a parchment, and today played him like a child's pipe. Gods up-in-arms, it was easy. His favorite line today was "With every breath." Brilliant. Pilate was his from that moment on, and it was only impulse that had made him say it, impulse that made him stare longingly to sea. "With every breath, Excellency." Ha. He missed Spain, not Rome. Spain he looked to, past that stinking city with its ungrateful rulers.

They had waited two abominably long hours on the wharf. Caratacus didn't show, of course. He never would. Decimus Vitellus Caratacus, *Primipilaris*, was dead.

Publius's letter had arrived a week ago.

To Prometheus Longinus, from your cousin Publius Cassianius, greetings.

*You may have heard by now of the death of Decimus
Vitellus Caratacus. The gangrene took him, after a wound to
the foot. He served twenty years in the Imperial Army only
to drop a leaden tub on his foot and come down with the
gangrene. They amputated, but it was too late. Too bad, too,
he was a good fellow. Good soldier. Heard he was about to
set sail for Palestinia. Did I ever tell you I served under him?
Princeps.*

*I know you stole my brooch, you old dog. You shouldn't
have been so interested in it. I don't miss it, but I wanted you
to know I know. Tell Pilate I said hello. How is the ambitious
old fox? Did he ever marry Antonia?*

Curious, that Pilate did not know. He probably didn't have any
friends who corresponded with him—Sejanus had his troubles with
Tiberius, and maybe Decimus was his only other friend. Maybe
Decimus wasn't high enough in the ranks to have his death published in the official posting from Rome. Especially if he died of
something as inglorious as the gangrene. A shameful death for a
distinguished military man.

Pilate would know eventually, and until then, dear cousin Publius
had given Prometheus enough to ingratiate himself to the prefect of
Judea. And dear Orion didn't know his position was now in jeopardy.
His smile broadened, until he saw Raman's waiting mug.

Prometheus poured the greasy Raman another swallow from the
amphora. "The scroll contained changes to the original plans for
the granary. Who authorized the changes?"

Raman considered the wine like a purveyor. "It must pay to
be the undersecretary to Orion Galerinius Honoratus. This is
delicious."

"I am undersecretary to Pontius Pilate."

Raman blanched and set down his cup. "That's what I *meant*, of course."

"The scroll . . . ," Prometheus prompted wearily.

"Ah, yes. I do not remember the name of the architect who made the changes, but his signature is on the scroll. It's all in order, sir."

"And Pilate approved it. The document had Pilate's seal."

"Of course! I know Pilate's seal." Raman was righteously indignant. "We would not go ahead with the changes without it."

"I want the scroll. Bring it to me tomorrow night. Not a word of this to Orion Galerinius."

Raman glanced about the tavern. "Of course not, sir. I am to be trusted. They did not make me foreman for nothing." His tone was carefully solicitous.

His payment should have been having a drink with Prometheus Longinus, but Prometheus could not afford Orion finding out. He took a denarius, one of Augustus's coins, and slid it across the table. He took his helmet and rose. "Leave in a quarter hour," Prometheus told Raman.

Raman nodded and lifted his mug. "Good-bye, my friend!"

One table over, hidden from view by the broad form of the Roman soldier at his table, Janus Bifrons peeked out and watched Prometheus leave the drinking house. He shook down his bracelets and looked thoughtfully at the other man Prometheus left behind.

10

"Has he given any indication what he will do?" Pontius Pilate asked as they trod down the stone steps of the stairwell.

"Pardon, Excellency?"

Pilate pressed his belly against his wide leather belt so Orion wouldn't see it jiggle. When did he have time for the gymnasium? "The Jew, the stonemason on my Tiberateum. His holy day begins this evening." The day after tomorrow Pilate would either hear squeals like a pig or the silence of compliance. He wasn't sure which he hoped for.

Thinking on the Tiberateum, it was time to hire a stonecutter for his dedication piece. Long had he worked on the right words for the cornerstone. He had two versions and couldn't decide which was better.

". . . not exactly sure what he has decided."

"I need you to hire a stonecutter for the Tiberateum cornerstone. I'd also like you to take a look at what I have composed for it. It is to be stately but not pretentious. I have two versions and would like your opinion."

"Of course, Excellency," Orion said.

"Do you think I should attend the work site today? You can point out the stonemason. If he sees me, perhaps it will affect his decision."

They came out at the bottom of the stairwell, and Pilate stopped. Orion stopped immediately.

"I am merciful, after all, Orion. I do not wish for this man to suffer. Perhaps seeing me will adjust his sensibilities." And if Orion could not answer him, well, Pilate could understand. He merely kept his gaze on him a measure longer, then turned the subject again to the cornerstone.

"I am thinking about something like this: 'Pontius Pilate, Prefect of Judea, has given this Tiberateum to the Citizens of Caesarea.' Or something more like, 'In Honor of Tiberius, from his servant, Pontius Pilate, Prefect of Judea, Governor of this Imperial Province of Rome, for the Citizens of Caesarea.' What do you think?"

❦

Orion dropped his tablet onto his writing table. "What do I think? Why don't you just call it the Pilateum?"

"Orion Galerinius Honoratus?" came a timid voice at his door. It was Lucretia, one of the cook's slaves, bearing a tray. "Cook sends this. He said you did not eat at breakfast and you did not eat at midmeal."

"Take it away and inform the cook I eat when I want to. Tell him to tend his duties, not my appetite."

"The cook would say your appetite is his—"

"Take it away!" Orion roared.

She jumped, and turned to run into—gods and goddesses—Janus Bifrons. The upset tray and all its contents bobbled between them, then clattered to the floor.

"Forgive me!" the girl exclaimed. Her face went crimson, and she knelt and began to quickly clean up the mess. "Forgive me!"

"No harm," Janus assured. He brushed the front of his vestments clean, then pulled the edge of his robe from the mess and knelt to help her.

Orion stood at his writing table, hoping Janus would leave with the girl. When all was silent and he thought it was safe, he looked over his shoulder—and hastily at his desk again. Janus leaned against the doorway.

"What do you want?" Orion said, with a grimace Janus could not see.

"Would you rather have the slave girl stay?" Janus asked dryly. He didn't wait for an answer. "I want to know why you are sore vexed these days, Orion Galerinius. And why you're not eating."

Orion squeezed his eyes shut and leaned stiff-armed on his writing table. "I—have a case of distressed bowels."

"If Prometheus could cause distressed bowels, I would believe you."

Slowly Orion's eyes came open. He peered over his shoulder. "What do you mean?"

Janus leaned back to look up and down the corridor. He came in and shut the door and went to the corner stool, arranging his vestments as he sat. "Orion, you've sought me out for matters of delicacy before. I hope that means you trust me. I am here out of curiosity and out of concern. This little display with the cook's tray deepens it. You are not a man given to outbursts of anger."

Bifrons's manner had not a trace of flirtation in it. This was the Janus Bifrons he liked. Orion relaxed. Had it all been his fancy these past years? He took his stool. "What did you mean about Prometheus?"

Janus's graying pointed beard poked his necklaces as he regarded a little gob of barley on the embroidered edge of his vestment. His bracelets clattered as he scraped it from the golden fabric with a long fingernail. "I was at the soldiers' drinking house on the quay last night. I overheard a conversation. Most of it. Why does Prometheus seek a certain scroll, Orion?"

An arrow through his gut. Orion kept his face fixed. Bifrons's lips moved, and he focused on them but the words were as easy to grasp as smoke. Orion blinked, tried to clear his head, tried hard to hear him.

". . . what a good man like you has to do with Prometheus Longinus . . ."

The lips were moving, his gut was roiling.

". . . foreman at the granary going up in the southeast quadrant. He is a coarse man, singularly uncivilized and . . ."

Raman. Sold by Raman. Rivkah's tree will be cut down. And Pilate might attend the Tiberateum today. He said he might. He'll know I didn't give the order. Everything over, all at once.

He looked about his room. What to take? He had to leave, now. Theron came yesterday and asked him to the Sabbath meal. He had to leave this moment, find the next ship out of Caesarea—could he leave without saying good-bye to Theron and Marina? He would never see them again.

"Did I ever tell you how I got my name?"

Orion wet his lips, shook his head to clear the daze, pulled his mind to the words spoken. "I don't care."

Janus smiled reflectively and folded his arms, settling in for a tale. "Well. I was the firstborn, and my mother—"

"Janus. Everything is over. My career . . . everything. My life."

"—wanted to dedicate her son to the god of beginnings—Janus. Now, if you will recall what you learned as a schoolboy, if you paid any attention at all, he is also the god of doorways."

"I could arrange my own murder. Visit a poppy tent first. I've never been."

"Orion, will you listen? Now. Just as a door has two sides, looking in opposite directions, so in that form is the god called Janus Bifrons. My mother liked the idea of her son being like a doorway." The reflective smile dwindled. His eyes narrowed on Orion. "I fancy you are much like that, Orion Galerinius. More than I have ever been."

What was Janus churning out of his mouth? Gods, he had to *think*. He scruffed up his hair. "Why don't you—will you just leave?"

"You protect them."

Orion stilled.

"You feed them Pilate's leftovers. Don't look at me like that— you think the young soldiers' program is a secret around here? And the little boy is safe at the side of the laundress because of the mercy of one—you think that has escaped notice? Acts like that roll like thunder in this palace."

Orion put a hand over his eyes, pressed his fingers into them.

"What is that you hold?"

Orion looked down at his lap. When had he taken the box? He snorted softly. "This is what kept me here when I long wanted to leave." He opened the box and took out the collar. He unwrapped it and handed it to Janus Bifrons. "That was fashioned for my father when he was a child."

Janus sent a swift look at Orion. "He must have made free for you to hold office. Or is that a nasty secret . . ."

Orion watched as Janus examined the collar. "He made free. When he was taken a captive in Gaul at eight years old, he vowed to save every copper he could find, every copper he could earn to buy his freedom. And he did. He vowed he would only marry in freedom, and he did. He vowed his children would be born free, and I was. At the age of forty-seven, at his manumission ceremony, his name became Appius Galerinius *Libertus*—Freedman." Tears came, and he worked his fingers over his eyes. When he could, he said, "He gave me the collar to remind me there was nothing I could not do."

"Hah!"

Startled, Orion looked up in time to catch the iron collar Janus tossed at him.

"Fine words, Orion Galerinius. Takes more than a collar."

Orion put the collar on his wrist and turned it around. "Yes, it does." He would have never believed it before. He knew it for truth now. He never once thought of the collar to help him forge the granary plans.

Janus rose and shook out his vestments. His lip curled as he picked off another bit of barley. "There is a man in the marketplace. I go and we talk of our gods. He has but one." Janus smiled a little and lifted his eyes to Orion. "It is part of my duty to know the local gods, and his is an interesting one. The man tells me he is a *jealous* god, quite possessive of his people. I have been learning of him to add him to our own." He fell into a frown. "Tricky, he is. Elusive. Unlike the gods we know. Some Jews believe he is connected to the Jew Pilate crucified; some say the Jew was his son. While, of course, the notion of sons of gods is not a new notion, this case is interesting because—" He caught himself.

"Well. I sit with the man in the marketplace, and we eat bread and dates. I have been learning much. One thing I have learned from this man is that the god is pleased when kindness is shown, particularly to his own people, and I wonder if he has not heard the thunder in the palace. Orion Galerinius Honoratus, I believe more than a collar stays you to your task. I believe you are as a door. One side looks to Rome, and one side looks to a sorely vexed humanity."

He went to the doorway and paused before he left. "Whatever troubles you, be it Prometheus or Pilate, perhaps you have the favor of the god of the marketplace Jew." He glanced up and down the corridor and added lightly, "And if you tell Pilate I am meeting with a Jew, I'll cut off your temple offerings."

Janus Bifrons left. Orion listened to the clatter of wooden ornaments until it died away. He turned the collar on his wrist. The favor of the god of the marketplace Jew—Theron's god. Well, Prometheus discovered the scroll—that was sore favor. And if Pilate visited the Tiberateum site this afternoon, he would hardly call that favor.

To my beloved father, from your favorless son, greetings.

I dance the bull's dance, and they have daubed my middle with red. I have never known more fear than I have right now, and I am even wearing your collar. Janus Bifrons was right. It's only metal.

He smoothed his hand over the calendar. He could feel the slight spongy bulge from Theron's documents beneath. He had to get rid of them immediately. If Prometheus did indeed have the scroll, anything could happen. If he found these papers . . .

Treason, treason, the breath of the Furies singsonged.

"Orion, come quickly."

Orion jumped. Marcus's burly form filled the doorway. He never heard the hobnails.

"What is it?"

"The two young apprentices of Theron."

"They are still here?" This morning Marcus had fetched him when they arrived.

"I passed by the archway a moment ago and saw Prometheus with them—the young girl Jorah is weeping."

Orion tossed the collar on his table and left his workroom with the guard at the double step.

11

A WHOLE WEEK WORKING in the palace, and Joab could not get over the wonder of it. He wanted to tell someone. Write home to Mother and Father. After upbraiding him for working in a Gentile establishment, they would be proud. The Praetorium Palace, Herod the Great's home! Their own Joab!

The upper part of the palace, the Praetorium, was where government business was transacted. Judgments, decrees, hearings, assemblies. Even parties. Two days ago they had to conduct their work discreetly while Pilate entertained a group of dignitaries from Syria. Pilate brought them over to observe Theron the Great at work—most had heard of him—and they looked on while Joab tried his best to look professional.

Jorah had felt the eyes too; she had assumed a superior air as she tamped in a tile board, giving it more critical attention than it needed, all the while seemingly unaware of the gaggle of people gawking. Once she had sneaked a glance at Joab, eyes dancing, and they both had to stifle sudden smiles. Only Theron did not notice. He wore his usual scowl and fumed about the inferior lighting in the corridor. He growled at Joab to remind him to speak to Orion about more sconces for the walls. If he noticed the crowd at the other end of the walkway, it was only because they blocked his light.

The lower part of the palace, the private part, was forbidden to them. Orion Galerinius made that perfectly clear the first day on the job. He seemed to drive it home to Joab, as if Joab were even tempted.

"Orion Galerinius Honoratus doesn't like you," Jorah now informed Joab as she wiped grout from the surface of a board with a sponge. She sat back on her knees, examined the effect, then dipped the sponge in the bucket and squeezed out the excess.

"I don't like him either," he replied. The walkway had been burrowed through several feet of concrete, connecting the public area to the private wing—Pilate's grand living quarters. He heard there was a swimming pool down there. "Don't you wonder what it's like down those stairs?"

"Theron would say we're not paid to wonder. Why don't you like Orion? I think he's interesting."

Joab didn't have much thought for Orion right now.

Where's your fat master? The undersecretary, Prometheus Longinus, had scorned at them this morning when they had arrived at the Praetorium with new boards.

He's back at the shop, working on a board, Joab had replied, eyes downcast.

The man had leered at Jorah. *Sure has a pretty helper. Even if she is a Jew.*

They were not given leave to enter. Prometheus Longinus sat back at his table and enjoyed looking at Jorah. Joab didn't know what would have happened if Orion hadn't arrived. Thinking on it, how was it he appeared at the right time? Vaguely he remembered one of the guards disappearing as soon as they climbed the steps to the palace.

Joab frowned as he dug his spatula for more grout. It made his guts clench, the way the man looked at Jorah. She didn't seem to notice the danger. She wouldn't. Always kept her eyes properly on the ground.

What did Joab feel toward her? Mitzvah? Hah. In the one week he had worked with her, he at least learned one thing: Jorah could take care of herself. In one week she'd already established herself as chief apprentice. *Joab, this color is too rusty. Joab, that mortar isn't thick enough. Joab, can you cut me some more of these tesserae?* She acted as though she'd worked there all her life.

"That's not enough," Jorah said, eyeing the amount of grout Joab pushed between two boards. "It will pull away from the tile when it dries."

"Would you like to do it yourself?"

"I'm just saying it's not enough."

He didn't reply.

Jorah said tartly, "You don't have to be so offended. I mean . . . I didn't mean to offend."

He hid his slight smile as he prodded more grout between the tesserae. What tedious work! Why anyone would want to become a mosaicist . . . or the *apprentice* to a mosaicist . . . He could easily find a job in a dye works around here if he tried hard enough. Why stay? His knees ached from kneeling, but he didn't want to take the time to wrap them with those ridiculous cloths as Jorah did. Jorah did anything Theron did.

"Marina says we are having company at the Sabbath meal tonight. She didn't say who, but she is acting so fussy. Have you noticed? She's acting as if the governor himself is coming. She's so distracted."

He slipped a glance at her and frowned. He needed to tell her the warning he felt every time they came to the palace. Every time he saw the undersecretary. He wished Theron would deal with it. She'd listen to Theron.

Presently he snapped, "You need to be careful around Prometheus Longinus." He glanced at the public end of the walkway. He'd said it too loudly.

Jorah stopped with her sponge. "What do you mean?"

Joab scowled. No, she wouldn't know. She was the sister of the Teacher, probably as sheltered as a bug under a rock. Girls like her were blind as—

She threw her sponge down and leaned back on her heels. "Are you talking about that bloated swine on the steps every day?"

He grinned and stopped pressing grout. He sat back on his own heels.

"Next time he tips back on that chair to look at me like I'm fresh from a brothel . . ." She pressed her lips, and her eyes glittered darkly.

So she did notice, for all that serene composure. "I like him less than Orion."

Jorah scraped at a dried patch of mortar on her wrist. "Why don't you like Orion?" she asked again.

Joab stuck the spatula in the grout pan. He had made Marina cry, but that wasn't the only reason. "He dismisses me. I hate that. He thinks I'm too young to have a valid opinion."

"I know how *that* feels. My brothers made me feel that way my whole life."

"Or he thinks I'm just another Zealot."

"Are you?"

"I have never been a Zealot." He held her gaze a moment, then looked away. The subject was dangerously close to Avi, and that made it close to Nathanael. Did she feel the sudden thickness in the air? He picked up his spatula again, but toyed with it. He felt the palms of his hands grow moist. After a long moment he risked a look at her.

He couldn't read her face. Expressionless. She was staring at her board. *Ask me, Jorah. Ask me what happened that day.*

She picked up her sponge, dipped it, and wrung it dry. She bent over the board again. After a moment, Joab took his spatula and scraped grout from the pan.

"I wish the only person to talk with me about Nathanael wasn't you."

His spatula froze inches above the board. He put his hand to his nose and quipped, "Ouch—am I bleeding?" He glanced at her—her face wasn't expressionless anymore.

Her hands clenched the sponge fast in her lap. Water seeped from it, a dark spot grew on her tunic.

He slowly set down his spatula. He felt his way backward to the archway wall. All week long, all he had wanted was for her to ask him.

He could still see the brown loaf of bread. Nathanael had come around the corner with the loaf, singing loudly so he wouldn't frighten anyone.

Jorah released the sponge. She crawled to the other side of the wall. Opposite one another they sat. She said quietly, "It was his idea for you to join our party. So you would feel safer."

"He brought bread."

"His idea. Joab . . . I'm afraid to ask you."

"I'll tell you . . . if you want."

Face blank, she nodded.

He told how Nathanael came bearing bread on the Passover pilgrimage to Jerusalem. How Avi had recognized him from where he spied, high on a boulder in the rocky pass. How Avi had whispered thanks to God as they took position and waited. How Avi dropped from the boulder, pulling Nathanael to the ground.

"It was all part of Avi's plan," Joab said, staring at a tile. The loaf of bread had pitched into the air. "Avi wanted to blackmail Jesus. Hurt his family or hold them hostage until he joined his powers against Rome. Nathanael was unexpected."

"Nathanael had shamed Avi that day," Jorah whispered.

Joab nodded, numb. They had visited the Teacher's home to try and persuade them to join the cause. The apprentice had chased them out with an adze. He had humiliated Avi, and Avi never forgot.

"Life with Avi was like . . . dwelling under a thick veil, only you didn't know it until later. It was confusing, it was madness. It's . . . hard to explain." Hard, but how he wanted to. "He was so certain about things. That's what I admired about him, in the beginning. I envied him. He hated Rome with all his heart, and I didn't hate anything and it occurred to me that maybe I should. Avi equally hated the ones who tolerated Rome, and I thought that sounded good too. He said they had no right to call themselves Jews. For the first time I heard that the cause was everything." He put his head to the side as he considered this. "It was the first lie I ever believed. That I know of."

"You know it to be a lie?" Jorah asked.

After a moment, Joab said, "It was Nathanael who made that clear to me."

"Nathanael?" Jorah was crying. Her eyes were puffy, and she pressed her sleeve to her nose.

"He reminded me of me. I realized later that he chased us out of your home because the land wasn't the issue for him—if it was, he would have listened to Avi. Deep down, the land wasn't an issue for me either. I didn't hate Rome enough." He scratched the back of his neck. "I tried to make up for that. I tried to make myself hate, and be as passionate as Avi was. I felt worthless because I wasn't." He scratched his neck harder.

She didn't want to hear this part.

"So. Avi came up with this plan—"

"I used to feel worthless when my brothers talked about important things and left me out."

"I could not imagine leaving you out of anything." He swallowed. Did his own words put the heat in his cheeks, or was it the way Jorah was looking at him? The way she was beginning to smile. He made it light. "I'd be afraid you'd take an adze to me yourself, the way you order me about."

Her smile only deepened. Their eyes locked, and Joab felt a strange ripple in his gut. Then Jorah's smile faded, and they both remembered what they were talking about.

"So. Nathanael came around the corner. Avi jumped him. They fought on the ground, and Nathanael got up. He didn't see me, and I—" He gripped the back of his neck. Tell it. Just tell it.

"See, the whole time I held Nathanael, I thought Avi was just hitting him, you know, just roughing him up. Thought it was okay, he was just getting back at him, and there's nothing wrong with that. But then Nathanael screamed—at first I thought, you sure are soft, can't take a few hits. And then—I saw the knife. And I realized Avi wasn't hitting him. And I—" His hand went to his mouth and he pinched his lower lip. "I was holding him." He rolled his lip in the pinch, frowning hard. "When I realized it I thought someone tore out my middle."

Jorah covered her face with her sleeve.

Horror and truth—the two were the same—had blazed about him in that moment, leaping and searing, dissolving the veil. Joab screamed—he had screamed. This moment was the first he remembered it.

A soft low croon came from Jorah. The croon became a choking sob. The sob settled down and became a croon again, like the low howl of a distant wolf.

"I swung Nathanael around, took the knife from Avi and stuck it in his chest."

That croon reached down in him, a barbarian claw dragging out his heart. He dropped his head and grimaced hard. Clawing him to shreds.

Avi was so surprised. Astonished. He staggered back and looked down at that knife sticking out of his chest. He stared at Joab and babbled words Joab couldn't understand, nonsensical words of a dying man. He dropped to his knees and fell sideways.

Sunlight came in by the window at the staircase and sat in a yellow disc by the steps. The croon was gone. Jorah still had her sleeve pressed to her face, but she was quiet. Joab had his head against the wall. Such a strange feeling inside. He felt as though he'd been holding his breath. As though he had been holding it since the day in the pass.

"I am so sorry, Jorah," he whispered. "I wish I would've known it was all a veil."

The sleeve was still over her face. Muffled, she said, "That? I cried my last for Nathanael before I came to Caesarea. That was for you."

He stiffened. "Me . . ."

"I saw you in the commonyard, and something . . . broke all down. You were so huge before then. I saw you as you are—the way Annika sees people." She sniffed, and her tone went wistful. "I want to be like Annika."

She cried for *him*? Did *that* make sense? He shifted in place, unaccountably angry. "Why would you cry for me . . ."

"I feel bad for you. It wasn't your fault. I—know that now. I hope you do too."

"Will you take your sleeve away?"

Muffled, "I can't."

"Take it away."

"No!"

"Why?"

"I'm a mess."

A pause. "I can talk to a mess. I can't talk to a sleeve."

"My nose gets huge when I cry. Red and huge. My eyes swell, my face gets all blotchy. It's quite hideous, trust me. I'm doing you a favor. Some women cry and they are beautiful. I am not one of them."

Softly, "I need to see you."

Slowly her sleeve came down. True, her nose was swollen and red. Her eyes were smaller for the puffiness, her face had red patches. She gave a sudden all-teeth smile, putting her thumbs under her chin and waggling her fingers to display her face. "See? I should go to that swine on the steps and let him see me now."

Why were those tears for him? What right had he to any compassion of hers?

She read his questions, and the all-teeth smile gentled. She sighed, and her gaze went distant. "You want to know why I really came here? I came to tell her she never deserved him. She did some things. . . . Joab, I hated her for it. I still can't think about it, I get so . . . And that's not the only reason: I wanted a chance to be unrelated to Jesus."

She shook her head. "But somehow—I can't explain it—things are starting to feel different. It started when I saw you in the commonyard." She hesitated.

Joab watched her face melt into a wretched earnestness. He watched tears come.

She dug them away with her fist. "I hate hating. It feels like a part of me up and left. It feels like God left."

"Then how could you cry for me?"

She blinked, bringing her filled eyes to him.

"I don't think you could cry for someone if God left."

She searched his eyes. Her look made his breath catch, it was so—wanting to believe. Maybe believing. Her lips trembled, and the tears spilled. The sleeve went over her face.

"Please, Jorah, don't hide from me."

Muffled, "I'm not."

"Can I see you?"

"No," she snapped. She added, "I cried for you because—"

Joab waited. The silence got long. "Yes . . . ?"

She still wasn't answering. Finally, muffled and sounding as though she had a cold, "It's pretty ridiculous if I have to tell you *why*." She spoke with a tartness that cheered Joab. "I have great hopes that you are not that dense."

"May I see you?"

She blotted her face and dropped her arm into her lap, resignation in the act. And by the tilt of the chin, defiance as well.

He rose and stepped over the grout pan, eased around the freshly laid board to Jorah. He went to his haunches. He rested his eyes on every detail of her face, and smiled. He touched his fingertips to her cheek, took her face, and gently kissed her. "I wanted to do that when you would never be more beautiful."

Her lips trembled. "Uh-oh. I'm getting beautiful again."

"I will kiss you again."

"I'm not sure this is the appropriate place." She smiled through the tears.

"I don't care."

"You are not paid to lounge," came a crisp voice at the public end of the walkway.

Joab scrambled to his feet, Jorah to hers a heartbeat later.

Prometheus Longinus stood holding a tablet to his chest. His look on Joab was sour, but when it went to Jorah . . . it changed, and slid back to Joab. He began a slow stroll toward them. "Well . . . what have I come upon?" He folded his arms, tucking the tablet beneath them. "What did you do to her, Jew? Perhaps I have misread you."

Joab's mouth fell open, he looked at Jorah—and his stomach seized. That face! Jorah was already protesting, but Joab knew it wouldn't matter. Sure enough, the undersecretary didn't even listen to her. He simply enjoyed his stroll to them.

"Not very pretty *now*, is she, but that doesn't matter much. Does it. Jew."

"He didn't do anything," Jorah protested.

"Yes, and he's probably very angry with me about that," Prometheus said with a glittering wicked grin at Joab. The grin went to Jorah and became a leer as his eyes traveled over her.

In one step Joab put himself between Jorah and Prometheus. He dared not make eye contact with him, only kept his gaze down and set himself for what would come. His heart pounded in his stomach. Thick-soled sandals came into view. They stopped a pace away.

"I should have you arrested," Prometheus breathed down on Joab. "We have a nice set of jail rooms, newly completed. I'll put you in one and finish what you started in another. At least you can listen. Jew."

Joab felt Jorah grasp a fistful of the back of his tunic. Yes, he knew enough to restrain himself. Knew he walked the edge of a knife.

"Please, sir," Jorah whispered. Both of her hands clutched his tunic now. She was trembling. Ha—he was trembling. "He didn't do anything."

Prometheus laughed. "You suppose I care about a Jewish maiden's honor? Not unless the honor is all mine."

Joab looked from hooded eyes to see the eyes of Prometheus slither over Jorah. His blood surged hot, he felt himself tense.

Jorah firmed her grasp on him and whispered, "Don't you dare."

"I don't care if he does anything or not." Prometheus's tone dropped to a honeyed lowness. "But I am very interested in what can happen next." He reached around Joab to finger the edge of Jorah's head covering.

Joab threw his shoulder into the Roman's middle, drove him toward the wall, thought he had a moment of surprise to—but the Roman dug his hands into Joab's shoulders and, using his momentum, slammed him face-first into the wall.

Patches of black and skittering bits of silver. He clawed for balance or a bit of Prometheus, but Prometheus wasn't there to break his fall.

Joab was on all fours, watching the skittering silver until his vision began to clear. He saw his blood dripping into a larger patch of red. He looked up to see Orion Galerinius and the guard Marcus. Marcus had Prometheus against the wall by the throat, and Orion stood protectively next to Jorah. Joab didn't like that much. He liked less the cold glare on Orion's face, aimed at himself.

"Can somebody tell me what is going on?" Orion asked.

"He assaulted me," Prometheus shouted, and shoved Marcus away. "Get your hands off me, who do you think you are?" He looked at Orion. "He was assaulting her, in the very act, and when I tried to pull him off he assaulted me."

Marcus glowered at Prometheus, which seemed strange to Joab, but then he sent an uncertain look first to Orion, then Joab.

"It's not true!" Jorah cried. "Orion Galerinius, it is not true!"

"Explain, Joab."

"I won't explain anything to you," Joab replied, watching his blood drip. He ran his tongue over his front teeth. He'd lose one or two of them.

"Why do you question him?" Prometheus demanded incredulously. "I just told you what happened. Do you disbelieve me, Orion?"

Orion only gave him a considering glance and looked again at Joab. "Tell me exactly what you were doing when Prometheus came upon you," Orion said.

"Kissing her," Joab slurred. His lips were fast growing thick. He lifted his head. The warmth of the blood felt queasy-strange on his numb lips. It dripped off his chin and he went to wipe it—but suddenly it seemed, by the silence around him, that his response was a very wrong one. What had he said? His head still rang from the wall. He went to rise, but Orion planted his foot on his back, pushing him flat.

"My word was not good enough for you."

"*Please,* Orion Galerinius! It's not what you think!"

The men ignored her.

"No, you had to question him."

"Put him in a cell," Orion said to Marcus, and pulled his foot away.

"It's not what you think," Joab said, though it was useless to protest. Jorah continued to plead with Orion, but Joab said, "Don't bother, Jorah. He wants this."

Marcus came and hauled him up by the neck of his tunic. As he led him away, Joab said over his shoulder, "You think I'm just another Zealot."

"He *assaults* a Roman officer, and you . . ." was the last thing Joab heard from Prometheus before Marcus guided him around a corner.

❧

The jail cell still smelled of plaster and was quite small. It had only three walls. A rolled pallet stood in one corner and a bucket in the other. It had no windows. The only light came in at the top and bottom of the door. This room was at the very end of the Praetorium; if Joab pressed his ear to the long wall he could hear faint cheering from the Great Stadium. Theron had told him there was a chariot race today.

Four paces on the door side, five on the stadium side. A tight pivot, and three paces back to the door. The room was the size of a sneeze, so small the pallet went up part of the wall when he unrolled it. That wasn't the problem, Joab could sleep in a tight place. The bucket was the problem. Its stink would fill the tiny room. He would hold off using it as long as he could.

He sat against the five-pace wall, knees up. He waited maybe an hour, wondering if Orion would show up to question him or at least let him know his fate. What consequence followed an assault on a Roman officer? With luck, with a great deal of luck, Jorah could set the matter straight. She would explain it to Theron, and Theron would come and demand justice. Orion would listen to him. With luck he would be out of here soon. Maybe Theron was on his way right now. It was nearly sundown—Sabbath. Poor Marina. What would become of her meal? What would she tell her mysterious guests?

An hour now, at least. It did not look as though Orion would come. So he let out the reins of thought inch by inch.

That puffy blotched face. Then she was self-mocking, with that grin and the flourish of her hands to display her face like a daisy. He put his head against the wall. Did it matter that his own face felt like a plate of mashed olives? Jorah cried for him. That was enough to think on for the next hour.

And what of the words that had troubled him since Jerusalem?

He had debt to Nathanael. He was charged to carry the words of a dying man. The words brought up images: Jesus with his followers. Indignant men dragging a woman.

She has been caught in adultery—the very act! The Law of Moses commands us to stone such a woman. What, then, do you say?

They waited for his response, heard only an echo of Torah-backed judgment. Maybe that's why he waited, down in the sand—so they could hear their own words again and again before he responded.

He ignored them, and it wasn't very polite. Because they didn't know what else to do, because they had to save face, because they couldn't just walk away, they pressed him for an answer. And he spoke the words of infamy.

He who is without sin among you, let him be the first to throw a stone at her.

He went back to his scrabbling in the sand, and the accusers regretted getting out of bed that morning.

Joab knew now why they did it: they dropped the stones because Jesus disarmed them.

The words made him want to pull a carpet of earth over his head. They were the biggest words he had ever heard. Words to explode, expose, destroy. Words to make utterly new. Full of terrible hope.

Deep in their hearts they wanted what he said. Deep in their hearts they cried out for such an answer. Else they never would have dropped the stones.

No wonder Nathanael died as though he knew something good.

12

"HE DIDN'T DO *anything* to me, Theron!"

"Orion wouldn't have locked up Joab for any old reason."

"Theron, *please*! It's my fault he's in there!"

"Yes, explain that again. What did he do to make you cry? He makes you cry, I'll make him cry."

Jorah took hold of the curtain flap, bunched it up, and screamed into it. She said some words too, but Theron couldn't catch them. He strained to hear, they sounded interesting. She even stamped her feet a few times. Yes, she had the makings of a great mosaicist.

It was just as she let the curtain flap go, and smoothed her tunic and her head covering in a nice display of haughty dignity (despite a face the color of a pomegranate), that Marina came in the front door.

She set down her basket and kicked the door shut, pulled off her shawl, and then froze at the scene before her. "Jorah," she gasped. "Whatever is wrong?"

"Trouble at the palace, Marina, and Joab is in the thick of it," Theron boomed. "He made Jorah cry, and Orion locked him up."

"He did *not* make me *cry!*" Jorah screamed. Then she burst into tears.

Theron threw up his arms. "I give up. Maybe you can get it out of her." He went to the peg and took his outer robe. "I'm going to the palace. Maybe I can talk to the scoundrel and see what he has to say."

"Yes! And tell that Orion Galerinius I said—"

"I was speaking of Joab," Theron said dryly. He looked at Marina and rolled his eyes. Then he kissed her on the cheek, said "Good luck," and ducked out the door.

Marina hurried over and drew her to the kitchen table, where she made Jorah sit. All the while murmuring words of comfort, she dipped a napkin in a bowl of water, wrung it out, and smoothed it over the girl's face. Then she hurried to the alcove to fetch a crock of watered wine and cups.

"Troubles, no matter how thickly they come, surely must come to an end," Marina said in a lilt as she poured wine into Jorah's cup. "My mother used to say that. There's more, but I've forgotten it." She sat on the bench next to Jorah. "Now, child, straight from the beginning. I want to hear it all."

Jorah stared at the crumpled napkin in her hands. All? Where could she start? That's what got Theron so frustrated, because when she came right down to it . . . how could she tell them why she cried? At the heart of it all was Nathanael.

What was she to do? It seemed there should be a consensus for telling everything, but Joab wasn't here. It would all be over! Maybe they couldn't work here anymore! Theron would not tolerate liars on his project . . . it would taint the work somehow.

Suddenly she wondered why it was such a good idea to keep *anything* secret at all. She could not remember the last time she had told a lie, much less lived one. Suddenly, to keep from them the death of a boy they knew . . . to keep it from his mother . . . was a very horrible thing indeed.

Jorah pressed the napkin over her face and wailed.

⁂

"Stinks in here," Theron said, crumpling his face. He held the candle aloft, searching out the reason. When he found it, his face crumpled more. He went to the other side of Joab and nudged him aside—closer to the bucket—to make room to sit. "It belongs to you. You sit by it, not me," Theron said when Joab glared at him.

"You could ask them to *empty the bucket for me*," Joab hollered at the crack at the bottom of the door. He resumed his slouch against the wall. "I pounded on the door for an hour, but no one came. I thought you were a guard."

"No, but I had to pay one dearly to speak to you," Theron grouched. "Orion is not around. Where could he be at this hour? He was supposed to come for the Sabbath meal. I looked for him on the way." He held the candle so he could inspect Joab. "You look terrible. What happened?"

"If you can't get them to release me tonight, could you ask them to send some water?"

Theron set the candleholder on the ground near the door. He grunted as he eased his bulk to the ground. He settled against the wall and folded his hands over his gut. "Take a moment to tell me why you made Jorah cry, and I'll get you some water." He looked around the room and shrugged. "A tiny place, but sure is quiet. Wouldn't mind spending a night here myself."

"That's because you can leave," Joab answered absently. An

uneasy feeling was settling on him. For the first time, he wondered . . . what did Jorah say to Theron and Marina? Why hadn't he thought of that until now? He had all that time to come up with something to tell Theron when he arrived, but no, he had spent it musing on the Teacher.

What on earth did she say? How did she explain her tears? It all came to Nathanael, and their deception toward Rivkah. Their stories would never ever match, not this side of the sun, unless they both told the truth.

"Oh, Theron," Joab groaned. He went to drag his hand down his face, but that was a mistake. His nose was broken. "We're going to be here a very long time."

"We are?" Theron laboriously stood to his feet. "Then first I see about that bucket."

❧

Marina had no jaunty quips now. Nothing her mother taught her could be given to this maiden. Jorah had done more living and dying than Marina ever had, and she was thirty years older.

Shock-faced, she sat next to Jorah. The wine gathered fruit flies she no longer brushed away. She heard the shofar sound, telling people to begin to prepare for Sabbath, but she could not move. Rivkah would arrive soon; Marina had a dish of vegetables in the common oven; the pistachio pastry needed another coat of honey. She could not move.

She could tell Jorah of the pain of not having children. Twenty-five years married to Theron, with a womb as dry as the Judean desert; twenty-five years of bringing meals to new mothers and watching the children of her friends while they went to the market or stole a moment of peace with their husbands. She could tell of that pain, to join their sorrows and gain strength in the joining . . .

but Marina had never lost a lover to a Zealot's knife, much less a brother to the agony of a Roman cross.

This sweet, honest, precious girl next to her—no, not a girl. A woman, for all her pain. A woman, she was seventeen. This woman . . . this child . . . what could Marina say to her?

"Do you hate me?" Jorah said at length.

"Do I—" Marina gasped. "Child . . ."

"I lied to you, Marina. Lied by not telling the truth."

Rivkah's boy was dead. That bouncing sprite Nathanael, such a wild little thing who couldn't sit still to save his life, who gave them such bedevilment, who made Theron laugh . . . the last they'd seen him he was about ten. So long ago, and now he was dead.

Rivkah sat vigil at the tree of her dead son. Rivkah went yearly to prune it like the other mothers who had planted wedding trees. She had fought Rome for her tree, like a fierce little gladiator, Orion said. That tree was the only dignity Rivkah afforded herself. The only claim to a normal, untarnished life she had allowed. There would be no wedding canopy for Nathanael.

"I don't know how to tell her," Jorah whispered.

Heart laden with misery, Marina looked at the door. A knock would soon sound there. What Jorah did not know how to do, she would do soon.

The bucket was emptied, Joab had his water, and Theron helped him clean up his face. Then the boy told a story Theron did not expect at all.

The candle had only a few inches left. Theron had stared into it for the duration of Joab's tale. Its white wavering flame was clear reality in a tale as surreal as it was heartbreaking. Poor Jorah, his own Jorah.

"He died the day after her brother did," Joab said in that soft murmur. "I took the box to him. I thought it could heal him. Seemed right at the time."

That poor child. So much for one so young to carry. The murder of her lover, the murder of her brother. He felt old and weary of a wicked world.

That little Nathanael.

"You have to tell her," Theron said, staring at the flame.

"I know."

"Orion needs to know. It's the only way you're going to get out of here."

Joab groaned and gripped the sides of his head. "I'd rather stay here than tell *him* the whole thing."

Theron eyed his apprentice. "Your contempt is misplaced. Orion Galerinius Honoratus deserves his name. He's one of the few Romans I've seen with a conscience. You don't know him, Joab."

"I know how he makes me feel."

Theron shrugged. "So who is perfect? But if I'm going to get you out of here, I'd better go see where he is." He moved to get up.

Joab looked at him. "Theron? How do I tell a mother her son is dead?"

Theron froze on his way up, then dropped his shoulders and settled back down. Nathanael . . . such a funny little kid. Never stopped moving, never stopped talking. Always into everything. And forget trying to have a conversation with him. He never listened, always interrupted, blurting another question before he got the first answered. A naughty little stinker, Marina called him— with a twinkle in her eye.

She had urged Theron to try and be like a father to him. He'd made a few awkward attempts, once asking Nathanael if he wanted to go fishing with him. The boy seemed embarrassed, as though he knew what Theron was trying to do, and he declared he hated to fish. Then after a while Rivkah stopped coming around.

Joab stared into the flame. "I don't know why I thought it would be easier because she was a prostitute. Maybe I thought a prostitute wouldn't feel as bad. That's dumb, huh? When I gave her the box I tried to tell her. . . ." He squeezed his eyes shut. "I was looking right in her eyes."

"She has pretty eyes," Theron said sadly.

"I have more to tell her. Nathanael himself sent me here, just before he died. He said some things I have to tell her. I'm not sure which will be the harder." He fell silent. "Theron? What am I going to do?"

"One tile at a time, boy. First we get you out of here. That will take some explaining, and I do not know where Orion is. Perhaps he has returned by now. You may end up spending the night here."

Joab shrugged bleakly.

Theron used Joab's shoulder as leverage to rise, then patted it. "Don't worry, boy. If you wish, I will be there when you tell Rivkah. Me and Marina both."

"That would . . . I would be grateful, Theron."

Theron banged on the door with his fist. The padlock clanked, and a guard slid it out of its fastening.

Rivkah never came. Orion never came. Theron was still gone. It had to be close to midnight. Strangest, eeriest, worst Sabbath evening Marina had ever passed.

She sat at the table, head on her fist, watching the flame of the only lit candle in the room. The dish of burned vegetables sat just beyond it. A neighbor had noticed it when she fetched her own dish from the common oven.

Jorah was curled on one of the couches, fast asleep. She had waited in miserable expectation for Rivkah's knock, had fallen asleep in the waiting.

Marina had her suspicions as to why Rivkah never showed. But where was Theron? Where was Orion? What would happen to Joab? Grief for Rivkah and grief for Jorah made her more tired than she'd ever been. She should wait up for her husband, but could not stay awake another minute. Marina wet her fingertips and pinched out the flame.

⁂

Orion's panic was nearly gone. It had abated at the clarity of his fate.

Well, and his life as a corrupted official did not last long. Perhaps the warning from Janus Bifrons had prepared him. But the panic left behind a nameless dread.

Now he sat across from Prometheus Longinus at the counsel table in the small audience hall. On the table between them was a scroll.

A guard stood at the entrance, one who belonged to Prometheus. The loyalty of each Praetorian guard belonged to either Prometheus or to Orion. It should have belonged purely to Rome, but this was the way of things. In Rome, anywhere, men chose allegiance. Problem was, Orion did not know who, if anyone, was allied to him. He'd never thought about it, never really paid attention. Didn't know it would be important one day. He could trust Marcus, that was all he knew. But Marcus had the day watch and had left after he threw Joab into a cell. He didn't know Orion Galerinius Honoratus had fallen.

Orion had been summoned to the audience hall from his private quarters not long afterward. He had been pacing his room, trying to order his thoughts, trying to wrest from a blank mind a course to take. Pilate, by the favor of Theron's god, did not attend the Tiberateum after all. That allowed Orion to think on Janus Bifrons's news, and decide whether he should take action before action came to him. He had just decided to leave for Theron's place, talk it over with them, when the abrupt knock came.

He should have suspected the manner of the guard; it was a wisp too confident. But he had been too annoyed at the interruption to really notice—too annoyed to realize action had come.

When he had entered the counsel room, he saw Prometheus's face first, fixedly impassive; then he saw the scroll. He could not help the initial shock, but had the forewarning from Janus to at least prevent a gasp. And Prometheus's cold manner actually helped summon his own.

"I could have gone straight to Pilate," Prometheus said now.

"Why didn't you?"

While Prometheus considered this, Orion looked away. How he hated the arrogance on that cold, handsome face. It was the end of everything for Orion. It did not matter what happened to him—it was Father. Father alone mattered. The scroll on the table before him mocked every sacrifice his father had ever made, every dream he ever had, for surely, the son of the freedman would end up a slave. Or worse.

"I suppose I felt grateful enough for this opportunity that I wanted to give you a chance to leave," Prometheus mused.

"There's some Roman decency."

Prometheus leaned back and studied him, genuine puzzlement on his face. "Orion, why did you risk it for a Jew?" He looked at the scroll. "Why make her Pilate's whore? If Pilate ever found out— you've lit your funeral pyre."

Now, instead of a funeral pyre, exile or slavery or suicide. And Prometheus did not even know of the stonemason. Despair began to fill him. Prometheus did not know of little Benjamin, but he would soon find out. He did not know of young Cornelius's program.

To my beloved father . . .

"What happens now?" Orion said. Despair tinged his voice; he could not keep it back.

"You leave," Prometheus said lightly. "Tonight. I'll give you one hour to pack your belongings and write a letter to Pilate. You're on your own after that. You should have enough time to get a ship out of the harbor before your absence is discovered. Do you want help penning your resignation? Put in something like, 'I was too Jewish for you.' Something like, 'Rome comes fully to the palace.' Yes. I like the sound of that."

"I have a favor to ask."

Prometheus's brows came up and he smiled, clearly amused. "Do you?"

Orion's eyes narrowed on the scroll. "I could deny it."

Prometheus smiled a nasty hard smile. "You're too Jewish for him. He is going to welcome this, you know that for truth. No, Uncle Pontius likes me much better. I'm more Roman than you have ever been. And why is that, do you suppose? Oh yes. Perhaps because I've actually served in the army. Perhaps because I have scars from battle on my body. You were nothing but a small man." He put his hands behind his head. "But what can I do for you, Orion Galerinius *Honoratus*? My first official act as chief secretary will be to see how I can accommodate the former chief secretary."

"Let the new granary plans stay as they are. It does no harm to let them stay." *Don't let it be for nothing. It cannot be for nothing.* "It is only a granary. Only a tree."

Prometheus shrugged. "It's done because I do not care. Anything else?"

"No," Orion said, and felt it descend on him entirely. An hour ago he was Pilate's number one. Now he was lucky to leave Caesarea. He would never see Theron again. He would never see Rivkah. He would never see his father again, for he could never, ever return to Rome. He was a fugitive heading for *exsilium*.

"My guard will escort you to your quarters. He will remain with you until you leave the palace."

Orion nodded, now breathless and numb, now sick. He started from the table, but struck it hard and without mercy. His voice hollow in his ears, he heard himself say, "Prometheus—we must go over the status of the palace."

Everything was transferring to this man. Everything! Did he know Pilate preferred his barley mashed with—Did he know Pilate suffered greatly if he ate anything with mint? Did Prometheus know Orion allowed the coalman to—

"Pilate is not good with names. He always forgets the name of the city engineer; it is Lippus. Lippus. The guest list for the Festival of Luna isn't complete. Laertes, the charioteer, cannot attend Pilate's luncheon tomorrow, he has a fever. Prometheus, the coalman cannot obtain Pilate's preferred—Decimus will arrive any day, keep the triclinium in readiness. . . ."

He didn't remember how Prometheus answered, or if he did at all. The guard pulled him staggering from the audience hall, and now walked beside him in the torchlit corridor.

Sometimes the responsibility was a chain and sometimes like bristlebane to stop his breathing. Nothing was ever really *done*. The interruptions alone could make a task-oriented man splay his neck on the block and cheerfully part with his head.

Now all he wanted was the chain and bristlebane, for suddenly it occurred to Orion that no matter how harshly he judged his own performance, no matter how short he fell in efficiency in some areas, he did not fall short in others. The nameless dread gained form: suddenly the most irresponsible thing of all was not walking away from it as he had often fantasized; it was that he had allowed it to be taken away.

The letter of the law came now to the Praetorium Palace, and Jews and Gentiles alike would suffer for it. Orion's father was old and good and had taught him ways of mercy as only an ex-slave could. Taught him to listen, taught him to look into the eyes. Long had Orion berated himself for not running a perfect palace. Now he could only wish for the chance to run it again with imperfections rampant and little Ben fast at his mother's side. The responsibility, too often like weights to snag him at the bottom of the sea, was now cut loose. He was released and set adrift, and why ever had he once wished to be free? He felt himself floating away. Soon others would be adrift as well. Orion Galerinius had fallen, taking others in the fall.

The hobnails from the guard's sandals ground and squeaked on the pavement.

Rufus, Clemidius, Alexandria, Aelius. The names were a mad cadence he could not silence, a murmuring backdrop to every minute in his workroom. He had been taken to his apartment and in a daze had stuffed things into a bag. He stood now in his workroom, just as bewildered.

He took his mother's tiny banded amphora, dropped it into the bag. He took his pearwood pipe. He took the new writing tablet from his father. He stood motionless at his writing table, gazing at his calendar and the notes bordering it. His table would be sifted by Prometheus in the morning. He didn't have a chance to explain everything, he didn't have a chance. . . .

Simon and Lydia. Mary and Sophoccles. Benjamin and his mother. The old man who came once a month with a bag of dates; Prometheus would demand coin for his taxes, not dates. He would report him to the *Publicani*. The old man would go to debtors' prison and there he would die.

The only thing Orion could do for them now was watch them go down in his wake.

"It is time," the guard said at the door.

Galen. Firmicus. He did not know there had been so many.

"I have to write the letter."

"Do so quickly."

He dropped onto his stool for the last time, and for the last time slipped a clean parchment out of his drawer. He dipped a pen that shook and touched the excess to a crumpled piece of ruined parchment. In five years he had lied twice to Pilate. Once about a stonemason. Once about a tree. He would tell his last lies to Pontius Pilate.

To Pontius Pilate, Prefect of the Eastern Imperial Province of Judea.

  With a heavy heart I put my pen to paper this evening. I have served you with pride these past five years, but fear I cannot remain another day: I have allowed indiscretions within my administration. For conscience's sake I must go. For the good of Rome I resign my post.

  Rome fully comes to the palace now. Prometheus Longinus will serve you well.

  I have learned much from you.

                    Orion Galerinius Honoratus

Pilate lowered the letter that had arrived on his breakfast tray. His gaze drifted to his sandals on the floor, to the leather laces curled beside them. His gaze went to the freshly whitened toga hanging by the open window, the edge newly dipped in shellfish purple. The air had a faint bite of sulfur from the whitening.

He was long gone by now. First ship out of the harbor with dawn's light. That's what Pilate would have done, and Orion was no fool.

"So falls a martyr of Rome," Pilate murmured. "Hail and farewell, Orion Galerinius."

13

MORNING CAME to the quay. The evening revelers had drifted away. A few drunks were sleeping where they fell. With dawn came the muster to ships, and crewmen came in to report from all directions. The sailors were a mixed lot: Thracians and Gauls, Germans and Spaniards and Macedonians. Some from Egypt, many from Judea.

From the doorway of Falnera's import shop, Orion watched the three large vessels in the harbor. He couldn't tell yet which were ready to leave. He would have inquired earlier but did not want to show himself; there were Roman soldiers on the harbor too.

Expulsion from the palace, those first steps away, brought clear thinking. He couldn't gallop from Caesarea Maritima in a huff and lather; he had to close out his Ostia fund with Justinian the banker. He would not be happy to see Orion, not this time—Orion had never withdrawn from his account.

At least here in the province he made more interest on his money than he would have in Rome. His father told him interest rose and fell between 6 and 10 percent back home. Here on the dangerous edge of the empire he would clear 12 percent, and that on over five years' worth of savings . . . Orion would be a fairly rich exile at least.

Those first steps away had brought to mind one thing he had forgotten. The slave collar he had deliberately left, wasn't sure why, it had been his amulet for years. But the collar sat upon the wide cut of parchment that was his calendar, and under that calendar was more to implicate him for Jewish doings than a forged scroll. Under the calendar was the sheaf of papers from Theron. Nothing would ensure the charge of treason faster than those documents.

Physical evidence of collusion with a subjugated people. How could he have been so stupid? He took his mother's tiny banded amphora, took the red charioteer, but left the papers. Why hadn't he destroyed them the second Theron left his room? The granary plans were laughable in comparison. Even when they discovered that Orion had protected the stonemason, a lawyer could easily argue that Orion had forgotten to give the order.

But once Prometheus found those documents—and he would—he'd have all the evidence he needed to prosecute Orion for treason. Treason was a public offense, not a matter of private law. What a way for Prometheus to start his term, revealing to all that he had single-handedly discovered Orion Galerinius Honoratus to be a traitor. The glory Prometheus would bathe in for a year.

Treason meant execution. *Exsilium* had a sudden warmth to it.

Orion could go to Spain, but too many Roman veterans retired there. He was considered in military service because of his appointment to Pilate—Spain was hardly the place for anonymous exile of a non-civilian official. Briton was an alternative, but he had heard horror stories of the climate. He hated the cold.

He could go the route of Herod the Great's son, Archelaus.

Archelaus had been deposed nearly thirty years ago, with a succession of equestrian-class Romans to rule in his place. Ironic, that one who would dwell in the same palace years later would also find himself on the lookout for a winsome place of banishment. Where had Archelaus gone? Gaul, wasn't it? If he was still alive, he was an old man now. Orion should look him up. They could trade expulsion stories.

How did you lose your job, Orion?

Oh, I was an idiot. Didn't know which favor would be one too many. So how is the weather around here? Do you happen to have an extra room?

A sleepless night on the quay left him with two clear options, Roman options, the two that had been obvious at the start no matter how he sifted it and tried to make it come out otherwise. It was suicide or exile.

Suicide was the more stylish way to go, but Orion had long considered suicide to be an act of impassioned petulance. Exile held more interest. The life he knew was over, and Orion had to say it many times to himself to make it true. Maybe there was another life out there, waiting to be lived. Maybe he would find it in Gaul.

Seagulls began their harbor cries. No one noticed him in the shop's doorway, and as he watched the growing activity on the harbor, he inched backward into the shadows. Falnera would arrive soon; perhaps he could spare some bread and figs before Justinian opened for business.

Yesterday he had his choice of breads. Yesterday he ate Dothan figs from Samaria because Pilate would have none other. Today he sat in a smelly doorway, probably smelling like the doorway himself. He had two finely woven sacks of all he possessed and no real plans, save escape. If a laughing fit wouldn't end with him flinging himself on a sword he would laugh himself to hysterics. Then Orion saw the big Roman soldier. He doused any notion to laugh.

No mistaking that profile; it was the drillmaster, Cornelius. He was in full Roman soldier rig, metal plates like scales overlapping on his shoulders, a belted leather cuirass over his chest, from which a sword hung stiffly at his thigh. The rust-colored cape was short, clasped low at his throat with a silver brooch. Orion wouldn't have been too concerned; he'd seen five soldiers already, at least. But Cornelius was looking for someone.

His back was to Orion, and he strode slowly on the dock, pausing occasionally to scan the ships or the people passing. Orion watched the back of the capped bronze helmet slowly turn . . . enough for him to see the scalloped cheek guard and leather chin strap . . . then turn again toward the sea. Orion soundlessly pushed back as far as he could go. The big soldier was not more than ten feet away.

Cornelius did not belong to Prometheus. Neither did he belong to Orion, exactly, but it was Cornelius who had come to him a few years ago and made his unusual request.

Orion saw the cheek guard again and held his breath; now he saw an eye and the side of his nose. Then the burly centurion was looking in his direction, and it was then that Orion saw the tip of his own sandal in the early sunlight—the same time Cornelius did.

The man looked at the toes exposed in the shadowed entrance, then looked around before he strolled over to Falnera's. He leaned against the wall next to the entrance, folding his arms. To anyone else it would appear that he had found a place to stand and wait. To Orion, the man softly said, "I was hoping to find you."

"You found me," Orion replied, his scalp prickling.

"I seek information. By the way—I am sorry to see you go."

Fractionally, Orion relaxed. He had not had many dealings with this man, but if he wasn't a friend, exactly, he wasn't an enemy. "Your gleaners' program is about to end," Orion muttered. "I'm sorry about that, Cornelius."

"It lasted four years. I am grateful to you. So are the poor of Caesarea. They know you for a friend, Orion Galerinius Honoratus."

The poor of Caesarea. Wonderful. Add the entire population of the poor to the litany of names. "They know me?" he said dully. "I do not know them."

"You have fed them for years. They all know your name."

Orion blinked. "That was not my idea. It was yours."

Cornelius scratched under his chin strap. "It was your backside on the line. True, it was safer in the beginning while Pilate tried to figure out the Jews, but we all know what you risked. This last year . . . we've been watching carefully. Many of us knew it was only a matter of time." His voice took a grim note. "Things are only going to get worse."

"What do you mean, 'we've been watching carefully'? Who's 'we'?"

"It would be wise if we do not exchange too much information."

"Good. Because I don't know what we're talking about."

Cornelius chuckled and shifted his arms as he looked out on the harbor. "We're talking about what you have done to ease the burdens of innocent people over the years. We're talking about people who have been spared misery because of what you did or did not do. I have many Jewish friends. They consider you a righteous man."

A righteous man. Orion pressed on his eyelids. He was tired and didn't need to get emotional right now. He pulled a dead leaf off his toga and crumpled it between his fingers. "I could have done much more. It could have lasted longer, had I not—" But Orion stopped himself. No point deciding where the line should have been drawn.

"I want no details," Cornelius quickly said. "But I know the difference between you and Prometheus Longinus. Things are going to be different, and quickly." Almost to himself he muttered, "You can already feel it."

"Tell your poor I'm sorry."

The man lifted his chin as he surveyed a ship. "Don't worry about that. Their god will take care of them. He did for years, through you. No offense, but it seems to me their god is bigger than you are, Orion Galerinius."

Wearily Orion pushed his eyelids up under his brows, but they fell down. "Someone else told me that once." A thought came to make him chuckle. Here, grubby and cowering in the corner of a shop entrance, even here in his newfound lowliness were—interruptions. "Good Cornelius, you say you seek information. What information could you possibly seek from an ex–chief secretary?"

"A person came to me late last night, after he learned of your—"

"You can say *fall*, Cornelius, I won't be offended."

"He came to see if I could give aid in a certain situation."

"Which is . . . ?"

"There is a boy named Joab locked up in the new facility."

Orion's eyes widened, then he groaned. "The person who came to see you . . . a big short hairy man?"

"Yes. His name is Theron."

"Joab." Another name adrift. "I forgot all about him. I was a bit preoccupied."

Cornelius risked a sideways glance at Orion. "I need to know if he should be released. We have to act quickly because the boy is Jewish."

Orion stiffened. The documents. If Prometheus finds the documents while Joab is still imprisoned . . .

Gods and goddesses and all their flaming mincing offspring. He kneaded his forehead hard. Ho, never mind the fact that Joab has past ties with Raziel of Kerioth, and the gods grant he keeps his mouth shut. No, the documents plus Jews working in the palace under the traitor Orion Galerinius would look like . . . Should he forget the bank account and swim from the harbor? If they found out Theron the Great had supplied him with the documents, Tiberius would hear Prometheus scream *Plot!* all the way to Capri. Theron and Marina and anyone associated with them would be in peril. They would be brought in for questioning. Anything could happen.

A harmless tree and the back of a stonemason started it all. Orion Galerinius Honoratus would be remembered as the engineer of a plot, in collusion with the despised Jews to overthrow Roman rule.

To my beloved father, from your infamous son . . .

The infuriating thing was, Orion loved his country. He believed in what the Roman Empire represented. Civility. Strength. Strength of character, strength of mind. Morality and education and opportunity. The very people who had enslaved his father offered him the chance to redeem himself.

Pax Romana. Orion believed in Rome, as Rome would never believe in Orion.

"Who else knows Joab is there?" Orion said, voice hoarse from lack of sleep.

"Besides Prometheus, and unless he told anyone else, only two guards: Marcus and Vitellus."

"And Vitellus . . . ?"

"Is one of mine."

Orion let out a breath; then the boy had a chance. If he deserved one. "What did the short fat hairy man have to say about Joab?"

"That his arrest was a misunderstanding. He had not touched the maiden. The maiden herself was with Theron, and confirmed—most emphatically—the misunderstanding. But I will not arrange for Joab's release unless assured that this Theron—"

"Theron's word can be—" He broke off at a cautioning flick of Cornelius's fingers.

Two sailors were passing. They ducked their heads at Cornelius and he nodded back at them.

Orion peeked to see that they had passed. "—trusted."

"Release him, then?"

"Yes. And quickly. It must be done before Prometheus finds some documents under the calendar on my writing table." Orion looked up at the man. "Joab has past association with the Zealot factions. He spoke the name of Raziel of Kerioth in my presence, last week at a meal." The changing look on Cornelius's face put a battering ram in Orion's stomach. "The documents have nothing to do with Joab, but could implicate him—and many others. It is terribly important that they are destroyed."

Treason, treason. The word lilted in a macabre singsong, and a chill chased on Orion's arms . . . he imagined if he had smoke, he could reveal the presence of the Fury.

Cornelius's face went grim, and he exhaled hard through his nose. "This will be trickier than I thought." He looked to the harbor. "What are the documents?"

"They are letters from proconsuls. Precedents from other provinces regarding the treatment of Jews. How local government would not interfere with their liaisons to Jerusalem, how contributions to their Temple would be allowed. Cornelius . . . those papers must be destroyed."

"Where are they?"

"In my workroom. Underneath the calendar on my writing table."

"Who in the palace is with you?"

This was not the time to wish he had been friendlier with the staff. After a moment, Orion said, "The priest, Janus Bifrons." He added, "I think."

"Who else?"

"I don't know. Marcus. That's it."

Cornelius watched the growing activity on the quay. He was silent for a length of time. "What I can do, I will do." He risked a quick look at Orion. "What about you, sir?"

"What do you mean?"

"How can I help you?"

Orion thought fast. He'd ponder this man's generosity when he had more time. "I have an account with Justinian the banker. His booth is located in front of the Temple of Rome and Augustus, north side. I was—trying to figure out how to withdraw my money without bringing down the palace on my head."

"His booth opens at the fourth hour?"

"Yes."

"I too bank with Justinian. He will trust me. How much does he owe you?"

"Three hundred and forty-seven dinars. Plus interest."

Cornelius gave an appreciative grunt. "A nice job you had."

"Yes. It was." For the first time he realized he had just lost his pension. On retirement, soldiers received a large retirement grant of thirteen to seventeen years' worth of pay. That was all gone.

"How are you getting out of Caesarea?"

"I run a—I *ran* a palace, Cornelius, I did not plot escapes." He gestured to the harbor. "You may not be exceedingly impressed by my strategy, but all I plan to do is chat with a captain on one of those ships and secure a place in his hold. First I need my passage money."

The soldier did not answer right away. Then he said, "Look—I don't know what kind of an arrangement you had with Prometheus that got you a head start from the palace, but if he finds those documents—assuming he hasn't yet—he will regret any favor he did for you. If you cast your shadow you are in danger."

Orion pinched the space between his eyes. "Prometheus thought I only had Jewish sympathies . . . those documents would declare me their messiah. Pilate would have another king to crucify."

Nausea rose. Crucifixion wasn't a punishment for Roman citizens, but treason implied an abandonment of citizenship. Suicide was a welcome option, hardly petulant.

"I will do what I can. I will also see to your exit from Caesarea. Is there a place you can stay for a few hours?"

Orion looked at the sky. It was early morning, still dim, but the light came fast enough. If he left Falnera's immediately, likely he would not be recognized, not if he kept his head down. "Yes. I have a place to stay. I should leave immediately if I am not to be recognized."

"I would escort you, but—"

"No, the guards will change soon. You must go." Orion rose slowly, easing out cramped muscles as he stood.

"Where will you be?"

"Joab knows the way. Cornelius, I have one last favor."

"Yes . . . ?"

"Bring some bristlebane. In case things do not go well."

"I will ask the priest. Go carefully, Orion Galerinius Honoratus."

The men risked a full look at one another. The last time they had seen each other's eyes was four years ago, when a young man came to a chief secretary with a strange request for a soldier of Rome.

"Go carefully, Cornelius."

Orion waited tight in the shadows until Cornelius pushed off from the wall and strolled down the quay in the direction of the Cardo Maximus. Orion would soon head for that street too, though his way lay north on the Cardo to a home that bordered a common-yard with a standing-up mosaic in the front.

14

JANUS BIFRONS hummed as he sprinkled the grain on the oval brass pan in the corner of the triclinium. This particular *lararium* was a shrine of all shrines, the finest Janus had ever had occasion to construct. It was elegantly proportioned, the representation of each household god perfectly placed. Janus had arranged for the shrine to *flow* from the corner of the dining room, as though it was part of the dining experience. That was the way it should be. It annoyed Janus that Pilate's devotion to the *lares* and the *penates* was perfunctory at best. Military to the core, nothing religious about him. Except when he needed something.

Pilate was a thinker, he had that going for him. He and Pilate had had scores of interesting conversations over the years. Janus only wished Pilate would do more talking now. He would like to hear about the Jew from Nazareth.

Janus noticed that the rug on the floor in front of the small altar was slightly askew. He tugged it into alignment with the mosaic tiles, stood back to regard the effect. Well, a few weeks ago Pilate had come to Janus to arrange for a special petition at the Temple of Rome and Augustus. That was something. He pulled the rug a fraction more, then flicked a dead insect off the bronze head of a god. It was a strong petition, more than a mere prayer; it was a vow, and Janus had it recorded for Pilate on the votive tablet in the temple. Along with the sacrifice of the pig, Pilate gave an offering: an elegant golden pitcher for libations. He also purchased a small plot of land, just south of the palace, to be made into a park for dedication to the god or goddess who answered his petition. Janus never told Orion about the petition.

Orion was his friend, but he would anger a god or goddess if he breathed the vow anywhere but the sacred firmament of the temple. It had troubled Janus these many days, knowing that Orion's position as chief secretary was in peril. With a heavy heart, he had inscribed on the votive tablet these words: *Blessed be the Capitoline Triad, Jupiter, Juno, and Minerva: hear my prayer and accept my vow. With the sacrifice of this pig, I entreat your gracious favor and ask of you this: that Decimus Vitellus Caratacus accept the position of chief secretary in my administration. If you will do this for me, I will do this for you . . .*

Janus had taken the pig and hired the services of the *popae* and the *victimarii*. He had hired the flute player, and the *tibicen* played as the sacrifice commenced, his music warding off all sound of ill omen throughout the ritual. Janus had worn his toga over his head during the sacrifice, guarding also against any sound or sight of ill omen. He had hummed along with the flute music, filling his head and his ears with only that which would be pleasing to the god and goddesses of the Triad.

He had hummed as he dribbled the wine over the pig's head and sprinkled the sacred cake. He hummed as the *popa* lifted the sacrificial knife and sliced the throat of the swine, hummed as he held the bowl to catch the blood. The entire ritual had gone very well, every nuance performed with precision. His *genius* was in rhythm with Pilate's request, despite the fact that if the sacrifice was accepted it meant the end of Orion's career.

Janus realized he was humming the tune of the tibicen and stopped. Strange, that the Primipilaris had not yet arrived. He sighed. But that he would, and soon. The palace would lose a good man. The Jews would suffer again.

Janus went to his knees on the rug before the *lararium* and murmured the prayers to the *di penates*. His *genius* was not at all in rhythm today. He was thinking more on the latest words from the marketplace Jew.

He had even copied them to a parchment, ostensibly because he needed them for the archives. They were words from one of the Jew's holy books, a tricky title called Deuteronomy. As he whispered other words before the shrine, he thought on the Deuteronomy words: "And now, Israel, what does the Lord your God require from you, but to fear the Lord your God, to walk in all his ways and love him, and to serve the Lord your God with all your heart and all your soul."

The Jew said this is what his religion was all about.

". . . protect this household and all therein . . ."

All your heart and soul. Ha—Janus explained to the marketplace Jew that Romans were free to believe and think whatever they wanted about their gods, no heart and soul about it. They had only to be certain that the rituals were performed correctly by priests and priestesses. The marketplace Jew came every week with a different scroll; in Rome, there were no sacred writings, save the formulation of prayers.

His god seemed unusually possessive. Roman gods didn't care so much. They cared more about themselves than mortals, and that was as it should be.

". . . guard the pantry stores that no pestilence may come upon them . . ."

Another text had Janus in bafflement. The text the Jew called the *shema*, also from the Deuteronomy scroll.

"Hear O Israel, the Lord your God the Lord is one. You shall love the Lord your God with all your heart—" Janus bit his lip when he realized he had spoken the words aloud.

"Forgive the deviation of the aforesaid prayer, O Capitoline Triad, mighty in splendor above all others, Jupiter Optimus Maximus, Juno Regina, Sulis Minerva . . ."

It made Janus irritable. Love this god with all his heart? The audacity. It was . . . delightful. Janus liked fervor. It seemed this god brimmed over with it. Roman gods were nothing if not passionate—disconsolate, temperamental, moody, and above all, capricious—but it was an aloof passion when it came to mortals. Boil down Judaism, on the other hand, and what's left in the pot is this: their god is about his people, and his people are about their god. It seemed like a love affair, from which Janus felt distinctly alienated. And maybe a little jealous.

Affection was not required of a priest . . . but hadn't Janus felt gratitude for the beauty of a Palestinia sunset? Or the fragrant humid mornings when he strolled the harbor and watched the world turn from blue gray to lavender gray to dove gray? His heart could lift in joy at such times, but which god would share his joy? He could offer thanks to the nameless local weather god, but would he feel the reciprocation that seemed to accompany this Jewish religion? Was there any joy to be returned to Janus Bifrons? Did any god take the same delight in him that he took in fragrant dove-gray mornings?

The Jew seemed to think the god had joy toward his people. Janus glanced at the array of household gods and wondered if one of those gods kept his eye on Janus; as the Jew knew, he *knew*, he had the eye of his god.

And it seemed wonderfully compact, this one-god Judaism. Stifling, at the same time. Didn't this god want company? It was the business of Janus Bifrons to see to the local gods, acquire them into the Roman pantheon. But chatting with Elias revealed one certain thing: this god did not seem interested in membership.

". . . do this for us, and for you we shall . . ."

There were Jews back in Rome, they came and they went according to the mood of the authorities, whether they were in a Jew-hating fancy or not. Persecution alone should have perked Janus's interest in the Jews—curious he had not thought of it before—but this was the first time he had been in close contact with a Jew. Talking with one, eating with one. Some Jews would not eat with him, but this Jew took it upon himself to teach Janus of his god—that seemed to make up for it.

"Janus Bifrons."

Did he hear his name? Surely not, who would ruin the morning supplications? He would have to start the whole thing over, every syllable. He would have to offer a sacrifice against the ill omen of indifference and impropriety—

"Janus Bifrons."

Murmuring doubtfully, he squinted at each household god. Did insect head take umbrage at—but he sensed a presence, and inched his widening gaze from the shrine to the doorway of the triclinium. The words of the prayer died. There stood one of the soldiers—inside the triclinium, pressed against the wall to conceal himself from anyone passing.

Indignation rose as Janus did. "Dare you to—"

The soldier put a finger to his lips. Whispering, he said, "Are you for him or against him?"

"Am I—"

"Orion Galerinius needs your help."

"Where is he?" Then he dropped his tone to match the soldier's. "Why would he need my help?"

"Have you not heard?"

"Heard what?"

"Orion Galerinius Honoratus has fallen. Prometheus Longinus has taken control."

Janus Bifrons stared. Prometheus Longinus. The business with the scroll. "When did this happen? How fares Orion, is he safe?"

"Not for long. I need to know . . . are you for him or against him?"

⁊⬥

Morning light from the window made the candlelight fade. Prometheus Longinus blew out the flame. Morning had broken on his new view of the Mediterranean. Murky blackness now became the moving blue of the sea. His last workroom had no window, and was the size of one of the jail cells in the new part.

He couldn't sleep last night, not that he had tried very hard. Too many plans whirled about in his head, too many ideas long held in reserve, now free for implementation. Better than the best wine, better than an entire evening in a poppy tent, even surrounded with beautiful whores; there were no ill effects with power. It came to reside in him like a second self, it filled his *genius* with fluttering intoxicants. It was more than he had felt when he put on his first adult toga. More than when he first commanded a cohort. Every time he achieved a new rank he felt this exhilaration, and there was nothing to compare. He felt huge inside, he felt like a god.

He had known he would have this one day, had never doubted it, not once. He smoothed his palms over the Augustus calendar on his new writing table, then folded his arms and lounged on it. Smiling, and that was something he couldn't stop doing, he reached to flick one of the styli in the vase, touched one of the neatly arranged tablets.

The respect! He laughed out loud. Gods, the new respect he already commanded. The fear. He'd had a measure of it as undersecretary, but everyone knew who was in charge of the palace. Orion had ruled the palace with an apparently offhanded touch; no one saw the imperiousness as Prometheus had. So haughty. Orion the Beneficent. Gods-up-in-arms, he would remember that look on his face till the day he died. Prometheus drew a long luxurious breath, half closing his eyes, as though he were drawing in the smoke of a poppy tent. Power and respect and fear were intoxicants no merchant could concoct.

He pulled back and regarded the large parchment on the writing table. He couldn't wait to destroy the Augustus calendar. It was filled with Orion's handwriting. He tilted his head and smoothed the curling edges of the calendar with his fingertips. No, there was actually something quite satisfying about seeing Orion's handwriting. It was a reminder of the way Prometheus had suddenly ousted him. Eventually, he would destroy everything about Orion in this workroom. It even smelled like Orion in here, but not for long.

The faint sound he had heard in the hallway, now growing, could only be the clacking and clattering of Janus Bifrons. He was about the palace early. Surely he had not heard the news of Orion's fall, not yet; wouldn't he be surprised to find Prometheus Longinus at Orion's table. He assumed an easy pose on the stool, gazing out the window while toying with a stylus. Then he dropped the stylus and rested his chin on his fist. He couldn't stop the smile, so he made it a wistful smile over the beauty of the morning.

The clacking stopped. "Greetings, Prometheus Longinus. Congratulations on your new posting."

The smile pinched, and Prometheus slid a look over his shoulder. Janus was holding a wooden box, fussing over items in it. He wasn't even looking at Prometheus. He muttered as he plucked at things in the box. "*Auspicium hilarem . . . imagines exitus.* Where is that chicken's foot?" He came into the room and set the box down, then knelt and began to rummage through it.

Prometheus sat back on his stool. "How did you hear?"

"The gods told me." He rummaged, then held something up. "My rooster wattle! Will you look at that—I'd forgotten all about this. That was no ordinary rooster. . . ."

"What are you doing?"

"Taking an auspice. Lemon verbena . . . oh, look here—one, two . . . nine black beans. Black beans for an auspice, that's a laugh." Janus Bifrons stopped suddenly and glanced at Prometheus. "You didn't *touch* anything, did you?"

Prometheus looked at the box. "No. Of course not. What is that box?"

Janus first gave a relieved sigh, then bent to his rummaging. "This box was given to me by an *augures* when I left Rome. With it I cleanse the rooms of the former occupants and ensure the welfare of the new. I also take the auspice to find out if your appointment will have divine approval."

"I've not heard of this custom. . . ."

Janus stopped, looked at Prometheus from under hooded eyes. "Are you a priest?"

"No . . ."

"Then stop your chatter and let me do my work." He shrugged.

"Unless, of course, you are not interested in the favor of the gods. If you are not—though I cannot imagine a military man who is not religious—I will not waste my—"

"No, no, no! Please, proceed. Am I supposed to do anything?"

"Yes. Leave. If your resident *genius* clashes with the exit of the *genius* of Orion Galerinius Honoratus . . ." Janus shook his head, face grim. Then an eyebrow rose. He sat on his heels and grasped his pointed beard. "Of course, that might be interesting. I have heard of violent upheavals in the celestial firmaments when *genii* clash. It is unnatural and ugly, like trying to mate a sheep and a goat, but it would be interesting to find out what really happens.

"Speculation is all we have, that and a revolting story I heard from a priestess in Syria. She had cleansed the apartment of a pro-consul—" Janus began to chuckle—"only to discover that the new appointee was in the apartment, fast asleep and rolled up in a carpet after a night of drunken revelry." The chuckle disappeared. "Within a week, the new appointee was found on the steps of the temple . . . the parts that were left of him, anyway." He gazed at nothing, then brightened and turned back to the box. "Where is that chicken's foot?"

Prometheus worked up enough spit to swallow. "I will leave you to your ministrations. Is there anything I should—can you suggest a course for me in the interim?"

Janus unfolded a paper packet and sniffed the contents. He took a pinch of the powder and tasted it, then nodded. "Hmm . . . ? Oh. If it were me, I would take myself down to the triclinium and wait there. Safety at the *lararium*, you know. But I insult you—of course *you* would know that, a military man." His face puckered. "Truly, though, it is surprising you did not know not to enter his workroom before the ritual was complete. Well. There is nothing for it. At least you didn't touch anything, thank the gods."

"Yes, well . . ." Prometheus paused to nervously pat Janus's shoulder, then he snatched his hand back and wondered if it was a bad omen to touch the priest before the ritual. "Just . . . do your best. Maybe a few times."

Janus gave him a burning look. "Once is enough, with a good priest."

"Yes, well . . ." Prometheus wiped his hands on the sides of his tunic, glad for the confidence Janus had in himself. Truly, his was a comforting presence. The way he poked around in that box, with a bored sort of ease like he'd done it a hundred times. Priests and priestesses walked between the gods and the mortals . . . you had to be some kind of strong person to do that, capricious as the gods and goddesses were.

Prometheus backed out of the room, murmuring his thanks. He eyed the corners of the ceiling, adding a tremulous thanks to whoever was there.

"*Ex voto,* Pontius Pilate, *votum solvit laetus libens merito,*" Janus Bifrons droned, as he shook out the contents of the packet to the floor. "*Di parentes,* Orion Galerinius Honoratus . . ."

Prometheus's eyes widened, and down the corridor he fled.

Janus held the box against his hip and shook the wooden bracelets down to his elbow as he made for the new part of the Praetorium. He had been in the new part only once, when Orion had taken him to hear the protestation of a man doomed for the headsman. He paused just before he crossed the walkway to the new part, murmuring a prayer to Limentinus, a god of the threshold. He wasn't sure if this was a threshold, but it was a crossing over of sorts. One couldn't be too sure.

Last cell on the left. Cornelius would meet him there. A strange place indeed to meet the young soldier. He passed by the cell on the right where he had spoken with the young man who had died last year. His chosen god was Apollo, a good choice for a dying man. He had also named the Capitoline Triad for good measure.

He had given Janus the only thing he had for an offering, a pathetic length of tarnished brass links. The boy must have seen the doubt Janus felt, because he went pale and began to stammer. And Orion, who had been waiting aloof in the corner, was instantly at his side.

My mother's god was Apollo. I have a beautiful bracelet of hers. I will give it to the priest and he will offer it on your behalf. You will find great favor, for my mother was gracious and good.

And the boy had wept his thanks.

The amazing thing was that Orion showed up at his apartment door the very next day and handed the bracelet to Janus. Never said a word, simply handed it to him and walked away.

There would be no such acts from Prometheus Longinus.

Janus stopped at the last cell on the left, and glanced over his shoulder down the hallway. Nobody around, not yet, thank the Triad. Breakfast was not delivered to prisoners until the palace staff had theirs, and that was at least an hour off. He murmured a prayer to the god of the threshold, in case he forgot upon entering, then tapped on the door. It was then he noticed the iron padlock on the door.

"Who is there?" came a muffled voice within, certainly not that of Cornelius. "Are you going to empty the bucket?"

Where was Cornelius? At a loss, Janus stared at the padlock, then down the hallway again. He suddenly felt very aware of the documents in the bottom of his box.

"Hello?" said the muffled voice.

Janus cleared his throat and spoke to the padlock. "I was told to meet Cornelius here."

Silence. Then, "I am Joab. You have the wrong cell."

Janus tapped his lips. How to proceed?

"Could you please tell someone to empty the bucket? This is a small room."

Last cell on the left, wasn't it? Janus looked at the cell opposite; the door was ajar, and the room was empty. Janus went to the room and looked in the crack of the door, just to be sure.

"Please . . . have you any news of Theron the mosaicist? Did he succeed in his petition to Orion Galerinius Honoratus?"

Janus blinked. What events were afoot? Did this have to do with Orion's deposal?

"Are you still there?" The voice grew bleak. "Hello?"

There is no concealing the sound of hobnails on flagstone. Janus heard Cornelius before he saw him. "Thank the Triad. I don't know what I would have done."

With a rueful look, the soldier held up an iron ring with a key dangling. "I forgot this. Did you get them?"

Janus lifted his box. "Right here, covered up with enough implements of augury to keep an entire battalion safe for a decade."

"Prometheus?"

"He cowers in the corner of the triclinium, praying for my success. A man with a guilty conscience."

Cornelius opened the padlock and pulled open the door. Therein stood a young man, blinking at the sudden light. He gazed from Janus to Cornelius. "Who are you?"

"Friends of Orion. Lucky for you." Cornelius turned to Janus. "The documents, please." Janus set the box down and pulled out the papers. He glanced down the corridor and handed them to Cornelius, who folded them in half and slipped them down the front of his cuirass. To Joab he said, "Walk behind me and keep your mouth shut." He started down the hallway.

"Cornelius, the key," Janus said with a doubtful look at the iron padlock.

"We must leave it. They cannot find it on me."

"What do you want me to do now?" Janus asked, hurrying to catch up with them.

"Go to Prometheus and tell him the auspice is completed. Carry on as normal."

"Is there nothing else I can do for Orion?"

At that, the one named Joab looked sharply at him.

"What's happened to Orion?" he asked.

"I said keep your mouth shut," Cornelius snapped. The soldier turned to Janus. "Did you get the bristlebane?"

Janus scowled. "I don't know why he wanted bristlebane." Reluctantly he produced a packet of the leafy dried herb from a fold in his tunic. He went to hand it to Cornelius, but hesitated. "Bristlebane is commonly used before quite horrible events."

Cornelius took the packet without answer and dropped it down his front. Unhappily, Janus gave instructions as the soldier led them on. "Tell him to chew the leaves half an hour before—the result he desires. If the leaves were powdered it would work much faster, but this was the best I could do. Tell him to take it with water or wine."

They came to where the corridor crossed into the old part of the palace. Cornelius stopped and held up his hand. He carefully looked both ways, listened for as long as he had looked, then proceeded.

They reached the entrance to the great auditorium. Cornelius turned to Janus. "You have done much. You have the thanks of Orion Galerinius, and if you ever need it, you have my sword. Go carefully, Janus Bifrons."

"Go carefully, Cornelius. Tell Orion for me . . . this palace will miss him."

The soldier nodded, and with Joab as his shadow, walked quickly across the great auditorium. There a guard, the guard Marcus it looked like, pulled open the great Praetorium door and slipped outside. He reappeared and motioned to Cornelius. The soldier slipped out the door with his shadow, and the great door was pulled shut. The sound of its closing echoed in the vast room.

Janus stood at the entrance and absently shook down his bracelets. He realized he had taken up the tune of the tibicen, when it came back to him in a hollow echo. He glanced into his wooden box and chuckled. It was probably the first time since Romulus and Remus an augury was conducted in such a way. But Prometheus wouldn't know. He was a military man, just a superstitious military man.

His tune took a buoyant note as he headed for the private part of the palace to the triclinium. He should get himself some breakfast, make Prometheus wait awhile. A little time at the *lararium* wouldn't kill him. The thought of a worried and anxious Prometheus Longinus on the rug before the altar was a cheering thought indeed.

15

ORION SAT ON THE COUCH—not a Roman couch—in the reclining area of Theron's home. Roman couches were for, well, reclining. This couch was for sitting. It felt awkward. Though it didn't come close to the awkwardness he felt between these two women.

The maiden Jorah was quiet now, and that was pure relief. She was on another couch across from him, and had spent most of the time since Orion had come—a few hours now—between fits of weeping and moments of quiet. She didn't acknowledge him, not since he arrived and disappointed her with no news of her Joab.

It was Marina who had his wary attention. His life had fallen apart, and he would have appreciated a little normalcy in this part of his world. A little sympathy. Instead, Marina sat at the loom in the corner, though she neither twisted wool nor wove. The look on her face worried him. He'd never seen Marina beaten.

"I hate this waiting," Jorah muttered.

It seemed neither of them had slept. After Orion had given them the details of his plight, each had taken to her part of the room and settled in, waiting for Joab and Theron. Orion would rather be in Falnera's doorway.

He didn't question Marina about this strange silent vigil, but felt it from where he sat. "I have to visit the brush," he said, more for something to say than out of genuine need.

Marina lifted her head. "Use a bucket in the workroom. You must not show your face out there." She plucked at folds of her garment, then smoothed what was plucked.

"Joab must mean a lot to you," Orion said cautiously. "I've already told you, Cornelius is a good man, a good soldier. He'll do well by Joab. I expect them any time."

He wished Theron were here, but no, Theron waited at the commonyard foregate for Cornelius and Joab. He did it to escape the stifling atmosphere in his home, the coward, and Orion felt very abandoned.

"Why didn't she come?" the maiden finally said. She had a pillow on her lap and twirled one of the corner tassels with her finger.

"Perhaps she did not want to come," Marina answered.

Her voice was dull with sadness. Flaming gods, he wished he were with Theron.

"Why?" Jorah asked.

"I once tried to turn her from her ways," Marina said softly. "That was a mistake."

"Why would that be a mistake? You would have done her a favor."

But Marina did not answer. Jorah went back to twirling the tassel.

"Why didn't who come where?" Orion ventured.

Marina looked up at Orion, as if seeing him for the first time since he arrived at dawn. "A friend of yours. Rivkah. I made pistachio pastry." Her gaze drifted. "I almost wish you could stay, Orion, if it were safe for you. She will need friends."

"Why?"

"She will soon learn her son is dead."

"She will what?" Cold sliced him through. "She will *what?*" He sagged against the couch. No, not *her* son. Rivkah sitting at the tree, pulling down wind-lifted hair, gazing out to sea. No, this could not be. "Not Rivkah's son. That cannot be."

"He is dead," Jorah whispered. "I was there."

Orion stared at Jorah across from him. He looked at Marina. The thickness in the air was grief and worry and fear.

He would be gone soon, his first thought. He would be on the sea heading for a faraway port. He would not have to face a mother's grief. He would not face *her* grief.

Shame came on the heels. He scrubbed his hair. And he'd thought Theron a coward? Escape was all he ever wanted when horrible things came. Why didn't he have his father's collar? He fidgeted for it now.

How could he look on Rivkah in her grief? How could he see her pride decimated? Why did he have to learn this now? For surely he could not leave, not now, not like this. He rubbed his eyes. When was the last time he had slept?

"How did it happen?" he asked wearily.

"That's a long story," was all Jorah said.

"When did it happen?"

"Two months ago," Jorah said. "At Passover. He died when my brother did."

It took a moment. He watched the tassel twirl. Then he sat up. "Two months ago?"

"We were going to tell her sooner, Joab and I, but . . . it was hard."

"Hard?" The word was foolish on his tongue. "*When* could you have told her?"

She shrugged bleakly. "We could have come straight from Jerusalem. Nobody was thinking much." She twirled the tassel around her finger. "Joab tried. How do you tell a mother her son is dead?"

"You open your mouth!" Orion shouted. The women jumped, and Orion rose from the couch. "Marina, how long have you known?"

"A day. Half a day. Since last night, it doesn't really matter, Orion. Nathanael is dead."

Orion barely heard her. The implications paraded in full-flung mockery. "Doesn't matter? I'd be in the palace right now," he said, incredulous. "Everything it took to change those plans. The scroll and Prometheus and—the shame my father will know on learning his son is a traitor. All because you did not tell a woman she sat vigil at the tree of her *dead son!*" He sat down heavily, bewildered and utterly ambushed. "She wouldn't have made the petitions. Prometheus wouldn't have a forged scroll. I would be in the palace. . . ."

"How do you tell a mother her son was murdered?" It was Marina who spoke. "Rivkah's boy was murdered, Orion. How do you tell her that?"

Oh gods, he wanted the collar. He dropped his head and closed his eyes on the sight of Rivkah, her face saucy and her eyes dancing. "You open your mouth, Marina. You just open your mouth."

To my beloved . . .

Theron's god, hear me now. I have no collar, no priest for a petition. I have nothing. I cannot leave her to this news, neither can I stay. Theron's god, if you are there at all . . .

"We must go to her now," he heard his voice say. He lifted his head, opened his eyes. Jorah had a fearful gaze upon him. Fearful—but there was miserable hope in it.

Marina was shaking her head. "Orion," she said in gentle surprise. "What are you thinking?" She gestured to the door. "You cannot go out there, dear friend, it is not safe. It will be difficult enough to get you to the harbor without notice around here—unless you can instantly grow a beard."

"We go see her now. Not another hour will pass on her ignorance."

Marina rose when he did, glancing at the door. "What of Cornelius? He will be here any time. Orion, if you are *seen* . . ."

The door in the back of Theron's workroom led to a smallyard, and the smallyard opened to an alley. The alley led to the main street. Theron was all the way on the other side of the commonyard, he would not see them leave. Orion went to the curtain flap and waited for them to follow. Marina would know the way.

"Can Romans grow beards?" Jorah wondered as she and Orion followed Marina. She heard Marina's snort, but Orion's grim face had a wisp of a weary smile.

"Mine only comes in on my jawline. Even then, it is scanty."

"Like my brother Jude."

Orion displayed his jaw with his hand. "See? I haven't shaved in twenty-four hours."

"Not much there," Jorah agreed after inspection.

He's a brave man, for a Roman. She looked at him sideways without his notice. The brief moment with his smile passed. As Orion's face went back to its bleakness, Jorah's hand went to her stomach; did James feel like this with his stomach pains? She was on her way to tell a mother her son was murdered.

They had skirted the marketplace, taking to the alleys because it was a Jewish marketplace and people would stare. No man had a smooth face there. No man wore a toga. Past the Jewish marketplace they took a main street. Here they did not draw attention because here people kept to themselves. Nobody exchanged greetings. They hardly even looked up. Here were tunics *and* togas.

Jorah had been in the rough part of the city several days ago when she had a wild thought to find Rivkah and end the matter. She had only gone a short distance past the safety of the Jewish marketplace, clutching the dill Marina had sent her for, when her pounding heart sent her scurrying back to the comfort of ornery merchants and bickering wives. She had glanced behind her, and two men at a corner watched her go. The looks on their faces. She shuddered, remembering, and moved a little closer to Orion Galerinius.

The street began to ascend, and Marina kept her measured pace. The cobblestones alone told of a different place, where filth began to show between them. Care had to be taken not to step into a gap. In this part of Caesarea, thieves would patiently dig out the street stones and abscond with them, to what use Jorah did not know. Did they sell them? Fix their homes with them? Theron had told her of this practice, when Jorah had stumbled on a loose cobblestone on the way to the palace.

Here, mothers treated their children differently. Mothers everywhere yelled at their children, but here it was shrill and vexing. Here men cast looks at Jorah, looks she firmly refused to see. She kept her eyes on the dirty cobblestones, following Marina's heels.

The heels took a side street to the left, crossed the way, and stopped at the third wooden door on the right.

Every bit of her aflame, heart pounding in her stomach, Jorah stepped next to Marina and clasped her hand. Orion stood behind them. Marina lifted her chin, squeezed Jorah's hand hard, and knocked.

After a moment the door opened and a young woman appeared. She had a round painted face and curly hair dyed the color of wheat stalks. Her eyebrows were black. Her eyes narrowed upon seeing them. "Three of you now. Zakkai must be desperate." Over her shoulder she yelled, "Rivkah! Three this time."

"Tell them to go away," said a voice within the home. "Tell them I know Ezekiel."

"She knows Ezekiel," the woman said, and began to shut the door. Orion Galerinius planted his hand on the door.

"Rivkah," he called. "Please. We must speak."

Silence, and a clatter.

The young woman peered at him. She took in the fine toga, and maybe saw something Jorah didn't, because an appreciative half grin came. "You must be Orion. Rivkah was right. Look, if you don't want anything to do with her, then . . ."

A woman appeared behind the first, and Jorah wanted to die. The only other place she'd seen eyes that color was in the face of Nathanael.

Rivkah was hastily smoothing down thick waving black hair—until she saw Orion. Then she clasped her hands and lifted her chin.

Jorah's free hand sought Orion's. He gripped it hard.

Rivkah's eyes took in Marina, took in Jorah and all the hand clasping, came to rest on Orion. It seemed she knew Orion well enough because first came confusion, then fear, and then Rivkah knew something was terribly wrong.

"His tree," she said, voice low.

Orion Galerinius slowly shook his head. Though it all lay upon Jorah, though she was the one who bore the onus of the telling, he said softly, "No, Rivkah. It is Nathanael."

The amber eyes widened. They cut to Marina, back to Orion. "What of him? You do not know Nathanael."

"I did."

The bright eyes came upon Jorah; they grew wild with fear and challenge.

"What do you mean, you *did*?" the other young woman snapped. She put an arm around Rivkah's waist, gripped her shoulder.

"I loved him," Jorah whispered. Tears came and fell. "We wanted to marry."

Orion Galerinius said gently, "Rivkah . . . your son is dead."

Rivkah flung up her arms to drop from the arms of the other, twisted and fell to all fours. Orion dropped beside her, tried to pull her into his arms, but she scrabbled away, crawling as fast as she could, then flung herself flat on the floor of the home. No sound came from her, no wail, nothing. She lay silent on the floor, breathing hard.

Orion stayed where he was, put his forehead on his knee and squeezed his eyes shut. Marina went to Rivkah, sat down beside her, and began to weep.

She thought to speak to this woman of scars. She was spread facedown on the ground, arms splayed as if to embrace Sheol. Not a sound from her. Jorah felt for the front step and dropped to it. She placed her hands in her lap. "He died a good Jew," she whispered, though no one heard her. "Abishag told me to tell you."

༞

Apparently the Roman soldier wanted to make it appear that Joab was under firm escort—which was more than likely the case. When they stepped out of the Praetorium, he grabbed a large cloth-wrapped bundle, pushed it into Joab's arms, and ordered him to walk ahead of him.

Joab waited until they had left the palace grounds and had the Great Stadium well behind. "May I ask a question?" he said respectfully over his shoulder.

"Yes."

"What's in this bundle?"

"Whatever I could find. I want it to look like you're conscripted for a mile."

Joab was glad he couldn't see his half smile. The Teacher had said something about that; when someone conscripted you for a mile, and Roman law said it could only be a mile, you were to offer— *offer*—another mile. He shook his head. Crazy! He could never do such a thing for a Roman. But Joab could not stop thinking on the Teacher and his baffling words. All night long he had occupied Joab's thoughts.

They were passing a group of soldiers. Cornelius gave Joab a shove and said loudly, "I don't care if your mile is up. Have a little backbone and stop your whining."

"Greetings, Cornelius," one of the soldiers called.

"Greetings, Falcorus," Cornelius called back. "Did you hear about Orion Galerinius?"

"About ten minutes ago." The man glanced about before he added on the sly, "Dirty shame too."

Cornelius shook his head. "Palace is losing a good man."

"Longinus ain't so bad," one of the other soldiers said with a shrug. "I was next to him in battle. He accounted well."

"Sure, he's good at killing people, not managing them," Falcorus replied. He nodded at Cornelius and said, "Ranks will change. You'll be promoted. *Optio* Cornelius, that must sound good."

Cornelius gave Joab another shove. "If it gets me out of the auxiliaries, sure it sounds good. Get me an Italian cohort, and I can rest my heels by noon."

The soldiers laughed at this. Cornelius waved and continued with Joab on the Cardo Maximus.

Joab waited until the street was nearly empty. "Orion has been replaced?"

"You could say that. He's waiting for us. He said you would know the way."

"He must be at Theron's."

"So I thought. We must stop at his banker first. And see about securing a place for him in the hold of a merchant ship."

Joab's mind raced. Orion Galerinius was every inch in charge yesterday. What could have happened between last night and this morning? "Is Prometheus—"

"Stop your chatter. It would help if you acted like a subjugated Jew."

Who is carrying the bundle? Joab wanted to ask.

"Optio Cornelius," he heard the soldier mutter. "Orion's loss, my gain. If that isn't a bite of honeyed bristlebane."

16

THERE WERE ANTS on the floor. Rivkah watched one scuttle over the dead body of another, then pick it up in its jaws and begin a laborious march. She watched until it disappeared into the seam where the wall and floor met. What would be done with the dead ant? Did they eat it? Bury it?

There was an ax somewhere, buried in the junk room. That was the small alcove where Nathanael slept; she called it a junk room because it was always a mess. She once told him she'd feed him to the madman in the tombs if he didn't clean it up, and he told her the madman would find him delicious.

She had known after the first full moon that he wasn't coming back. Kyria had too.

Where would she find the ax? Beneath his cot? In the unholy

mess in the corner where he piled everything when she told him to clean his room? She told him rats had babies in that pile. Was the ax on a shelf against the wall? The shelves he'd built when he was ten.

It came unexpectedly, a pulling from her gut, a dragging up and dragging out. Rivkah, who had lain silent on the floor all day, long enough for Marina and the young girl to leave, long enough for the sun to disappear, now began to wail. Kyria came and knelt on one side, Orion on the other. Orion, who had a palace to run. He had told her enough times he had a palace to run—

The crying time lasted as long as the silence, and rose and fell like the keening of a madwoman. When she thought it was done it came again, for she would never—oh God—never see Nathanael again, never tell him how sorry she was for the scars on his leg, scars identical to her own and those of her mother. Mother was dead, took her scars to her grave, and Nathanael now took his.

Nathanael, her bright-eyed mouthy scoundrel, her fierce and forgiving rogue, he who defended her in the face of sundry accusers, scorning their scorn and sometimes throwing rocks. She cried the sorrow of her lifetime for her baby, for the boy she had never deserved, for the life that stretched out bleak before her.

※

"She is still sleeping? I wish she didn't have to wake to that news."

Orion had been dozing. He looked up to find the young woman offering him a plate and a mug. He sat up and took them, murmuring his thanks. He was sitting in the small entryway, Rivkah curled on the floor next to him. The young woman settled to the ground on the other side and eyed Orion curiously.

"My name is Kyria," she whispered, with a glance at Rivkah. "In case she never told you about me. Did she?"

Orion went to work on the bread. He was so hungry, so tired he couldn't remember what Rivkah had said. He shrugged and gulped down some wine.

"What happened to Nathanael?" the girl asked.

The girl was younger than Rivkah, probably in her midtwenties. He could tell she had been crying; traces of kohl smudged her face. Her ringlet hair was not naturally blonde—the eyebrows were as dark as Rivkah's. She was a trifle plump, with softly rounded cheeks.

"I don't know," Orion answered quietly. He did not want to tell her the boy was murdered. It would do no good to offer that, he did not know the details.

Tears slipped down the rounded cheeks as she looked at her sleeping friend. After a time she wiped her face, rearranging the kohl smears. "He was a good kid. I helped raise him. I used to take him to the chariot races when Rivkah had a client. He loved those races. He'd stick his little thumb up or down like Pilate himself. I used to laugh at that." She smiled a little, remembering.

"Rivkah had fits, me bringing him there. I told her he'd end up a woman-man if he didn't do manly things, him without a father. Chariot races are just the sort of thing for a boy. I did my best by him. Taught him lots of things, taught him how to . . . clean fish and—" She suddenly stopped, face tightening. "I'm going to cry again, Roman."

Despite her words, she didn't cry just yet. Instead, she looked at Orion with a sudden grin, eyes sparkling with tears. "You know what she always called him? My baby. Always called him *my baby* no matter how big he got. Called him *my baby* in front of his friends, gods, how he hated that. 'Where's my baby going?'"

Orion found he liked listening to her. Her manner of speech had the coarse tang of the uneducated, but it was not offensive. Her voice was a little hoarse, as though used to going on full tilt at a louder pitch. It was . . . charming. Poignant.

"Was he like her? I've often wondered."

"In some ways. Had her temper. Had her foul mouth. Had her eyes."

The tears fell, and Orion put his attention on his plate.

"He used to drive me crazy when he was little, I'll say that. When he got older we missed him, he didn't stay around much."

"Why is that?"

Kyria wiped her nose and snorted. "Why do you think, Roman?"

"Oh." Orion looked at Rivkah's still form. He would not ordinarily ask such a thing, but he did not feel uncomfortable, asking Kyria. "Can you tell me this? Why does she do it? She could do anything she wanted."

Kyria nodded. "She could be a cloth merchant. She's got an eye for color. She's got taste, she can tell you what goes with what . . . that sort of thing. I'm no good at that. She made that pillow over there."

Orion twisted around. Through the archway he saw a large indigo pillow on a low couch.

"She makes lots of pillows. Sometimes she sells them to our friends. She dyed the fabric herself on that one, the indigo and the gold." Her gaze came back to Rivkah. "She does it because she makes herself. I do it because I'm not good at anything else."

"Why would she—"

Kyria shook her head wearily. "I don't know. Has to do with her family. I'm glad her mother is dead." At Orion's surprise, Kyria said, "She used to come around here on unfortunate occasion. Wicked shrew. She came only to call Rivkah names and threaten to take Nathanael away. Rivkah once told her it was her fault, that she wouldn't be a whore if it weren't for her mother. Later I asked Rivkah what she meant by that, but she wouldn't tell."

Kyria gave Orion a small, bitter smile. "I got a theory. The priest

Zakkai sometimes sends around one of his boys to quote things to Rivkah. I think he's a guilty man. Rivkah won't say, but I'm not a fool—she once told me she was his wife's serving maid." A dark eyebrow went up.

Orion dropped his eyes to his plate, then looked at Rivkah.

"So she didn't grow up like me, but I wonder if it would be better if she had. Her father was as bad as her mother, used to beat her. You know how I know? Go to scratch your head around Rivkah, and she'll flinch like you're gonna hit her. Makes me sick. She still does it, twenty years after he died. At least I'm pretty sure it was her father. Could've been her mother. Could've been Zakkai." On sudden thought, she said, "Look—don't tell any of this to Rivkah, okay? She's kind of a private person."

"No . . . I won't."

Kyria stood and gazed down at Rivkah's sleeping form. "Look, I got an appointment at the inn. If I don't show up—"

"It's okay."

"I just don't want her to wake up alone, you know?"

"I won't leave her."

She looked at him, noticed the empty plate and cup, and took them. Then she said, "You know what? I wish Rivkah would've met you a long time ago." She went to put the dishes away.

Orion watched a few strands of black hair wave with Rivkah's breathing. Very quietly he said, "So do I."

Orion Galerinius was sleeping. He was unshaven, she'd never seen him like that. She preferred his face smooth, but the bristle wasn't unattractive. A little gray in it. His face was puffy with weariness, that was plain. His arms were folded, ankles crossed. His head listed only slightly, as if even in sleep he would not allow himself complete repose.

She touched his sandal, caressed the edge of its sole. She put her hand over his foot, drew closer to him, took a deep breath and sighed long, then went back to sleep.

❧

Orion woke to the sound of loud banging. He opened eyes that hadn't stayed closed long enough, then froze when he saw he was not in his apartment, not in his bed. His ears informed him faster than his eyes. That banging was not a palace sound.

Kyria stepped over him and hurried to the door. Orion scrubbed his face hard and looked groggily about. Rivkah was not in sight. It occurred to him that maybe he should not be either, though the why of that was vague.

Hushed murmurs at the door. Kyria opened it enough for Marina to slip in.

"Orion! You must come quickly. Cornelius has made the arrangements."

He looked up at her, clarity coming slowly. Arrangements. Those were good things. "What sort of arrangements, Marina?" His voice was as hoarse as the day after a chariot race, his mouth sticky and foul-tasting.

She squatted beside him. "There is a vessel in the harbor. Cornelius has secured another passage for you." Her dark eyes searched his. "There is something else—Pilate is looking for you. He went to the Tiberateum today."

Orion rubbed his eyes. "That is supposed to be significant. I can't think what it means."

Marina gave him a twisting pinch. "Wake up, Orion. It means we should have stayed put. Joab and Cornelius came yesterday morning after we left. Cornelius had a place for you. He paid the captain of the ship, and they waited as long as they dared. They couldn't find us."

"But Theron . . ."

"He didn't know where Rivkah lived. The ship sailed yesterday afternoon."

Alarm finished his waking. "Yesterday? Today is—"

"Day after Sabbath. Today the stonemason was to receive the forty-nine."

Dazed, Orion sagged against the wall. Pilate went to the Tiberateum—he knew he didn't give the order. *Gods and goddesses.* "What happened?"

"Cornelius arrived a short time ago. He said that Pilate visited the Tiberateum to inquire if the stonemason had changed his mind about working on the Sabbath. Nobody knew what he was talking about."

"I'll bet he's angry," Orion said.

"Angry? Cornelius says he's stalking the palace like the Furies on fire. Whatever that means."

"It means I'll be arrested and tried for treason. Exile seems particularly winsome right now. What of the stonemason?"

"Well, thank the Eternal, apparently Pilate was so infuriated with you he forgot about him."

"Ah. That's good," Orion said rather faintly.

"What treason?" Rivkah's voice came from down the hallway.

She stood at a curtain flap, one hand holding an ax at her side. Her face was newly aged with grief. Her voluminous black hair was disheveled, and the top of her head was coated with white and gray and black ashes. Ashes smudged her face where tears had been. Her outer tunic was torn down the middle, dusted with sooty ash.

He got to his feet, looking at the ax. The woman lost her son. Lost her battle with Rome. From of old came the usual working of his mind—though he knew it to be purely illogical, he wondered what he could have done to prevent the loss of her son.

What was this responsibility he felt for her? Part of the job, yes, to see to the matters of the Praetorium Palace. The day she put her petition before him, he became responsible. But protocol never demanded he should see it through to the end.

"Why do you put ashes on your head?" he asked.

"I don't know."

"Why do you tear your clothes?"

"Because we cannot tear out our hearts."

He regarded the coating of ash on her hair. Yes, it would probably violate another custom. It would call down Theron's god, and Orion would fry like a fish ball on a brazier. But there was nothing for him to do, with this lovely woman consumed in sorrow, but to push off from the wall and go to her, to reach and take of the ashes from her head and sprinkle them on his own.

She watched as he took and sprinkled, took and sprinkled, and tears flowed fresh down her cheeks, washing trails through the ashes. She took a fistful of his clothing and shook him gently, her face tight and her voice tight. "What treason does Marina speak of? What treason?"

"It's not important, Rivkah," he replied. "I can imagine what you're going to do with the ax. Let it be."

She regarded the ax and shook her head. "I have to cut it down."

"Another custom?"

"No." A tear splotched the ax head.

He took her shoulders until she looked at him. "Then let it be. They won't harm it anymore." He gripped her shoulders as if to give her strength.

She put her forehead on his chest and wept, and he put his arms around her and held her tight. "Let it live for him," he murmured against her hair. "It's still his tree. It's still his tree, Rivkah."

She moved her head back and forth. "I don't deserve to have it stand," she sobbed. "I don't deserve it."

Kyria came and put her arms around Rivkah's waist, laying her head on Rivkah's back. Orion couldn't hear her cry, but could feel her shake with sobs. He met Marina's eyes. It wasn't until he saw tears in hers that his own eyes blurred. He rested his cheek on Rivkah's hair, reached to pull in Kyria too.

The ex–chief secretary to the prefect Pontius Pilate held two crying women in one of the foulest places in town. In one grim recess of his mind, fear prevailed. If they caught him before he got to the port, he would be executed. In another recess, he tried to imagine a boy who looked like this woman, with golden eyes and a fiery temperament.

"I should like to die this loved," Orion whispered.

At his words, Rivkah's cries began to abate until finally she stood silent. Kyria's weeping subsided too, and she pulled away, wiping her face. Rivkah blotted her face on Orion's toga. She looked up at him, and he hardly heard her words for the rift of emotion at the sight of her face. She would never be lovelier than this, right now, with those damp golden eyes framed by dark wet lashes, strands of hair sticking to her face. He saw for the first time in the eyes a ring of green about the gold. Ashes and cosmetics made dark smears on her face. She pulled aside sticky hair as she searched his eyes, utterly unconscious of her messy loveliness.

"Don't you have a palace to run?" she asked.

He smiled slightly. "Not anymore."

"Orion," Marina said, blotting her face with her head covering. "We must go. Cornelius has made new arrangements, and they will not last. It will be harder than ever to get you to the harbor."

Kyria was against the wall, looking hard at Orion. "What is going on?"

"He must leave Caesarea," Marina explained wearily. "He is wanted for helping the Jews."

Orion watched Rivkah's face harden. Her jaw gained the set he knew well.

"You mean, for helping me."

"You and another," Marina replied. "And others and others. Orion, we must go. *Now*. Give us a chance to save your hide, will you?"

Anger flared in Rivkah's face. She shoved Orion away. "What have you done?"

Orion staggered backward, staring at her.

She pushed him again, hard, until he hit the wall. "What have you done?" she demanded again.

"I—"

She screamed, "What—have—you—done?" With every word she hit him with her fist.

He seized her wrist and shouted in her face, "I don't know! I don't know what I've done! I've lost it all!"

She used her other fist, hitting with every word, shrieking. "Why didn't you let them cut down the tree, you stupid fool of a—"

Kyria hauled Rivkah back. "Will you shut up so I can think?" To Orion she said, "What of treason, Roman? What's the punishment for that?"

Orion was glaring at Rivkah, who glared back. He dropped the look and muttered, "Treason is a public offense."

Rivkah tried to lunge for Orion, but Kyria hauled her back and twisted a handful of her sleeve to hold her in place. "That's supposed to explain it? I'm a prostitute, Your Excellency. A harlot. A whore. We don't get out much."

Marina wearily stated, "Cornelius said Roman law is either public or private. Treason against Rome is public. It carries the death sentence."

Kyria's eyebrow came up. She looked Orion up and down approvingly. "What did you do to earn that, Roman?"

"I didn't give an order," Orion answered, returning a slight smile.

Rivkah lunged for Orion again, but Kyria held her fast. "Theron told me Pilate said to cut it down," Rivkah hissed. She writhed and seethed in Kyria's hold, clearly intent on killing Orion. "That's the order you didn't give, you slick-faced Roman dog of a—what does a *tree* matter? Are you crazy? It never mattered, you pagan pig! You—"

As Rivkah brought out her curses, Orion watched her struggle, oddly, all of the struggle gone out of himself. "No, Rivkah. For that, I simply had to flee. The treason is for something different." A thought came, and he asked Marina, "Did Cornelius free Joab?"

"Yes," she replied with icy patience. "And Pilate has a garrison looking for you. They are all over the harbor. Lucky for you they suspect you've already left, so they're not looking too sharply. Cornelius is waiting at our place to bring you to the ship, and if we don't leave now then everything he risked for you is in vain."

"Where will you go?"

He had never heard her voice like that. Small and soft.

She had stopped her struggling. Kyria cautiously let her go. She looked as tired and disheveled as he felt.

"Are you going to hit me again?"

She shook her head, and the dark hollows of her eyes pulled at his heart.

"Wherever the ship is bound."

Marina grabbed his arm. "It's bad enough I'll never see you again, you risk your Roman life dawdling. The vessel puts out at dawn, which is only a few hours away. It has already been searched, lucky for—"

"Marina," Rivkah said in the same small voice. "How did Nathanael die?"

Marina's shoulders sagged. "Oh, child." She reached to arrange a coil of Rivkah's ash-covered hair. "There is time for that later. Joab has something quite remarkable to tell you. For now I must whisk our messiah away." She caressed her chin, then turned toward the door and looked out both ways. She slipped out and beckoned for Orion.

He gazed on Rivkah.

Her look was loss. She had her ax and her ashes, her torn outer robe and no more pride. He thought he could not bear to look on her in her decimated pride, but now he could not bear to look away. And for the great heaviness stealing on him, he could say nothing. Not even good-bye. Marina caught his arm and pulled him out, shut the door.

❧

The ax fell and gouged a chip in the hard-packed floor. Rivkah turned aside into her room, vanishing behind the long strands of beads. Kyria listened but heard nothing, save Rivkah falling on the bed.

Well, someone had to cry some more. Kyria settled on the couch and took the indigo pillow in her lap. Then she wept again, this time not for Nathanael but for Rivkah, and for the Roman, and maybe for herself.

17

PROMETHEUS PEERED into his cup. He swirled it gently, watching the wine swell to the edge and sheet down into the goblet. He glanced at Pilate, but nothing had changed. Still lost in his dark incredulity.

"It makes you wonder what the Primipilaris would think of all this," Prometheus mused as if to himself. As he expected, Pilate stirred a little at that.

"He knows Orion had Jewish sympathies," Pilate muttered over his own cup, gripped hard in his fist. "That I told him myself. This will not surprise him."

They were in the foreroom of Pilate's private quarters, a place Prometheus had never been. The luxury, the spaciousness, were not lost on him. He simply acted as though the grave matter at hand were more important. The vase on the corner table could pay his wages for six years, and gods-up-in-arms the walls were finished in powdered marble stucco—all of them. What of Pilate's inner room, was it finished in powdered gold? He tried to gain a surreptitious peek, but a curtain, an extravagantly brocaded curtain that could have been a tapestry itself, obscured his view.

"Clever of you to inform him, Excellency. What a perfect time for Orion's deceptions to be revealed," Prometheus said.

The prefect stirred again.

Prometheus could not stop the ensuing smile, so he made it into a smile respectful of Pilate's cleverness. "Orion's deceptions and his subsequent fleeing from Caesarea will underscore your warning to the Primipilaris." He shook his head. "He will learn upon arrival that your first in command fled like a madman before a horde of noisome Jews, as you yourself had intimated. I think, then, that the import of the Jewish situation will be greatly impressed upon him." Prometheus again shook his head in benign wonder.

For the first time, Pilate eyed him. "Yes. It will be, won't it?"

His tone had gained a hopeful edge. Perhaps he would allow himself beguilement from his despondency. Prometheus pressed in delicately.

"Now if Orion *didn't* flee Caesarea, and my sources are doubtful, well, that of course would be a gift from the Triad. His punishment would have to be very public. The Amphitheater, I would think. Or the Great Stadium, it would seat more. Caesarea would talk of it for months. The Primipilaris would see how you reward disloyalty to Rome."

"He would. Wouldn't he?" Pilate straightened in his chair and tugged down the sides of his toga.

"I do not envy you."

Pilate glanced sharply at him.

Prometheus started, as if surprised to be caught breathing so personal a thought. "I—well, truth be told, Excellency, I don't know how *I* would have ruled this province, these past several years. It's clear why the Triad fixed your stars the way they did." As if the thought just came, he lifted his cup to Pilate. "To Pontius Pilate, ruler of the Jews. No, this: To Pontius Pilate: he who conquered them at last."

Pilate considered him with a faint smile and lifted his cup. He was ready to drink . . . then hesitation flickered in his gray eyes. The faint smile vanished. He still held his cup in the air, unaware of it. "I lost a good man to the Jews."

The cup came down and wine sloshed over the edge, staining the linen tablecloth.

Prometheus barely prevented the sigh. He'd lost him again.

"He was poisoned to the core. What failed? Where do I lay the blame? On Orion himself, or on the Jews whose trickery . . ." He rose suddenly and resumed his restless stalking.

Prometheus groaned inside, settling in for another unending tirade. The mutterings worked into a growl.

"Why couldn't he have been strong?" Pilate paced his apartment with blind hate, only his familiarity with the room keeping his course. "There is no excuse for his actions. Do you know the *betrayal* I feel, the humiliation? Do you know how I felt at the Tiberateum? Nobody knew what I was talking about. He was my number one. Do you know what implications that will cast upon *me*? 'Pilate could neither handle the Jews nor his own men.'"

Prometheus rolled his eyes when he could safely do so. How could he get out of this? His position was too new to know exactly what was expected of him. Could he excuse himself, say he had duties to attend? Wouldn't Pilate understand about duty?

He had been here a few hours now, listening to the rise and fall of the prefect's moroseness. It was getting predictable. He'd slouch on the table in a stupor, then rise and bellow treachery. He'd stop in front of—yes, there he went now. Predictable as snot on an urchin's face. He stopped in front of the golden standard fixed to the wall and stared up at the image of his beloved Tiberius Caesar.

Prometheus waited for the murmuring. Yes, there it was.

"I didn't hate them before I came. This is where it all started. Right here." He touched the golden incense pan on the shelf built below the standard. "Sejanus was right, but his words made little sense to me then. I was assembling my staff. Packing. Making arrangements for leaving my home. Would that I had listened to my mentor."

Your mentor falls fast from the grace of Tiberius, my prefect. Let's hope Tiberius doesn't remember who Sejanus's friends are.

Prometheus took a sip of his wine and put weary eyes on the medallion.

It wasn't the full battle standard. The pole was probably in the *sacellum*, either in the barracks or in Jerusalem. The eagle was gone, the inscription of the legion was gone. Pilate only had the six-inch disk with the profile of Tiberius, bordered in a triumphal wreath, set on an ornately carved gilt charger and mounted on his powdered marble wall.

He broke tradition and burned incense daily to Tiberius's image on the medallion, as if a battle victory were won every day; blackened pucks of incense in the tray told of the constant ritual. It made Prometheus uncomfortable, a little nauseated, to see Pilate's adoration so clearly on his face. Adoration, longing. Devotion.

Or was it the sight of the dismembered standard that made him sick? Where was the eagle? Where was the inscription? Did the dismembered parts have battle scars on them? To Prometheus, a legionary soldier first, an appointee in Pilate's administration next, the standard entire was sacred. It was a man's unit. It was honor, fortitude, bravery, and strength. It was Rome, of course, though that was for the political prisses who never saw a day of battle: Rome and the gods be cursed, the standard meant the man on the other side. It meant survival.

So yes, Prometheus could understand a measure of Pilate's devotion. He could understand why he displayed the standards on the walls of the Antonia Fortress in Jerusalem, gods, yes; any Roman soldier could. Prometheus had applauded the act, as Orion worried about offending the locals. And offended they were. The Jews woke to find the standards winking down from the wall, the image of Tiberius smiling on the courtyard of their sacred Temple.

Orion Galerinius Honoratus was never a soldier. He was the only one to wonder what implications might come. He was the one who consulted with the former quaestor to Valerius Gratus, and reported the subsequent warnings to Pontius Pilate. They went ignored.

Prometheus remembered how they had called Pilate from his morning tea on his new balcony overlooking the Mediterranean. Remembered the shock on his face when the governor had to go out to the Jews, because they would not come in to him. How enraged they were, and how mystified Pilate was. It was his introduction to the freakish devotion to a solitary god. The beginning clash of misunderstandings between two cultures that could never be reconciled. It wasn't their god who kept them safe from Pilate in those early years; it was their appalling zeal.

Speak of appalling zeal.

"In Tiberius speramus . . ." Pilate murmured, pushing about a charred puck in the incense pan.

In Tiberius we trust? Caesar he may be, but how far could you trust one who spent all his time dallying at Capri with winsome youths? Fetching as it sounded, it wasn't a sensible way to run an empire, not when one left the Senate to itself.

"Me duce tutus eris . . ."

Prometheus choked back the laugh. *Under your leadership, Tiberius will be safe? Great gods up-in-arms, who do you think you are, Pontius Pilate? Nobody will even remember you, save for a few indignant Jews.*

He took his cup and lifted it again to Orion Galerinius for affording this opportunity, grim though it was at the moment. No, they wouldn't remember Pilate, but with the luck of the gods and possibly the good work of Janus Bifrons, they would remember Prometheus Longinus. He drained his cup and looked to see if the amphora had more.

⚜

The big Roman soldier was ill at his ease, pacing the room, unable to sit for long. Theron watched him from where he sat at the kitchen table. He didn't talk much, which was okay with Theron. Theron didn't know what to say to him.

He'd heard mention of this man in the past few years, in certain circles in which Theron occasionally turned. Cornelius, the soldier who ran the gleaners' project at the palace. He who was responsible for taking palace leftovers and doling them out to the poor. A curious act of kindness for such a big, burly . . . Roman.

The soldier had arrived around noon yesterday with Joab. If Theron expected a joyous reunion between the lad and Jorah, he was disappointed. She who had spent anxious hours waiting for his return, who had raised a mighty stink for his release, received Joab with cool regard, saying, "I hope you've learned what folly it is to attack a Roman official," and flounced off to tend to Cousin Thomas.

Marina was off fetching Orion, and Joab left sometime before dawn. That left Theron to entertain the big Gentile. Theron did not like to entertain. He'd rather be working on a mosaic. Actually, that would be a much better place to wait for Orion and Marina. Why not? Was it rude to work while you were supposed to be entertaining? He could talk much better in there. At the moment, things were fidgety awkward. He finally came up with something to say.

"What is your function in the army?"

"I am drillmaster of the auxiliaries."

Was Theron supposed to be impressed? He didn't know how the Roman army was set up. Drillmaster could be a very impressive rank. He settled on a cautious "Oh."

"I won't be for long," the man mused. "With Orion gone, ranks will change. I'll make Optio of the Legion X Fretensis, second in command to the centurion."

"Is that good?"

"For me, yes. I'll draw more pay. Better pension. But I can't think past what is happening to Orion." He stopped in the middle of his pacing, looked for a place to sit, chose the bench on the other side of the kitchen table. A good comfortable distance from Theron. "How is it you know Orion?"

"Marina picked him up in the marketplace a year or so ago. She does that, brings people home like strays. She saw Orion and knew he was lost."

"Lost?"

"You know, lost."

The man still had a blank look.

"He lost his way. Not in the marketplace—in life." Maybe that's why the fellow wasn't centurion yet, he wasn't too quick.

The soldier leaned back and appraised Theron curiously. "And did you find him to be . . . lost?"

"Sure. Marina has talent for that sort of thing. She can pick 'em out of a crowd. Never fails."

"How do you mean, 'talent'?"

It occurred to Theron he should offer his guest something. That went with entertaining. That's what Marina would do. "You want some wine or something? You hungry?"

"I'm fine, thank you. What about this talent of your wife's . . . and what do you mean, Orion Galerinius was . . . lost?"

Theron just prevented himself from rolling his eyes. How could he explain talent? How could he explain why he had a gift to make beauty with tiny little tesserae, and he had no gift to perceive a man lost or not? Marina did what she did, Theron did what he did. Trying to get him to explain was like making him explain a sunset. He scratched the back of his head, squinting hard for an answer.

"Well . . . I don't know what you believe about your gods. My God gives people treasures, special treasures we're meant to share with others. He gave Marina a treasure of . . ." Theron shrugged. "I don't know what you call it. I never had to put a name to it. She's got keen insight on folks. She knew one day at the marketplace that the short smooth-faced toga-wearing young man had heart troubles. She got to talking with him, and invited him to the Sabbath meal. He's been coming for a year now."

"He's been coming here every Sabbath?" Cornelius said. "For a year?"

Strangely, he didn't look too pleased with that. He even looked alarmed.

"Yes, a year," Theron said defensively. "And he's not lost anymore."

The Roman leaned on his knees, rubbing his hands together. "That won't look good. That won't look good at all. Don't mention that anymore, to anyone. Understand?"

Bewildered, Theron said, "What do you mean?"

"Orion Galerinius Honoratus was Pilate's First. Ordinarily it would do no harm, a Roman meeting with a Jewish family, but this is no ordinary province and Pilate is no ordinary prefect. He has strong anti-Jewish sentiment, and I know I state the obvious. But it should have been just as obvious to Orion, even a year ago, well before the Jesus of Nazareth incident. He should never have come here. Not once."

The Roman's words came hard. Theron thought on them unhappily, feeling a measure of what was supposed to be Orion's guilt. Orion had told them many times, half jokingly, half not, of the risk he took in being there. Theron had always laughed it off.

"He used to tell us it was dangerous. I guess I didn't take him seriously," Theron said slowly. He couldn't tell Marina this, it would break her heart. "I hope nothing we have done has harmed Orion."

"Orion's actions were all his own." A slight smile lifted the grim mouth. "Well, is he lost anymore?"

"I don't think so." Theron raised his chin. "Marina doesn't quit until it's time to."

"There you have it. Maybe it was worth it."

They exchanged a long look, and Theron decided he liked this fellow.

"I think maybe I would like to have you over for Sabbath meal sometime. If it isn't too dangerous for you," he added.

The soldier grinned. "Because I am lost?"

"I'll leave that to Marina." It was because Theron thought he'd enjoy his company, but of course he didn't say it. Theron didn't make friends often, and this was getting awkward. "Do you know Orion well?"

"No. There was never any time. I would have liked to know him better. I think many do. The palace is full of regretful people right now."

"You know, I always got the feeling Orion didn't think he had friends. Especially in the palace. Why is that?"

Cornelius snorted. "Just his nature, I guess. There are more for him than against him."

Theron grunted. "Except for Pilate and Prometheus."

"Let me ask you something," the soldier suddenly said. He rested his elbows on his knees again, rubbing his hands together. "How is it some of your Jewish number are taken to task for their infractions of your laws, but others are not?"

Theron shrugged. "Sometimes it depends on the community. Sometimes it depends on if a person has subjected himself to synagogue and the religious officials. If he has, he is liable."

"Meaning?"

"That I am safe." Theron chuckled at himself, then regarded this soldier with a squint. "I am considered as the *am ha-aretz* rabble, the Jews of the Land. We subject ourselves to no one—well, except for the one with the biggest stick, in this case, Rome. The religious leaders pay no mind to us, and the *am ha-aretz* do not trouble themselves over much with the Law. They try and stick to the Ten Commandments, they pay the half-shekel temple tax, that's about it. For many of them, being Jewish is an incident of birth. They just go with what they know."

"Is that how it is for you?"

"It's a little more than that." Theron's gaze drifted, and he nodded. "A little more than that." He opened his mouth and closed it. Then he cleared his throat in a growl and looked sharply about before he said, "I'm thinking about reading Torah again." He suddenly shook his finger at the Roman. "You say anything to Marina and I'll—"

He let the threat hang in the air, then warily continued. "Well. I've heard some of the lectures Jorah's brother gave—her brother was Jesus of Nazareth—and I find—"

"Her brother was the Nazarene? I heard him speak once." The

soldier shook his head. "Tell me Orion didn't know this when he hired her for the walkway. Tell me he wasn't that stupid."

"He didn't know." Theron's lip came out. "I was the stupid one."

The door opened, and the two men started. Marina and Orion slipped in, and Theron and the soldier exchanged a relieved glance. Marina quickly closed the door, then looked to make sure the windows were shuttered.

Of course they were shuttered—a great big Roman casting a shadow thrice Theron's size? His form filled the entire window; neighbors would have gathered just to see what the obstruction was.

Cornelius gave a great sigh and dropped his head. He looked up at Orion and said, "You're lucky."

"I'm in your debt. For all you have risked for me, I can never pay you back."

"You look terrible. Have you slept?"

"Some."

The soldier reached behind him and took a heavy pouch from the table. He tossed it to Orion. "There is your Ostia fund. Minus the two passages I had to pay."

Orion hefted the shifting bag in his hand. "You knew I was saving for a place in Ostia?"

"Everybody knew it." Cornelius rose from the table. He pulled out his leather cuirass and fished down the front. He first handed a small packet to Orion. "The bristlebane."

Then he pulled out a crumpled packet of papers. "Sorry. They are not very fresh, they've been in there over a day. Your priest friend got them for me. Pilfered them from right under Prometheus's nose."

"Janus Bifrons . . . ," Orion said wonderingly, taking the papers.

"He told me to tell you that you will be missed. We must go, Orion. I want to get there at muster of ships, it will be busier. More people around, more distractions."

Orion handed the papers to Theron. "Here. Get these back to your people."

Theron slowly took the sheaf and looked up at Orion, who was already asking Marina for the bag he had brought with his things. She went to fetch it while Orion and the soldier spoke together in low tones.

They had been waiting for hours. Now suddenly things were going much too fast. Theron scowled at Orion. The skinny funny man. He looked at the papers in his hands and swallowed fiercely.

"Have I told you how much I like the ribbon mosaic?" Orion said. "I think it's your best work yet. I think that's what they'll remember you for. They're going to put in better lighting, did I tell you that? Sconces will line the whole walkway, both sides. They're on order."

Theron glared at the papers. He had thought they would help the stonemason. They were worthless, after all his efforts to get them. Orion was right again, and Theron felt a fool. He had only endangered his friend by trying to play at subversion. Endangered him by hosting Sabbath meals. He kept his scowl on the papers and said, "Where will you go?"

"Wherever I can."

Theron nodded, biting his lip hard. Finally he said, "Send word."

"I will. Theron, I have a favor to ask."

He had not wanted to look at Orion's eyes, wished he would just get out and go. He growled his throat clear. "I got no time for favors. I got a mosaic to do." But, feeling miserable as a sick eel, he peered up at Orion.

The skinny funny man, with that chopped-up Roman haircut. Looked as if he hadn't slept in a week, and Orion was always prissy about appearances. Looked as if someone had rolled him down the street.

"Look in on Rivkah now and then, will you, Theron? Have her over for Sabbath sometimes."

"Yes, okay. I got a mosaic to do." He got up and went to the workroom without a backward glance.

Marina brought the sack to Orion. He opened it and rummaged through it, then handed Marina a tiny, brightly enameled amphora. "That was my mother's. I want you to have it."

Marina took it, clasped it tight in her fist and kissed her fist. "You're breaking hearts all over Caesarea," she said, eyes sparkling with tears. "That was Theron with a broken heart."

She nodded at Cornelius, who stood patiently, eyes averted, at the door. "So go, already. Be careful." She embraced Orion, stood him back to look at him, then pushed him to the door. And he was gone.

Theron, who was standing behind the workroom curtain, realized he was holding the papers. He shambled to the worktable, dropping them in a mortar bucket on the way.

18

Dawn had stolen in under a sky that hinted rain. The clouds would clear soon. Jorah was learning that coastal mornings were sometimes like this.

Another merchant vessel had arrived at the harbor entrance. She watched the sailors, tiny from where she sat, climb the rope grid and haul up the sail. They lashed the sail to the long wooden beam they straddled. It must be a great height, looking down from the top of the mast. Worse to see moving water at the bottom. Jorah wondered if they were ever terrified to look down.

The vessel cast its anchor and waited for a long time until a longboat rowed through the harbor and met it outside the huge, carved stone archway. Jorah would love to be on a boat that passed under there, to look up and see the stone that curved as gracefully as the bend of a daisy, all the way to the carved stone pillars on either side of the entrance.

The merchant vessel was in the shape of a great wooden smile. With the square sail rolled up, the ship looked curiously empty, as though the smile had lost the rest of its face. The triangular piece of sail at the very top looked like a hat from here, until the sailors rolled it away. Now it was just a plain smile, sectioned by the mast and crossed by the beam. It looked like a floating Roman cross, hideous with the grin.

Jorah settled her chin on her knees. Her arms were tight about her legs; she'd been in this position so long someone could pick her up and she'd stay this way. The sunburn on her cheeks and her nose and forehead stung with ocean salt spray. She had spent the entire day here yesterday after Joab returned. She went home to take care of Cousin Thomas and came back before dawn. She poked up the sleeve of her tunic; her forearm and hand were shades darker than the rest of her arm, tawny pink, glistening with sea mist.

She watched men from the vessel fling lines to the men in the longboat.

"I miss you," she murmured. "I've missed you for a very long time."

Now and then she went back in her fancy to the time when everything was perfect. Not that she would have thought it perfect then.

She and Devorah always argued fiercely. They got along much better after Devorah left for Bethany. Still, she remembered when she and Devorah and Mother would weed the terrace. She recalled one time when Mother was in a particularly light mood, and kept tossing her pulled weeds at Devorah and Jorah, pretending that she didn't, acting as though the girls did it themselves. How Devorah and Jorah had laughed. She wondered if Devorah remembered.

She remembered the certain place each sat around the kitchen table. Father and the boys ate first, then she and Mother and Devorah. Jorah remembered the backs of the boys. Father sat in a chair on the end, Jesus was first on the bench next to him. James's place was next to Jesus, then Joses and Simon, with Judas in the chair on the end. Mother always liked the table against the wall, underneath the window. They only pulled it out when company came. She could see late sunlight coming in, burnishing the heads of her brothers. She could see her brothers eat, see them pass the bread basket.

She remembered the day Simon rushed in to tell that Father had fallen at the well. Jorah was supposed to be fetching the water, but she was sick that day. Father had taken the jar, winking at her and telling her he'd decided to take up women's work. He had paused at her bed and felt her forehead, worry furrowing his own. Then he gave her a smile and quick caress and was gone. Gone.

Jesus's place moved to the chair on the end.

She remembered the day Jesus did not come back. She remembered seeing his place at the table empty. She didn't know, then, it would be empty ever after.

James's place moved to the chair on the end.

"I wonder if you missed me," she whispered.

She had a dance she did when she was little that made Jesus laugh. She'd twirl and give a hop, twirl and give a hop, and when she saw it delighted her oldest brother she'd do it time and again until the others groaned for her to stop. Jesus would still give her that crinkly smile, as if to make up for the others.

A pebble sailed just over her head and dropped on the head covering she'd abandoned to the sand. She stared at the pebble, then looked over her shoulder. Joab stood a short distance behind her.

"I didn't want to startle you," he called over the breeze.

"How did you know I was here?"

"I decided you weren't at the palace. I'm glad you didn't make me go there."

He came and dropped beside her. Then he sat up straight and looked under his hand at the vessel under tow, gliding for the harbor entrance. "That mast is going to hit the arch."

"No, it won't."

"Yes, it will, look—oh. No, it won't."

The men in the longboat pulled at the oars. The merchant vessel glided slowly under the archway, the mast clearing it by only a few feet.

"I watched one go in with a mast even taller than that one. Seemed like it would shear off, but it made it through."

"What happens when the mast is too tall?" Joab asked.

"They sit at anchor outside the harbor." She pointed at the northwest corner of the harbor. "The cargo gets ferried in the longboats. One left a little while ago." She glanced at Joab, noticing the bruises on his face. Purple spread from the sides of his nose to under his eyes.

"Have you been here long?" he asked, as she studied his nose, and his eyes, and his purple lips.

"Since before dawn. I couldn't sleep."

"Me either."

"What was it like, spending a night in jail?" she asked.

"Stinky."

"I'm glad you're out."

"Me too."

She looked at him a moment longer, then put her attention on the sea. "Rivkah knows."

"Marina told me."

"And now Theron and Marina know everything. I suppose there

is no more 'us.' No more pretending." She smiled a smile that felt older.

"I wish I had been there with you," he said, his face and voice dark. "It wasn't right that you had to tell her on your own."

"Why is that?"

"I—" He paused. "I don't know. It just wasn't right. I feel . . ."

"Responsible? For Nathanael's death? Didn't we talk about this? Just before Prometheus did that?" She nodded at his nose. "Tell me you don't feel responsible, Joab. You did what you could to prevent it."

Joab did not answer. After looking on the water for a while, he said, "Here we are again, same place. Talking about things that are—" He broke off and said suddenly, "You know, someday all I want to do is talk about—"

"Mortar."

"Yes. Or where I can get a decent pair of sandals."

"How about Theron's sniff? You ever notice that? I always want to blow my nose when I hear it."

"I always want to tell him to blow his own." After a time his smile faded. "At least your part is over. I still have to tell her Nathanael's last words."

"You want me to go with you?"

"No." Then, "Did you ever hear that story?"

Jorah picked up a handful of the shore and sifted the wet shells and gravel in her hands. "You said something about an adulteress and stones."

"That's the one."

"Bits of it. They always kept me from what he said or did." Her hands stilled at their sifting. "Tell me." She raised her eyes to his. The ache in her heart made it hard to keep the pleading from her voice. "Tell me everything you know that he said or did. I don't care how outlandish it sounds."

"Outlandish. Well, this was that—if you call putting the Torah on end and spinning it 'outlandish.'"

"That isn't funny."

"Of course not."

She gazed at her fistfuls of the shore. "Is this one of the stories of blasphemy? If it is, I don't want to hear it. Tell me how he walked on water. I like that one. I like the one about the demon man from Gerasene." She clenched her fists, making the shells and gravel squeak. "I like the healings. He did those things, Joab. My brother—" She stopped, because the pain came so sharply.

"Yes, he did those things," Joab said, looking out across the sea. "He did things and he said things I am having a frightful time ignoring."

She blinked rapidly. "Why don't you do what I do? Shut out the bad and try to think only on the good."

"It's the bad that's got my attention."

She watched a seagull feather tumble past, scurrying with the wind. Presently, in a very small voice, she asked, "How bad was this?"

"He defied Torah. She was an adulteress, she had stones coming to her. It was justice. I looked it up to be sure, it's in the book of Leviticus. See, some men had dragged her to him. And I don't think they really cared about the woman, they were just using her. Using her to taunt him because they knew . . . somehow they knew he might give a different answer from Leviticus. They wanted it so they could use it against him. And sure enough . . . he gave a different answer. 'He who is without sin among you, let him be the first to throw a stone at her.'"

Jorah considered the words. This was not what she expected, she'd heard worse behind the workroom curtain flap. She had heard he said, and this had to go down as the worst, "Before Abraham was born, I am." She had been wincing in anticipation of Joab's words, and now felt only relief. "What's so bad about that? It sounds like mercy to me."

"Exactly!" Joab snapped. "These words, of which *I* am courier, made every one of those men drop their stones. They shouldn't have done it. I wonder if they regretted it."

"Oh, really?" Jorah retorted. "You would have dropped your own stone if you were there. What makes you so different?" When Joab tried to speak she cut in with, "Why does this eat at you so? This was the last thing we talked about right here."

"Yes," Joab said bitterly, "and I'm no closer to figuring it out."

"What is so hard? It was mercy."

"Yes! It was mercy and it was defiance! Those men should have told him he defied *Law*. Instead, every one of them dropped his rock. That's what I heard—every one. The oldest ones first, and they should have known better. The Law is for deterrence from wicked ways, Jorah. She had stones coming to her." He sagged a little, as if some of the heat had gone out of him. "But he said no."

Jorah lifted her chin and tossed her hair back. "I think those are the best words he ever said."

"They were defiance."

"I'll treasure them," she snapped.

Joab didn't seem to hear. His gaze was on the water. And to Jorah's complete surprise, his lips trembled very slightly. Some strange emotion played all over his face—anger mostly. But were those tears in his eyes? He was unaware of her gaze, unaware as he talked to the sea. He had forgotten her, in fact, just as he had before.

"He said no, and they did something quite monumental by dropping those stones: they agreed with him. How could they do such a thing? That is what—" his fists balled, and the color deepened on his cheeks—"angers me so. I don't know *why* they did it. They were wiser than I am. Older than I am, more learned in the Torah. Do you know how long it took me to find the stones passage? They could probably quote it like the Ten Commandments."

He did not speak for a while, deep in his brooding glower. He took up again as morosely as before. "So what am I supposed to do? What am I supposed to do with his words, and how they responded? It's as if he said to them, 'This is what the Torah says, but I'm telling you something different.' And they agreed by dropping the stones." He dug at his eyes with the heel of his hand and shook his head. "That's terrifying, absolutely terrifying, because it was blasphemy or it wasn't, and I wish to God I didn't have to decide. Wish the words had been anything but those. I want to just tell her and run. Leave her to them. That's all I'm supposed to do anyway, right?"

An unexpected thought came to her, then, as she watched him watch the sea, that perhaps Joab was the only one to carry those words. Maybe he was meant to. She liked that thought. Another thought came after, that this was just the sort of man she wouldn't mind spending a lifetime with because he ignored her: clean forgot she was there for the pondering of things so deeply stirring that tears came from it. And *that* thought made her own tears come, because she hadn't expected to feel this way again.

Nathanael did that. Ignored her for the pondering of God things. No one was supposed to make her happy again, happy over being completely ignored. Maybe that was her own personal fate, because it had been happening all her life. For the first time she realized she didn't want it any other way.

"He said dizzying things," Joab murmured in grim wonder. "I feel as though I am at a great height when I hear them."

A tear tingled down the sunburn. "Oh, be quiet. I don't like talking with you, Joab."

Startled, he blinked and looked at her. "I'm sorry. I'll go if you want."

"Don't you dare." Jorah sniffed and wiped the grit off her hands with her tunic. She reached for her wadded head covering and shook it out to dab her face. "My nose is swelling, in case you're interested. You may want to kiss me."

His laughter was startling. She kept dabbing to hide her smile.

"I hear you raised a stink for my release," Joab finally said. "A 'mighty' stink. That's what Theron said."

Jorah shrugged and said loftily, "I'd have twice as much work to do, putting in that walkway."

"Why aren't you wearing your head covering?"

"Are you going to stone me for it?" When he laughed again, she eased back on her arms and nodded toward the harbor. "Look at that one. That one won't make it through."

Joab followed her glance and cocked his head. "I don't know. I'd bet a kiss on it."

"Oh, really. A kiss if it makes it or if it doesn't?"

"Either way."

This time Jorah laughed, and Joab grinned that small self-satisfied grin she was getting used to. It didn't last long, though. It was as if he would not allow himself to stray long from what was his burdened responsibility.

"'My kingdom is not of this world,'" Jorah offered, despite herself. "That's the one thing he said that stays with me. I heard it from my brother-in-law, Matthias. He said it to Pilate. 'My kingdom is not of this world.'" She glanced at Joab. "I suppose you'll be going to Jerusalem."

Surprise arrested him, made him gaze at her. As he searched her eyes, it occurred to her that another's eyes did not have to be golden to catch her attention. His were a deep brown, slightly turned down at the edges.

"How did you know—Jerusalem has been on my mind, but vaguely. Not even a solid thought." His gaze became curious.

"That's where they all go for answers about Jesus. I wonder if James and Jude found theirs. I wonder if any of them has."

"I'm curious about his followers, if they dispersed or stayed together. If they are together, who is their leader? What is their agenda? Most important of all . . . what conclusions did they come to about Jesus and his relation to the Torah? Is there a new kind of—" He pressed his lips, as if he couldn't quite say it.

"Judaism." Yes, saying it made her stomach dip. "I think, now, that I would like to know those things too."

Joab scooped up sand and let it drain through his fist. "What will Theron do without us . . . ?"

"We must finish the ribbon mosaic first."

"Yes."

"We can't leave him to that."

"No." He looked up from the sand. She could feel his eyes on her face, but didn't want to look yet, not with what she had just admitted. She was going to Jerusalem? For her, it was as close to proclaiming belief in her brother as she could get. But not yet. Not yet.

"How long do you think it will take us to—what's the matter?" Joab asked.

"I'm not sure," Jorah whispered. Her skin prickled all over, not from the breeze. "I have to think."

Nathanael's words. "Joab, what exactly were Nathanael's last words?"

He shrugged. "What I told you. About the stones and the accusers—"

"No, no, no. Exactly what he said."

His face softened in remembrance. "He said, 'Tell her, no stones. Go for me. Tell her what Jesus said.'"

"Tell her. Go for me . . ." Jorah whispered. It couldn't mean . . . It did mean.

She seized his arm. "Oh, Joab. He forgave her."

"Well . . . of course he did. I think that was the whole point."

"No—you don't understand. He *forgave* her. Not for the—But for the—" It was too much. She scrambled to her feet, hardly knowing where she walked.

No, no . . . how could he forgive her for that? How could . . . ? Yet his mother was his last thought on earth. His last wish was for her to know he forgave.

"Why are you crying?" Joab was at her side, following her weaving walk.

She lifted her arms and let them fall. "There he goes again, leaving me for God things. No, I wasn't his last thought on earth. It was for her. For the one who gave him scars. You'll be the same way, with my luck. Your last thought as you're drifting out of this earth will be all God and mercy."

With any luck at all, with all the fortune and blessing she could hope to find, that's exactly how it would go.

He caught her and held her, and it was pure relief to let go and rest against him.

She let herself be held, until she was holding too. "Don't stop where you're going, Joab. Don't you stop."

Maybe he didn't know exactly what she was talking about, but he whispered into her hair, "I won't."

❧

He was late for his appointment with the marketplace Jew, but Janus Bifrons made his way slowly up the Cardo Maximus. He didn't feel like talking of gods today. What he had witnessed today was enough to make Janus wish his mother had never dedicated him at all. Such an awful thing, seeing that child torn from his mother.

The shrew Rhodinia—and the gods stew him in the Styx if he ever gave an offering for her again—had rushed past him in the corridor, dragging the Jewish laundress to Prometheus. The child trotted trustfully behind, grasping his mother's tunic. Janus had paused to peek in at the triclinium, where Prometheus lounged at breakfast and considered the child before him.

The little boy gazed about the room in interest, oblivious to the shrieking woman. He blinked at the black-and-white mosaic on which he stood, cocked his head to look at it differently. He covered up one mosaic square with a toe, then moved his toe to peek at it again. He did this several times while the shrew carried on. Janus had watched the child, foreboding welling within, because Prometheus was not Orion.

Prometheus reclined on a couch, poking at a bowl filled with Dothan figs. He glanced at the child only once, when Rhodinia yanked him forward by the neck of his tunic. The child twisted, trying to see his mosaic piece. When he could see it no more, his soft gaze floated about until it rested on something Janus could not see. Something on the table at which Prometheus reclined. While words rose and fell about him, the child's gaze stayed on the certain object. He cocked his head, looking at it.

When Rhodinia marched in triumph from the room, with the child shoved in front of her and the Jewish mother wailing behind her, Janus observed the expression on the child's face. Vacant, yet unhappy. He knew something was wrong. He didn't know what. The mother screamed all the way down the corridor, and Prometheus Longinus popped a fig into his mouth and consulted his beeswax tablet.

Janus shook down his bracelets and stepped around a pile of donkey dung. Doing so, he banged into a man pushing a two-wheel cart and earned himself what was surely an Aramaic curse. Janus instantly jabbed the air with two fingers like snake fangs and muttered a cant to ward it off. The man pulled back, looking Janus up and down, then shook his head and wheeled the cart off.

Before he knew it he was in the marketplace and sitting on the overturned buckets with the Jew.

"I brought what you wanted," said the Jew, and produced a curled portion of papyrus cut from a scroll. The freshly printed Greek words could only be the Deuteronomy words that had recently intrigued Janus. He read and saw it was so. *For what great nation is there that has a god so near to it as is the Lord our God whenever we call on him?*

Janus nodded. "Yes. Fascinating."

"You said we would speak of Stoicism today," said the Jew.

"So I did. Yes. Stoicism. Official Roman policy. Seneca its current staunch proponent." *Did the little boy know by now? Did he understand it was forever?* "Stoics say you do not have a choice in what you've been given, only in how it is played out. You do your best with what you have."

The Jew considered it carefully. "To do one's best is always the wisest course. I think on some of Solomon's writings, how he said, 'Whatever your hand finds to do, do it with all your might.' This is similar, although it is . . ." and off he went in a round of words that Janus did not hear.

Stoicism was the most sensible belief system Rome had. The

gods hand you your fate. You do your best with what you've been given. *What if what you have been given is unholy unfair?*

What if you're a little boy? What then? The little Jewish boy, torn from his mother. That unsure, unhappy look. The anguish of the mother. They didn't have a choice; Prometheus was the stoic god who had dealt them their fate.

Janus had never once considered any fault line in Stoicism. Not until he saw the child, and saw the god mete out a fate that was never destined to be.

He grew aware of the Jew's face, leaning pointedly into his own. When he had his attention, the Jew drew back. "What troubles you, Gentile?"

"This and that and sundry others," Janus answered with a sigh. He watched a merchant open her stall. She layered lengths of fabric on a plank. "Tell me, my friend: when an ill wind rises, more foul than the last, most foul you've known, and it blows throughout the palace visiting every crevice and cranny, what is an aging priest to do? I am of the order of the *Fetiales*. Mine is a sacred trust. It is a religious and a diplomatic mission. What happens when I am suddenly indifferent?"

The eyebrows of the Jew came up. "Indifferent? Our conversations have gone that well?"

"Yes. I'm your first proselyte."

The Jew would know it for a jest, and so he did. He sat back in amusement and parried with his own jest. "We get a half-shekel for every proselyte we bring in. You just paid my temple tax."

"A half-shekel? I am a pagan priest, surely I am worth more." The Jew began that chuckle of his, and it encouraged Janus. "What of the queen across the Tiber? How much did her conversion fetch? Which lucky fellow brought her in?"

Whenever the marketplace Jew laughed, he took his time to do it. Janus enjoyed the sound; it was sorely needed in this wretched day. When at last the laughter subsided, the Jew considered him thoughtfully.

"I suspect we will not talk of our gods."

Janus thought of the stonemason, and of the tree of the prostitute. He thought of the palace leftovers, a program that would surely come to an end. And the little boy never did leave his thoughts.

"A good man has fallen. For deeds of compassion, he flees for his life. And I wonder, Jew, where in all of this is the morality of Rome? He broke law . . . but it was for mercy. He disobeyed a command because he knew it was wrong. Do you know what kind of rotten cistern we pry open with that kind of thinking? They don't want us to think like that. They want to keep the cistern closed." He frowned. "I should stick to my votives and auguries. A perfectly performed ritual is all that matters."

He waited for the Jew to respond, but that wasn't his style. He knew Janus had more to say, and would not comment until all was out.

Janus gave him a rueful look, then sighed. "Well, it isn't right. Is that what you want me to say? You of the solitary god? It isn't right. He broke law for mercy. What good it does for me to come to this conclusion I cannot imagine. It changes nothing. I only know the palace is the poorer for the absence of a good man."

"Things are not so different on my side."

"Prometheus is able enough, but cares only for expediency. He lacks Orion's—what did you say?"

"Things are not so different on my side."

Whatever Janus expected, it wasn't that. "How so?"

But the Jew drew himself up and gave Janus a haughty eye. "You think I will discuss with a Gentile what I have not yet discussed with my God?"

Janus smiled, and there it was again. That certain pang that made him feel a little left out. This time it didn't grate him as it had done before. "I wouldn't dream of it. Go and consult with your god. Tell him I said hello."

The Jew's eyes twinkled. Then he changed the mood and brightly said, "So. Back to that of which we are in common trade: religion. Tell me of your beliefs in Stoicism."

"I don't believe anymore."

That belief he had left on the palace floor when Rhodinia took the little boy away.

19

PILATE AND PROMETHEUS trotted down the stone steps, Prometheus pressing notes in the wax as he went. Twice Pilate had to wait for him to catch up; he had to stop and hold the tablet against his knee to press the stylus better. He must have left the tablet open and so hardened the wax, a careless and inefficient thing to do. They had just turned the corner for the final flight of steps when Prometheus had to stop again.

Pilate hated to hear sighs, but could not stifle his own. "I hope you will learn to use that thing more efficiently."

"Yes, Excellency."

"Next?"

"Ah . . . the family of the magistrate who died last week—they wish to know if they can use the Praetorium Palace chariot for the funeral procession."

"And what did you tell them?"

Prometheus's eyes snapped from his tablet to Pilate. "I—"

"That would never have made it to Orion's tablet. Take responsibility and make decisions, Longinus. Do not waste my time."

"Yes, Excellency."

"Next?"

"That's all, sir."

Pilate tugged down the sides of his toga. "I am going to Jerusalem this morning. Ready my escort and pack my things. Send a dispatch ahead to prepare the palace staff there. Clear my schedule for four days."

Prometheus raised a surprised face from his tablet. He dropped the stylus and scrambled for it. "You're going to Jerusalem, sir?"

He kept the sigh in check this time. "Why do I always repeat myself to you, Longinus? Is it because you cannot hear, or because you are questioning me? Yes, I am going to Jerusalem. I've gotten back a few reports, and I hear his followers are still meeting. My sources say they share meals together, which is a particularly Essene trait. Possibly a new cult is on the rise."

"Perhaps that is to be expected, with a recent martyr," Prometheus offered. "I wouldn't worry about it, Excellency. You certainly did the right thing. He was a threat to Roman sovereignty. . . ." His voice died away when he saw Pilate's hard gray stare.

"He was no threat. He was never a threat. He was only a religious fanatic. And if you try again to assure me of what I have or have not done, if you give your opinion without my request for it, the auxiliaries will have a new mess cook."

"Yes, Your Excellency."

"Have you learned nothing from Orion?"

"I—"

"He conducted himself more like a Roman officer than I have

seen from you yet." Pilate trotted down the rest of the steps, saying over his shoulder, "Send the swiftest rider if the Primipilaris arrives."

"Yes, Your Excellency," Prometheus called after.

It would take the man another half hour just to press in the last sentence. Gods, how he missed Orion. Gone two, three days? He would have to be patient. It would take time for a new secretary to learn his ways. He hoped Prometheus was a fast study. He didn't think so.

Pilate went to the archival room himself because it would take Prometheus ten minutes to write his request down and another ten to execute it. He wanted some reading material on his way to Jerusalem.

The material on Jesus of Nazareth was scanty for the three years he traveled about Judea and Galilee. Infiltrators had been sent from the beginning, when he began to draw crowds. They listened for key words that would alert them to possible seditious brewings. Words such as *weapons, arsenals, tactics,* any mention of names from the Hasmonean dynasties, and especially the Maccabees. The infiltrators were experts, and from the beginning saw no threat in the Galilean. The fact that he was Galilean gave the most interest, since Galileans were commonly known as troublemakers.

The word *kingdom* came up a few times, and that had alerted the spies. But he had always used the term in some esoteric way. Pilate got the last earful. *My kingdom is not of this world.* His own benediction, lucky for Pilate. It inspired him.

The flogging should have been enough. They wanted blood, Pilate gave them blood. It was a last-minute attempt to try and save his life, surely he must have known that. Surely he saw it for the true mercy it was. Pilate had watched for satisfaction when they saw the blood, but the Jews wanted more, and Tiberius said to keep the peace. Pilate wasn't being humorous when he put "King of the

Jews" over his head. He was defending his verdict. Covering his tracks. If blasphemy was a Jewish offense, declaring oneself king was a Roman one. If Pilate had to crucify him to keep peace with the hotheads, he had at least the man's claim to kingship to make it legal.

What were his followers up to? Had they decided his kingdom was indeed of this world? They were taking meals together, his sources found that noteworthy. What else were they doing?

He was no threat. He was never a threat.

The only reason Pilate was going to Jerusalem was for the benediction words: *My kingdom is not of this world.* Pilate would never say aloud what he had felt at the eerie moment those words were spoken. He'd never admit the fear—no, the force of those words. Never admit that at that instant he had known there was, indeed, a threat in the man.

꼭

Muster to ships brought seamen from everywhere, staggering in from wherever they'd dropped at inns, brothels, and gaming rooms. It was a busy time on the quay, a time Orion usually enjoyed because he loved the sailing industry. Loved everything about it, had ever since he was a boy.

Muster to ships was a time of on-loading and off-loading, of seamen giving orders and seamen obeying orders, of clamor and commotion and hustle and hurry, all with a backdrop of pleasant sounds: ship's bells and seagulls and loud guffaws and ornery shouts and bare feet trampling up and down gangplanks and on decks. Many shouts from the officer seamen were in Latin, because most of the ships were from Rome and their rigging came with Latin labels. Many of the sailors, however, were not from Rome. From where Orion and Cornelius waited, against a smokehouse close to a dock,

Orion watched in amusement as a few sailors puzzled through the orders. Some figured "check the *rudentis*" meant check the brails, and "once over the *pedis*" meant once over the sheets, and they were right. Orion watched as two Germanic-looking seamen received an order to haul in the *pons*. Their puzzled looks earned a contemptuous glare from the captain, who gave a jerk of his head to the gangplank.

When Orion was small, his father had worked at a grain warehouse in Ostia. When on break from his duties, he and Orion would take packets of hot peas purchased from street merchants and an amphora of Father's favorite fish sauce and go to the river mouth to watch the boats. The merchant ships could not travel upstream; they had to anchor at sea and unload to smaller vessels. The *naves codicariae* were the river barges that transported goods up the Tiber from Ostia to Rome.

Sometimes Orion saw wild animals bound for the circus. One day a merchant vessel got too close and grounded in the dangerous silty mouth of the Tiber. One of the barges pulled up close, and Orion watched as an elephant was transferred by tackle to the barge. The mighty three-masted vessel was grounded for days in the Tiber mouth, while the same elephant barge shuttled back and forth between Ostia and Rome at least a dozen times. Orion suspected his father would not miss the chance to present the moral, and he had not.

He smiled fondly now, remembering his father's charge: *You see the three-master? Not so powerful now. Consider the* nava codicaria, *my boy.*

"What are you thinking of, Orion Galerinius?" Cornelius asked at his side.

"Naves codicariae." And a beloved father.

To my beloved father, from your Orion. Thank you for being the father you were. Thank you for being the man you were. I was so fortunate, so very fortunate. . . .

"You won't find any river barges around here," Cornelius said. "See the two-master on the—soldiers, head low."

Orion ducked his head right as soldiers passed on his left.

Cornelius exchanged greetings with them. When they passed, he murmured, "You have a lot of friends, Orion Galerinius. They recognized you instantly. Acted like they never saw you."

Astonished, Orion nearly turned around. He didn't know anyone in the garrison except for the Praetorian guards. "Who were they?"

"Tullus, Horatio, and Demas."

"Never heard of them."

To this Cornelius only chuckled.

They waited until Cornelius received a prearranged signal from the captain of the two-master. With the soldier casting sharp but furtive looks about the dock, he made Orion walk ahead of him up the gangplank.

He wasn't wearing his dirty toga anymore; that was rolled up and stuffed into one of his sacks. Cornelius had made him buy a tunic in the marketplace on the way to the harbor. His sandals were stuffed in the bag too, though he wasn't sure that was such a good idea. He slipped two or three times on the gangplank, slick with dirty wash water slopped down from the deck of the ship. His feet alone could implicate him to any soldier on the lookout—they were as white as temple marble from years of confinement in the palace. The only sun they got was at the very occasional chariot races he attended.

He found himself smirking; Prometheus was a huge fan of the races. He was good friends with Laertes, the most popular charioteer in Caesarea. Prometheus was about to find out that one of his chief duties was to miss all the exciting events because he had to dash about seeing to the endless details that sustained them.

This was a single-cargo ship, and Cornelius got him into the hold immediately, out of sight and stashed away with bags of grain. The captain attended them briefly, informing them they were due to put out in a few hours after they got the clearance from a dock warehouse to load a shipment of barley from Ziklag.

Orion asked him where the ship was bound.

"We put in first to Alexandria, then sail for Rome."

He felt the blood drop from his face, and slid a look at Cornelius. The soldier was perfectly impassive. The captain nodded to them both and left.

"Rome?" Orion demanded. "How about a ship anywhere but?"

"Do you think Pilate sent a dispatch of your fall to Rome? You think he's going to admit his chief secretary was lost to the Jews? Not anytime soon. You've humiliated him. He'll wait as long as he dares to report the change in personnel. My guess is you'll be perfectly safe in Rome for at least a few weeks. I wouldn't risk any longer than that."

Orion gazed at Cornelius, allowing the shock to abate and the implications to come. "I could see my father."

Cornelius smiled. "I thought you could do that." He looked about the hold, cramped with grain bags and casks of watered wine for the crew. He had made Orion purchase food in the marketplace to cook for himself in the galley during the journey. Orion wouldn't have thought of that.

Other passengers were settling in or had been on board previously and were waiting to sail. Near the grain hold was a cramped area rigged with hammocks and a few small tents. People slept in the hammocks or ate or talked or stared back at Cornelius and Orion. He would have to get used to the smell, and fast. Greasy cooking odors, stale sweat, and the privy—a bucket in the corner, lashed to the hold with metal clasps. And an old smell of seasickness, as though it was soaked into the grain of the hull.

"Cozy," Orion murmured with a half smile at Cornelius.

"It's that." The soldier returned the grin. Then he reached out, and the men gripped hands. "Hail and farewell, Orion Galerinius Honoratus."

"Hail and farewell." Any attempt to thank the young soldier would be grossly inadequate. "Cornelius . . ."

"The honor was mine. I hope you land well. Send word when you can."

"I could never use my name in correspondence with you. How shall I sign myself?"

Cornelius thought on it, and grinned. "Sign yourself Judah the Maccabee."

Orion laughed out loud. "Orion Galerinius Honoratus might be safer."

"No, I like it. Fair winds, Judah."

Not for the first time he wished he had taken the time to get to know this soldier better. He would have liked to share a mug with him at the soldiers' drinking house. "May the favor of . . . Theron's god be upon you."

Cornelius touched his knuckles to his forehead, and was gone.

Raman waited around the corner of the smokehouse to be certain. Soon enough the big Roman soldier came down the gangplank of the two-master, this time alone; he paused on the dock, bending as if to adjust a strap on his hobnail. The foreman watched his eyes closely. Yes, the man was looking everywhere, scanning for Roman soldiers, wondering if he was being watched. The eyes did not seem to look for civilian spies.

❧

There is no mistaking the sound of hobnail boots in cadence. He had heard enough military drills to know it.

Orion had secured an unused hammock and rolled into it, sacks and all, the moment Cornelius departed. He was asleep instantly, and at the heavy footfalls above him on deck, instantly awake. Awake, but not quite coherent. How long had he slept? He only knew the sound above was a dreadful sound, for that is what filled him; and dread or just plain stupidity immobilized him. Later, he knew it would have done no good to hide. They would have lanced the grain sacks to find him.

Prometheus led the group of six Praetorian guards himself. He chose the Praetorians because they lent more elegance and direness to the situation than garrison soldiers. Later, Orion learned it would have been more if Pilate had not taken his escort to Jerusalem. So many to incarcerate one short man.

They dragged him from the hammock and put him in iron bonds and led him from the ship in the middle of the guard. He was still stupid from lack of any real sleep in the past several days, and gazed in confusion at faces staring at him. Later, he realized he was looking for faces he knew. Looking for familiarity as they marched him to the Praetorium Palace. He saw none he recognized, save one. That of the granary foreman whose name the bleariness could not produce.

It was the smallest cell they put him in, the three-sided cell, last one on the left. It hadn't been cleaned from its latest occupant, Orion knew the instant they pushed him in and clanked the door shut. The iron padlock slid into place, and he heard hobnails fade down the corridor.

Incarcerated in the Praetorium Palace, and not in a decent toga.

They'd relieved him of his two sacks. Orion stood for a while, swaying with fatigue, fingering the cloth belt securing the waist of this provincial tunic. It was a coarse weave and it itched everywhere, felt about as comfortable as the backing of a carpet. Orion considered the rolled-up pallet for a long moment before he conceived of its function. Then he took it and spread it out—it went up part of the wall.

The place wasn't fit for prisoners; he'd have someone check into it in the morning. He'd put Galen on it. Good servant, Galen, knew how to take an order, spoke perfect Greek, little bitty accent. Knew how to get things around the province, the coal Pilate liked. Best oranges. He'd talk to Pilate about making him a steward. Put it in his tablet, he'd forget if he didn't. . . .

He curled onto the pallet, back against the long-sided wall. Sconces for the walkway, they'd be in soon. Orion would measure them himself, he didn't trust this to the workers. He'd measure meticulously. Meticulously.

20

"Yes, okay, I am coming," Theron bellowed from the workroom at all the pounding. He came through the curtain and glared about for Marina. Then he remembered that she'd said something about a woman and a baby a couple doors down. Well, she should have heard this racket and come down to send the annoyance packing. Nobody bothered him this time of day, not anyone he knew.

He opened the door and did not know the boy soldier there. At least, he wore the rig of the Roman soldier, but his features were all Judean. He had to be younger than Joab.

"You are Theron?" he squeaked in an immature voice.

"Yes, and you are bothering him."

He had been in the middle of pinching strips of lead that would line a tesserae ribbon. A nasty job, though if tortured he would admit that even the nasty jobs of mosaic—maybe especially the nasty jobs—brought immense satisfaction. He could complain himself blue to Marina about lead pinching, and show her his injured fingertips, but he had long ceased to get sympathy out of her.

"Drillmaster Cornelius sends word: He has changed his mind about the pattern for his villa and would like you to bring a design from Ostia."

Theron held the door and squinted at the boy for a long moment. "Not good enough for him, eh?"

The boy shrugged. "Do you have a return word?"

"Yes. Ah . . . tell him he's a barbarian for changing the pattern. Tell him I'll be there in an hour." The boy nodded and turned to go, but Theron called him back. "Where does your drillmaster want to meet? At his villa or . . ."

"He is in the drillmaster office at the barracks; he'll be there until sundown. You can bring the design there."

"Yes, okay. Tell him he doesn't pay me enough for this." Theron shut the door before the boy could respond.

He rolled his lower lip in a pinch. Something was terribly wrong. Ostia had to mean Orion. Change in pattern, maybe that meant something changed between yesterday and today. Orion was supposed to be long gone from Caesarea. He was supposed to have left yesterday morning.

Theron chose two pattern boards, one of which was indeed from Ostia, though Cornelius might not know that. It was a classic black-and-white pebble mosaic of a ship going out to sea from the Ostia port. The other was a pattern from the same region, Naples. He had them on his shoulder and was nearly to the commonyard gate when someone stopped him.

"Theron!" It was Marina. And by her tone it was not the first time she had called him. She caught up with him, glancing at the pattern boards on his shoulder. "Where are you going?"

"Someone changed their mind about a design."

"You're going right now?" she said, surprised. She didn't wait for him to answer, but lifted a plate she'd been carrying and pulled back the towel to show what was underneath. "Look, Theron. So many people brought Mary and Laban food that she's giving it out. Sesame pastries." She offered the plate to him.

"I'm not hungry," he said absently.

Her smile fell. "Not hungry?" she snapped. "What's wrong?" She looked with suspicion at the pattern boards.

"Nothing. I have to check out something at the palace. When Joab returns don't let him work with the lead strips; tell him I'll finish it. But if Jorah comes, she can do it."

"Is there anything wrong?"

"No, nothing wrong." Then he looked into the eyes of his wife of twenty-five years. "Except maybe you should pray for Orion." He turned and went out the commonyard gate, latching it behind him.

Cornelius signed the young man and sent him off with Demas to find a bunk. Another for the auxiliaries, another sent by Shamash-Nadwar. Shamash-Nadwar had his eye on Roman citizenship and would likely get it with all the new recruits he sent his way. He would have to make mention of it to Undersecretary Prom—no. To Undersecretary Remus.

He pulled over the manual he had set aside to sign the recruit. He did not often have time to peruse old battle strategies, but had to allow the drillmaster-in-training time with the men. Ranks would officially change at the end of the month. Optio Cornelius. He couldn't deny he had wanted this. He just didn't want it this way.

He opened the leather scrip and found his place again. He'd been reading on the battle strategy of the Parthians during Crassus's defeat. Fascinating, how the bowmen were trained in their rapid-fire shot, and that from horseback. Pivoting on their mounts, firing volley after volley, opening the way for the ensuing charge of the cataphracts with their spears. How Crassus had underestimated his enemy. Roman pride and barbarian brilliance. A lousy tactician was Crassus. The eagles of seven—seven!—Roman legions ended up in Parthian hands. The infamy. Augustus Caesar had managed to soft-speak them back to Rome through treaty. Cornelius could only imagine the shame Crassus would have endured, had he not been killed at Carrhae. He would have fallen on his own sword if—

He shoved aside the manual and rose from the table. He wished he were with his men; the comfort of routine would take his mind off the fate of Orion Galerinius. Muster, calisthenics, weapons training, breakfast. Technique, calisthenics, foot drills, midmeal. Working parties, weapons, drills, evening meal. Postings and liberties, troops fall in. This had been every day of his life for years. He wanted to be in the Great Stadium, railing the idlers and praising the promising. He wanted to see if Justus the mouthy one was giving any trouble to Alexander, see how Alexander was handling it.

"You sure do a lotta pacing. That's all I see you do."

The short fat mosaicist stood in the doorway, dark with backlit sunlight. He had his arm over two boards on his shoulder.

Cornelius motioned him in. He glanced out the doorway, but nobody would be in the barracks at this time of day, not unless they were looking for a reprimand.

"I hear the pattern has changed," Theron said.

"It has."

Cornelius gestured at a stool in front of the table, the place new recruits sat while being sworn into the Roman auxiliary army. He sat behind his desk and watched as Theron lowered the boards to the ground, then took one of the boards and pushed aside the strategy manual to clear a space. He laid the pattern board on the desk and pulled up the stool.

"There. A pattern from Ostia." Theron glanced behind him, and lowered his voice. "Something has gone wrong."

Cornelius ran his fingers over the pebbled mosaic. It was the worst part of his job. Here one of his men would sit if he had bad news to tell him. A mother died, a father. He liked this interesting little man, and it troubled him deeply to give him news such as this.

"Orion has been taken." After everything, after all the painstaking details. How had it happened? Did one of the men sell him out? The thought made him nearly as heartsick as Orion's fate. Of course, the newer recruits would not know Orion. It had to be a new recruit, currying favor with the new chief secretary.

Theron nodded grimly. "That much I figured."

"I'm sorry I couldn't come, I'm on post until sundown. Sorry I had to send for you."

"What happens now?"

Cornelius glanced from the mosaic to the mosaicist. "Pilate is in Jerusalem. He won't be back for a few days."

"Yes, okay. What does that mean?"

Cornelius shifted in his seat. He wasn't making this easy. "It means . . . Prometheus does not have *imperium*. It means Orion will live a few days, until Pilate gets back." By the squinty look in the older man's eyes, Cornelius suddenly realized the man did not grasp the gravity of the situation in the least. Did he think he could get him another ship out of the harbor? "Theron—Orion is going to be executed."

Theron's expression did not change. "Yes, okay. How are we going to get him out?"

Cornelius blinked. "You don't understand. There is nothing we can do."

Theron's face went cold. "Then why did you bring me here?"

"Why—to tell you Orion is going to die. To—give you a chance to say good-bye to him. He's allowed visitors."

"You're not going to try to help him?"

Cornelius sat back in his chair.

"You told me yourself, there are more for Orion than against him." And the little mosaicist folded his arms over his gut and waited.

A thought began to take form as Cornelius gazed at the man. It was so faint he had to cock his head to listen hard for it. While he absently responded to Theron, something like, "It doesn't work that way. We cannot fly in and free him by force. The soldiers care more about their pensions than . . . ," blathering on with one side of his brain, the thought took form on the other.

"There must be a way," Theron insisted.

Silence, I am listening for it, he wanted to snap. He did not even realize he had gotten up to pace until he was suddenly looking into the face of Alexander. The man stood in front of him, his face red with the Palestinian sun. He was taking off his helmet, his hair was helmet-formed and dark with sweat.

". . . pretty well, though I took one to task for his insolent—"

Cornelius raised a hand to belay it. He stilled himself for the vague inner notion, hand poised in the air—and turned quickly on Theron. "It is not a military issue at all. Augustus, Theron."

"Of course, Augustus," Theron said with an uncertain glance at Alexander.

Cornelius came back to the table. He could feel his heart pound in his gut. It was a far-reaching chance and could put him on the block next to Orion.

"Would you like me to report back later, sir?" Alexander said, glancing at the mosaic board upon which Cornelius had a hard glare.

Cornelius lifted his gaze to Theron. "The documents."

"What of them?"

"Do you have them?"

"Of course."

Right next to Orion. A dual execution, and public. Treason demanded public display. The next words he spoke would utterly commit him, come what may.

He sat down, calm with decision. "Bring me the documents, Theron." He glanced at Alexander. "My drillmaster will escort you."

So lost he was in planning he hardly realized the two were gone. It would take the skill of a diplomat, and Cornelius thought he had a little diplomacy. It would take strategy, and not the Crassus kind. Augustus was his own hero, a man mightier in strategies of state than in military campaign. He glanced at the corner of the office where the image of Augustus was displayed upon a shelf with the other chosen gods of the Legion X Fretensis. He would need more than a supplication to the spirit of Augustus. He wondered if Janus Bifrons ever thought to supplicate the god of the Jews.

The visits began sometime after the noon meal. Orion had been sitting with his back against the long-sided wall, thinking that anyone incarcerated in the Praetorium Palace certainly did not eat this well—he had smiled when he recognized the special blend of herbs the cook had sprinkled on the barley—when the iron padlock slid from its fastening. He thought it was the guard come to take his tray away. It was not.

The Jewish laundress stood in the doorway until the guard told her to get in or go away. She told him she would only be a moment, and timidly came forward. When the door closed behind her, she pressed her back against the door and did not move the duration of the visit.

Orion rose, and stood as far away as he could, backed into the tight corner. The small room afforded no luxury of personal space. He felt a flood of embarrassment for all things at once: for the stink of the room and his unkempt appearance. For the lack of his toga, and for the utter decimation of his—*mincing offspring, this is what Rivkah would have felt to have her tree cut down*—pride. He managed a smile, though it did not stay long because the woman began to cry.

She was distressed long before she came, canals of dismay had been set in her face. She spoke her mangled Greek in a tight whisper. "My son she took away." She pressed her fingertips against quivering lips.

Oh, no. Little Benjamin. Anger flashed and rose. Prometheus. Only Prometheus could have reversed his decision. "I am so sorry."

Why was it his fate to be dragged back to the palace and live through all that his imagination had already hinted?

"I am sorry—" he could not remember her name—"good woman, but there is nothing I can do."

But she was shaking her head before he finished speaking. "I come for only thanks." She pressed her lips again, then continued. "Two more years, my Benjamin with me. Two more good years. You are a good man. My thanks, my thanks."

And then she dared to do what she never would have done if Orion Galerinius was still chief secretary. She came and took his hand and kissed it three times. Then, weeping, she turned from him and pounded on the door. She did not look at him again, and in a moment she was gone.

After the flushing astonishment of the hand kissing, he did not know why he was left with fury inside. After the woman left, because he could not cry out in rage lest someone would hear, he took the hand that was kissed and made a fist and smashed the wall as hard as he could. He dragged it down the whitewashed blocks, stamped with the insignia of the Legion X Fretensis, rubbing skin off as he dragged, and pounded one more time.

Her visit was the first. He tried to caution the others, tried to tell them they were foolish to visit someone accused of treason; it was a very risky thing to do. No one seemed to listen.

The cook came with his usual gloomy sense of humor. "Blame it all on me. I had wanted to say good-bye, and a god must have granted this wish. I would have preferred he grant the new mother-in-law wish." Before he left he slipped Orion a fresh loaf of honey-cake from a fold in his tunic.

The steward of the tricliniums came. "Prometheus is a slouch, Orion Galerinius. I never found any olive pits on the floor when you were here. And date pits and crab claws and nutshells," he sniffed. "Acts like he's Pilate himself. I hear it's treason for you. What a shame, Orion Galerinius. You should have been more careful."

Janus Bifrons came.

He thought he heard the clack and clatter, but it was such a familiar old sound and he was so deep in his thoughts that he didn't put it to Janus until the iron padlock slid, and there stood the priest in the doorway.

Upon sniffing the foul air in the room, he instinctively clutched his vestments to him. His lip curled when he located the source of the stink, and he turned to the guard before the door closed. "Empty this," he demanded, pointing to the bucket.

Orion had requested the same over an hour ago, but the guard acted deaf. With the priest it was a different matter. No one defied a priest. The man reluctantly removed the bucket and closed the door.

Holding his sleeve to his nose, Janus Bifrons said behind it, "No offense, Orion," and gathered up his vestments to settle on the pallet on the floor. Orion had folded it double to offer to his guests.

"They took my bristlebane away," Orion said.

"It wasn't a good quality," Janus replied from behind his sleeve. He cautiously removed it, not entirely satisfied with the outcome. "I cannot say it is good to see you again. What happened?"

Orion shrugged. "Does it matter? It was my fate."

To this, Janus gave a decidedly sour grimace. "Your fate," he muttered. "An undeserved fate if I ever saw one."

"What does it matter if it's undeserved? It is what it is."

"Stop with the rhetoric, I am not in the mood." He twisted off one of his bracelets and handed it to Orion. "There. You have a possession. A man should not be without a possession, however humble, to meet the afterlife."

Orion held the bracelet to the light, turning it in his hands. "This isn't . . ."

"A gift from Augustus to Mother. She served as one of the priestesses of Diana."

Silence settled, an awkward one. The same silence everyone else had tried to avoid, that between the living and the soon-to-be dead.

Janus asked in a tone supposed to be light, "Any regrets?"

A tightening in his gut, a surge of his blood.

The order of his workroom, the order of his writing table. His tablets and his pearwood pipe and his neat handwriting on papyrus. He rubbed the callus on his middle finger. He missed the feel of a stylus in his hand. His missed his bit of the sea.

I regret letting down those who depended upon me for small acts of mercy. Such small acts to him—so important to them. He knew that now. The litany of names still haunted him. Especially the look of the laundress.

Orion looked at the wooden bracelet, softly silver with age. "That is an unholy question, Priest of the Fetiales."

The bracelet had been recently cleaned, it was still damp and smelled of lye. He lifted it even with the eyes of Janus, closed one eye to peer through its circle and smile sadly at the priest.

Orion lowered the bracelet with his look. He was tired. Weary with heavy thoughts.

Janus rose and smoothed his vestments. He pounded on the door, and the iron padlock slid. The priest left the cell without another look, without another word.

⁂

Slam. Crash. Silence, then a scuffling noise. Marina's eyes went wider as she looked from the equally mystified Roman soldier in her home to the workroom curtain. A roar of oaths came from Theron, and Joab's name was involved. She gave the soldier a weak smile and excused herself.

"Theron, what on earth," she hissed as she came into the workroom. "What is that language—"

There was her man on all fours, his broadened end the only thing visible from where he crawled under a table. He came out with his face red in fury, and his eyes searching everywhere.

"If I get my hands on that Joab, he will be the next sacrifice at the Temple of Rome and Augustus!"

"Theron!" Marina gasped.

"He cleaned my workroom!" Theron roared. An oath followed and Marina gave his arm a hard twisting pinch.

"You watch your mouth. Of course he cleaned your workroom, he's the only one you let do it. You told me he couldn't pinch the lead strips, so he found something else to do."

Jorah, meantime, watched the scene from where she sat at a worktable, her face glowing with Marina's own astonishment.

"Where is that son of a Cretan?" Theron bellowed. "I knew those papers were important! If he threw them away I will—" And he sputtered and fumed to keep back the oaths that would earn him another pinch.

"Tell me what is happening," Marina demanded. "What is wrong with Orion?"

The fury abated at those words, and Theron turned to his wife. He explained everything in terse sentences. Jorah came beside them, her face now filled with worry.

"Orion has been taken?" Marina gasped.

"I need those papers. I don't know why, but the Roman knows what he's doing. What did Joab do with them? Where is he?"

"He left a little while ago. He—" Jorah hesitated. She looked at Marina. "He went to tell her Nathanael's last words. He wouldn't allow me to come, said he had to do it himself. He said he had to get it over with."

"But he wouldn't take those papers with him," Theron growled, still looking about the room. "The bin!" he hollered, and hurried out the back door with the women on his heels.

The bin was the common-use container shared by the neighbors on either side. He ran to it and tilted it to himself. The ensuing oath Marina did not seem to hear. The bin was completely empty. Theron looked, and the bin wrap was gone. It prompted another oath, and this time Marina heard. He rubbed his arm as his thoughts raced.

"He must have brought it to the heap," Marina said.

"Is it burning day today?"

"I don't know—I can't think," Marina fretted, rubbing her forehead. "Fourth from Sabbath is burning day." She counted on her fingers, then sent a sickened look to Theron. "How important are those papers?"

"They could mean Orion's life."

"Then we must go to the heap." Marina looked at Jorah. "Go and fetch the Roman soldier. We will need all the help we can get. Then run as fast as you can to Rivkah's. Ask Joab exactly where he dumped the bin wrap. We will be at the heap."

⁂

Joab dropped the smelly bin wrap on the side of the doorstep. The burlap was stiff with old filth and smelled like the inside of the bin itself. His father would have chided him for not burning the wrap with the trash, but the people from Caesarea seemed more inclined to save a pruta as long as they could. Frugal as a mother of twenty, the old saying went.

The door opened before he could knock. He'd let a bin wrap distract him as long as he could.

It was not Nathanael's mother, it was the girl he'd seen before. She looked as though she had been crying, which did nothing for his turmoil within. She looked ornery too, but the orneriness softened when she recognized him.

"Marina said you would be by."

"Is she here?"

The girl nodded and moved aside to let him in. "She's out back. I'll get her." She indicated a low couch and disappeared down a short hallway.

But Joab could not sit. He drew a deep breath, but nothing could settle him. He only had to say words Nathanael requested he say. He was not responsible for their accuracy. It did not matter one dried-up fig what Joab ben Judah thought of the words, he only had to deliver them. Just deliver them, and deliver his soul of their onus. What did he care what they meant. He was only a courier.

"Just a courier," he whispered to himself. "I'm only a courier."

She came in from the back, and by the look on her face she was miserably eager to hear what Joab had to say. It was a face struck like a new coin with grief.

It brought back flitting images of the day in the pass. The scuffle. Kicked-up dust. The grunts and the first gasp of pain.

"You have words from my son," the woman said.

Like looking into the eyes of Nathanael himself. The last he'd seen Nathanael, he lay on the pillows at the doctor's house. These amber eyes looked out from a frame of cosmetics—those from greasy, lavender-hued lids.

Tell her for me . . . no stones.

"How did he die?"

The plaintive words came from the other one. She was leaning against the wall, arms folded, gazing at him as intently as Nathanael's mother.

"He died as I could only hope to die," Joab answered. "He died bringing bread to people he didn't know. He died loved. He died with—" And the words caught because suddenly, looking into the golden eyes, he knew why they dropped the stones.

Because they were there. That was the only difference between Joab and the ones with the stones, they were there. They saw her eyes and knew Law didn't matter anymore in the face of one who needed much more. They saw her eyes and saw down to the misery at the bottom and felt a compassion that Law could never give.

He'd been afraid to come, afraid to bump against the sin of this woman's life, afraid it would contaminate him or set him on a wayward track. Afraid of her pain. And now . . . now there wasn't any fear. There was only unexpected compassion, calm compassion, because Joab knew he had something good to tell her. He knew, he knew why they dropped the stones.

Tears were streaming from the eyes. Liquid ran from her nose. She fumbled blindly for something to wipe her face, and her friend snatched off her own head scarf and handed it to her.

Joab took her gently by the hand and led her to the low couch. First he told the woman how Nathanael died. He told it as he knew it, leaving a few hard details to his memory alone. Then he told the miserably eager mother of a son's last words, and found that it wasn't hard at all. Then he explained the words, and told about an adulteress and accusers and a Teacher who did not allow them to throw stones.

The women cried quietly the whole time Joab spoke, constantly wiping tears. Kyria held Rivkah's hand hard, crying as much as her friend.

He finished and sat on the couch with quiet marvel inside. What peace was this? Worst thing he ever had to do, yet the peace he felt at the words he spoke brought something he'd never known.

She didn't realize the implications of the words of Jesus, he could see that, she was too wounded to understand. Maybe too uneducated. The ones who knew the Torah best understood the infamy of the words the most. But no longer did he feel fury at them.

He felt the good in them.

A frantic pounding on the door. Jorah pushed her way in, searching—she shook the bin wrap at him. "Joab! Where did you dump the trash?"

He stared at the brandished wrap. "What—?"

"The trash! Orion's life depends on it!"

"What of Orion?" Rivkah gasped at the same time as the other girl asked, "What happened to the Roman?"

Jorah jumped in place with furious impatience. "The trash,

Joab, are you so thick? Where did you dump it? If those papers are burned, then something awful will happen!"

"To Orion?" Rivkah demanded.

"What will happen?" Joab asked, utterly bewildered.

"I don't know!" Jorah screamed.

"Are you talking about the papers in the mortar bucket? Why would I throw them away?"

Anguish became astonishment. "You mean you didn't?"

"Of course not. Who would burn papers? They looked legal."

She grabbed Joab's arm. "Where are they?"

"Next to the pattern plates. I put a tile on them to—Jorah! Where are you going?"

But Jorah had rushed out the door and was flying down the street, her dark-blue head covering flapping.

The three sent one another fleeting glances before dashing out the door after her.

21

Pontius Pilate gazed at the mosaic on the floor of the triclinium. The mosaics in Herod's Jerusalem palace were different from the Caesarean mosaics. One would think Herod a pious Jew with the mosaics found here. Barely ornamental at all, with patterns that could not offend his god, much less his people. Simple crests of the sea was all. Or borders like a crenellated tower. Scrupulous in design. Yet in the palace back in Caesarea, in Pilate's own quarters, were mosaic depictions of things like a bowl of fruit with a dove perched on the edge. Pilate knew of Herod the Great's hypocrisy as his own people did not. His people were more devoted Jews than he had ever been.

"They expect a wide berth about that devotion without a care for my own," he murmured to himself. The presence of the servant roused him from his thoughts.

"Excellency? A dispatch has arrived from Caesarea." The servant handed a sealed papyrus roll to Pilate.

A flush of excitement replaced his bitter musings. Decimus! He snatched the roll and glanced at the seal. Prometheus had pressed the image of the Pegasus into the wax, the insignia of the legion in which he had served. Loyalty to one's legion never died. He smiled and broke the seal.

Eagerness withered as his eyes traveled the script of his new secretary. He read the short message again, and thrice, before he lowered it into his lap.

"Excellency?" the servant questioned unhappily. Unhappy news for Pilate was unhappiness for everyone. "Will there be a return word?"

He had just arrived. He hadn't had time to receive the infiltrators of the new cult.

"Ready my escort, I am returning to Caesarea." He shifted his jaw as he looked at the roll in his lap. "I am the return word."

※

The sun would soon set on a second night in the cell. Long periods of boredom followed flurries of visitors. Each time a new person came he wished he could go to the baths; the humiliation of being without a toga was rivaled only by his own stink. What a sight he must be. Unshaven and looking as though he'd been dragged up and down a Caesarean alley.

He wondered if she had heard by now. He wondered if she would come.

Why would she come? She just learned her son was dead. She had other things to think about. He had his good-bye, the sight of her standing in disheveled sorrow. That was the good-bye he would take to the block. That was the *her* he would remember when the soldier produced the blade to send him to the afterlife. But every time the padlock rattled, his heart jumped.

He noticed his hand. He made the fingers clench. It was unthinkable. His hands would swell and rot and the whole of him would become a mass of corruption. This body so alive would be so dead in a day or two. It was absurd.

The padlock rattled. The door swung open and it was—Kyria. It was so bizarre to see her standing there that comprehension left for a moment. He could not rise, could not speak. Perhaps because of disappointment that she was not another.

"Hello, Roman," she said cheerily. "We have five minutes, so the guard says."

He stayed in his corner and knew he could not conceal his dismay. What was wrong with him, what weakness was this? Where was his self-collection? Little things like an unexpected face could bring on the swell of a whimper.

"Forgive me, I am not Rivkah," she said, and the door pushed her forward as it closed. "She's really angry at you, by the way." She began to inspect the room, pulling back when she looked into the bucket. She picked up the wooden bracelet he had given pride of place on the pallet. "Who's this from?"

He felt himself relax, and realized it was good to see her. "A gift from a friend."

"Is that a Roman custom?" She looked at him. "You give gifts before you die? Seems a little late."

She put the bracelet on and held her arm out to admire it, then settled on the pallet. He realized he was breathing something other than stink, realized it was her perfume. At least he managed not to close his eyes when he inhaled.

"She thinks it's her fault you're here," Kyria said, looking at the light on the ceiling. "Not much of a view, Roman."

Orion felt a nudge of despair. She just found out her boy was murdered. Did she need the guilt of his own death? "The idea of someone else taking my guilt is appealing, but inform her my actions were my own."

"I'm not supposed to tell you something," Kyria announced, self-satisfied. Her eyes glittered as she smiled deeply.

He couldn't help smiling back. "What are you not supposed to tell?" He thought of the first time he saw Rivkah, on the other side of the table on the Praetorium Palace steps.

She rolled her eyes. "I don't *know*, Roman. They won't tell me."

A fraction of disappointment. A blinking off of a vagary that maybe Rivkah had confided something to her. . . .

"We were all in the barracks and oh! that soldier was angry. I thought he was nice looking the second I saw him, but furious? Ho. Anyway, he said, 'What is this, a delegation?' He said, 'Why don't you just parade the palace?' He was *so* mad." She smiled dreamily. "Kicked us out the second we got there. I told him he was pushy. Anyway. He forbade Theron and Marina and Rivkah and Joab and Jorah from visiting you. That's why I'm here. I thought you might want to know, in case you felt bad, their being your friends."

"I did wonder." Theron and Marina were the only friends he had. The only ones not to visit. "Thank you for telling me."

"The angry soldier said it was dangerous. Rivkah said she didn't care." Kyria paused, then said delicately, "Roman, they had to drag her home."

"They did?" Curse him for his wistful tone.

"They did. She finally settled down when they told her it wouldn't do you any favors, her being Jewish. What with the tree and all."

They sat in a silence Orion did not notice, so companionable was her company. It comforted him greatly, if he allowed himself to admit it. She was Rivkah's friend, and so brought with her a little bit of Rivkah.

So they had to drag her away. He smiled a little. That sounded like Rivkah. Did she—really want to see him that much? Would he let himself believe it? Well, lately he'd allowed himself to think other things . . . about Rivkah. . . .

"What are you thinking of?" Kyria said with that knowing smile.

For answer, he did something very un–chief secretary: he made his own smile as roguish as he could.

And she put her head back to laugh.

He laughed too, mincing offspring how long had that been, and shook his head at the craziness of being in a cell and laughing with a prostitute.

"Kyria." He had her attention. "It was kind of you to come. Truly kind."

Her merriment dwindled. "Well. I guess my five minutes are up." She rose and dusted off her backside. She noticed the bracelet on her arm, took it off, and set it on the pallet, then she rapped on the door. "By the way, the guard told me you're forbidden any other visitors. He said Prometheus Longinus is probably jealous."

"How did you get in?"

"I'm a prostitute, Roman. I told the guard I was your dying wish." Then, as she studied his face, the sauciness disappeared, replaced by an anxiousness that didn't fit.

The door swung in, and after a faltering smile she left, taking with her the comfort of her presence. The little bit of Rivkah.

He would not see her one last time. Nothing mattered anymore. He sank into the corner, and there was greeted by a monstrosity he had held at bay. Despair fell on him in full, despair too great for a whimper.

22

"I will have your bema seat removed to the stadium," Prometheus was saying briskly—an imitation of Orion if Pilate ever saw it. As if imitating his tone could produce his actions. "I've put out notice, Excellency, and they are posting it in the public squares. The sentence will be passed this afternoon. Execution is set for noon tomorrow."

"I want the stonemason there. Today, at the reading of the sentence."

Prometheus raised an uncertain gaze from his tablet. He caught himself and took his stylus to scratch it into the wax. His consternation was evident, however, when he had to use the flattened end of the stylus to press out a mistake.

Don't think I didn't see.

❧

The rattle of the padlock. So familiar now, familiar as other things used to be.

The door swung open. "On your feet, Orion Galerinius."

He stepped into the corridor, wincing at the light. When they got to the end of the corridor another Praetorian joined them. Their steps in perfect cadence, the towering soldiers flanked Orion, and he actually felt secure between them. Such a ludicrous thought it nearly set him laughing.

He used to try not to notice the respect he commanded in the palace. Didn't know how much he had enjoyed the respect until now. At one time they would have swapped palace small talk—the silence of the Praetorians let him know he was no longer chief secretary. He knew these two marching beside him, Ancus and Livy. Knew they belonged to Prometheus.

They didn't take the back way to the Great Stadium, this was too official. They went through the auditorium where Pilate held court—past the conspicuous absence of the bema seat—out the great oaken doors of the Praetorium Palace.

The Great Stadium ran north and south along the coast, a perfect place for entertainment, where sea breezes on a good windy day could soothe the crowds in the stands. The Praetorians walked him to the wide public archway where stragglers dashed in late from places of employment or repose. Some glanced at Orion, unsure if this was the criminal spoken of in the posted notices.

They came out from the archway, and Orion saw more people than he had expected in the stone tiers. Surprising, since sentence day was not nearly as entertaining as execution day. Tomorrow the place would be at capacity, ten thousand people packed tight.

Punishment for crimes against the *populus Romanus* had to be carried out in a public fashion. For military personnel a humane death was prescribed. It was the only cheering thought as the soldiers led him on the hard-packed track toward the bema. Decapitation was swift and much more dignified than crucifixion.

The wooden rectangular dais of the bema rose in the middle barrier of the Great Stadium, across from Pilate's traditional seat in the games. The purple-cushioned throne had been placed upon the dais, and on the cushions in his imperial slouch sat Pontius Pilate.

They stopped in front of the dais. Orion could not lift his gaze to the man seated there. Nausea from unaccustomed sun, dread of his fate. Or did shame prevent him? Six years he had served the man on the bema. He could neither defend his actions nor explain them. Excuses were for the weak.

A guard shoved him to his knees, and the noise of the crowd died.

The voice of Janus Bifrons.

"Capitoline Triad, we invoke you this day. Attend and preside. Nemesis, goddess of vengeance and justice, we invoke you this day. Attend and preside. Portunus, protector of harbors, we invoke you this day. Attend and preside. May the proceedings please all gods present, known and unknown. Blessed be the Capitoline Triad."

How many times had he heard that invocation, with Janus at his side instead of above him?

The voice of Prometheus Longinus.

"Orion Galerinius Honoratus, Chief Secretary in the administration of government in Judea, the Imperial Province of Rome; quaestor to His Excellency Pontius Pilate: You are guilty of insubordination, being the failure to issue an imperial decree. His Excellency Pontius Pilate."

If the crowd was earlier stilled, it was now perfectly silent.

"Rise, Orion Galerinius Honoratus."

A murmur from the crowd, confusion within Orion. This was not procedure. A guard hauled him to his feet. Against his will he rose, but Pilate was not looking at him. He was looking at Prometheus.

Prometheus read from the large ornamental tablet used only in legal proceedings.

"Nicanor of—" he hesitated over the pronunciation of the Hebrew name—"Barzillai. Come forth." He raised his head and looked toward the tribunal.

Coming across the tracks toward the dais was a man flanked as he had been with two Praetorian guards. He was nearly as tall as the guards, lean, with long wavy hair held in place with a leather string. He had a way of walking that was strange to Orion's eye, as though he walked against a gentle wind. There was elegance in it, a certain grace that made Orion wonder if the man was a performer in the spectacles. He had a grim calm in his face and, strangely, eyes only for Orion. The three halted before the dais.

Prometheus was nervous. His fingers convulsively gripped the edges of the large tablet.

"Nicanor of—Barzillai, is it true you were conscripted for the skill of your workmanship to imperial employment on the Tiberateum?"

Orion felt as though a horse were galloping through him, a phantom image from the races.

"It is true," the man said clearly.

"You are by trade a stonemason?"

"I am."

"You are Jewish."

His head lifted a fraction. "I am."

"You refused to work at the Tiberateum on your holy day."

Just as clearly as before, "I did."

"At any time did the man on your right, Orion Galerinius Honoratus, read to you in the presence of the Tiberateum conscription this imperial decree: 'The Jewish stonemason Nicanor of Barzillai shall be flogged with seven times seven for every day he chooses not to work, lest he entice others by wicked example'?"

The man hesitated, eyes dropping from Prometheus, eyes not quite going to Orion. "I have since heard of the decree."

"It was never read to you?"

"No."

At that, Prometheus lowered his tablet.

Pilate rose tall from the purple-cushioned throne. "It shall be read to you this day."

Orion's skin leapt an inch.

Pilate took a tablet from a small table next to the bema—Orion's own tablet. He opened it, and the stylus fell out. Prometheus scrambled for it, but it rolled off the dais and fell to the ground. One of the guards retrieved it and handed it up to Pilate. It was the stylus Father had given him.

Pilate took the stylus, then noticed the inscription on the flattened end. He read it, puzzled, and looked at Orion. He would wonder why "river barges" was inscribed in ivory. *Naves codacariae*, he had read.

Orion had only seen the stonemason in distant profile when he went to see if the man was a good worker. He had never seen his face up close.

Lean and brown. Deep lines. An inscrutable look in the eyes that slid to his. Orion held the look a moment, sharing strong sensation with the man—impending dread, common lot—then dropped his eyes.

Pilate tucked the stylus into the loop. "Approach the bema, Orion Galerinius Honoratus."

Orion stepped forward, his chest inches from the wooden platform. Into his downcast view came his tablet, offered by Pilate. Crowd murmurs rose. Orion looked up.

Pontius Pilate leaned on his knee, offering him his old tablet. For his ears only, Pilate said, "Let's have no more foolishness. A tunic looks ridiculous on you." And he smiled. An old weary smile, an affectionate one, like something they traded regularly. That strange sensation of having his hair tousled . . .

"Yes, Excellency," he whispered from habit, from confusion and fear, and took the tablet with trembling hands.

Pilate withdrew into his cushions.

Prometheus's eyes had been resting on Orion, filled with the same old contempt—at least there was comfort in that familiarity. He consulted the ornamental tablet once more.

"By the grace of Pontius Pilate, Orion Galerinius Honoratus shall read the decree formerly entrusted to him and so reinstate himself as chief secretary without remonstrance or delay, that the beneficent ways of Rome and her protectors may be known to Caesarea Maritima and its hinterlands." Prometheus lowered the tablet.

Orion looked down at his tablet. He smoothed his hand over the wooden cover and opened it. He saw on one side the last list he had made. Scratches through every line including the last—*Order scourging.* Inscribed on the other side of the tablet was the decree. In the center of the tablet, in the worn leather loop long in need of replacement, was the stylus.

Naves codacariae. Trembling fingers touched the ivory.

The simple little moral his father tried to impress. All the little morals his father tried hard, sometimes too hard, to instill. Sometimes it disappointed him that Father thought him so dull he had to drive home the lessons over and over and over. It made him think Father did not believe in him.

If Father's old collar had no courage to instill, this inscription had no conscience. The collar was old iron and this was old ivory.

We find courage in the going, Orion, beloved boy. Do not wait until it comes to you. It never will. Find it on the way.

For Father he had wanted so desperately to keep his office and bring no shame; for Father he had to relinquish it, for only shame would come. The swing of the sword was a moment; the shame of a blighted conscience, a long and weary lifetime.

I don't know if you were ever loved, Pilate, as I was.

To order a scourging for the man of conscience beside him simply wasn't right. It wasn't right. He closed the tablet, smoothed his hand on its cover, and laid it on the platform.

A moment of silence followed, then commotion. He felt as though an explosion had rendered him deaf, as though he existed in surreal silence while all around were messages he could not comprehend. Pilate was speaking and it looked loud, but Orion could not hear. Janus Bifrons had an expression as incomprehensible as everything else—was it relief? Seemed like pride. How odd. But the look became stricken and slid past him to Pilate. Something the prefect had said did not please him in the least.

It surprised the crowd, too, and the bubble burst and into it rushed a cacophony. One voice he heard over all, a cry he knew to be significant. He looked into the patches of color but could not discern any one face familiar to him.

"Silence!" Prometheus thundered, and held up Pilate's signifier's staff. At the sight of brandished authority the crowd quieted.

"Punishment will commence at noon tomorrow. You are dismissed."

The crowd surged from the tiered stone seats, eager to be on their way with the news. Hundreds were gone in moments. Pilate stepped down from the dais and left with his entourage. The stonemason followed, flanked by his guards. They headed for the starting gates, the back way to the palace. Why didn't they leave the usual way, through the public arch where pomp could attend their leaving?

Apparently the proceedings had loosed the tongues of the Praetorians. They talked over his head as they led him to the archway.

"He'll go down on the seventh," Ancus said confidently. "That's where my bet goes."

Livy looked Orion up and down. "I don't know. He's got something in him; he defied Pontius Pilate. I say the seventeenth."

"Seventeenth!" the other exclaimed.

Livy nudged Orion. "Don't let me down."

"Why did they take him out the back way?" Orion wondered.

The guards exchanged looks. "Why?" Ancus laughed. "You just humiliated the governor of Judea. The races have never seen the crowds that will be here tomorrow."

With shock Orion realized his words were true. The prefect had offered him clemency; Orion had stuffed it in his face. That's how everyone must perceive it.

"The soldiers' house is going to be packed," Ancus said. "They'll take bets until midnight."

Something ominous in that. "Bets on what?" Orion asked.

That exchange of glances again. "On which stroke will take you down. You heard him—you're due for the forty-nine."

23

CORNELIUS STALKED into the drillmaster's office, furious with the two who sat forlornly at the worktable but barely aware of them. Pilate had thrown all his plans into a pyre and set them aflame.

It wasn't Pilate he could blame, it was his own cursed surprise. Everything was over before Cornelius knew, so intent he had been on the unusual proceedings. He should have suspected something when he saw the stonemason with the Praetorians. He should have acted precisely the moment Pilate arose from the bema—

A timid knock came at the doorway. One glance and Cornelius exploded a bellyful of oaths. He stepped aside to fling an arm at the worktable. "Go ahead. Join them. No one seems to care I'll lose my head for it."

Theron and Marina crept into the office and went to the

worktable where the prostitutes—Orion surely had a strange group of companions, Jews and prostitutes—had taken refuge. The one called Rivkah rose and embraced Marina, sobbing onto the older woman's shoulder. The one called Kyria sat with her arms folded, glancing at Cornelius himself now and then. Not that he really noticed.

"You curse like a soldier," Theron commented, joining him away from the women. "I can't get away with anything, with her." He jerked his head at Marina.

Cornelius did not answer. He was too busy trying to salvage plans. He resumed his stalking.

All the careful planning, the precise timing, the drama. All for nothing! (He didn't know he had cursed until he noticed the anxious look Theron threw at Marina.) His gut was in shreds as he waited near the stonemason and the guards, unaware of their imminent role—

"Poor Orion," Theron was saying.

Cornelius glared at him from hooded eyes. Couldn't he see he was trying to *concentrate*? He thought he had anticipated every single angle, like any good tactician. He'd even drawn a schematic of the Great Stadium in the dirt outside the barracks, outlining where Pilate would be and where Cornelius should stand—

"How many do you think he can take?"

Cornelius eased a vicious scowl Theron's way. "Why are you even—" He stopped and studied the man, considered him for a long moment. He tilted his head. "Not many," he said slowly.

Theron nodded. "He is not a big man. Not much meat on his bones. I could take double, and you—" He gave an appreciative snort as he looked at the soldier's form. "You could take the entire forty-nine and get up to dance a jig."

"No one can take forty-nine," Cornelius replied absently.

He gazed at the huge drooping lip. What the mosaicist saw so clearly had been to Cornelius a black wall. Truth was, five years ago Orion Galerinius had given a pledge to the poor of Caesarea. Truth was, on hearing Pilate's verdict he'd allowed horror and sentimentality to put him in a quandary. What sort of response was that for a Roman soldier? Emotion had ruled—in time of battle that was unforgivable.

"It will be harder," he said with a glance at the women. They didn't know the plan. The one called Kyria was watching him.

"It will be harder," Theron agreed unhappily.

The one called Kyria got up and came over. She glanced at Marina and Rivkah, who were in weepy conversation. "What will be harder?" she asked softly.

"You are a woman," Cornelius told her. "Do you think we will discuss any plans with women?"

"What plans?"

Cornelius glared at her, anger flaring. Anger for all of them, yes; much more for himself. "Why did I let you in?" He pointed at the door. "Out. All of you. Comfort yourselves at home, this is no place for—"

Alexander, his drillmaster, came clattering in, face white. He hissed, "Cornelius! It's Remus."

"Oh, help us," Cornelius whispered, stomach plunging. His glance darted from the Jews in the back to the Jews at his side. He heard the coming steps, saw the shadow at the doorway. He put his back to the doorway, seized Kyria, and pulled her in for a long kiss.

A very long kiss. He broke it off with, "You had to bring her *now*, Theron? I'm on post!"

Fortunately, after a breathless second the girl caught on, returning with a playful, "You have bunks in the barracks, don't you?" Then she pulled him down for another kiss.

He allowed it as long as he thought he should, a little longer for good measure, a few more seconds to make it convincing, before he pulled away. "Now, what kind of example would I be to my men?"

He turned her around and gently pushed her toward Theron. "Theron, with all due respect, take your women out of here. Policy says they're not allowed in the barracks."

"Yes, it does," came a cheerful voice behind him.

He started and turned, came to attention. Remus was pressing back a smile, amused to have caught his *optio* in shenanigans.

"Undersecretary Remus," Cornelius said stiffly. "They were just leaving."

"I can see that," he said, watching Theron usher them toward the door.

"It won't happen again; he was not aware of our—"

"I am not Prometheus, Optio Cornelius. Your secret is safe with me." He gave him a wink. "But be a little more discreet in the future."

"Yes, sir." As Remus came in, the others left.

Kyria caught his eye on the way out. She whisked him an up-and-down look and disappeared.

⁂

Twilight came for his last night on earth, and he should have important thoughts to think. He wanted it over so he could think no more. They were doing him a favor, releasing him from a world that had closed around his neck. He wanted it to end.

Forty-nine lashes, the guards had said, and they would not stop when he fell unconscious. That was without precedent, a cruelty not conceived. Any flogging ended if the man fell unconscious. Not for Orion. Forty-nine in full, and if the forty-nine did not kill him, thirst and exposure would; his body was ordered to remain fast at the flogging posts until he was declared dead. No decapitation for Orion. He may as well be crucified.

"What a cruel thing to do," he mused aloud, surprised, as if the punishment were for another. He sat with his knees drawn up, one moving idly back and forth. "You must have really wanted me back. It's flattering, Pilate, but between you and me I should have trained Prometheus much more efficiently."

Cruel and revolting. Orion had a flash of pity for the one who held the scourge. He would have to flog an unconscious heap because Orion wouldn't last more than—

His gut seized, his fist went to his mouth.

It wasn't death he feared, only the hellish pain of getting there. He knew how it would go, he'd officiated enough times. It was all in the numbers. On which downstroke would he break? Everyone broke. Most broke before the tenth—some merely upon seeing the flogging posts. Oh gods, goddesses, he knew how it was going to go. He'd end up like all the rest, he'd break and howl like a gibbering fool and scream until the sound became a pitiful rasping shriek. Until the sound of anguish wrote itself on the memory of every man present.

A flogging was the decimation of everything within, the laying out not only of flesh but of pride. Of dignity—every man he'd seen at the posts had lost control of everything: bowels, stomach, mind. It was the utter ruination of a man. It was said that a flogging made a bad man worse and broke a good man's heart.

What of the man who flogged? Did it make him worse or break his heart?

"Pity yourself, Orion," he muttered.

How many times had he tried not to see a man flogged? Strange to have to endure a flogging in a completely different way. He remembered the first time he witnessed it: the shocking brutality had taken his breath as every downstroke took the breath of the criminal. He had endured it by flinching, wincing, looking away. In time he learned to endure it by hating every scream he heard at the post, hating the man at the post because he had brought it on himself and could have prevented the torment. Veteran witnesses had not much mercy for the one being flogged.

Forty-nine. What a horrible thing to witness. He prayed into his fist that Rivkah wouldn't be there.

⁂

"I'm sorry. He is not allowed visitors."

"Why?" Rivkah demanded. "He is going to die tomorrow."

The guard looked down the hallway over Rivkah's shoulder. His returning gaze was hesitant. She quickly pressed her request. "Please. You can search me, I have no bristlebane or implements of escape, nothing." She pulled off her circlet of bangles and pushed it toward him. "Here, take this. It's worth at least ten dinars."

The guard gently pushed it back. "Keep it. You have five minutes."

"Thank you," she breathed. While he took his key to open the iron lock, she refitted the circlet and hurriedly arranged her veil, parting it in the middle and smoothing it down with her hair on either side of her face. She wore no cosmetic, figuring she would cry it off anyway; she wanted no smears of kohl on her face. She lifted her chin and drew a quick breath.

The guard pulled open the door and held it for her. Then he took the oil lamp on the small table near his chair and gave it to her. Stomach fluttering, she entered the jail cell.

He had been sleeping, curled on a pallet. He pushed up, squinting at the light spilling on him from the flickering sconce in the corridor. The door closed behind, nudging her into the tiny room.

It took a few moments to get used to the dimness, even with the flame from the lamp. She placed it on the floor near his pallet.

Orion rose and stood with his hands behind his back, pressed into the corner. He broke the silence first. "It's really you, isn't it," he said in a near whisper. "It's not my imagination. Tell me it's not."

She pressed her fingers hard on her lips. He didn't need to hear a sob, he needed her to be strong. She swallowed fiercely, brought her hands down to smooth the sides of her tunic. "We have five minutes. I have much to say."

"He always says five minutes. He's a softhearted man."

She could see him better now. He had more growth in the gray-and-black grizzle on his face. The color accentuated the white in the rest of his face, a face that seemed thinner than she'd last seen, brown eyes more large. "You look tired."

He did not respond. She could not look in his eyes long. She broke from them to look about before she sat on the floor.

He lowered himself in his corner.

"Orion, I have something to tell you—" And what was so carefully rehearsed all the way from her home now choked in her throat. Then it dissolved before him in a way she never intended. Her hands flew to her face. "I'm so sorry! Orion, I'm so *sorry!*"

He was on his knees before her, arms pulling her in, their foreheads touching. He whispered and murmured, but she would not allow him to comfort.

"The tree never mattered," she wept. "I was playing a game! I made it important because of what I did to my son—don't you see? It had nothing to do with his chuppah. It never did." She put her head down and covered it with her arms and cried.

When the crying subsided, Orion spoke.

"Think, Rivkah. Please, you must *think*. If you were at the stadium today your ears told you the truth. It is for the order of the stonemason that I am here. Did Pilate ever mention a tree?"

She was still. Then she shook her head. She wasn't ready to release herself of blame, but couldn't bear for him to worry about her. Couldn't bear for this night to be about what she should or shouldn't have done. She had to be strong for him. Strong and the way he liked her to be.

A thought bloomed, the one she did not much think on because it was so new and so saturated with hope, and hope was something that had always ended in bitter disappointment. But with the thought came a lifting from herself.

She raised her head from her lap. "I have something to tell you."

He studied her face, a smile growing. "This will be better, I think." He sat back to listen.

She wiped her nose. "You have no idea." She smiled a little herself. "You have *no* idea. You will not believe what Jesus of Nazareth did. Joab came and told me Nathanael's last words, and you will not believe it."

She told him the story of the prostitute before Jesus, how they were both on the ground while the others with the stones stood over them. She told the astonishing thing Jesus did, how he made them drop their rocks with that devastating line: *He who is without sin, throw the first stone.* He said it to learned ones! Respectable ones! And *they dropped their stones!*

"I've heard this story," Orion said softly. "We talked about it one Sabbath. I thought the woman was an adulteress."

Rivkah shook her head. "No. She was a prostitute." She could feel that effusing hope swell to flush her cheeks. "Then he said, *Go and sin no more.* Orion—" Her hands worked as she tried to explain. "There are no words big enough for that. It's monumental. We hide so much. But Jesus knew. They looked and saw the whoring, but Jesus looked past it. . . ."

The hope became a heady fluttering. "He saw much more than they did, and he made them drop their rocks anyway." She shook her head at the astounding mystery. "He said go and sin no more and of course she did just that, she went and sinned no more, because who could after that kind of . . ." She couldn't find the word.

"Mercy."

She nodded. "Yes. It was mercy."

When the look they shared lengthened into distraction from the subject, she blinked and tried to pull it back. But she thought of something else, the other thing she could barely think on for the hope it offered.

"Orion, listen to me—" She glanced at the door, and her tone dropped to a hush. "Kyria told me there might be a plan for your rescue."

She waited expectantly, but the words did not change a thing on his face. He only looked away.

"A plan, Orion. They wouldn't tell her, but Theron and Cornelius . . ."

His look would not listen. His look would not believe. His look was despair and determination, many things forming a hard bleakness she'd not seen in that confident face. "What are you thinking right now?"

In a voice thin and distant, he replied, "I am thinking I will never see your hair turn silver."

"Don't talk like that—there's a plan. . . ."

"It doesn't seem fair." His eyes traveled her hair.

She crawled over to him, into his arms, and curled in his lap. He buried his face in her hair.

He held her long and he held her tightly, and she agreed with him, whispering, "It doesn't seem fair." How could she finally feel secure, as if she had dropped down a long-heavy load, knowing—

In defiance, she lifted her face to his, searching his eyes. "Orion, there *is* a plan. If Kyria of all people has hope . . ."

He began to kiss her face. Her forehead and her eyes, her cheeks and her neck, her chin and finally her mouth. He kissed her, and she him, until a sob broke from her, and he held her tight. She cried into his neck, "There's a plan, Orion, there's a plan . . . there has to be a plan. . . ."

The guard did not tap at the door until long after the weeping within had ceased.

24

THE SUN STOOD OVER the Great Stadium, shining hot upon the people packed in the stone tiers. Half the population of Caesarea had to be in the stands, ten thousand people thick. The ones at the top were luckiest. They couldn't see as much blood, no, but they were ones who caught the breezes coming down northeast from the sea.

Vendors on the walkway to the public entrance sold loaves of bread for ten prutas. They offered spiced peas and roasted nuts, chunks of honeycomb and handfuls of raisins . . . tiny cups of date juice or ladles full of watered wine. They lined the walkway because Pilate had long since banned their presence from the inside arena when disputes arose over the placement of their stalls. The Circus

Maximus back home had no such ban, had an entire concourse devoted to food and bookstalls and souvenirs.

Orion waited with four Praetorian guards in the public entrance because Pilate was only now settling on his cushions. There would be announcements before they led him out. It wasn't often ten thousand people were gathered all at once, and the magistrates lost no opportunity to inform citizens of a new tax or new policy or new law or news in general.

The citizens of Caesarea took most seriously their responsibility to witness public punishment. Some came to see the blood and guts, truthfully most, but incumbent upon them foremost was their duty to witness the fulfillment of justice. The authorities also supposed public punishment to be a deterrent from any wayward inklings to misdeeds. Deterrent or entertainment, it didn't matter. No one knew if it worked, no one cared.

Billows of wide-eyed hysteria, insane flourishes of thought capriciously seized Orion as he waited with the guards. He would soon die a horrible death, and he was powerless against it. The thoughts bade him run, tear away, crash through the phalanx of the four guards circling him.

The last billow deposited his gaze on the leather armguard of the Praetorian in front of him. The short cloak usually worn was abandoned today in favor of the sun shining off the overlapping bronze scales that rounded the soldier's shoulders. They would look like a floating circle of gold when they came into the arena.

Then they were moving, and insane thoughts leapt. Plead, rage—do anything, Orion, you're going to die. They moved slowly under the archway and onto the hard-packed track. They were walking past the turning post at the far end of the raceway. They walked precisely in the middle of the east-side track—he was near enough the stands to see ostrich feathers waving at flies. He saw a little boy chewing honeycomb. A little boy shouldn't have to watch this.

He remembered the day his father gave him the tiny red charioteer.

He remembered his first chariot race.

Through the wavering heat off the stadium floor he saw the dais ahead on the right, in the center barrier, across from the governor's traditional seat in the stands. Pilate's bema seat had been removed from the dais. Pilate would be on his purple cushions in the governor's box. The two figures on the dais were Prometheus and Janus Bifrons. Past the dais another figure stood in the center barrier, and he could see the flogging posts, mere sticks from this distance.

To my beloved father, from your Orion . . . hail and farewell.

He walked in rhythm with the four, their perfect steps luring his own to cadence. Five to go, four to return. Insane thoughts flourished.

Theron's standing-up mosaic. The look of the Jewish laundress.

Rivkah . . . he looked to see, but his rhythm faltered, and the guard behind goaded him to cadence once again.

A white-clad group in the stands, those had to be the Essenes.

Ostrich feathers waving.

He could not discern faces in his glimpses of the stands. He could feel his stomach screw tight like a well winch as he walked. *Gods and goddesses this could not be.*

Pilate on the left in his high-backed seat, flanked by servants, not meeting his gaze. It meant he was even with the dais, and the flogging posts were just beyond it; how ever did their slow march travel so fast? After halting for presentation before the governor, the circle of shining gold continued.

Prometheus announced his sentence as they passed the dais on the right.

He kept his eyes straight ahead on the starting gates as long as he could, until the circle veered right for the center barrier.

The man at the post held the scourge at his side as if to hide it from Orion. But Orion saw the dangling cords, six or seven or eight of them—thin leather strips with bits of bone and metal threaded at the ends, wiped clean after each stroke so they should not clump with blood and flesh and so deaden the effect. The most merciful scourger was he who flogged the hardest; open the back quickly, let the blood gush forth, and so hasten the death of the criminal.

Sawdust between the two posts to soak up blood. A stain would be unsightly in the games. Leather thongs at the top of each post to secure each wrist.

Pushed to his knees between the posts. Stripped bare save his loincloth. His white back exposed to the stadium. A Praetorian pulled his right wrist to the post and lashed it there with the thong. He gazed down his arm to the lashed wrist, bewildered. His consciousness wavered like the heat off the tracks, insane thoughts leaping.

The softly plump face of his mother, eyes kind and merry. A mist of lavender with the image, the color she loved so much.

Father with one hand on Orion's back and the other pointing to a constellation. Dark starry sky . . .

"Tense yourself hard, lad." It pricked through the black and the stars, because the scourger never spoke to the scourged. "Brace against the bonds, bow your back with all your might. I'll give 'em as hard as I can."

Tears leapt to his eyes. Mercy from the scourger. Mercy everywhere he turned these days. For a prostitute, for a former chief secretary.

Left wrist lashed to the post.

His breath came hard, fast, and erratic. His hands tingled—and what was this, his knees were still on the ground—not procedure. He was supposed to be suspended between the posts, knees two hand spans from the ground so he could not brace against the blows. The guard who lashed his wrists paid out rope enough to let him brace.

Muscle would be cut quicker. Mercy from the guard.

"Thank you," he whispered to guard and scourger alike.

He bowed his back and squeezed his face shut.

⚘

Cornelius waited beneath an arch in the starting gates. He kept to the edge of the shadows, drawing back if he noticed any attention his way. It was the closest he could be to the proceedings without gaining notice. The distance made him nervous, but the schematic he had drawn of the Great Stadium clearly showed him this was the only place he could be.

He swallowed the bile that constantly rose as he watched for Orion to enter.

"Excellency, I have news . . . ," he whispered. "It has come to my atten—Your Excellency, it will behoove you to take note of these papers—documents—to take note of these *edicts*." He wet his lips. Yes, edicts. "Excellency, I have the most astonishing . . ."

He straightened stiff, peering at the far end of the arena. Here they came. Four guards, as he expected. Orion in the middle.

He wet his lips and gripped the parchments, then shuffled through them without seeing a word. He scanned the track for the hundredth time to make sure no obstacle lay between him and Pilate's seat. He and Theron figured on five, no more. Orion could take five downstrokes. Five was plenty cruel, Pilate would be appeased. At the fifth, Cornelius would tear into the arena like a madman.

>❧

The crowd rippled to a hush when they saw the group of five enter the arena.

Rivkah and Kyria leaned forward on their stone bench, clutching one another. They had taken their seats hours earlier, placing themselves on the third tier halfway between the governor's seat and the starting gates. They knew the Praetorium Palace was connected to the Great Stadium by a walkway through the starting gates. Surely any rescue for Orion would come from there. The distance from the public archway to the flogging post was too great. He'd take too many lashes before rescue reached him.

"Look! There." Kyria discreetly kept her hand in her lap as she pointed out the presence of the big Roman soldier waiting in one of the starting gates. "I told you he had a plan," she whispered.

"Where?" Rivkah said, straining to see.

"In the shadows—see? He probably has a whole cohort behind him."

A whole cohort. "If God hears the prayers of a prostitute," Rivkah whispered.

>❧

The five moved inexorably along the stadium floor. Marina's tears started the moment she saw Orion. Theron pulled her close, and she wept quietly on her man. She did not see the furtive glances he sent to one particular starting gate.

"This is wrong," Joab hissed on the other side of Theron. He glowered at the short man in the center of the soldiers.

Jorah took his hand to her lap and held it hard.

"This is wrong."

"He did not obey their law," Jorah whispered, and Joab felt a tear on his fist.

"He did what was right," Joab muttered, helpless misery growing as the five approached the governor's chair.

He did not prevent the death of Nathanael. He could not prevent the death of this one. What could he do? Tolerate it, as the Jews always did. You'd die if you raised an opinion—just look at Jorah's brother. Shake your head and say it's awful, go back to fishing and be glad the Romans weren't bothering *you* today. The day would come when the Jews would rise again. Until then the blood of good men would spill, but what could you do? Bide your time and be patient and wait until all are united for an uprising.

"We will *never* be united," Joab growled. Everyone knew why Orion Galerinius Honoratus was at the posts. Officially, because he disobeyed an order, a Roman matter. Unofficially? He tried hard to spare the life of a Jew. The man on the purple cushions didn't try hard enough.

It began low in his throat and came through his clenched teeth. He didn't know he had made a sound until Jorah lifted her head to stare. He rose from his seat to his tallest and planted his feet.

"What are you doing?" Jorah gasped.

"I don't know."

"Sit down!" she hissed, pulling on his sleeve. He yanked his arm away. He felt a heave in his chest as he watched Orion walk the racetrack. He would stand, he would not cry.

"Joab," Theron began, glancing about at the stares coming their way. "This is not a good time to tell the world you are angry."

"I don't care."

"You are not doing anything to help Orion. He can't even see you."

"I don't care." He firmed his mouth. "I never liked him anyway."

🙖

Rivkah and Kyria clutched one another harder as Orion's tunic was stripped from his back. The guard tossed the garment aside and took his wrist and pulled it to a post. Frantically Rivkah looked to the starting gate.

"Why don't they come?" she gasped.

Kyria stared at the arch. She glanced at Orion, back to the arch.

The Praetorian guard went to the other side and pulled his other hand to the flogging post. He took the leather thong and lashed it tight.

Rivkah did not breathe. And the tall figure in the shadows did not move.

She lunged from her seat and clawed her way over spectators for the starting gates.

🙖

What was this? The scourger, *speaking* to Orion? Cornelius stared hard—they were rigging him for a mercy killing, he realized in shock. Three lashes then, no more. Three would do the damage of five. He'd run and shout on the third downstroke. Sweat sprang to his scalp. He poised, intent on Pilate's seat in the stands. It was halfway down the tracks on the right, third tier up. No horse was more ready to leap from the starting gate.

The kindhearted guard and scourger did not realize their mercy jeopardized any chance Orion had at all. It was another tactical error that could cost Orion his life; Cornelius had not conceived of mercy from the executioners.

Janus Bifrons stepped forth for the invocation of the gods.

"Capitoline Triad, we invoke you this day. Attend and preside. Nemesis, goddess of . . ."

A flash of green was his only warning—he threw up his arm to block a hurtling form. It bounced back and came again.

"Where is the cohort?" the woman hissed, murder in her wild golden eyes—the prostitute from the barracks.

He snapped his gaze to the priest, then shoved her into the shadows with enough force to send her sprawling, enough, he hoped, to—

The second hurtling form knocked him against the stone arch, crushing the parchments between him and the wall. He cursed and checked the parchments, then threw the other form aside to frantically peer for Janus Bifrons—he still spoke to the sky, thanks be to the True One.

"Apollo, chosen of Orion Galerinius Honoratus, attend and preside."

The one called Kyria shoved her face into his, screeching, "You and Theron have a plan, where is the plan?"

As if he had time to sip *wine* over it! Streaming oaths, he grabbed her shoulders and took a precious moment to ensure he plowed her into the other one. He whipped around to the proceedings, suddenly aware of the new attention from those closest in the stands, who looked to see what the ruckus was in the starting gates.

"Unknown god, whom I suspect to be the god of the Jews . . . I invoke you this day. Attend and preside."

Breathing hard, papers clutched, Cornelius suddenly realized what the priest said and looked at Pilate. Yes, the prefect had drawn his head slightly to the side, he was wary; Pilate just heard an invocation like no other. But Bifrons merely shared an inscrutable look with the governor, then withdrew to his place beside Prometheus.

Fully aware of the two tangled on the ground behind him and the Praetorian striding toward him upon referral from those in the stands, Cornelius held his breath as Prometheus lifted the signifying staff and brought it down with a dull thud on the dais.

The scourger raised his arm.

Cornelius breathed, "Third downstroke," and crouched to spring—and sprawled forward as a body leaped to his back, buckling his knees, snapping his head back. He crashed to the tracks and bit his tongue as his chin dug the pavement, trying even as he slid to throw off the form, frantic for the center barrier.

❦

The thin cords whistled—

The force of the blow knocked his breath clean, then pain knocked his senses clean. It sliced his mind as it sliced his back, pain so unimaginable nothing at all could be conceived. Bewilderment rang his senses, his breath would not come, would not come—he writhed and thrashed for air.

"Brace, lad!" the scourger hissed.

Orion could not. The blow had flung him forward against his bonds, like a sail taut in the wind.

"Brace!"

His breath returned in a strangulating gasp.

"One!" Prometheus called out.

Snarling, he hauled back and braced.

❦

"You said there was a *plan!*" Kyria shrieked and proceeded to deliver a hail of kicks to his side.

He seized her ankle and yanked. She fell hard on her bottom with an "Ooof!"

"I *am* the plan, you vixen shrew!" He spat blood and shook the parchments, struggled to rise.

"Optio Cornelius and his women."

It wasn't a Praetorian. Undersecretary Remus stood over him, and this time he was not amused. "Can you not arrest your appetites until an opportune time? For example . . . any other time than an execution, and that of a Praetorium official? You disgust me."

"One!" Prometheus called. Cornelius scrambled to his feet and looked to the posts.

❦

Undersecretary Remus looked more closely. He took in the fistful of crumpled parchments, the blood at his optio's mouth and the scrape on his chin. He took in the anguished appearances of the women, who had fled to each other when Prometheus called the number. He took in the way his optio ignored him for the proceedings at the barrier.

"What is going on?"

But his optio did not answer. He breathed hard and gazed intently at the scourger.

Remus saw the sweat on his face, glanced at the clutched parchments. "What are you thinking, Optio Cornelius?"

Optio Cornelius wasn't listening. Then his face jerked in a wince, and Prometheus called out, "Two!"

One of the women collapsed in a wail, the other swooped down to her. Cornelius was a sweating statue, this time sliding his eyes from the barrier to—

Remus turned to see. The prefect.

That terrible, intent stare. Suspicion raised his neck hairs. He instinctively widened his stance to block the soldier's way. "I asked you a question, Optio."

Nothing changed. It was as if the man saw through him to Pilate.

"What are those papers you have?" Remus demanded.

No response.

"Let me see them." He held out his hand.

"Three!" Prometheus called.

彩

Cornelius charged.

He plowed straight through Remus because it would catch him off guard—and so it did; he caught an instant of the shock on his face as he went down. But Remus was quick to respond, and as Cornelius leapt Remus clawed for his leg and snagged a bootlace. He staggered for a moment, dragging him behind, then Remus wrenched and Cornelius went down hard.

On impact he twisted to face the undersecretary, and while the other man hauled him in by the bootlace, Cornelius reared his other foot and brought it crashing down on his face. Remus crumpled and Cornelius scrambled to his feet, and this time charged not for Pilate's seat but for the barrier itself. Orion had taken three or four mercy blows, the fifth would kill him.

He bellowed all the way to the barrier, holding up the papers as though he charged with a standard. The scourger was intent on his grisly task and did not hear him as he wiped the cords clean and raised the scourge for another.

Janus Bifrons saw, and Janus Bifrons leapt from the dais and tumbled to the ground with the scourger.

Cornelius skidded to a halt before the bloody heap sagging between the posts.

He swung around, waving the papers, frantic to find—and there was Pilate on his feet in his governor's box, leaning forward, hands gripping the rail.

25

"Excellency—" Cornelius croaked. He lifted his voice. "Excellency! I have news!" He held the papers high.

The entire crowd was on its feet. The guards were poised uncertainly, gazing from him to Pilate, ready for a word from their prefect.

Pilate leaned on the rail. After a long moment he called, "Bring it to me."

"Punishment must cease until you read these, Excellency," Cornelius called back. "You will understand why."

"So be it." Pilate nodded to the scourger.

Cornelius ran for the governor's box as the golden-eyed one flew past him for Orion. He trotted to the short barrier wall between the tracks and the first stone tier of the stands and jumped over the wall. People leaned aside to let him through, and he used their shoulders to pull himself to the governor's box. He handed the papers up to Pilate.

Pilate shuffled through them, glancing at the faces peering at him, and jerked his head to indicate that Cornelius should join him. He disappeared from the rail.

Cornelius went around to the opening of the stone enclosure. He'd never even been near Pilate's box. He went in and waited at the opening until Pilate would bid him to come forward.

The high-backed chair was carved gilt, inset with purple fabric, bordered with overlapping golden leaves. Cornelius worked on breathing evenly while his prefect examined the papers.

Rivkah dropped beside the ruin of Orion Galerinius, for the moment ignoring his back, which floated as a red blur in her mind.

He was unconscious, or so it seemed, only his bonds holding him up. His face was greasy white, vomit and foam dripped from his chin. She reached a trembling hand to wipe it away.

"Cut his bonds," she told the scourger.

"He cannot," said the priest, on the other side of Orion. "We must wait and see what Cornelius can do."

"It is too late," she whispered, tears falling as she moved to crouch in front of him. Her knee slid in the vomit; she righted herself and reached to put shaking hands on either side of his face. Drops of sweat trembled and dripped from the tips of his soaked hair.

"I don't think so," said the priest, wiping his nose on his sleeve. "You're not done with us yet, Orion Galerinius Honoratus. Not you. You've rolled thunder for us."

So white against the black-and-gray bristle. But he was breathing. Head sagging, body utterly slack between the posts, but he was breathing.

She crept forward to put her shoulder beneath his chest and prop him to ease the strain on the bonds. Then she cried out when she saw his ribs—the ends of the cords had curled around his back to the front. Bloody lines edged his ribs like fringe. Staring at the dripping furrows, she cried to the priest, "How bad is it?"

After a moment the priest replied, "It is bad."

"*Please* cut the bonds!"

The face of the priest appeared, white as Orion's. "He cannot. It must come from Pilate. Don't you understand?"

❧

Pilate had a fingertip at the corner of his eye, massaging as he read.

He tried to concentrate, but marshaling cognition at this time was nigh unto impossible. He kept attention on the parchments, however, kept his eyes moving on the lines as if each word made sense and he could render a verdict accordingly. For surely a verdict was required. His former chief secretary was unconscious at the posts. That he saw past Cornelius.

The parchments were battered and dirty, spattered with blood—not Orion's, he had seen bloody spittle at the soldier's mouth. Dates. Names. *Concentrate, Pontius. Proconsuls and the half-shekel and provinces of Rome.* He held the paper at arm's length to see it better.

He read through one parchment. Then started it over, same parchment, reading slowly this time. He put the first to the back and read the next. He lifted his eyes to the waiting soldier. He saw it all in an instant. He rested against his chair, then, let the hand with the papers drop to his lap.

The soldier before him thought him a fool.

He leaned his elbow on the chair arm, put his head on his fist. The soldier had his eyes fast on the top of his chair.

"Come forward."

The soldier came forth and stood at rigid attention. His appearance was disheveled for a Roman soldier. He knew this man: Cornelius, drillmaster of the auxiliaries.

"Where did you get these?" Pilate finally asked.

"A member of the Jewish Council brought them to me. When I realized their significance I got them here as fast as I could."

"When you realized their significance . . ." He worked the corner of his eye with his fingertip. Pilate could laugh. He was good, this one was. "I'll have to watch my back around you."

Startled, the soldier flitted his glance at Pilate, then away.

He sighed. Well, maybe he had it wrong. Maybe he was an easily impressed fool. The half-shekel practice had nothing to do with Sabbath-day observances, they could whine implications all they wanted. Surely the Jews had taken this man to market.

Should he ask for names? Find out which member of the Council was desperate enough to dig these up? What did that say of Orion? How far, how deep did his deception run? Just how deeply involved was he in Jewish affairs? His resignation spoke of "indiscretions." Should he put forth an inquiry and get to the bottom of them, or should he treat this like a nest of adders?

He felt weary then, old and weary of everything in sight. What he wouldn't give to sit as a common spectator in the Circus Maximus and cheer for the Reds. Sit in an arena for the reason it was built, for spectacle and entertainment and the cheer of hearts weary of daily toil. What he wouldn't give to watch the *quadrigae* career around the turning posts, hooves and dirt clods flying, the roar of the crowd vibrating within.

Once as a boy he'd scrambled with his friends and brought home in triumph a puck of horse dung from the arena. No ordinary horse dung—it came from Compressore, the Red horse of charioteer Scipios. Scipios, the greatest charioteer to live.

On a dare from Decimus he had gone to one of the lap counters at a turning post, the one with the bronze dolphins. He tried to remove one of the dolphins, but it turned on an axle that was bolted to the form. He looked to show Decimus that he had tried, but Decimus had betrayed him, leaving Pilate to the Circus steward, who dragged him out of the arena by his ear. His ear had torn a little, he still had the scar. At least he could boast about the scar to his friends. Good old Decimus.

The soldier was waiting.

Sitting back, he could see the Mediterranean, not the center barrier nor what waited there. The soldier's head, down on the right, marred a perfect picture.

"How did you get that scrape on your chin?"

"I fell, Your Excellency."

It could turn out to be a good thing. It could show his willingness to be persuaded for justice. Throw them a little chicken feed and things could simmer down in Caesarea for a time. His eyebrow quirked: and if Decimus did show, he'd find a Caesarea with the appearance of control, for the Jews would live on their meager triumph for months. Appeased, they would give an appearance of placid compliance, all the while scheming behind their backs for another foothold.

Tolerate them, Tiberius had told him. Tolerance, Pilate had come to see, was a smile on the face and a knife behind the back.

"I am not a fool, and I want you to know that before I tell them to release him." He glared at one of his attendants. "Summon Prometheus. Tell him to bring his tablet."

He held out the parchments to Cornelius, and eyed him with intrigue. "I don't know where to place the . . . *triumph* of this day. Seems well enough to lay it at your feet. Well done, soldier."

26

THE AFTERLIFE SMELLED like Rivkah. Sweet and spicy and earthy-fresh, like a breeze off a lush field. The afterlife was also dreadfully painful. If he moved he wanted to die all over again. If he moved, his consciousness swept him away and he could no longer attend to the words of the spirits about him.

"What is the difference between *deportatio* and *exsilium*?"

"Cornelius says not much. Except Orion could have chosen the place of his banishment. *Deportatio* means they have chosen."

Strange thing for spirits to speak of. They spoke of other strange things too. Sometimes many spirits seemed to be congregated in conversation, sometimes only one or two. He learned that spirits wept and whispered and cursed like mortals. He learned that they prayed, which seemed odd. They also inflicted an outrageous amount of pain, pain resulting in his own weak cries. One she-spirit, who sounded remarkably like Rivkah—perhaps a relative who had gone on before—had cried along with Orion while other spirits picked over his back and doused it with flame.

"Why won't Theron come?"

"He is too miserable. He will not work, he will not eat. He only goes to the sea."

He breathed deeply of the pillow that smelled like Rivkah and drifted to the place where no pain could touch him.

⁂

"He needs to drink. We must get him to drink, Rivkah."

"I try! I soak cloth and press it to his mouth. I cannot turn him, Marina. The pain is too great for him."

"We will have to bear the pain just as much as he. We must be strong for him. We must hurt him to heal him, Rivkah. Do you understand?"

"I do."

To my beloved father . . . do you hear her cry for me?

"Rivkah . . . ," Orion whispered, and the gods grant the she-spirit can hear. *Get me a straw of hay and I will drink for you. I will do anything for you.* Did he think it, did he speak it? Gods grant her to hear. Gods grant . . .

⁂

"You really should clean yourself up, Rivkah. You are beginning to smell. You're not doing any favors for the Roman with a stink like that. . . .

"What? I'm not trying to offend, I'm on your side. Don't be so touchy. Anyway, did you *see* the way he stood between Orion and Pilate? Did you see the way he waved those papers?

"I will die to have him. I will lie down and die. I will change all my wicked ways and those of my neighbors to have him. We will raise our children in a charming southern villa. Or a flea-infested rat hole, Rivkah, I don't care. I must have him. I will have him. I will die six hundred and eighty times until I do have him."

Orion heard a gasp. "I kicked him. I kicked him! I can't believe I did that. . . ."

❧

"How is he doing today?"

"He opened his eyes! He looked straight into my eyes, and he knew it was me! And he is taking water through a straw, Marina! Lots of it. You won't believe how much he is drinking. . . ."

More weeping, Father. Do you hear that? I will do anything for her. Anything.

❧

The gods and all their relations conspired to swamp him in pain.

"I'm finished."

A clatter. A rushing of feet. The rush brought a wave of air, and on it, the fragrance of Rivkah's hair. "Orion? Did you say something?"

He wet his lips. "I'm finished." The words sounded hoarse, but even he could hear the words spoken not by a disembodied spirit but by a miserable mortal. He felt soft fingertips brush aside the hair on his forehead.

"Finished with what?"

"Pain. It can stop now. I'm all done."

He felt the whisper-touch of kisses on his eyebrow, his cheek.

"I just breathe and it hurts."

He opened his eyes and saw the most beautiful face he had ever seen. She tilted it sideways so he could look straight into her eyes. No goddess was this beautiful. No goddess would have tears dripping off her nose for him.

He smiled, and it was a puckery ridiculous smile because he was lying on his stomach on Rivkah's bed. He reached to touch a tear on her nose, groaning at the pain the movement ignited . . . the tear dripped off before he got to it so he touched her cheek instead.

She smiled and took his hand to kiss it again and again.

"How long have I been here?"

"Four days. Cornelius said as soon as you can walk by yourself, you are to be deported."

"Where?"

"Northern Britannia."

"Ah. That figures."

The amber eyes glittered. "You didn't think Pilate would send you to a nice Greek island, did you? A few slaves in tow and a nice fat purse filled with gold?"

He could look on that smiling face forever. "Don't leave me," he whispered drowsily as fatigue suddenly came. She kissed his fingers and held them to her cheek, and he knew he could sleep because she would be there when he woke.

❦

"How is he doing?"

"He refuses to go in a bucket. He says it's bad enough to be held up by two women so he can relieve himself." Rivkah's brows came together. She rubbed her thumbnail over a spot on the table. "He—vomits every time we take him to the brush. It makes the wounds bleed."

Marina reached to clasp her hand. "It's all right, Rivkah. The physician says he will heal, it will only take time. There is no sign of infection. You've been doing a wonderful job."

It was the first time in years Rivkah sat at Marina's table. The first time in a week she had left her home. She stopped rubbing the spot.

"You remember the day you took me to buy cloth at Collina's?"

Marina was shelling pistachios in her lap. She tossed the cleaned ones into a bowl on the table. "I remember."

"I'll never forget that." Rivkah reached into the bowl to take a pistachio and examine it, turning it over in her fingers before popping it in her mouth. "I'm going with him, you know."

"I thought you might."

"I'll take care of him the rest of my life."

Marina pitched a few more pistachios into the bowl. "He's a fortunate man."

Rivkah dug in the bowl, let the nuts sift through her fingers. "I'm the fortunate one. And I'm going to tell him about the scars, Marina. Mine and Nathanael's. I'm going to tell him everything. I used to think he'd hate me if he knew, but . . ."

Her lips trembled, but she pressed them. She took two pistachios and tapped them together. "The night before the flogging I told him what Jesus of Nazareth said. About the stones and the prostitute."

"It's a good story."

Rivkah nodded. "Yes, it is." She put the nuts in the bowl and rested her chin on her fist, looking out the window.

Marina observed Rivkah without seeming to. The look on that face could make her fling up her arms and dance. Jesus of Nazareth, whether he lived or not, had her thanks. Look at that face! Marina tried for a year to get a look like that. One little story from one she didn't even know, and it sets her to softness and thought. Ha—and

Marina thought *she* was talented in heart matters. For the story of the stones alone Marina would find out more about that lad. She'd like to pick up a few tips in their common trade. If he lived, maybe they could sit and talk. Trade ideas.

"I miss Nathanael," Rivkah murmured on her fist. "You know he forgave me, Marina. He asked Joab to come tell me those words. It's like—" She wiped her nose as tears came. It was a moment before she could continue. "It's like he was taking care of me with those words. You know what I mean?"

Marina reached to clasp Rivkah's hands. She held tight and smiled through her own tears. "I do, child."

"Such a boy I had . . ." She stopped in the middle of wiping her nose. "Did Jorah tell you about the tefillin she gave me? *Nathanael's* tefillin?" She shook her head, snorting softly. "Makes you wonder what that family was like. I like that Jorah. She's been over every day to look after Orion. She brings me flowers as though I were her own mother. Acts like I'm not even a prostitute. Imagine that." She pushed Marina's arm. "You never did either. You never acted like I was a prostitute."

Marina patted Rivkah's arm and got up to go to the alcove. She made her voice light, saying over her shoulder, "You want some wine?" Then she gripped the counter's edge and kept her back to Rivkah, so she could not see the tears stream down her face.

"No stones, Marina," she heard Rivkah murmur. "Imagine that . . ."

※

"Your wife told me I would find you here," Theron heard behind him. He turned to see the big Roman soldier picking his way through sea grasses to where Theron sat on a boulder on a rocky outcrop overlooking the sea. He looked about for a place to sit, and finally settled down on the edge of the outcrop, legs dangling. He unbuckled his helmet and set it on the ground, ruffed up his hair, and sighed contentedly at the view.

Theron leaned his elbows on his knees. He rubbed his hands together and nodded at the sea. "Isn't that a sight? I've lived here for years. Never took time to come and sit."

"Orion is doing well," Cornelius commented, squinting at the sun off the sea.

"So I hear."

"We've got passage booked for him. He leaves in three days. The Jewish Council took up a collection for him to pay the passage, with some pocket change left over. It was good of them. Pilate confiscated his Ostia fund, you know." He looked at Theron thoughtfully. "How come you haven't gone to see him?"

Theron shrugged. "I already said good-bye."

"Marina says you haven't worked since the flogging." Cornelius eyed him. "Looks like you've lost some weight too." He pointed and said, "I swear that lip looks a little smaller."

"You want to see what I got?" Theron reached beside himself and produced a scroll. "This belongs to Cousin Thomas. I thought maybe he'd fall backward if I asked to borrow it, but he acted like I was borrowing soap."

"What is it?"

"You read Hebrew?"

Cornelius chuckled. "No."

Theron laid it on his lap and ran his curved palm gently over it. "It's a scroll of psalms. The psalms are a collection from our holy writings. It says some pretty good things in here." Theron squinted at him. "What's the new thing they call you?"

"Optio."

"Well, you know what, Mister Optio?"

Cornelius grinned at the man. "What is that, Mister Mosaicist?"

Theron's look fell upon the scroll. He sniffed and nodded, then looked to the sea. "I need him. You know—*him*."

Cornelius's grin faded. He looked to the sea too, and thought that he did, indeed, know what Theron meant.

The two men gazed long upon the vast hazy expanse, listening to the waves, enjoying the warmth of the sun tempered by sea breezes, enjoying the company of each other.

Theron scratched his ear. "You in any trouble with the palace for what you did for Orion?"

"I don't know. They'll be watching me, that's certain."

"You think maybe you want to come over for Sabbath meal sometime? Marina makes the best—" Theron broke off, and out came the mighty lip. He cleared his throat with a growl. "I'm gonna miss that funny man."

"He'll land well, Theron," Cornelius assured. "Don't you worry about him. He's got somebody who loves him to take care of him. What more could you want?" After a time, eyes following a distant vessel, he went to speak but hesitated. Then he stated, "That scroll speaks of the god. The *one* god."

"Yes."

Silence. Then, "The one *true* god."

"Yes."

"The God of the Jews."

"Yes."

"What kind of things does it say?"

Theron's gaze went back to the scroll. An affectionate smile came. "A whole lot of things. 'The Lord is near to all who call on him.' Things like that."

Cornelius leaned back on his arms. After a while he said, "I'd be honored to attend your Sabbath meal sometime."

❦

The boards for the ribbon mosaic began to take up a great deal of space on the floor of Theron's workroom. Jorah and Joab did not have Theron to consult to ask whether the tesserae had set well enough to prop the boards against the wall. They left them flat on the floor until he decided to show up. They did not feel comfortable going to the palace to install the boards without him—not with Prometheus in charge. Jorah shuddered at the memory of his eyes on her—so the boards accumulated, waiting for Theron as they did.

It worried Jorah. She'd grown immensely fond of the grouchy little man. It wasn't like him not to be in his workroom. It had been a week now, since Orion's flogging. Every day Marina had Joab run some food out to Theron at the place he'd taken possession of by the sea. Joab said Theron would only give a little wave to acknowledge him, then go back to his sea observance.

Jorah consulted Theron's original pattern board and placed a tessera on the grooved mortar of her board accordingly.

"If Theron were in Jerusalem, this pattern would show up everywhere within a year," she commented. "There'd be bad imitations from Masada to the Antonia Fortress."

"I hope he comes out of it soon," Joab muttered. He stood at a worktable, grading sand and gravel. He filled the small burlap bags Marina had made and marked them according to coarseness. "I want to get out of here."

Jorah did too, but she didn't want to agree with Joab when he was in such a contrary mood. Moodiness irritated her, and more so when she had to drag every tiny detail out of Joab to get him to tell her why.

"Why can't you just tell me why you're so crabby? I'm tired of tiptoeing around your mood."

Joab's hand with the scoop froze on the way to a bucket filled with pebbly sand. "I'm sorry," he said, the tightness at his forehead smoothing.

If there was one thing she loved about him, it was his quickness to recognize his own folly—when she pointed it out. She shook her head. Clearly this man needed her for the rest of his life.

He lowered his hand with the scoop. "I want to go to Jerusalem. And I want to get away from . . ."

"*Her?*"

He sat back on the stool and thought it over.

If there was another thing she loved about him, it was the way he stopped to consider his words before he spoke them. She wasn't like that. At all.

"I think so. I think it's because—I feel disappointed in the way she took the words."

Jorah sat back on her heels. "What do you mean?"

He turned on his stool toward her. "I watched her reaction when I told her the story. I didn't leave anything out, and I told it to her very carefully and not at all fast. I even told her where it's found in Leviticus. But—she didn't respond the way I . . . thought she would. It was as though she didn't hear me. Or didn't care. Or didn't understand exactly the—implications of what Jesus said."

Jorah kept a smile from surfacing. He goes about silent for days, and now there is no stopping him. She leaned back on her arms to enjoy this conversation.

His troubled gaze fell to the scoop in his hands. "It doesn't seem as if it meant much to her."

"What did it mean to you when you first heard it?"

Joab looked up. He thought on it. "Well—not much," he admitted. "Nathanael was dying. I only tried hard to memorize what he was saying."

"So it all came later."

"Well—yes."

Jorah shrugged as if to say there you have it.

Joab smiled a little, but it faded. He toyed with the scoop. "It's hard to leave her to it, without trying to explain. The words are so—"

"Huge. I know, I know—you've said it a hundred times. Let her be smart, will you? *You* figured it out."

"But—"

"Well, what conclusions do you want her to come to?" Jorah asked. She innocently arched her brows and fluttered her eyelids. "Maybe that the words Jesus spoke were . . . oh . . . *mercy*?"

He looked at her for a long time. He didn't answer, and she was not like that—she would have blurted any old thing. But he merely kept his thoughtful gaze on her until a little smile came. Then he turned back to his sandbags. "How long do you think it will take to put in the walkway?"

"Four, five months. And that's only if Theron decides to show up."

Jorah waited, but Joab did not respond. She grimaced, and reluctantly returned to her tesserae. It was the longest conversation they'd had in days. She picked up a tiny tile and rubbed it between her thumb and finger.

Presently Joab commented, "It won't be decent for us to travel to Jerusalem by ourselves."

"I was thinking that."

"Maybe we should travel properly. If we were—*betrothed*, people wouldn't wag their tongues."

Jorah glanced at Joab. "I was thinking that."

After a moment Joab paused at his sandbag. "I mean a real betrothal."

Jorah's heart jumped, and a flush of joy ran through her. She therefore acted as though it was the only conclusion any idiot could come to. "Of course." She couldn't stop the smile, though, and bent over the board to hide it.

"Your brothers will string me up when we get to Jerusalem, for not asking them first," Joab grumbled.

"You could ask Cousin Thomas," Jorah said quickly. Too quickly. She tried to add something flouncy and tart—but couldn't think of a single thing.

The sounds in the room returned to the whisper rush of sand filling burlap bags and the scrape of a spatula on tesserae. After a moment the curtain flap, which had been parted an inch or two, eased back into place.

Discussion Questions

1. Which character in the book could you most easily identify with? Why?

2. In what ways is Theron "a bad Jew"? How do you think Jesus would have regarded Theron's views?

3. When the story opens, Orion is in the habit of helping the Jews in "small ways," but then the stakes begin to rise. In what ways does Orion's true character begin to show under this pressure? Has there been a time in your life that you had to start making hard choices about right and wrong?

4. Marina says Rivkah is loved by God and made in his image, but "she does not believe this. Not yet." When and how does Rivkah come to understand her value in God's eyes? What part do Jorah and Joab play? Who or what first convinced you of your value to God—or is this something you are still unsure of?

5. How did you feel when you learned the identity of Nathanael's father? Have you ever been betrayed by someone you should have been able to trust? Why is this even more devastating than being hurt by someone or something impersonal?

6. Janus Bifrons tells Orion that the God of the Jews is pleased "when kindness is shown, particularly to his own people," and that perhaps Orion has God's favor. Would you agree? What are some examples from Scripture?

7. What did you think of Janus Bifrons's assessment of God's relationship with his people? "Their god is about his people, and his people are about their god. It seemed like a love affair."

8. Jesus' words, which Joab is charged to tell Rivkah, are "He who is without sin among you, let him be the first to throw a stone at her." (The biblical account of this incident is found in the Gospel of John, chapter 8.) Joab thinks these are "the biggest words he had ever heard. Words to explode, expose, destroy. Words to make utterly new. Full of terrible hope." How do these words affect Joab? Jorah? Rivkah? You?

9. What bothers Orion most is the certainty that he has let his father down. If you were Orion's father, how would you feel about his choices?

10. Were you surprised when Cornelius stepped forward to help Joab and then Orion? Have you ever been helped by an unexpected ally? (For more on Cornelius, see Acts 10 in the Bible.)

11. When Orion learns of Nathanael's death, he is glad that he will not have to face Rivkah's grief. Yet he feels ashamed that "escape was all he ever wanted when horrible things came." When have you wanted to escape from a painful situation or truth? Why is this a universal human experience? What might give a person the courage to stay and face it?

12. Janus says of Orion, "He broke law . . . but it was for mercy. He disobeyed a command because he knew it was wrong." What parallels do you see between Orion's behavior and the ministry of Jesus?

13. Orion is surprised to find he has so many friends. In prison, he has a succession of visitors come to express their appreciation for his acts of kindness. Why do we often wait until it is too late to thank those who have made a difference in our lives? Who can you reach out to this week to express appreciation, perhaps overdue?

14. What is the significance of Orion's memory of his father's words about river barges? "You see the three-master? Not so powerful now. Consider the *nava codicaria*, my boy." How does remembering this help Orion know what to do when he stands before Pilate?

15. Why does Rivkah insist that the woman in the story of Jesus and the stones is a prostitute, not an adulteress? Does it matter? Why or why not?

About the Author

TRACY GROOT is the author of three Christy Award–winning novels—*Madman, Flame of Resistance,* and *The Sentinels of Andersonville*—along with *The Brother's Keeper, The Stones of My Accusers,* and most recently *The Maggie Bright.*

She loves books, movies, knitting, travel, exceptional coffee, dark-chocolate sea foam, and licorice allsorts. She lives with her husband, Jack, in a Michigan home where stacks of books must be navigated to get anywhere, and if she yet lives at the reading of these words, she is likely at work on her next historical novel.

For more information about Tracy and her books, visit www.tracygroot.com.

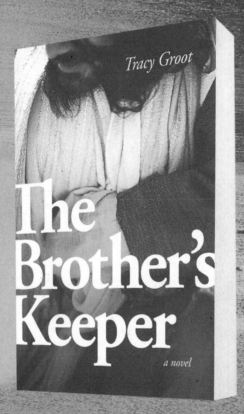

1

HE DID NOT KNOW what to call them. They were not Essenes, nor were they Zealots. Some were not even Jewish. He watched the latest two retreat down the slope that led to his home. The tall one, the ruder of the two, looked over his shoulder to stare boldly at James. The fact that these pilgrims never got what they came for pleased him greatly. To be sure, the shorter one carried away a pocketful of sawdust, scooped from the floor when he thought James was not looking; no matter. The fool had more sawdust in his head than in his pocket.

They were heading for the village. And how would these visitors find Nazareth? Would they be disappointed to see that it was no different than their own hometown? They would see the same filthy beggars and the same people who did not notice them. The same smelly streets, the same noisy marketplace. They would hear women arguing prices with the merchants. They would see the usual mix of people in typical Galilean villages: Jews, Gentiles, a few strutting Romans, traveling foreigners. They would see people who lived the hard facts of life, people who sweated and smelled like them.

Would they be as disappointed with Nazareth as they always were with James and his family?

James leaned against the workroom doorway and watched until the two disappeared down the hill. When the first of these strangers had come to visit, James and his brothers had treated them politely. Answered questions, showed them around. Pointed out the corner workbench; they always liked to see that. In the beginning the attention was entertaining. It amused them; truth to tell, it even flattered. Nearly three years later, James was no longer amused.

Many carried away tokens of their visit: a curled shaving from the workroom floor, a pebble from the path, a handful of stone chips from a roof roller James was chiseling. Once he caught Jorah giving tours of the home for two copper prutas per person. Though Mother put an end to that, James thought it time for recompense. At least someone had the sense to make these strangers pay for their intrusions.

What did they expect the home to be like? James saw it all the time, the looks that said their Teacher's home fell short of their expectations.

Those who made it past the workroom, and precious few did, came to the smallyard, an area where the sleeping rooms, the main courtyard, and the workroom converged. In the smallyard was the cistern. If there the stranger turned right, he would walk a few steps through a cool stone passage that opened left into the foreroom where the brothers slept, then the aftroom where Mother and Jorah slept. If instead the stranger went past the smallyard, he would find himself in the courtyard. There he would see Mother's oven in one corner, those corner walls blackened from smoke. He would see pots to dye wool, pans for cooking, a grindstone for wheat and barley, a small loom for cloth. He would see a shelter of coarse cloth covering half the courtyard, under which Mother and Jorah made food, cleaned and carded wool, and mended baskets, tunics, and sandals.

The strangers would see a home much like their own, if they were neither poor nor rich. They would see nothing remarkable. Nothing to account for an unordinary man in an ordinary world.

But they needed a name. James had a few he called them privately, names of which Mother would not approve. He rubbed his lower lip, looking at the place where the last two had disappeared. The tall one had looked long at James and the home . . . perhaps to put them in his memory to tell his grandchildren.

What would James tell his own?

He shoved off from the doorway to turn into the workroom and noticed the gouge in a ridge of sawdust on the floor. He bent and picked up a handful himself, rubbing the coarse wooden filings between his fingers. What did they do with it? Sprinkle it on sick relatives? He shook it away and went to his bench.

Jesus-ites. Nazarites would work, except it was taken. *Nazarenes* would fit, but were not all the occupants of Nazareth called Nazarenes? He could just imagine how the villagers would take it, mistaken for followers of Joseph's son.

He picked up a hunk of cypress, hefted it in his hand, looked down the length of it. Five palms long, four fingers wide. He picked up his measuring stick, ever hearing his father's voice when he did so—*"Twice measured is once cut—"* and rechecked the measure. He would soon fashion the length into a replacement support for a threshing sledge. He ran his thumb over a knot, traced calloused fingertips along the grain, then tossed the chunk of wood onto the ground next to the thresher and wearily rubbed his eyebrows.

They came more frequently now—two, three times a week. Some were shy, some as rude as this last visitor. Some came to argue the Torah and the Prophets, some to rouse support for another go at an uprising. Some treated James and his family with a sickening awe, others with pity, as from a strange self-righteousness. He was not sure which he hated more.

Those in the village were too eager to give directions to the seekers. James did not blame them, after all. Fair trade for the notoriety inflicted upon Nazareth. Last week he overheard a merchant giving cheerful directions: "Straight up the main road, past the well; you will come to a home on the left; that would be Eli's place. The home past that one, up the hill, is Joseph's place." The seeker had turned away, with the trader calling after him, "Be sure to ask for a relic! They love to give away relics!" Then he laughed with the customers at his stall.

James knelt and looked under his workbench. In the corner against the wall was a box full of seasoned pieces of wood for carving. He dragged the box to himself and brought it to the top of the bench, where he rummaged through it, holding certain pieces out from under the awning to see them in the sun. He remembered this one with the crook at the end. A remnant of the olive tree he had sectioned off last summer. He had thought to fashion a water dipper out of that crook. He laid it on the table and rummaged some more.

Time was when he was James ben Joseph. Time was when James, Joses, Simon, Judas, Devorah, and Jorah were all children ben Joseph, the carpenter. Now he was James, brother of the scourge of Nazareth.

Here was an oblong chunk of sycamore. Maybe Jude had put it into the box; he didn't remember it. Perhaps left over from the synagogue project. He turned it over. Make a nice platter, maybe a good oblong bowl. When was the last time he had carved? With jobs and projects and the time-wasting seekers to fill their days, he didn't often have the leisure for this pastime.

"This is the carpenter's home?"

He slowly put the piece of sycamore back into the box, resting his hands on the edge.

He looked over his shoulder and squinted at the young man who stood in the doorway, gazing at the workroom. He was younger than James by at least ten years—maybe eighteen or nineteen. He had wild reddish-brown hair barely kept in place with a thin leather tie circling his head. A vain attempt at a beard gave him a dusky jawline. When James did not answer, the lad's wandering gaze came back, showing his brightly colored eyes.

"Is this the carpenter's—"

"We are bread makers," James cut him off, with a gesture at the workroom. "What do you think the wood and stone is for?"

On the heel of the young man's startled look came a grin. "You must be James. Annika said I remind her of you."

For the first time since the seekers left, the knot inside began to loosen. "You are Nathanael?"

The young man nodded and stepped inside, inhaling deeply. "Smells wonderful in here." He picked up a handful of stripped cypress bark and held it to his nose, closing his eyes as he breathed deeply. "I love cypress. I've missed it."

James noticed that Nathanael did not kiss the mezuzah fixed to the doorjamb, but he did not care. Religious Jew or nonreligious Jew, as long as he was not one of the seekers. Annika hadn't said much about Nathanael, only that he was new to Nazareth and in need of work.

"Have you worked with wood before?"

"I apprenticed with my uncle. Once in a while."

Hands clasped behind his back, Nathanael gave himself a tour. He strolled under the shade of the awnings, erected at the top of the walls to shelter the workbenches from the late-winter rains. He came first to Judas' bench, appraising every detail. Most of Jude's tools were hung neatly on a rack above the bench; some were jumbled less neatly on the table. He passed James' bench; James watched his amber-hued eyes, a different color for these parts, whisk eagerly over everything. He stopped at Father's bench near the passage to the smallyard. Father's bench looked more like what it had become, the catchall spot for odds and ends. Opposite Father's bench was the fire pit. He crossed the room to the pit, looked it over, then walked past Joses' bench and Simon's bench and came to stand at the bench in the corner.

The corner workbench was the only one without wood chips near it. It was as neat and tidy as the day it was left. The tiny wooden boat James had carved when he was seven still lay where it always had, on the shelf above the bench in the corner, tilted on its side. A little vase Jorah had made was on the other side of the shelf. Jesus would put a sprig of fresh herbs or a posy of wildflowers in it.

Nathanael reached for one of the tools. James gave an involuntary start but held fast. It was the first time in three years . . .

Nathanael did not see his reaction. He turned the heavy gouge adze over in his hands, thumbed the curved blade. "It's a little rusty. Needs a fresh edge. Where is your grinding stone?"

"Outside, by the steps to the roof." Nathanael started for the door, but James said, "We need to talk first."

Nathanael stiffened. Studying the adze edge, he said flatly, "You hired someone else."

James regarded the young man, who now had a defiant set to his jaw. Annika, the woman who could not spare her tongue to save her life, had not offered much information about this lad.

James took a stool and gestured to another by Joses' bench— away from the corner. "Please, sit. Rest yourself. Don't I get a full ear of how far our place is every time Annika brings the eggs?"

"What is far?" Nathanael muttered. "She is an old woman."

On the way to the stool he studied the adze as though he would rather be sharpening it. He took the stool, then looked straight at James with those strange-hued eyes. "If you do not want me, just say it."

James pulled back. "If we do not want you . . . ? That is not the question. The question is if you want us. Our apprentices come and go. Nobody wants to stay."

"Why not?"

James cocked his head, squinting at him. "What did Annika tell you about us?"

The lad shrugged. "That you needed an apprentice. And that you have a pretty sister."

Annika the matchmaker. Annika the meddler. "She did not say anything else?"

"What's there to say? You need help; I need work."

A movement at the doorway caught James' eye. "It isn't that simple," he muttered as he took in the group of three now standing at the door.

The familiar knot returned to his stomach, hardening to a fist of iron.

The girl in the middle chittered to the boys next to her in a lordly way, gesturing toward the workroom. Keturah. She used to come for carving lessons, trading cucumbers for instruction. But the young men with her, near Nathanael's age, he had never seen before. James rose from his stool.

"Hello, James," the girl said airily, as if she spoke to him in the market all the time. To the boys she said, "That is his brother, the next oldest. His other brothers, Joses and Simon, are still away on a trading trip. Aren't they, James?" When James did not answer, she chattered on. "Judas just left for Capernaum; he should be back in a week or so."

She pointed to the corner workbench. "Over there. That is where he worked. He was the one who taught me to carve. He was the best wood-carver in Galilee."

"Simon is the best," James stated.

She only glanced at him. "He carved a bowl for my grandmother," she told the boys. "Finest bowl I have ever seen. It's her favorite."

The girl would not be able to tell apart a bowl carved by Simon or—

"Do you have business here, Keturah?" James asked, and reached for his mallet.

Her brown-eyed look flickered over him. "So, you remember my name." Some of her lordliness softened.

"I remember," James said quietly.

He used to feel like a lumbering fool around her. Every time she came to the shop, every time he saw her in the marketplace . . . instant idiot is what he would become. But after her favorite wood-carver left, she stopped coming around. And James' trips to the market became fewer. He glanced at her tunic. She was wearing lavender again.

He realized he did not feel stupid around her anymore, and strangely, the thought brought a flicker of sadness.

She was already pointing out another attraction to the boys.

"Do you have a loom that needs mending?" he said, his voice tight. "Stones to be cut, a tool to be sharpened? Do you have *business* here, Keturah, or are you here to waste my time?"

He had learned something about the seekers: the ruder he was, the quicker they left. He had never been so rude when his father was alive. He never imagined he could be so rude.

She broke off midsentence to stare at him. "I—no. I was only—"

"I have work to do," James snapped. He pointed with the mallet to the outdoors beyond them. He did not miss the darkening of her cheeks.

"This is his brother?" one of the lads muttered, looking James up and down as he crossed the threshold and sauntered into the workroom.

"Not much like him, is he, Avi," the other commented, upper lip pulled to sneer.

The iron fist lurched painfully in James' stomach, and he gripped the mallet handle convulsively as the hatred flared. They did this. They touched off something inside him that ought never have been touched.

God of Israel, help me now, because I surely want to kill them.

The one called Avi pulled himself tall. "How is it you are not out there with him? Why does not a single brother of his help him?" He snorted. "I would give anything to be one of his twelve. Anything! You are his own brother, and you cannot find the time of day even to listen to him."

"The Teacher said it himself, Avi." The other lad shrugged and stepped into the workroom after his friend. "'A prophet will have honor, but not from those of his own household.'"

God of Israel . . .

Any words but those . . . any words that filtered back to the workroom but those words. The images of the one day Jesus had come back to Nazareth, and what happened in the synagogue . . . the memory rioted his senses, flooding his gut with torment.

"You do not even care." Avi's voice dripped scorn, and he shook his head. "This whole village is crazy."

Keturah's fists went to her hips. "I did not bring you here to flail your tongue. Come. It is time for us to leave."

"The greatest leader our people have seen since Judah the

Maccabee, and we sit around sawing wood," Avi scoffed. He brushed past Keturah as he strolled to the bench in the corner.

"*Now* is the time to throw off the Roman yoke! We did it to the cursed Syrian Greeks; we can do it to the cursed Romans. And throw out all the rest of the Gentiles as well. This is *our* land. God has seen and heard, and the time of the Jew has come once more."

His dark eyes glittered as he placed both palms lightly on the surface of the workbench, either in wonder or perhaps to infuse himself with residual power.

"The time is coming soon, I can feel it," he whispered. "He will declare soon, and I will be there when he does."

Oddly, the rage in James' stomach diffused and died away.

"Just leave," James whispered. The crooked piece of olivewood, his whittling knife . . .

Day after day, for nearly three years, he had heard it all. From the passioned Zealots like this one, from the gentler and much more polite Essenes. From the Pharisees, the Sadducees. From other sectarians whose tenets blurred into the rest. From synagogue leaders, and once a Temple leader. Even from Annika the meddler. Everybody had an opinion about Joseph's son.

Interesting, the effect these people had on his family. They set Simon to studying with fury, draping himself over the family's two scrolls any chance he could get. They caused gentle Joses to plead and argue. They made Judas hide. And all James wanted to do was carve.

"Five hundred years of foreign domination! Persia, Greece, Egypt . . ."

If it were not for the fact there wasn't any money in it, not real money, he would carve all day and fashion beauty out of jagged castoffs of sycamore, cedar, and oak. He would save for some fancy imported pieces, get them from Amos in Gaza.

". . . has heard and he will give us back our land. Jesus is our prophet to speak the word of God and *unite* us! That's the key! Unity!"

Satinwood from the East, that sparkled in the sun. Purpleheart from Africa, with a hue so deeply rich and luxuriant no stain could ever match it. Rub it with olive oil is all.

"Somebody needs to talk to him! I have tried, but those fool fishermen will not let me near him. He needs to know the plan! Raziel from Kerioth—"

James looked at Avi sharply. "Do not say that name here."

"What? You do not wish to have your brother's name associated with a man of real courage and honor?"

"My brother is not an insurrectionist," James said between his teeth. He flicked a glance out the workroom door. All it would take was one passing Roman . . .

"None of his brothers believe in him. They are all cowards," Avi's friend said scornfully.

"You are right, Joab." Avi's tone oozed disdain. "The only one with courage is the Teacher himself. Out there daily with the *people*."

On her way to escort out her overly zealous guest, Keturah leaned toward James and whispered, "I am sorry."

She took Avi's arm and said, "We must go." He angrily shook her off.

"Are you all blind? The time is now! We have to be united! All he has to do is say the word, and thousands will be at his side! The cause is everything. Everything! Anyone who does not agree is not Jewish."

To his left, James caught movement. Jorah stood in the passageway to the smallyard with the sackcloth flap pulled to the side. "What is all the shouting in here?" she demanded, brushing aside a curled wisp of hair with floury fingers.

"With his powers and our swords, we could gouge the side of Rome and bring Caesar's empire crashing down!"

Jorah rolled her eyes. "Not again," she groaned, and let the flap fall back into place.

"Never before has Israel seen these miracles! I myself tasted of the bread he brought down from heaven. I have never tasted anything more delicious. Surely a thousand times better than manna."

James had heard others claim the same, yet Joses had been there that day. He reported that it tasted no different than Mother's loaves. It was probably where Jesus got the recipe.

"... realize what can be done? No need to pack supplies! Do you realize what kind of strategic military advantage that would have? Raziel says all we have to do is—"

"Don't say that name!" James thundered at him.

"I have to get to Jesus!" Avi thundered back.

"How would you like a personal audience with him?" Nathanael drawled.

The Zealot snapped his mouth shut, blinking in surprise. James slowly turned to stare at the lad on the stool who toyed with the gouge adze.

"You—you could do this?" Avi stammered, with a fast exchange of glances with his friend. "You could get me a personal audience?"

"Of course." Nathanael shrugged, as if it were a petty thing. He rose from the stool and strolled to Avi at the corner bench, all the while inspecting the curved blade of the heavy adze. He lounged conversationally against the bench, thumbing the adze blade. He lifted the blade even with his eyes, then looked at Avi beyond it and with a wicked smile softly said, "I will give you a chance to experience his healing powers firsthand."

It had been so long since James had laughed, his own outburst startled him.

The greedy excitement in Avi's face shriveled to contempt.

Nathanael spread his arms wide, carelessly swinging the adze so that Avi jumped aside. "What?" Nathanael asked innocently. "It's perfect! What better way to get his attention? He heals you; you tell him the plan . . . brilliant." He suddenly frowned and puffed out his cheeks. "Of course you might bleed to death before you get to him, and that would not be good. But the cause is everything, right? We have to be willing to take a little risk." He went to drape his arm about Avi in brotherhood, but Avi ducked away.

James could not stop laughing. He sat down hard on his stool and laughed himself to aching. The curtain flap twitched aside, and Jorah's wondering face appeared.

Avi was slinking away.

"Avi!" Nathanael reproached, arms wide. "Brother! I said I could get you an audience." His face lit in sudden inspiration. "We could practice on your friend! Find out exactly how long it takes him to bleed to death. What is your name? Joab? Come here, Joab." He traced a few practice swoops in the air.

Joab ducked out the door with Avi close behind him. Keturah ran to the doorway, where she stopped and yelled, "My coppers, you thieves!" Over her shoulder she flashed a smile at Nathanael and James, then flew out the door, shouting, "Stop, you thieving cheats!"

James went to the doorway and watched the three race down the path. He laughed again delightedly and yelled, "Look at them run!"

Mother joined Jorah at the curtain, smiling a mystified smile at her boy. "What was that all about?" she said.

Jorah folded her arms and looked at Nathanael, who, with a pleased grin on his face, twirled the adze between both forefingers. James came away from the doorway, shaking his head at Nathanael and chuckling.

"Too bad Judas missed that," James said.

"I don't know who you are," Jorah said to Nathanael, "but I have not heard my brother laugh in forever. For that you will join us for the midmeal."

Grinning, Nathanael looked from the adze to Jorah, and his grin promptly faltered. James caught the look, and his own smile finally came down. He knew well the look. Probably how he appeared the first time he saw Keturah.

Jorah swept an up-and-down look at Nathanael, then whirled away.

Mother nodded at the young man. "You must be the lad Annika told us about."

Nathanael straightened and ducked his head respectfully. "Yes, I am."

Mother folded her arms and, with her eyes twinkling, said, "How do you like living with Annika?"

Nathanael darted a look at James. "I—she—"

"Annika is a wonderful woman, I am sure you have discovered," Mother said.

"That she is," Nathanael replied, not meeting her eyes.

"Do join us for the meal," Mother urged. She glanced at James. "I want to know what made my son laugh." She disappeared behind the curtain.

Visibly relieved, Nathanael resumed his slouch at the workbench.

James went to the passage and held the curtain aside to watch Mother's retreat. Then he let the curtain fall back and turned to Nathanael. "Now, what do you *really* think of Annika?"

Nathanael snorted. "Sounds like you know her."

James straddled a stool at his bench and picked up the crooked piece of olivewood. "All my life. She is more of an aunt than a family friend. She is a grandmother to every child in Nazareth; they all adore her. The opinions of the adults are different."

Nathanael hesitated, then said quietly, "I have never met anyone like her."

James raised his eyes from the wood. He watched the lad look around the shop.

"My uncle never kept his place so neat." Nathanael shook his head. He jerked a thumb at Jude's bench. "The amount of tools you have . . . I have never seen so many, let alone so many sizes."

James pried off a piece of bark from the olivewood. "Tools are a hobby for Judas. We have a decent set for every bench. 'He who does not teach his son a trade brings him up to be a robber.' My father used to say that."

"My father is a drunk."

James pursed his lips, nodding. He broke off more bark. "Anything else?"

Nathanael folded his arms. "My mother is a whore."

James shifted his jaw, then offered, "My brother walks on water."

"Anything else?"

James studied him long before he could answer. He liked what he saw in those strange bright eyes, liked the defiant tilt in the chin. He liked this boy, and he already feared for him.

"Yes, I am afraid there is something else," James said, resting the olive piece on his lap. "Work for me, and you will regret it. You will be scorned and ridiculed, sometimes refused trade in the market-place. Some cowards will throw things at you when you pass. They will spread rumors about you and shun you in the synagogue. Some will cross to the other side of the street when they see you coming, people you have known all your life. People who used to be friends.

"Your chances of a decent marriage will be ruined, unless you choose to marry one of the—seekers. You will have more interruptions to your work in one day than you will have visits to the brush. You will deal with fanatics and with fools. And if you are used to being liked, forget about it. Forget all about it, because you will be hated." He broke off to smile grimly. "Work for me, Nathanael, and your life will be misery."

A gleam came into Nathanael's eye, and with it a slow grin. "I have not had such an offer in a long time."

"I hope you refuse it. I like you."

Nathanael stretched his legs out and folded his arms. "Let me see . . . they won't have much chance to shun me in the synagogue since I am a bad Jew and do not go. If they throw things at me, well, I can hit a gecko at fifty paces—I will keep a rock or two handy. Being scorned and such . . ." He lifted his hands and shoulders. "My mother is a whore. I have been scorned since birth. So I hate to disappoint you, but I accept your offer."

James smiled. "You will live to regret it."

"From what you tell me, I can only hope so." He looked about the shop. "Where do you want me?"

James hesitated. All of the other apprentices had worked at Father's bench, or alongside Judas and James. The corner bench had been vacant for three years.

He had hoped . . .

Jorah called them from the courtyard to the midday meal.

Nathanael looked at James, who waved him on. "I will join you in a moment."

Nathanael set the gouge adze down on the corner bench and went to the passage. The curtain flap swished behind him.

James lingered to look at the tools hanging above the corner bench.

Sounds and smells drifted into the workshop from the almost-spring day outside: the bray of neighbor Eli's cantankerous donkey, some children shouting to one another, the fragrance of rain and of wet grasses and of early spring wildflowers. From the courtyard he heard Jorah laugh, heard the soft clatter of a lid on a cook pot.

He remembered the way it used to be. On a day like today it might be his turn to check the barley crop on their terraced strip of land. Or he might have gone to Capernaum with Jude. He might have been on the way home from the late-winter trip to Gaza, back when Jesus and James did much of the trading.

He had not taken a journey since the last one with Jesus, three and a half years ago. James could not even remember the last time he had walked their own land, one terrace up from Eli's. Simon had taken over the planting and weeding, and in the late spring and summer, the watering. And Jude went on the trips alone, or with Joses. James stayed here, under the sky within these four walls.

"Somebody has to stay," he whispered to himself.

"James, are you coming?"

"Yes." He cleared his throat. "Yes, I'm coming."

He tossed the crooked olive piece back into the carving box, set the box on the floor, and shoved it into the corner. He set his mallet on the pegs, then went to the corner bench, where he replaced the gouge adze on the empty peg just so, then adjusted it. He stepped back to look, because he would not see it this way again. Then he saw the tiny, tilted boat on the corner of the shelf.

On sudden furious impulse, he lunged for the toy. He ran out the doorway, stumbling as he went. He reared back and whipped the little boat as far as he could. It sailed long in the air, then bounced and skittered down the slope.

Experience history like never before
with more great fiction from

Tracy Groot

"We are rebels, are we not? Then let us
rebel against what is not us."

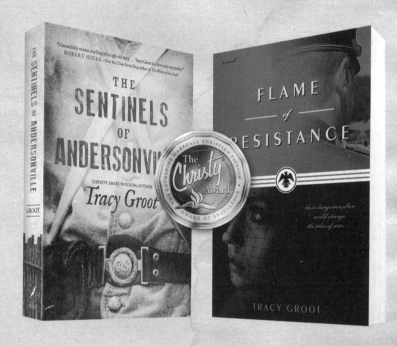

Their dangerous plan could
change the tides of war.

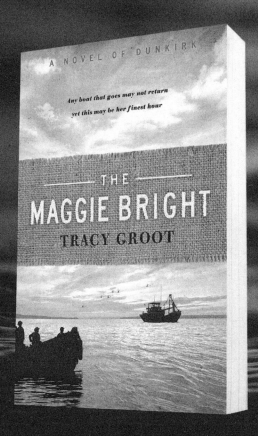

TYNDALE HOUSE PUBLISHERS IS CRAZY4FICTION!

Fiction that entertains and inspires

Get to know us! Become a member of the Crazy4Fiction community. Whether you read our blog, like us on Facebook, follow us on Twitter, or receive our e-newsletter, you're sure to get the latest news on the best in Christian fiction. You might even win something along the way!

JOIN IN THE FUN TODAY.

 www.crazy4fiction.com

 Crazy4Fiction

 @Crazy4Fiction